The invitation to be a damned fo
my office.

Not chiseled out on a marble slab, no, but neatly typed on
high-quality note paper.

Reading it, I sank down in my office chair, my face cold,
my hand tempted to clench and wad the note and throw it
aside.

It said:

GREEN GLADES PARK. Halloween.
Midnight tonight.
Center rear wall.
P.S. A great revelation awaits you. Material for a best-
selling novel or superb screenplay. Don't miss it!

Now, I am not a brave man. I have never learned to drive.
I do not fly in planes. I feared women until I was twenty-
five. I hate high places; the Empire State is pure terror for
me. Elevators makes me nervous. Escalators bite. I am
picky with food. I ate my first steak only at age twenty-four,
subsisting through childhood on hamburgers, ham-and-pickle
sandwiches, eggs, and tomato soup.

"Green Glades Park!" I said aloud.

Jesus, I thought. Midnight? Me, the guy who was mobbed
by bullies down the middle of adolescence? The boy who hid
under his brother's armpit the first time he saw *The Phantom
of the Opera*?

That one, yes.

"Dumb!" I yelled.

And went to the graveyard.

At midnight.

A GRAVEYARD FOR LUNATICS

ALSO BY RAY BRADBURY

The Toynbee Convector

Death Is a Lonely Business

Something Wicked This Way Comes

The Haunted Computer and the Android Pope

The Stories of Ray Bradbury

Where Robot Mice and Robot Men Run Round
in Robot Towns

Long After Midnight

Dandelion Wine

When Elephants Last in the Dooryard Bloomed

The Halloween Tree

The October Country

I Sing the Body Electric!

Switch on the Night

The Illustrated Man

The Martian Chronicles

R Is for Rocket

Dark Carnival

The Machineries of Joy

The Anthem Sprinters

A Medicine for Melancholy

Moby Dick (screenplay)

Fahrenheit 451

Golden Apples of the Sun

S Is for Space

Classic Stories 1

Classic Stories 2

A GRAVEYARD FOR LUNATICS

ANOTHER TALE OF TWO CITIES

RAY BRADBURY

BANTAM BOOKS

NEW YORK · TORONTO · LONDON · SYDNEY · AUCKLAND

*This edition contains the complete text
of the original hardcover edition.*
NOT ONE WORD HAS BEEN OMITTED.

A GRAVEYARD FOR LUNATICS

*A Bantam Book / published by arrangement with
Alfred A. Knopf, Inc.*

PRINTING HISTORY
Knopf edition published 1990
Bantam edition / January 1992

Library of Congress Cataloging-in-Publication Data

Bradbury, Ray, 1920–
  A graveyard for lunatics / Ray Bradbury.
    p.   cm.
  ISBN 0-553-35477-9
  I. Title.
PS3503.R167G74   1992
813'.54—dc20   91-16642
                                                    CIP

Published simultaneously in the United States and Canada

PRINTED IN THE UNITED STATES OF AMERICA

FFG   0 9 8 7 6 5 4 3 2 1

With love, to the living:
SID STEBEL,
who showed me how to solve
my own mystery;
ALEXANDRA, my daughter,
who cleaned up after us.
GEORGE BURNS,
who told me that I was a writer
when I was fourteen.

And to the dead:
ROUBEN MAMOULIAN,
GEORGE CUKOR,
JOHN HUSTON,
BILL SKALL,
FRITZ LANG,
and JAMES WONG HOWE.

And to
RAY HARRYHAUSEN,
for obvious reasons.

A GRAVEYARD FOR LUNATICS

1

Once upon a time there were two cities within a city. One was light and one was dark. One moved restlessly all day while the other never stirred. One was warm and filled with ever-changing lights. One was cold and fixed in place by stones. And when the sun went down each afternoon on Maximus Films, the city of the living, it began to resemble Green Glades cemetery just across the way, which was the city of the dead.

As the lights went out and the motions stopped and the wind that blew around the corners of the studio buildings cooled, an incredible melancholy seemed to sweep from the front gate of the living all the way along through twilight avenues toward that high brick wall that separated the two cities within a city. And suddenly the streets were filled with something one could speak of only as remembrance. For while the people had gone away, they left behind them architectures that were haunted by the ghosts of incredible happenings.

For indeed it was the most outrageous city in the world, where anything could happen and always did. Ten thousand deaths had happened here, and when the deaths were done, the people got up, laughing, and strolled away. Whole tenement blocks were set afire and did not burn. Sirens shrieked and police cars careened around corners, only to have the officers peel off their blues, cold-cream their orange pancake makeup, and walk home to small bungalow court apartments out in that great and mostly boring world.

Dinosaurs prowled here, one moment in miniature, and the next looming fifty feet tall above half-clad virgins who screamed on key. From here various Crusades departed to peg their armor and stash their spears at Western Costume down the road. From here Henry the Eighth let drop some heads. From here Dracula wandered as flesh to return as dust. Here also were the Stations of the Cross and a trail of ever-replenished blood as screenwriters groaned by to Calvary carrying a backbreaking load of revisions, pursued by directors with scourges and film cutters with razor-sharp knives. It was from these towers that the Muslim faithful were called to worship each day at sunset as the limousines whispered out with faceless powers behind each window, and peasants averted their gaze, fearing to be struck blind.

This being true, all the more reason to believe that when the sun vanished the old haunts rose up, so that the warm city cooled and began to resemble the marbled orchardways across the wall. By midnight, in that strange peace caused by temperature and wind and the voice of some far church clock, the two cities were at last one. And the night watchman was the only motion prowling along from India to France to prairie Kansas to brownstone New York to Piccadilly to the Spanish Steps, covering twenty thousand miles of territorial incredibility in twenty brief minutes. Even as his counterpart across the wall punched the time clocks around among the monuments, flashed his light on various Arctic angels, read names like credits on tombstones, and sat to have his midnight tea with all that was left of some Keystone Kop. At four in the morning, the watchmen asleep, the two cities, folded and kept, waited for the sun to rise over withered flowers, eroded tombs, and elephant India ripe for overpopulation should God the Director decree and Central Casting deliver.

And so it was on All Hallows Eve, 1954.

Halloween.

My favorite night in all the year.

If it hadn't been, I would not have run off to start this new Tale of Two Cities.

How could I resist when a cold chisel hammered out an invitation?

How could I not kneel, take a deep breath, and blow away the marble dust?

2

The first to arrive . . .

I had come into the studio at seven o'clock that Halloween morning.

The last to leave . . .

It was almost ten o'clock and I was making my final walk-around of the night, drinking in the simple but incredible fact that at last I worked in a place where everything was clearly defined. Here there were absolutely sharp beginnings, and ends that were neat and irreversible. Outside, beyond the stages, I did not much trust life with its dreadful surprises and ramshackle plots. Here, walking among the alleys just at dawn or twilight, I could imagine I opened the studio and shut it down. It belonged to me because I said it was so.

So I paced out a territory that was half a mile wide and a mile deep, among fourteen sound stages and ten outdoor sets, a victim of my own romance and infatuated madness over films that controlled life when it ran out of control beyond the Spanish wrought-iron front gates.

It was late, but a lot of films had fixed their schedules to end on All Hallows Eve, so that the wrap parties, the farewell binges, would coincide on various sets. From three sound stages, with their gigantic sliding doors thrown wide, came big-band music, laughter, explosions of champagne corks, and singing. Inside, mobs in film costumes greeted mobs from outside in Halloween garb.

I entered nowhere, content to smile or laugh as I passed. After all, since I imagined the studio was mine, I could linger or leave as I wished.

But even as I moved into the shadows again, I sensed a certain tremor in myself. My love of films had gone on too many years. It was like having an affair with Kong, who fell on me when I was thirteen; I had never escaped from beneath his heart-beating carcass.

The studio fell on me the same way every morning when I arrived. It took hours to fight free of its spell, breathe normally, and get my work down. At twilight, the enchantment returned; my breathing suffered. I knew that someday soon I would have to get out, run free, go and never come back, or like Kong, always falling and always landing, it would one day kill me.

I passed a final stage where a last burst of hilarity and percussive jazz shook the walls. One of the assistant camera operators biked by, his basket loaded with film on its way to an autopsy under the razor of a film editor who might save or bury it forever. Then into the theatres or banished to the shelves where dead films go, where only dust, not rot, collecteth them.

A church clock, up in the Hollywood hills, struck ten. I turned and strolled back to my cell block in the writers' building.

The invitation to be a damned fool was waiting for me in my office.

Not chiseled out on a marble slab, no, but neatly typed on high-quality note paper.

Reading it, I sank down in my office chair, my face cold, my hand tempted to clench and wad the note and throw it aside.

It said:

GREEN GLADES PARK. Halloween.
Midnight tonight.
Center rear wall.
P.S. A great revelation awaits you. Material for a best-selling novel or superb screenplay. Don't miss it!

Now, I am not a brave man. I have never learned to drive. I do not fly in planes. I feared women until I was twenty-five. I hate high places; the Empire State is pure terror for me. Elevators make me nervous. Escalators bite. I am picky with food. I ate my first steak only at age twenty-four, subsisting through childhood on hamburgers, ham-and-pickle sandwiches, eggs, and tomato soup.

"Green Glades Park!" I said aloud.

Jesus, I thought. Midnight? Me, the guy who was mobbed by bullies down the middle of adolescence? The boy who hid under his brother's armpit the first time he saw *The Phantom of the Opera?*

That one, yes.

"Dumb!" I yelled.

And went to the graveyard.

At midnight.

3

On the way out of the studio I veered toward the Men's, not far from the Main Gate, then veered away. It was a place I had learned to stay away from, a subterranean grotto place, with the sound of secret waters running, and a scuttling sound like crayfish backing swiftly off if you touched and started to open the door. I had learned long ago to hesitate, clear my throat, and open the door slowly. For then various interior doors of the Men's shut with thuds or very quietly or sometimes with a rifle bang, as the creatures that inhabited the grotto all day, and even now late because of the stage-set parties, panicked off in retreat, and you entered to the silence of cool porcelain and underground streams, tended to your plumbing as soon as possible and ran without washing your hands, only to hear, once outside, the sly slow reawakening of the crayfish, the doors whispering wide, and the emergence of the grotto creatures in various stages of fever and disarray.

I veered off, as I said, yelled to see if it was clear, and ducked into the Women's across the way, which was a cold, clean white ceramic place, no dark grotto, no scuttling critters, and was in and out of there in a jiffy, just in time to see a regiment of Prussian guards march by toward a Stage 10 party and their captain break ranks. A handsome man with Nordic hair and great innocent eyes, he strode unknowingly into the Men's.

He'll never be seen again, I thought, and hurried through the almost midnight streets.

My taxi, which I couldn't afford, but I was damned if I'd go near the graveyard alone, pulled up in front of the cemetery gates at three minutes before the hour.

I spent a long two minutes counting all those crypts and monuments where Green Glades Park employed some nine thousand dead folks, full time.

They have been putting in their hours there for fifty years. Ever since the real-estate builders, Sam Green and Ralph Glade, were forced into bankruptcy and leveled their shingles and planted the tombstones.

Sensing there was a great piece of luck in their names, the defaulted bungalow court builders became simply Green Glades Park, where all the skeletons in the studio closets across the way were buried.

Film folks involved with their shady real-estate scam were believed to have put up so the two gentlemen would shut up. A lot of gossip, rumor, guilt, and ramshackle crime was buried with their first interment.

And now as I sat clenching my knees and gritting my teeth, I stared at the far wall beyond which I could count six safe, warm, beautiful sound stages where the last All Hallows revelries were ending, the last wrap parties wrapping up, the musics still and the right people drifting home with the wrong.

Seeing the cars' light beams shifting on the great sound-stage walls, imagining all the so-longs and goodnights, I suddenly wanted to be with them, wrong or right, going nowhere, but nowhere was better than this.

Inside, a graveyard clock struck midnight.

"Well?" someone said.

I felt my eyes jerk away from the far studio wall and fix to my driver's haircut.

He stared in through the iron grille and sucked the flavor off his Chiclet-sized teeth. The gate rattled in the wind, as the echoes of the great clock died.

"Who," said the driver, "is going to open the gate?"

"*Me!?*" I said, aghast.

"You *got* it," said the driver.

After a long minute, I forced myself to grapple with the gates and was surprised to find them unlocked, and swung them wide.

I led the taxi in, like an old man leading a very tired and very frightened horse. The taxi kept mumbling under its breath, which didn't help, along with the driver whispering, "Damn, damn. If anything starts running toward us, don't expect me to stay."

"No, don't expect me to stay," I said. "Come on!"

There were a lot of white shapes on each side of the graveled path. I heard a ghost sigh somewhere, but it was only my own lungs pumping like a bellows, trying to light some sort of fire in my chest.

A few drops of rain fell on my head. "God," I whispered. "And no umbrella."

What, I thought, in hell am I doing here?

Every time I had seen old horror movies, I had laughed at the guy who goes out late at night when he should stay in. Or the woman who does the same, blinking her big innocent eyes and wearing stiletto heels with which to trip over, running. Yet here *I* was, all because of a truly stupid promissory note.

"Okay," called the cab driver. "*This* is as far as I go!"

"Coward!" I cried.

"Yeah!" he said. "I'll wait right *here!*"

I was halfway to the back wall now and the rain fell in thin sheets that washed my face and dampened the curses in my throat.

There was enough light from the taxi's headlights to see a ladder propped up against the rear wall of the cemetery, leading over into the backlot of Maximus Films.

At the bottom of the ladder I stared up through the cold drizzle.

At the top of the ladder, a man appeared to be climbing to go over the wall.

But he was frozen there as if a bolt of lightning had taken his picture and fixed him forever in blind-white-blue emulsion: His head was thrust forward like that of a track star in full flight, and his body bent as if he might hurl himself across and down into Maximus Films.

Yet, like a grotesque statue, he remained frozen.

I started to call up when I realized why his silence, why his lack of motion.

The man up there was dying or dead.

He had come here, pursued by darkness, climbed the ladder, and frozen at the sight of—*what*? Had something behind stunned him with fright? Or was there something beyond, in studio darkness, far worse?

Rain showered the white tombstones.

I gave the ladder a gentle shake.

"My God!" I yelled.

For the old man, on top of the ladder, toppled.

I fell out of the way.

He landed like a ten-ton lead meteor, between gravestones. I got to my feet and stood over him, not able to hear for the thunder in my chest, and the rain whispering on the stones and drenching him.

I stared down into the dead man's face.

He stared back at me with oyster eyes.

Why are you looking at me? he asked, silently.

Because, I thought, I *know* you!

His face was a white stone.

James Charles Arbuthnot, former head of Maximus Films, I thought.

Yes, he whispered.

But, but, I cried silently, the last time I saw you, I was thirteen years old on my roller skates in front of Maximus Films, the week you were killed, twenty years ago, and for days there were dozens of photos of two cars slammed against a telephone pole, the terrible wreckage, the bloody pavement, the crumpled bodies, and for another two days hundreds of photos of the thousand mourners at your funeral and the million flowers and, weeping real tears, the New York studio heads, and the wet eyes behind two hundred sets of dark glasses as the actors came out, with no smiles. You were really missed. And some final pictures of the wrecked cars on Santa Monica Boulevard, and it took weeks for the newspapers to forget, and for the radios to stop their praise and forgive the king for being forever dead. All that, James Charles Arbuthnot, was you.

Can't be! Impossible, I almost yelled. You're here tonight up on the wall? Who put you there? You can't be killed all over again, *can* you?

Lightning struck. Thunder fell like the slam of a great door. Rain showered the dead man's face to make tears in his eyes. Water filled his gaping mouth.

I spun, yelled, and fled.

When I reached the taxi I knew I had left my heart back with the body.

It ran after me now. It struck me like a rifle shot midriff, and knocked me against the cab.

The driver stared at the gravel drive beyond me, pounded by rain.

"Anyone *there*?!" I yelled.

"No!"

"Thank God. Get out of here!"

The engine died.

We both moaned with despair.

The engine started again, obedient to fright.

It is not easy to back up at sixty miles an hour.

We did.

4

I sat up half the night looking around at my ordinary living room with ordinary furniture in a small safe bungalow house on a normal street in a quiet part of the city. I drank three cups of hot cocoa but stayed cold as I threw images on the walls, shivering.

People can't die *twice*! I thought. That couldn't have been James Charles Arbuthnot on that ladder, clawing the night wind. Bodies decay. Bodies *vanish*.

I remembered a day in 1934 when J. C. Arbuthnot had got out of his limousine in front of the studio as I skated up, tripped, and fell into his arms. Laughing, he had balanced me, signed my book, pinched my cheek, and gone inside.

And, now, Sweet Jesus, that man, long lost in time, high in a cold rain, had fallen in the graveyard grass.

I heard voices and saw headlines:

J. C. ARBUTHNOT DEAD BUT RESURRECTED.

"No!" I said to the white ceiling where the rain whispered, and the man fell. "It wasn't *him*. It's a *lie*!"

Wait until dawn, a voice said.

5

Dawn was no help.

The radio and TV news found no dead bodies.

The newspaper was full of car crashes and dope raids. But no J. C. Arbuthnot.

I wandered out of my house, back to my garage, full of toys, old science and invention magazines, no automobile, and my secondhand bike.

I biked halfway to the studio before I realized I could not recall any intersection I had blindly sailed through. Stunned, I fell off the bike, trembling.

A fiery red open-top roadster burned rubber and stopped parallel to me.

The man at the wheel, wearing a cap put backward, gunned the throttle. He stared through the windshield, one eye bright blue and uncovered, the other masked by a monocle that had been hammered in place and gave off bursts of sun fire.

"Hello, you stupid goddamn son of a bitch," he cried, with a voice that lingered over German vowels.

My bike almost fell from my grip. I had seen that profile stamped on some old coins when I was twelve. The man was either a resurrected Caesar or the German high pontiff of the Holy Roman Empire. My heart banged all of the air out of my lungs.

"What?" shouted the driver. "Speak up!"

"Hello," I heard myself say, "you stupid goddamn son-of-a-bitch you. You're Fritz Wong, aren't you? Born in Shanghai of a Chinese father and an Austrian mother, raised in Hong Kong, Bombay, London, and a dozen towns in Germany. Errand boy, then cutter then writer then cinematographer at UFA then director across the world. Fritz Wong, the magnificent director who made the great silent film *The Cavalcanti Incantation*. The guy who ruled Hollywood films from 1925 to 1927 and got thrown out for a scene in a film where you directed yourself as a Prussian general inhaling Gerta Froelich's underwear. The international director who ran back to and then got out of Berlin ahead of Hitler, the director of *Mad Love, Delirium, To the Moon and Back*—"

With each pronouncement, his head had turned a quarter of an inch, at the same time as his mouth had creased into a Punch-and-Judy smile. His monocle flashed a Morse code.

Behind the monocle was the faintest lurking of an Orient eye. I imagined the left eye was Peking, the right Berlin, but no. It was the monocle's magnification that focused the Orient. His brow and cheeks were a fortress of Teutonic arrogance, built to last two thousand years or until his contract was canceled.

"*What* did you call me?" he asked, with immense politeness.

"What *you* called *me*," I said, faintly. "A stupid," I whispered, "goddamn son-of-a-bitch."

He nodded. He smiled. He banged the car door wide.

"Get in!"

"But you don't—"

"—know you? Do you think I run around giving lifts to just any dumb-ass bike rider? You think I haven't seen you ducking around corners at the studio, pretending to be the White Rabbit at the commissary. You're that"—he snapped his fingers— "bastard son of Edgar Rice Burroughs and *The Warlord of Mars*— the illegitimate offspring of H. G. Wells, out of Jules Verne. Stow your bike. We're *late!*"

I tossed my bike in the back and was in the car only in time as it revved up to fifty.

"Who can say?" shouted Fritz Wong, above the exhaust. "We are both insane, working where we work. But you are lucky, you still *love* it."

"Don't *you?*" I asked.

"Christ help me," he muttered. "*Yes!*"

I could not take my eyes off Fritz Wong as he leaned over the steering wheel to let the wind plow his face.

"You are the stupidest goddamn thing I ever saw!" he cried. "You want to get yourself killed? What's wrong, you never learned to drive a car? What kind of bike is that? Is this your *first* screen job? How come you write that crap? Why not read Thomas Mann, Goethe!"

"Thomas Mann and Goethe," I said, quietly, "couldn't write a screenplay worth a damn. *Death in Venice*, sure. *Faust?* you betcha. But a good *screenplay?* or a short story like one of mine, landing on the Moon and making you *believe* it? Hell, no. How come you drive with that monocle?"

"None of your damn business! It's better to be blind. If you look too closely at the driver ahead, you want to ram his ass! Let me see your face. You *approve* of me?"

"I think you're funny!"

"Jesus! You are supposed to take everything that Wong the magnificent says as gospel. How come you don't *drive?*"

We were both yelling against the wind that battered our eyes and mouths.

"Writers can't *afford* cars! And I saw five people killed, torn apart, when I was fifteen. A car hit a telephone pole."

Fritz glanced over at my pale look of remembrance.

"It was like a war, *yes?* You're not so dumb. I hear you've been given a new project with Roy Holdstrom? Special effects? Brilliant. I *hate* to admit."

"We've been friends since high school. I used to watch him build his miniature dinosaurs in his garage. We promised to grow old and make monsters together."

"No," shouted Fritz Wong against the wind, "you are *working* for monsters. Manny Leiber? The Gila monster's dream of a spider. Watch out! There's the menagerie!"

He nodded at the autograph collectors on the sidewalk across the street from the studio gates.

I glanced over. Instantly, my soul flashed out of my body and ran back. It was 1934 and I was mulched in among the ravening crowd, waving pads and pens, rushing about at première nights under the klieg lights or pursuing Marlene Dietrich into her hairdresser's or running after Cary Grant at the Friday-night Legion Stadium boxing matches, waiting outside restaurants for Jean Harlow to have one more three-hour lunch or Claudette Colbert to come laughing out at midnight.

My eyes touched over the crazy mob there and I saw once again the bulldog, Pekingese, pale, myopic faces of nameless friends lost in the past, waiting outside the great Spanish Prado Museum facade of Maximus where the thirty-foot-high intricately scrolled iron gates opened and clanged shut on the impossibly famous. I saw myself lost in that nest of gape-mouthed hungry birds waiting to be fed on brief encounters, flash photographs, ink-signed pads. And as the sun vanished and the moon rose in memory, I saw myself roller-skating nine miles home on the empty sidewalks, dreaming I would someday be the world's greatest author or a hack writer at Fly by Night Pictures.

"The menagerie?" I murmured. "Is *that* what you call them?"

"And here," said Fritz Wong, "is their *zoo!*"

And we jounced in the studio entrance down alleys full of arriving people, extras and executives. Fritz Wong rammed his car into a NO PARKING zone.

I got out and said, "What's the difference between a menagerie and a zoo?"

"In here, the zoo, we are kept behind bars by money. Out there, those menagerie goofs are locked in silly dreams."

"I was one of them once, and dreamed of coming over the studio wall."

"Stupid. *Now* you'll never escape."

"Yes, I will. I've finished another book of stories, and a play. My name will be remembered!"

Fritz's monocle glinted. "You shouldn't tell this to me. I might lose my contempt."

"If I know Fritz Wong, it'll be back in about thirty seconds."

Fritz watched as I lifted my bike from the car.

"You are almost German, I think."

I climbed on my bike. "I'm insulted."

"Do you speak to *all* people this way?"

"No, only to Frederick the Great, whose manners I deplore but whose films I love."

Fritz Wong unscrewed the monocle from his eye and dropped it in his shirt pocket. It was as if he had let a coin fall to start some inner machine.

"I've been watching you for some days," he intoned. "In fits of insanity, I read your stories. You are not lacking talent, which I could polish. I am working, God help me, on a hopeless film about Christ, Herod Antipas, and all those knucklehead saints. The film started nine million dollars back with a dipso director

who couldn't handle kindergarten traffic. I have been elected to
bury the corpse. What kind of Christian are you?"

"Fallen away."

"Good! Don't be surprised if I get you fired from your dumb
dinosaur epic. If you could help me embalm this Christ horror
film, it's a step up for you. The Lazarus principle! If you work
on a dead turkey and pry it out of the film vaults, you earn points.
Let me watch and read you a few more days. Appear at the
commissary at one sharp today. Eat what I eat, speak when
spoken to, yes? you talented little bastard."

"Yes, Unterseeboot Kapitän, you *big* bastard, sir."

As I biked off, he gave me a shove. But it was not a shove to
hurt, only the quietist old philosopher's push, to help me go.

I did not look back.

I feared to see *him* looking back.

6

"Good God!" I said. "He made me *forget!*"

Last night. The cold rain. The high wall. The body.

I parked my bike outside Stage 13.

A studio policeman, passing, said, "You got a *permit* to park
there? That's Sam Shoenbroder's slot. Call the front office."

"Permit!" I yelled. "Holy Jumping Jesus! For a *bike?*"

I slammed the bike through the big double airlock door into
darkness.

"Roy?!" I shouted. Silence.

I looked around in the fine darkness at Roy Holdstrom's toy
junkyard.

I had one just like it, smaller, in my garage.

Strewn across Stage 13 were toys from Roy's third year, books
from his fifth, magic sets from when he was eight, electrical
experiment chemistry sets from when he was nine and ten, comic
collections from Sunday cartoon strips when he was eleven, and

duplicate models of Kong when he turned thirteen in 1933 and saw the great ape fifty times in two weeks.

My paws itched. Here were dime-store magnetos, gyroscopes, tin trains, magic sets that caused kids to grind their teeth and dream of shoplifting. My own face lay there, a life mask cast when Roy Vaselined my face and smothered me with plaster of paris. And all about, a dozen castings of Roy's own great hawk profile, plus skulls and full-dress skeletons tossed in corners or seated in lawn chairs; anything to make Roy feel at home in a stage so big you could have shoved the *Titanic* through the space-port doors with room left over for *Old Ironsides*.

Across one entire wall Roy had pasted billboard-sized ads and posters from *The Lost World, Kong,* and *Son of Kong,* as well as *Dracula* and *Frankenstein*. In orange crates at the center of this Woolworth dime-store garage sale were sculptures of Karloff and Lugosi. On his desk were three original ball-and-socket dinosaurs, given as gifts by the makers of *The Lost World,* the rubber flesh of the ancient beasts long melted to drop off the metal bones.

Stage 13 was, then, a toy shop, a magic chest, a sorcerer's trunk, a trick manufactory, and an aerial hangar of dreams at the center of which Roy stood each day, waving his long piano fingers at mythic beasts to stir them, whispering, in their ten-billion-year slumbers.

It was into this junkyard, this trash heap of mechanical avarice, greed for toys, and love for great ravening monsters, guillotined heads, and unraveled tarbaby King Tut bodies, that I picked my way.

Everywhere were vast low-lying tents of plastic covering creations that only in time would Roy reveal. I didn't dare look.

Out in the middle of it all a barebone skeleton held a note, frozen, on the air. It read:

CARL DENHAM!

That was the name of the producer of *King Kong.*

THE CITIES OF THE WORLD, FRESHLY CREATED, LIE
HERE UNDER TARPAULINS WAITING TO BE DIS-
COVERED. DO NOT TOUCH. COME FIND ME.

THOMAS WOLFE WAS WRONG. YOU CAN GO HOME
AGAIN. TURN LEFT AT CARPENTERS' SHEDS, SECOND
OUTDOOR SET ON THE RIGHT. YOUR GRANDPARENTS
ARE WAITING THERE! COME SEE! ROY.

I looked around at the tarpaulins. The unveiling! Yes!

I ran, thinking: What does he mean? My grandparents? Waiting? I slowed down. I began to breathe deeply of a fresh air that smelled of oaks and elms and maples.

For Roy was right.

You can go home again.

A sign at the front of outdoor set number two read: FOREST PLAINS, but it was Green Town, where I was born and raised on bread that yeasted behind the potbellied stove all winter, and wine that fermented in the same place in late summer, and clinkers that fell in that same stove, like iron teeth, long before spring.

I did not walk on the sidewalks, I walked the lawns, glad for a friend like Roy who knew my old dream and called me to see.

I passed three white houses where my friends had lived in 1931, turned a corner, and stopped in shock.

My dad's old 1929 Buick was parked in the dust on the brick street, waiting to head west in 1933. It stood, rusting quietly, its headlights dented, its radiator cap flaked, its radiator honey-comb-papered over with trapped moths and blue and yellow butterfly wings, a mosaic caught from a flow of lost summers.

I leaned in to stroke my hand, trembling, over the prickly nap of the back-seat cushions, where my brother and I had knocked elbows and yelled at each other as we traveled across Missouri and Kansas and Oklahoma and . . .

It wasn't my dad's car. But it *was*.

I let my eyes drift up to find the ninth greatest wonder of the world:

My grandma and grandpa's house, with its porch and its porch swing and geraniums in pink pots along the rail, and ferns like green sprinkler founts all around, and a vast lawn like the fur of a green cat, with clover and dandelions studding it in such profusion that you longed to tear off your shoes and run the whole damned tapestry barefoot. And—

A high cupola window where I had slept to wake and look out over a green land and a green world.

In the summer porch swing, sailing back and forth, gently, his long-fingered hands in his lap, was my dearest friend . . .

Roy Holdstrom.

He glided quietly, lost as I was lost in some midsummer a long time back.

Roy saw me and lifted his long cranelike arms to gesture right and left, to the lawn, the trees, to himself, to me.

"My God," he called, "aren't we—*lucky?*"

7

Roy Holdstrom had built dinosaurs in his garage since he was twelve. The dinosaurs chased his father around the yard, on 8-millimeter film, and ate him up. Later, when Roy was twenty, he moved his dinosaurs into small fly-by-night studios and began to make on-the-cheap lost-world films that made him famous. His dinosaurs so much filled his life that his friends worried and tried to find him a nice girl who would put up with his Beasts. They were still searching.

I walked up the porch steps remembering one special night when Roy had taken me to a performance of *Siegfried* at the Shrine Auditorium. "Who's *singing?*" I had asked. "To hell with singing!" cried Roy. "We go for the Dragon!" Well, the music was a triumph. But the Dragon? Kill the tenor. Douse the lights.

Our seats were so far over that—oh God!—I could see only the Dragon Fafner's left *nostril!* Roy saw nothing but the great flame-thrown smokes that jetted from the unseen beast's nose to scorch Siegfried.

"Damn!" whispered Roy.

And Fafner was dead, the magic sword deep in his heart. Siegfried yelled in triumph. Roy leaped to his feet, cursing the stage, and ran out.

I found him in the lobby muttering to himself.

"Some *Fafner!* Christ! My God! Did you see?!"

As we stormed out into the night, Siegfried was still screaming about life, love, and butchery.

"Poor bastards, that audience," said Roy. "Trapped for two more *hours* with no *Fafner!*"

And here he was now, swinging quietly in a glider swing on a front porch lost in time but brought back up through the years.

"Hey!" he called, happily. "What'd I *tell* you? My grandparents' house!"

"No, *mine!*"

"Both!"

Roy laughed, truly happy, and held out a big fat copy of *You Can't Go Home Again.*

"He was wrong," said Roy, quietly.

"Yes," I said, "here we *are*, by God!"

I stopped. For just beyond this meadowland of sets, I saw the high graveyard/studio wall. The ghost of a body on a ladder was there, but I wasn't ready to mention it yet. Instead, I said: "How you doing with your Beast? You *found* him yet?"

"Heck, where's *your* Beast?"

That's the way it had been for many days now.

Roy and I had been called in to blueprint and build beasts, to make meteors fall from outer space and humanoid critters rise from dark lagoons, dripping clichés of tar from dime-store teeth.

They had hired Roy first, because he was technically advanced. His pterodactyls truly flew across the primordial skies. His brontosaurs were mountains on their way to Mahomet.

And then someone had read twenty or thirty of my Weird Tales, stories I had been writing since I was twelve and selling to the pulp magazines since I was twenty-one, and hired me to "write up a drama" for Roy's beasts, all of which hyperventilated me, for I had paid my way or snuck into some nine thousand movies and had been waiting half a lifetime for someone to fire a starter's gun to run me amok in film.

"I want something never *seen* before!" said Manny Leiber that first day. "In three dimensions we fire *something* down to Earth. A meteor drops—"

"Out near Meteor Crater in Arizona—" I put in. "Been there a million years. What a place for a *new* meteor to strike and . . ."

"Out comes our *new* horror," cried Manny.

"Do we actually *see* it?" I asked.

"Whatta you *mean*? We *got* to *see* it!"

"Sure, but look at a film like *The Leopard Man*! The scare comes from night shadows, things unseen. How about *Isle of the Dead* when the dead woman, a catatonic, wakes to find herself trapped in a tomb?"

"Radio shows!!" cried Manny Leiber. "Dammit, people want to see what scares them—"

"I don't want to argue—"

"Don't!" Manny glared. "Give me ten pages to scare me gutless! You—" pointing at Roy—"whatever he writes you glue together with dinosaur droppings! Now, scram! Go make faces in the mirror at three in the morning!"

"Sir!" we cried.

The door slammed.

Outside in the sunlight, Roy and I blinked at each other.

"Another fine mess you got us in, Stanley!"

Still yelling with laughter, we went to work.

I wrote ten pages, leaving room for monsters. Roy slapped thirty pounds of wet clay on a table and danced around it, hitting and shaping, hoping for the monster to rise up like a bubble in a prehistoric pool to collapse in a hiss of sulfurous steam and let the true horror out.

Roy read my pages.

"Where's your Beast?" he cried.

I glanced at his hands, empty but covered with blood-red clay.

"Where's yours?" I said.

And now here it was, three weeks later.

"Hey," said Roy, "how come you're just standing down there looking at me? Come grab a doughnut, sit, speak." I went up, took the doughnut he offered me, and sat in the porch swing, moving alternately forward into the future and back into the past. Forward—rockets and Mars. Backward—dinosaurs and tarpits.

And faceless Beasts all around.

"For someone who usually talks ninety miles a minute," said Roy Holdstrom, "you are extraordinarily quiet."

"I'm scared," I said, at last.

"Well, heck." Roy stopped our time machine. "Speak, oh mighty one."

I spoke.

I built the wall and carried the ladder and lifted the body and brought on the cold rain and then struck with the lightning to make the body fall. When I finished and the rain had dried on my forehead, I handed Roy the typed All Hallows' invitation.

Roy scanned it, then threw it on the porch floor and put his foot on it. "Somebody's got to be kidding!"

"Sure. But . . . I had to go home and burn my underwear."

Roy picked it up and read it again, and then stared toward the graveyard wall.

"Why would *anyone* send this?"

"Yeah. Since most of the studio people don't even know I'm *here!*"

"But, hell, last night *was* Halloween. Still, what an elaborate joke, hoisting a body up a ladder. Wait, what if they told *you* to come at midnight, but *other* people, at eight, nine, ten, and eleven? Scare 'em one by one! That would make sense!"

"Only if *you* had planned it!"

Roy turned sharply. "You don't really think—?"

"No. Yes. No."

"Which *is* it?"

"Remember that Halloween when we were nineteen and went to the Paramount Theatre to see Bob Hope in *The Cat and the Canary* and the girl in front of us screamed and I glanced around and there you sat, with a rubber ghoul mask on your face?"

"Yeah." Roy laughed.

"Remember that time when you called and said old Ralph Courtney, our best friend, was dead and for me to come over, you had him laid out in your house, but it was all a joke, you planned to get Ralph to put white powder all over his face and lay himself out and pretend to be dead and rise up when I came in. Remember?"

"Yep." Roy laughed again.

"But I met Ralph in the street and it spoiled your joke?"

"Sure." Roy shook his head at his own pranks.

"Well, then. No wonder I think maybe you put the damn body up on the wall and sent me the letter."

"Only one thing wrong with that," said Roy. "You've rarely mentioned Arbuthnot to me. If I made the body, how would I figure you'd recognize the poor s.o.b.? It would have to be someone who really knew that you had seen Arbuthnot years ago, right?"

"Well . . ."

"Doesn't make sense, a body in the rain, if you don't know what in hell you're looking at. You've told me about a lot of other people you met when you were a kid, hanging around the studios. If *I'd* made a body, it would be Rudolph Valentino or Lon Chaney, to be sure you'd recognize 'em. Correct?"

"Correct," I said lamely. I studied Roy's face and looked quickly away. "Sorry. But, hell, it *was* Arbuthnot. I saw him two dozen times over the years, back in the thirties. At previews. Out front at the studio, here. Him and his sports cars, a dozen different ones, and limousines, three of those. And women, a few dozen, always laughing, and when he signed autographs, slipping a quarter in the autograph book before he handed it back to you. A quarter! In 1934! A quarter bought you a malted milk, a candy bar, and a ticket to a movie."

"That's the kind of guy he was, was he? No wonder you remember him. How much'd he give you?"

"He gave me a buck twenty-five, one month. I was *rich*. And now he's buried over that wall where I was last night, isn't he? Why would someone try to scare me into thinking he'd been dug up and propped on a ladder? Why all the bother? The body landed like an iron safe. Take at least two men, maybe, to handle that. Why?"

Roy took a bite out of another doughnut. "Yeah, why? Unless someone is using *you* to tell the world. You *were* going to tell *someone* else, yes?"

"I might—"

"Don't. You look scared right now."

"But why should I be? Except I got this feeling it's more than a joke, it has some *other* meaning."

Roy stared at the wall, chewing quietly. "Hell," Roy said at last. "You been back over to the graveyard this morning to see if the body is *still* on the ground? Why not go see?"

"No!"

"It's broad daylight. You chicken?"

"No, but . . ."

"Hey!" cried an indignant voice. "What you two saps *doing* up there!?"

Roy and I looked down off the porch.

Manny Leiber stood there in the middle of the lawn. His Rolls-Royce was pulled up, its motor running silent and deep, and not a tremble in the frame.

"Well?" shouted Manny.

"We're having a *conference!*" Roy said easily. "We want to move *in* here!"

"You *what*?" Manny eyed the old Victorian house.

"Great place to work," Roy said, quickly. "Office for us up front, the sunporch, put in a card table, typewriter."

"You *got* an office!"

"Offices don't inspire. This—" I nodded around, taking the ball from Roy—"inspires. You should move *all* the writers out of the Writers' Building! Put Steve Longstreet over in that New Orleans mansion to write his Civil War film. And that French bakery just beyond? Great place for Marcel Dementhon to finish his revolution, yes? Down the way, Piccadilly, heck, put all those new English writers there!"

Manny came slowly up on the porch, his face a confused red. He looked around at the studio, his Rolls, and then at the two of us, as if he had caught us naked and smoking behind the barn. "Christ, not enough everything's gone to hell at breakfast. I got two fruitcakes who want to turn Lydia Pinkham's shack into a writers' cathedral!"

"Right!" said Roy. "On this very porch I conceived the scariest miniature film set in history!"

"Cut the hyperbole." Manny backed off. "Show me the *stuff*!"

"May we use your Rolls?" said Roy.

We used the Rolls.

On the way to Stage 13, Manny Leiber stared straight ahead and said, "I'm trying to run a madhouse and you guys sit around on porches shooting wind. Where in hell is my Beast!? Three *weeks* I've waited—"

"Hell," I said reasonably, "it takes time, waiting for something really new to step out of the night. Give us breathing space, time for the old secret self to coax itself out. Don't worry. Roy here will be working in clay. Things will rise out of *that*. For now, we keep the Monster in the shadows, see—"

"Excuses!" said Manny, glaring ahead. "I don't see. I'll give you three more days! I *want* to see the Monster!"

"What if," I blurted suddenly, "the Monster sees *you*! My God! What if we do it all from the Monster's viewpoint, looking out!? The camera moves and *is* the Monster, and people get scared of the Camera and—"

Manny blinked at me, shut one eye, and muttered: "Not bad. The *Camera*, huh?"

"Yeah! The Camera crawls out of the meteor. The Camera, as the Monster, blows across the desert, scaring Gila monsters, snakes, vultures, stirring the dust—"

"I'll be damned." Manny Leiber gazed off at the imaginary desert.

"I'll be damned," cried Roy, delighted.

"We put an oiled lens on the Camera," I hurried on, "add steam, spooky music, shadows, and the Hero staring *into* the Camera and—"

"*Then* what?"

"If I *talk* it I won't *write* it."

"Write it, *write* it!"

We stopped at Stage 13. I jumped out, babbling. "Oh, yeah. I think I should do *two* versions of the script. One for you. One for me."

"Two?" yelled Manny. "Why?"

"At the end of a week I hand in *both*. You get to choose which is right."

Manny eyed me suspiciously, still half in, half out of the Rolls.

"Crap! You'll do your *best* work on *your* idea!"

"No. I'll do my damnedest for you. But also my damnedest for *me*. Shake?"

"*Two* Monsters for the price of one? Do it! C'mon!"

Outside the door Roy stopped dramatically. "You *ready* for this? Prepare your minds and souls." He held up both beautiful artists' hands, like a priest.

"I'm prepared, dammit. Open!"

Roy flung open the outside and then the inside door and we stepped into total darkness.

"Lights, dammit!" said Manny.

"Hold on—" whispered Roy.

We heard Roy move in the dark, stepping carefully over unseen objects.

Manny twitched nervously.

"Almost ready," intoned Roy across a night territory. "Now . . ."

Roy turned on a wind machine, low. First there was a whisper like a giant storm, which brought with it weather from the Andes, snow murmuring off the shelves of the Himalayas, rain over

Sumatra, a jungle wind headed for Kilimanjaro, the rustle of skirts of tide along the Azores, a cry of primitive birds, a flourish of bat wings, all blended to lift your gooseflesh and drop your mind down trapdoors toward—

"Light!" cried Roy.

And now the light was rising on Roy Holdstrom's landscapes, on vistas so alien and beautiful it broke your heart and mended your terror and then shook you again as shadows in great lemming mobs rushed over the microscopic dunes, tiny hills, and miniature mountains, fleeing a doom already promised but not yet arrived.

I looked around with delight. Roy had read my mind again. The bright and dark stuff I threw on the midnight screens inside my camera obscura head he had stolen and blueprinted and built even before I had let them free with my mouth. Now, turnabout, I would use his miniature realities to flesh out my most peculiar odd script. My hero could hardly wait to sprint through this tiny land.

Manny Leiber stared, flabbergasted.

Roy's dinosaur land was a country of phantoms revealed in an ancient and artificial dawn.

Enclosing this lost world were huge glass plates on which Roy had painted primordial junglescapes, tar swamps in which his creatures sank beneath skies as fiery and bitter as Martian sunsets, burning with a thousand shades of red.

I felt the same thrill I had felt when, in high school, Roy had taken me home and I had gasped as he swung his garage doors wide on, not automobiles, but creatures driven by ancient needs to rise, claw, chew, fly, shriek, and die through all our childhood nights.

And here, now, on Stage 13, Roy's face burned above a whole miniature continent that Manny and I were stranded on.

I tiptoed across it, fearful of destroying any tiny thing. I reached a single covered sculpture platform and waited.

Surely this must be his greatest beast, the thing he had set himself to rear when, in our twenties, we had visited the primal corridors of our local natural history museum. Surely somewhere in the world this Beast had hidden in dusts, treading char, lost in God's coal mines under our very tread! Hear! oh hear that subway sound, his primitive heart, and volcanic lungs shrieking to be set free! And had Roy set him free?

"I'll be goddamned." Manny Leiber leaned toward the hidden monster. "Do we see it *now*?"

"Yes," Roy said, "that's it."

Manny touched the cover.

"Wait," said Roy. "I need one more day."

"Liar!" said Manny. "I don't believe you got one goddamn bastard thing under that rag!"

Manny took two steps. Roy jumped three.

At which instant, the Stage 13 set phone rang.

Before I could move, Manny grabbed it.

"Well?" he cried.

His face changed. Perhaps it got pale, perhaps not, but it changed.

"I know that." He took a breath. "I know that, too." Another breath; his face was getting red now. "I knew *that* half an hour ago! Say, god damn it to hell, who *is* this!?"

A wasp buzzed at the far end of the line. The phone had been hung up.

"Son of a bitch!"

Manny hurled the phone and I caught it.

"Wrap me in a wet sheet, someone, this is a madhouse! Where was I? You!"

He pointed at both of us.

"Two days, not three. You damn well get the Beast out of the catbox and into the light or—"

At which point the outer door opened. A runt of a guy in a black suit, one of the studio chauffeurs, stood in a glare of light.

"Now what?" Manny shouted.

"We got it here but the motor died. We just got it fixed."

"Move out, then, for Christ's sake!"

Manny charged at him with one fist raised, but the door slammed, the runt was gone, so Manny had to turn and direct his explosion at us.

"I'm having your final checks made up, ready for Friday afternoon. Deliver, or you'll never work again, either of you."

Roy said quietly, "Do we get to keep it? Our Green Town, Illinois, offices? Now that you *see* these results you got from us fruitcakes?"

Manny paused long enough to look back at the strange lost country like a kid in a fireworks factory.

"Christ," he breathed, forgetting his problems for a moment, "I got to admit you really *did* it." He stopped, angry at his own praise, and shifted gears. "Now cut the cackle and move your buns!"

And—bam! He was gone, too.

Standing in the midst of our ancient landscape, lost in time, Roy and I stared at one another.

"Curiouser and curiouser," said Roy. Then, "You really going to do it? Write two versions of the script? One for him, one for *us*?"

"Yep! Sure."

"How can you *do* that?"

"Heck," I said, "I been in training for fifteen years, wrote one hundred pulp stories, one a week, in one hundred weeks, two script outlines in two days? *Both* brilliant? *Trust* me."

"Okay, I do, I do." There was a long pause, then he said, "Do we go *look*?"

"Look? At *what*?"

"That funeral you saw. In the rain. Last night. Over the wall. Wait."

Roy walked over to the big airlock door. I followed. He opened the door. We looked out.

An ornately carved black hearse with crystal windows was just pulling away down the studio alley, making a big racket with a bad engine.

"I bet I know where it's going," said Roy.

8

We drove around on Gower Street in Roy's old beat-up 1927 tin lizzie.

We didn't see the black funeral hearse go into the graveyard, but as we pulled up out front and parked, the hearse came rolling out among the stones.

It passed us, carrying a casket into the full sunlight of the street.

We turned to watch the black limousine whisper out the gate with no more sound than a polar exhalation from off the northern floes.

"That's the first time I ever saw a casket in a funeral car go *out* of a cemetery. We're too late!"

I spun about to see the last of the limo heading east, back toward the studio.

"Too late for what?"

"Your dead man, dummy! Come on!"

We were almost to the cemetery back wall when Roy stopped.

"Well, by God, there's his tomb."

I looked at what Roy was looking at, about ten feet above us, in marble:

J. C. ARBUTHNOT, 1884–1934 R.I.P.

It was one of those Greek-temple huts in which they bury fabulous people, with an iron lattice gate locked over a heavy wood-and-bronze inner door.

"He couldn't have come out of there, *could* he?"

"No, but something got on that ladder and I knew his face. And someone else *knew* I would recognize that face so I was invited to come see."

"Shut up. Come on."

We advanced along the path.

"Watch it. We don't want to be seen playing this stupid game."

We arrived at the wall. There was nothing there, of course.

"Like I said, if the body was ever here, we're too late." Roy exhaled and glanced.

"No, look. There."

I pointed at the top of the wall.

There were the marks, two of them, of some object that had leaned against the upper rim.

"The ladder?"

"And down *here*."

The grass at the base of the wall, about five feet out, a proper angle, had two half-inch ladder indentations in it.

"And here. See?"

I showed him a long depression where the grass had been crushed by something falling.

"Well, well," murmured Roy. "Looks like Halloween's starting over."

Roy knelt on the grass and put his long bony fingers out to trace the print of the heavy flesh that had lain there in the cold rain only twelve hours ago.

I knelt with Roy staring down at the long indentation, and shivered.

"I—" I said, and stopped.

For a shadow moved between us.

"Morning!"

The graveyard day watchman stood over us.

I glanced at Roy, quickly. "Is this the right gravestone? It's been years. Is—"

The next flat tombstone was covered with leaves. I scrabbled the dust away. There was a half-seen name beneath. SMYTHE. BORN 1875–DIED 1928.

"Sure! Old grandpa!" cried Roy. "Poor guy. Died of pneumonia." Roy helped me brush away the dust. "I sure loved him. He—"

"Where're your flowers?" said the heavy voice, above us.

Roy and I stiffened.

"Ma's bringing 'em," said Roy. "We came ahead, to find the stone." Roy glanced over his shoulder. "She's out there now."

The graveyard day watchman, a man long in years and deep in suspicion, with a face not unlike a weathered tombstone, glanced toward the gate.

A woman, bearing flowers, was coming up the road, far out, near Santa Monica Boulevard.

Thank God, I thought.

The watchman snorted, chewed his gums, wheeled about, and strode off among the graves. Just in time, for the woman had stopped and headed off, away from us.

We jumped up. Roy grabbed some flowers off a nearby mound. "Don't!"

"Like hell!" Roy stashed the flowers on Grandpa Smythe's stone. "Just in case that guy comes back and wonders why there're no flowers after all our gab. Come on!"

We moved out about fifty yards and waited, pretending to talk, but saying little. Finally, Roy touched my elbow. "Careful," he whispered. "Side glances. Don't look straight on. He's back."

And indeed the old watchman had arrived at the place near the wall where the long impressions of the fallen body still remained.

He looked up and saw us. Quickly, I put my arm around Roy's shoulder to ease his sadness.

Now the old man bent. With raking fingers, he combed the grass. Soon there was no trace of anything heavy that might have fallen from the sky last night, in a terrible rain.

"You believe now?" I said.

"I wonder," said Roy, "where that hearse went to."

9

As we were driving back in through the main gate of the studio, the hearse whispered out. Empty. Like a long autumn wind it drifted off, around, and back to Death's country.

"Jesus Christ! Just like I guessed!" Roy steered but stared back at the empty street. "I'm beginning to enjoy this!"

We moved along the street in the direction from which the hearse had been coming.

Fritz Wong marched across the alley in front of us, driving or leading an invisible military squad, muttering and swearing to himself, his sharp profile cutting the air in two halves, wearing a dark beret, the only man in Hollywood who wore a beret and dared anyone to notice!

"Fritz!" I called. "Stop, Roy!"

Fritz ambled over to lean against the car and give us his by now familiar greeting.

"Hello, you stupid bike-riding Martian! Who's that strange-looking ape driving?"

"Hello, Fritz, you stupid . . ." I faltered and then said sheepishly, "Roy Holdstrom, world's greatest inventor, builder, and flier of dinosaurs!"

Fritz Wong's monocle flashed fire. He fixed Roy with his Oriental-Germanic glare, then nodded crisply.

"Any friend of *Pithecanthropus erectus* is a friend of mine!"

Roy grabbed his handshake. "I liked your last film."

"*Liked!*" cried Fritz Wong.

"*Loved!*"

"Good." Fritz looked at me. "What's new since breakfast!"

"Anything *funny* happening around here just now?"

"A roman phalanx of forty men just marched that way. A gorilla, carrying his head, ran in Stage 10. A homosexual art director got thrown out of the Men's. Judas is on strike for more silver over in Galilee. No, no. I wouldn't say anything funny or I'd notice."

"How about passing through?" offered Roy. "Any funerals?"

"Funerals! You think I wouldn't notice? Wait!" He flashed his monocle toward the gate and then toward the backlot. "Dummy. Yes. I was hoping it was deMille's hearse and we could celebrate. It went *that* way!"

"Are they filming a burial here today?"

"On every sound stage: turkeys, catatonic actors, English funeral directors whose heavy paws would stillbirth a whale! Halloween, yesterday, yes? And today the true Mexican Day of Death, November 1st, so why should it be different at Maximus Films? Where did you find this terrible wreck of a car, Mr. Holdstrom?"

"This," Roy said, like Edgar Kennedy doing a slow burn in an old Hal Roach comedy, "is the car in which Laurel and Hardy sold fish in that two reeler in 1930. Cost me fifty bucks, plus seventy to repaint. Stand back, sir!"

Fritz Wong, delighted with Roy, jumped back. "In one hour, Martian. The commissary! *Be* there!"

We steamed on amidst the noon crowd. Roy wheeled us around a corner toward Springfield, Illinois, lower Manhattan, and Piccadilly.

"You know where you're going?" I asked.

"Hell, a studio's a great place to hide a body. Who would notice? On a backlot filled with Abyssinians, Greeks, Chicago mobsters, you could march in six dozen gang wars with forty Sousa bands and nobody'd sneeze! That body, chum, should be right about here!"

And we dusted around the last corner into Tombstone, Arizona.

"Nice name for a town," said Roy.

10

There was a warm stillness. It was High Noon. We were surrounded by a thousand footprints in backlot dust. Some of the prints belonged to Tom Mix, Hoot Gibson, and Ken Maynard, long ago. I let the wind blow memory, lifting the hot dust. Of course the prints hadn't stayed, dust doesn't keep, and even John Wayne's big strides were long since sifted off, even as Matthew, Mark, Luke, and John's sandal marks had vanished from the shore of the Sea of Galilee just one hundred yards over on Lot

12. Nevertheless, the smell of horses remained, the stagecoach would pull in soon with a new load of scripts, and a fresh batch of riflemen cow pokes. I was not about to refuse the quiet joy of just sitting here in the old Laurel and Hardy flivver, looking over at the Civil War locomotive, which got stoked up twice a year and became the 9:10 from Galveston, or Lincoln's death train taking him home, Lord, taking him home.

But at last I said, "What makes you so sure the body's here?"

"Hell." Roy kicked the floorboards like Gary Cooper once kicked cow chips. "Look close at those buildings."

I looked.

Behind the false fronts here in Western territory were metal welding shops, old car museums, false-front storage bins and—

"The carpenters' shop?" I said.

Roy nodded and flivvered us over to let the dog die around the corner, out of sight.

"They build coffins here, so the body's here." Roy climbed out of the flivver one long piece of lumber at a time. "The coffin was *returned* here because it was made here. Come *on*, before the Indians arrive!"

I caught up with him in a cool grotto where Napoleon's Empire furniture was hung on racks and Julius Caesar's throne waited for his long-lost behind.

I looked around.

Nothing *ever* dies, I thought. It always returns. If you *want*, that is.

And where does it hide, waiting. Where is it reborn? Here, I thought. Oh, yes, *here*.

In the minds of men who arrive with lunch buckets, looking like workers, and leave looking like husbands or improbable lovers.

But in between?

Build the *Mississippi Belle* if you want to steamboat landfall New Orleans, or rear Bernini's columns on the north forty. Or rebuild the Empire State and then steam-power an ape big enough to climb it.

Your dream is *their* blueprint, and these are all the sons of the sons of Michelangelo and da Vinci, the fathers of yesterday winding up as sons in tomorrow.

And right now my friend Roy leaned into the dim cavern behind a Western saloon and pulled me along, among the stashed facades of Baghdad and upper Sandusky.

Silence. Everyone had gone to lunch.

Roy snuffed the air and laughed quietly.

"God, yes! Smell *that* smell! Sawdust! That's what got me into high school woodshop with you. And the sounds of the bandsaw lathes. Sounded like people were *doing* things. Made my hands jerk. Looky here." Roy stopped by a long glass case and looked down at beauty.

The *Bounty* was there, in miniature, twenty inches long and fully rigged, and sailing through imaginary seas, two long centuries ago.

"Go on," Roy said, quietly. "Touch gently."

I touched and marveled and forgot why we were there and wanted to stay on forever. But Roy, at last, drew me away.

"Hot dog," he whispered. "Take your pick."

We were looking at a huge display of coffins about fifty feet back in the warm darkness.

"How come so many?" I asked, as we moved up.

"To bury all the turkeys the studio will make between now and Thanksgiving."

We reached the funeral assembly line.

"It's all yours," said Roy. "Choose."

"Can't be at the top. Too high. And people are lazy. So—this one."

I nudged the nearest coffin with my shoe.

"Go on," urged Roy, laughing at my hesitance. "*Open* it."

"You."

Roy bent and tried the lid.

"Damn!"

The coffin was nailed shut.

A horn sounded somewhere. We glanced out.

Out in the Tombstone street a car was pulling up.

"Quick!" Roy ran to a table, scrabbled around frantically, and found a hammer and crowbar to jimmy the nails.

"Ohmigod," I gasped.

Manny Leiber's Rolls-Royce was dusting into the horse yard, out there in the noon glare.

"Let's go!"

"Not until we see if—there!"

The last nail flew out.

Roy grasped the lid, took a deep breath, and opened the coffin.

Voices sounded in the Western yard, out there in the hot sun.

"Christ, open your eyes," cried Roy. "Look!"

I had shut my eyes, not wanting to feel the rain again on my face. I opened them.

"Well?" said Roy.

The body was there, lying on its back, its eyes wide, its nostrils flared, and its mouth gaped. But no rain fell to brim over and pour down its cheeks and chin.

"Arbuthnot," I said.

"Yeah," gasped Roy. "I remember the photos now. Lord, it's a good resemblance. But why would anyone put this, whatever it is, up a ladder, for what?"

I heard a door slam. A hundred yards off, in the warm dust, Manny Leiber had got out of his Rolls, and was blinking into the shade, around, about, above us.

I flinched.

"Wait a minute—" Roy said. He snorted and reached down.

"Don't!"

"Hold on," he said, and touched the body.

"For God's sake, quick!"

"Why looky here," said Roy.

He took hold of the body and lifted.

"Gah!" I said, and stopped.

For the body rose up as easily as a bag of cornflakes.

"No!"

"Yeah, sure." Roy shook the body. It rattled like a scarecrow.

"I'll be damned! And look, at the bottom of the coffin, lead sinkers to give it weight once they got it up the ladder! And when it fell, like you said, it would really hit. Look out! Here come the barracudas!"

Roy squinted out into the noon glare and the distant figures stepping out of cars, gathering around Manny.

"Okay. Let's go."

Roy dropped the body, slammed the lid and ran.

I followed in and out of a maze of furniture, pillars, and false fronts.

Off at a distance, through three dozen doors and half up a flight of Renaissance stairs, Roy and I stopped, looked back, craned to ache and listen. Way off, about ninety to a hundred feet, Manny Leiber arrived at the place where we had been only a minute ago. Manny's voice cut through all the rest. He told everyone, I imagine, to shut up. There was silence. They were opening the coffin with the facsimile body in it.

Roy looked at me, eyebrows up. I looked back, unable to breathe.

There was a stir, some sort of outcry, curses. Manny swore above the rest. Then there was a babble, more talk, Manny yelling again, and a final slam of the coffin lid.

That was the gunshot that plummeted me and Roy the hell out of the place. We made it down the stairs as quietly as possible, ran through another dozen doors, and out the back side of the carpenters' shop.

"You hear anything?" gasped Roy, glancing back.

"No. You?"

"Not a damn thing. But they sure exploded. Not once but three times. Manny, the worst! My God, what's going on? Why all the fuss over a damned wax dummy I could have run up with two bucks' worth of latex, wax, and plaster in half an hour!?"

"Slow down, Roy," I said. "We don't want anyone to see us running."

Roy slowed, but still took great whooping-crane strides.

"God, Roy!" I said. "If they knew we were *in* there!"

"They don't. Hey, this is fun."

Why, I thought, did I *ever* introduce my best friend to a dead man?

A minute later we reached Roy's Laurel and Hardy flivver behind the shop.

Roy sat in the front seat, smiling a most unholy smile, appreciating the sky and every cloud.

"Climb in," he said.

Inside the shed, voices rose in a late-afternoon uproar. Someone was cursing somewhere. Someone else was criticizing. Someone said yes. A lot of others said no as the small mob boiled out into the hot noon light, like a hive of angry bees.

A moment later, Manny Leiber's Rolls-Royce streamed by like a voiceless storm.

Inside, I saw three oyster-pale yes-men's faces.

And Manny Leiber's face, blood-red with rage.

He saw us as his Rolls stormed past.

Roy waved and cried a jolly hello.

"Roy!" I yelled.

Roy guffawed, said, "What came *over* me!?" and drove away.

I looked over at Roy and almost exploded myself. Inhaling the wind, he blew it out his mouth with gusto.

"You're nuts!" I said. "Don't you have a nerve in your body?"

"Why should I," Roy reasoned amiably, "be scared of a papiermâché mockup? Hell, Manny's heebie-jeebies make me feel good. I've taken a lot of guff from him this month. Now someone's stuck a bomb in *his* pants? *Great!*"

"Was it *you*?" I blurted, suddenly.

Roy was startled. "You off on *that* track again? Why would I sew and glue a dimwit scarecrow and climb ladders at midnight?"

"For the reasons you just said. Cure your boredom. Shove bombs in other people's pants."

"Nope. Wish I could claim the credit. Right now, I can hardly wait for lunch. When Manny shows up, his face should be a riot."

"Do you think anyone saw us in there?"

"Christ, no. That's why I waved! To show how dumb and

innocent we are! Something *is* going on. We got to act *natural*."

"When was the last time we did *that*?"

Roy laughed.

We motored around behind the worksheds, through Madrid, Rome, and Calcutta, and now pulled up at a brownstone somewhere in the Bronx.

Roy glanced at his watch.

"You got an appointment. Fritz Wong. Go. We should both be seen *everywhere* in the next hour except *there*." He nodded at Tombstone, two hundred yards away.

"When," I asked, "are you going to start getting scared?"

Roy felt his leg bones with one hand.

"Not yet," he said.

Roy dropped me in front of the commissary. I got out and stood looking at his now-serious, now-amused face.

"You coming in?" I said.

"Soon. Got some errands to run."

"Roy, you're not going to do something nutty now, are you? You got that faraway crazed look."

Roy said, "I been thinking. When did Arbuthnot die?"

"Twenty years ago this week. Two-car accident, three people killed. Arbuthnot and Sloane, his studio accountant, plus Sloane's wife. It was headlined for days. The funeral was bigger than Valentino's. I stood outside the graveyard with my friends. Enough flowers for the New Year's Rose Parade. A thousand people came out of the service, eyes running under their dark glasses. My God, the *misery*. Arbuthnot was that loved."

"Car crash, huh?"

"No witnesses. Maybe one was following too close, going home drunk from a studio party."

"Maybe." Roy pulled at his lower lip, squinting one eye at me. "But what if there's more to it? Maybe, this late in time, someone's discovered something about that crash and is threatening to spill the beans. Otherwise why the body on the wall? Why the panic? Why hush it up if there's nothing to hide? God, did you hear their voices back there just now? How come a dead

man that's not a dead man, a body that's not a body, shakes up
the executives?"

"There must've been more than one letter," I said. "The one
I got, and others. But I'm the only one dumb enough to go see.
And when I didn't spread the word, blurt it out today, whoever
put the body on the wall had to write or call in today to start
the panic and send in the funeral hearse. And the guy who made
the body and sent the note is in here right now, watching the
fun. Why . . . why . . . why . . . ?"

"Hush," said Roy, quietly, "hush." He started his engine.
"We'll solve the half-ass mystery at lunch. Put on your innocent
face. Make like naïve over the Louis B. Mayer bean soup. I gotta
go check my miniature models. One last tiny street to nail in
place." He glanced at his watch. "In two hours my dinosaur
country will be ready for photography. Then, all we need is our
grand and glorious Beast."

I looked into Roy's still burning-bright face.

"You're *not* going to go steal the body and put it back up on
the wall, are you?"

"Never crossed my mind," said Roy, and drove away.

11

In the middle of the far-left side of the commissary there was
a small platform, no higher than a foot, on which stood a single
table with two chairs. I often imagined the slavemaster of a
Roman trireme warship seated there crashing down one sledge-
hammer, then another, to give the beat to the sweating oarsmen
locked to their oars, obedient to panics, pulling for some far
theatre aisle, pursued by maddened exhibitors, greeted on shore
by mobs of insulted customers.

But there never was a Roman galley coxswain at the table,
leading the beat.

It was Manny Leiber's table. He brooded there alone, stirring his food as if it were the split innards of Caesar's fortuneteller's pigeons, forking the spleen, ignoring the heart, predicting futures. Some days he slouched there with the studio's Doc Phillips, testing new philtres and potions in tapwater. Other days, he dined on directors' or writers' tripes as they glumly confronted him, nodding, yes, yes, the film was behind schedule! yes, yes, they would hurry it along!

Nobody wanted to sit at that table. Often, a pink slip arrived in lieu of a check.

Today as I ducked in and shrank inches wandering through the tables, Manny's small platform place was empty. I stopped. That was the first time I had ever seen no dishes, no utensils, not even flowers there. Manny was still outside somewhere, yelling at the sun because it had insulted him.

But now, the longest table in the commissary waited, half full and filling.

I had never gone near the thing in the weeks I had worked in the studio. As with most neophytes, I had feared contact with the terribly bright and terribly famous. H. G. Wells had lectured in Los Angeles when I was a boy, and I had not gone to seek his autograph. The rage of joy at the sight of him would have struck me dead. So it was with the commissary table, where the best directors, film editors, and writers sat at an eternal Last Supper waiting for a late-arriving Christ. Seeing it again, I lost my nerve.

I slunk away, veering off toward a far corner where Roy and I often wolfed sandwiches and soup.

"Oh, no you *don't!*" a voice shouted.

My head sank down on my neck, which periscoped, oiled with sweat, into my jacket collar.

Fritz Wong cried, "Your appointment is *here. March!*"

I ricocheted between tables to stare at my shoes beside Fritz Wong. I felt his hand on my shoulder, ready to rip off my epaulettes.

"This," announced Fritz, "is our visitor from another world, across the commissary. I will guide him to sit."

His hands on my shoulders, he forced me gently down.

At last I raised my eyes and looked along the table at twelve people watching me.

"Now," announced Fritz, "he will tell us about his Search for the Beast!"

The Beast.

Since it had been announced that Roy and I were to write, build, and birth the most incredibly hideous animal in Hollywood history, thousands had helped us in our search. One would have thought we were seeking Scarlett O'Hara or Anna Karenina. But no . . . the Beast, and the so-called contest to find the Beast, appeared in *Variety* and the *Hollywood Reporter*. My name and Roy's were in every article. I clipped and saved every dumb, stillborn item. Photographs had begun to pour in from other studios, agents, and the general public. Quasimodos Numbers Two and Three showed up at the studio gate, as did four Opera Phantoms. Wolfmen abounded. First and second cousins of Lugosi and Karloff, hiding out on our Stage 13, were thrown off the lot.

Roy and I had begun to feel we were judging an Atlantic City beauty contest somehow shipped to Transylvania. The half-animals waiting outside the sound stages every night were something; the photographs were worse. At last, we burned all the photographs and left the studio through a side entrance.

So it had been with the search for the Beast all month.

And now Fritz Wong said again: "Okay. The Beast? *Explain!*"

12

I looked at all those faces and said: "No. No, please. Roy and I will be ready soon, but right now . . ." I took a fast sip of bad Hollywood tap water, "I've been watching this table for three weeks. Everyone always sits at the same place. So-and-so up here, such-and-such over across. I'll bet the guys down there don't even know the guys over here. Why not mix it up? Leave spaces so every half hour people could play musical chairs, shift, meet someone new, not the same old guff from familiar faces. Sorry."

"Sorry!?" Fritz grabbed my shoulders and shook me with his own laughter. "Okay, guys! Musical chairs! *Allez-oop!*"

Applause. Cheers.

Such was the general hilarity as everyone slapped backs, shook hands, found new chairs, sat back down. Which only suffered me into further confused embarrassment with more shouts of laughter. More applause.

"We will have to seat this maestro here each day to teach us social activities and life," announced Fritz. "All right, compatriots," cried Fritz. "To your left, young maestro, is Maggie Botwin, the finest cutter/film editor in film history!"

"Bull!" Maggie Botwin nodded to me and went back to her omelet, which she had carried with her.

Maggie Botwin.

Prim, quiet lady, like an upright piano, seeming taller than she was because of the way she sat, rose, and walked, and the way she held her hands in her lap and the way she coifed her hair up on top of her head, in some fashion out of World War I.

I had once heard her on a radio show describe herself as a snake charmer.

All that film whistling through her hands, sliding through her fingers, undulant and swift.

All that time passing, but to pass and repass again.

It was no different, she said, than life itself.

The future rushed at you. You had a single instant, as it flashed by, to change it into an amiable, recognizable, and decent past. Instant by instant, tomorrow blinked in your grasp. If you did not seize without holding, shape without breaking, that continuity of moments, you left nothing behind. Your object, her object, *all* of our objects, was to mold and print ourselves on those single bits of future that, in the touching, aged into swiftly vanishing yesterdays.

So it was with film.

With the one difference: you could live it again, as often as need be. Run the future by, make it now, make it yesterday, then start over with tomorrow.

What a great profession, to be in charge of three concourses of time: the vast invisible tomorrows; the narrowed focus of now; the great tombyard of seconds, minutes, hours, years, millennia that burgeoned as a seedbed to keep the other two.

And if you didn't like any of the three rushing time rivers? Grab your scissors. *Snip.* There! Feeling *better*?

And now here she was, her hands folded in her lap one moment and the next lifting a small 8-millimeter camera to pan over the faces at the table, face by face, her hands calmly efficient, until the camera stopped and fixed on me.

I gazed back at it and remembered a day in 1934 when I had seen her outside the studio shooting film of all the fools, the geeks, the autograph nuts, myself among them.

I wanted to call out, Do you remember? But how could she?

I ducked my head. Her camera whirred.

It was at that exact moment that Roy Holdstrom arrived.

He stood in the commissary doorway, searching. Finding me, he did not wave but jerked his head furiously. Then he turned and stalked out. I jumped to my feet and ran off before Fritz Wong could trap me.

I saw Roy vanishing into the Men's outside, and found him standing at the white porcelain shrine worshiping Respighi's *Fountains of Rome*. I stood beside him, noncreative, the old pipes frozen for the winter.

"Look. I found this on Stage 13 just now."

Roy shoved a typewritten page onto the tile shelf before me.

The Beast Born at Last!
The Brown Derby Tonight!

Vine Street. Ten o'clock.
Be there! or you lose *everything!*

"You don't believe this!" I gasped.

"As much as you believed *your* note and went to the damn graveyard." Roy stared at the wall in front of him. "That's the *same* paper and typeface as *your* note? Will I go to the Brown Derby tonight? Hell, why not? Bodies on walls, missing ladders, raked-over prints in grass, papier-mâché corpses, plus Manny Leiber screaming. I got to thinking, five minutes ago, if Manny and the others were upset by the scarecrow dummy, what if it suddenly disappeared, then what?"

"You didn't?" I said.

"No?" said Roy.

Roy pocketed the note. Then he took a small box from a corner table and handed it to me. "Someone's using us. I decided to do a little using myself. Take it. Go in the booth. Open it up."

I did just that.

I shut the door.

"Don't just stand there," called Roy. "*Open* it!"

"I am, I am."

I opened the box and stared in.

"My God!" I cried.

"What do you see?" said Roy.

"Arbuthnot!"

"Fits in the box real nice and neat, huh?" said Roy.

13

"What made you *do* it?"

"Cats are curious. I'm a cat," said Roy, hustling along.

We were headed back toward the commissary.

Roy had the box tucked under his arm, and a vast grin of triumph on his face.

"Look," he said. "Someone sends *you* a note. You go to a graveyard, find a body, but don't report it, spoiling whatever game is up. Phone calls are made, the studio sends for the body, and goes into a panic when they actually have a viewing. How else can I act except out of wild curiosity. What kind of game is this? I ask. I can only find out by countermoving the chesspiece, yes? We saw and heard how Manny and his pals reacted an hour ago. How would they react, I wondered, let's study it, if, after finding a body, they lost it again, and went crazy wondering who had it? *Me!*"

We stopped outside the commissary door.

"You're not going in there with that!" I exclaimed.

"Safest place in the world. Nobody would suspect a box I carry right into the middle of the studio. But be careful, mate, we're being watched, right now."

"Where?!" I cried, and turned swiftly.

"If I knew that, it would all be over. C'mon."

"I'm not hungry."

"Strange," said Roy, "why do I feel I could eat a horse?"

14

On our way back into the commissary I saw that Manny's table still stood empty and waiting. I froze, staring at his place.

"Damn fool," I whispered.

Roy shook the box behind me. It rustled.

"Sure am," he said gladly. "Move."

I moved to my place.

Roy placed his special box on the floor, winked at me, and sat at the far end of the table, smiling the smile of the innocent and the perfect.

Fritz glared at me as if my absence had been a personal insult.

"Pay attention!" Fritz snapped his fingers. "The introductions continue!" He pointed along the table. "Next is Stanislau Groc,

Nikolai Lenin's very own makeup man, the man who prepared
Lenin's body, waxed the face, paraffined the corpse to lie in state
for all these years in the Kremlin wall in Moscow in Soviet
Russia!"

"Lenin's *makeup* man?" I said.

"Cosmetologist." Stanislau Groc waved his small hand above
his small head above his small body.

He was hardly larger than one of the Singer's Midgets who
played Munchkins in *The Wizard of Oz*.

"Bow and scrape to me," he called. "You *write* monsters. Roy
Holdstrom *builds* them. But I rouged, waxed, and polished a
great red monster, long dead!"

"Ignore the stupefying Russian bastard," said Fritz. "Observe
the chair next to him!"

An empty place.

"For who?" I asked.

Someone coughed. Heads turned.

I held my breath.

And the Arrival took place.

15

This last one to arrive was a man so pale that his skin seemed
to glow with an inner light. He was tall, six feet three I would
imagine, and his hair was long and his beard dressed and shaped,
and his eyes of such startling clarity that you felt he saw your
bones through your flesh and your soul inside your bones. As he
passed each table, the knives and forks hesitated on their way
to half-open mouths. After he passed, leaving a wake of silence,
the business of life began again. He strode with a measured tread
as if he wore robes instead of a tattered coat and some soiled
trousers. He gave a blessing gesture on the air as he moved by
each table, but his eyes were straight ahead, as if seeing some
world beyond, not ours. He was looking at me, and I shrank, for

I couldn't imagine why he would seek me out, among all these accepted and established talents. And at last he stood above me, the gravity of his demeanor being such it pulled me to my feet.

There was a long silence as this man with the beautiful face stretched out a thin arm with a thin wrist, and at the end of it a hand with the most exquisitely long fingers I had ever seen.

I put my hand out to take his. His hand turned, and I saw the mark of the driven spike in the middle of the wrist. He turned his other hand over, so I could see the similar scar in the middle of his left wrist. He smiled, reading my mind, and quietly explained, "Most people think the nails were driven through the palms. No. The palms could not hold a body's weight. The wrists, nailed, *can*. The wrists." Then he turned both hands over so I could see where the nails had come through on the other side.

"J. C." said Fritz Wong, "this is our visitor from another world, our young science-fiction writer—"

"I know." The beautiful stranger nodded and gestured toward himself.

"Jesus Christ," he said.

I stepped aside so he could sit, then fell back in my own chair.

Fritz Wong passed down a small basket full of bread. "Please," he called, "change these into fish!"

I gasped.

But J. C., with the merest flick of his fingers, produced one silvery fish from amidst the bread and tossed it high. Fritz, delighted, caught it to laughter and applause.

The waitress arrived with several bottles of cheap booze to more shouts and applause.

"This wine," said J.C., "was water ten seconds ago. Please!"

The wine was poured and savored.

"Surely—" I stammered.

The entire table looked up.

"He wants to know," called Fritz, "if your name is really what you say it is."

With somber grace, the tall man drew forth and displayed his driver's license. It read:

"Jesus Christ. 911 Beachwood Avenue. Hollywood."

He slipped it back into his pocket, waited for the table to be silent, and said:

"I came to this studio in 1927 when they made *Jesus the King*. I was a woodworker out back in those sheds. I cut and polished the three crosses on Calvary, still standing. There was a contest in every Baptist basement and Catholic backwash in the land. Find Christ! He *was* found *here*. The director asked where I worked? The *carpenter's* shop. My God, he cried, let me *see* that face! Go put on a *beard*! 'Make me look like holy Jesus,' I advised the makeup man. I went back, dressed in robes and thorns, the whole holy commotion. The director danced on the Mount and washed my feet. Next thing you know the Baptists were lining up at Iowa pie festivals when I dusted through in my tin flivver with banners "THE KING IS COMING," "GOING ON BEFORE."

"Across country in auto bungalow courts, I had a great ten-year Messiah run, until vino and venality tattered my smock. Nobody wants a womanizing Saviour. It wasn't so much I kicked cats and wound up other men's wives like dime-store clocks, no, it was just that I was Him, you see?"

"I think I see," I said gently.

J. C. put his long wrists and long hands and long fingers out before him, as cats often sit, waiting for the world to come worship.

"Women felt it was blasphemy if they so much as breathed my air. Touching was terrible. Kissing a mortal sin. The act itself? Might as well leap in the burning pit with an eternity of slime up to your ears. Catholics, no, Holy Rollers were worst. I managed to bed and breakfast one or two before they *knew* me, when I traveled the country incognito. After a month of starving for feminine acrobats, I'd run amok. I just shaved and lit out across country, pounding fenceposts into native soil, duck-pressing ladies left and right. I flattened more broads than a steamroller at a Baptist skinny dip. I ran fast, hoping shotgun preachers wouldn't count hymens and hymnals and wallop me with buckshot. I prayed ladies would never guess they had enjoyed a laying on of hands by the main Guest at the Last Supper. When I wore *it* down to a nubbin and drank myself into a stupor, the studio'd pick up my bones, pay off the sheriffs, placate the priests in North Sty, Nebraska, with new baptismal fonts for the birth of my latterday kids, and tote me home to a cell on the backlot, where I was kept like John the Baptist, threatened with losing both my heads until they finished one last fish fry at Galilee and one more mystery tour up Calvary. Only old age and a dilapidated pecker stopped me. I was sent out to the bush leagues. Which was great for I ravened for leagues of bush. There was never a more woman-oriented man than this lost soul you see here. I was undeserving to play J. C. when, in thousands of theatres across country, I saved souls and lusted for dessert. For many years I have solaced myself not with bodies but with bottles. I'm lucky Fritz renovated me for this new film, in long shots, with tons of makeup. That's it. Chapter and verse. Fade out."

Applause. The whole table clapped hands and called praise.

Eyes shut, J. C. bowed his head, left and right.

"That's quite some story," I murmured.

"Don't believe a word of it," said J. C.

The applause stopped. Someone else had arrived.

Doc Phillips stood at the far end of the table.

"My God," said J. C. in a strong, clear voice. "Here's Judas *now!*"

But if the studio doctor heard, it was not evident.

He lingered, studying the room with distaste, fearful of encounters. He resembled one of those lizards you see on the edge of a primeval forest, glinting his eyes around, terribly apprehensive, sniffing the air, touching the wind with probing claws, lashing his tail in little twitches, doom in all directions, no hope, only nervous response, ready to spin, rustle, run. His gaze found Roy and for some reason fixed on him. Roy sat up, stiffened, and smiled a weak smile at the doc.

My God, I thought, someone saw Roy stealing off with his box. Someone—

"Will you say grace?" called Fritz. "The Surgeon's Prayer— O Lord, deliver us from doctors!"

Doc Phillips glanced away as if only a fly had touched his skin. Roy collapsed back in his chair.

The doc had come, out of habit. Beyond the commissary, out there in the bright high-noon sun, Manny and a few other fleas were doing backflips of anger and frustration. And the doc had come here to get away from it or search for suspects, I could not tell which.

But there he was, Doc Phillips, the fabulous physician to all the studios from the early handcranked cameras to the advent of shrieks and screams in sound to this very noon when the earth shook. If Groc was the eternal jolly Punch, then Doc Phillips was the glum curer of incurable egos, a shadow on the wall, a terrible scowl at the back of theatre previews, diagnosing sick films. He was like those football coaches on the sidelines of victorious teams, refusing to flash their teeth just once in approval. He spoke not in paragraphs or sentences, but clips and chops of shorthand prescription words. Between his ayes and nays lay silence.

He had been on the eighteenth green when the head of Skylark Studios sank his last putt and dropped dead. It was rumored he had sailed off the California coast when that famous publisher threw an equally famous director overboard to "accidentally" drown. I had seen pictures of him at Valentino's bier, in Jeanne Eagels's sickroom, at some San Diego yacht race where he was carried as sunstroke protection to a dozen New York movie moguls. It was said he had happy-drugged a whole studio star system and then cured them in his hideaway asylum somewhere in Arizona, near Needles. The irony of the town's name did not go unsaid. He rarely ate in the commissary; his glance spoiled the food. Dogs barked at him as if he were an infernal mailman. Babies bit his elbows and suffered stomach cramps.

Everyone flinched and pulled back at his arrival.

Doc Phillips fastened his glare here and there along our group. Within instants, some few of them developed tics.

Fritz turned to me. "His work is never done. Too many babies arrived early behind Stage 5. Heart attacks at the New York office. Or that actor in Monaco gets caught with his crazy operatic boyfriend. He—"

The dyspeptic doctor strode behind our chairs, whispered to Stanislau Groc, then turned quickly and hurried out.

Fritz scowled at the far exit and then turned to burn me with his monocle.

"Oh master futurist who sees all, tell us, what the hell *is* going on?"

The blood burned in my cheeks. My tongue was locked with guilt in my mouth. I lowered my head.

"Musical chairs," someone shouted. Groc, on his feet, said again, his eyes on me, "Chairs. Chairs!"

Everyone laughed. Everyone moved, which covered my confusion.

When they had done with churning in all directions, I found Stanislau Groc, the man who had polished Lenin's brow and dressed his goatee for eternity, directly across from me, and Roy at my side.

Groc smiled a great smile, the friend of a lifetime.

I said, "What was Doc's hurry? What's going on?"

"Pay no attention." Groc calmly eyed the commissary doors. "I felt a shudder at eleven this morning, as if the rear of the studio had struck an iceberg. Madmen have been rushing around ever since, bailing out. It makes me happy to see so many people upset. It makes me forget my melancholy job of turning Bronx mud ducks into Brooklyn swans." He stopped for a bite of his fruit salad. "What do you guess? What iceberg has our dear *Titanic* struck?"

Roy leaned back in his chair and said, "There's some calamity at the prop and carpenters' shop."

I shot Roy a scowl. Stanislau Groc stiffened.

"Ah, yes," he said slowly. "A small problem with the manatee, the woman's figure, carved from wood, to go on the *Bounty*."

I kicked Roy under the table, but he leaned forward:

"Surely that wasn't the iceberg you mentioned?"

"Ah, no," said Groc, laughing. "Not an Arctic collision but a hot-air balloon race, all the gas-bag producers and yes-men of the studio are being called into Manny's office. Someone will be fired. And then—" Groc gestured toward the ceiling with his tiny doll hands—"falling upward!"

"What?"

"A man is fired from Warner's and falls upward to MGM. A man at MGM is fired and falls upward to 20th. Falling *upward*! Isaac Newton's *reverse* law!" Groc paused to smile at his own wit. "Ah, but you, poor writer, will never be able, when fired, to fall upward, only down. I—"

He stopped, because . . .

I was studying him as I must have studied my grandfather, dead forever, in his upstairs bedroom thirty years ago. The stubble on my grandpa's pale waxen skin, the eyelids that threatened to crack and fix me with the angry glare that had frozen Grandma like a snow queen in the parlor for a lifetime, all, all of it as clean and clear as this moment with Lenin's necrologist/cosmetician seated across from me like a jumping jack, mouse-nibbling his fruit salad.

"Are you," he asked, politely, "looking for the stitch marks over my ears?"

"No, no!"

"Yes, yes!" he replied, amused. "Everyone looks! So!" He leaned forward, turning his head to left and right, skinning his hairline and then his temples.

"Lord," I said, "what fine work."

"No. Perfect!"

For the thin lines were mere shadows, and if there were flea bite stitch scars, they had long since healed.

"Did you—?" I said.

"Operate on myself? Cut out my own appendix? Perhaps I am like that woman who fled Shangri-La and shriveled into a Mongol prune!"

Groc laughed, and I was fascinated with his laughter. There was no minute when he was not merry. It was as though if he ever stopped laughing he would gasp and die. Always the happy bark, the fixed grin.

"Yes?" he asked, seeing that I was studying his teeth, his lips.

"What's there so funny to laugh at," I said, "always?"

"Everything! Did you ever see a film with Conrad Veidt—?"

"The Man Who Laughs?"

That stopped Groc in mid-dust. "Impossible! You lie!"

"My ma was nuts for films. After school, she'd pick me up from first, second, third grade to go see Pickford, Chaney, Chaplin. And . . . Conrad Veidt! The gypsies sliced his mouth so it could never stop smiling all the rest of his life, and he falls in love with a blind girl who can't see the awful smile and he is unfaithful to her but, scorned by a princess, crawls back to his blind girl, weeping, to be comforted by her unseeing hands. And you sit in your aisle seat in the dark at the Elite Cinema and weep. The End."

"My God!" exclaimed Groc, and almost not laughing. "What a dazzling child you are. Yes!" He grinned. "*I* am that Veidt character, but I was not carved into smiles by gypsies. Suicides, murders, assassinations did it. When you are locked in a mass grave with ten thousand corpses and fight upward for air in nausea, shot to death but not dead. I have never touched meat since, for it smells of the lime pit, the carcass, and the unburied slaughter. So," he gestured, "fruit. Salads. Bread, fresh butter, and wine. And, along the way, I sewed on this smile. I fight the true world with a false mouth. In the face of death, why not these teeth, the lascivious tongue, and the laugh? Anyway, *I* am responsible for *you!*"

"Me?"

"I told Manny Leiber to hire Roy, your tyrannosaurus buddy.

And I said we needed someone who wrote as well as Roy dreamed. *Voilà! You!*"

"Thanks," I said, slowly.

Groc preened over his food, glad that I was staring at his chin, his mouth, his brow.

"You could make a fortune—" I said.

"I already do." He cut a slice of pineapple. "The studio pays me excessively. Their stars are always booze-wrinkling their faces, or smashing their heads through car windows. Maximus Films lives in fear that I might depart. Nonsense! I will stay. And grow younger, each year, as I cut and stitch, and stitch again, until my skin is so tight that when I smile my eyes pop! So!" He demonstrated. "For I can never go back. Lenin chased me out of Russia."

"A dead man chased you?"

Fritz Wong leaned forward, listening, mightily pleased.

"Groc," he said, gently, "explain. Lenin with new roses in his cheeks. Lenin with brand-new teeth, a smile under the mouth. Lenin with new eyeballs, crystal, under the lids. Lenin with his mole gone and his goatee trimmed. Lenin, Lenin. Tell."

"Very simply," said Groc, "Lenin was to be a miraculous saint, immortal in his crystal tomb.

"But Groc? Who was he? Did Groc rouge Lenin's smile, clear his complexion? No! Lenin, even in death, improved *himself*! So? Kill Groc!

"So Groc ran! And Groc today is where? Falling upward . . . with *you*."

At the far end of the long table, Doc Phillips had come back. He advanced no further but, with a sharp jerk of his head, indicated that he wanted Groc to follow.

Groc took his time tapping his napkin on his little rosebud smile, took another swig of cold milk, crossed his knife and fork on his plate, and scrambled down. He paused and thought, then said, "Not *Titanic*, Ozymandias is more like it!" and ran out.

"Why," said Roy, after a moment, "did he make up all that guff about manatees and woodcarving?"

"He's good," said Fritz Wong. "Conrad Veidt, small size. I'll use that little son of a bitch in my next film."

"What did he mean by Ozymandias?" I asked.

16

All the rest of the afternoon Roy kept shoving his head into my office, showing me his clay-covered fingers.

"Empty!" he cried. "No Beast!"

I yanked paper from my typewriter. "Empty! Also no Beast!"

But at last, at ten o'clock that night, Roy drove us to the Brown Derby.

On the way I read aloud the first half of "Ozymandias."

> I met a traveller from an antique land
> Who said: Two vast and trunkless legs of stone
> Stand in the desert . . . Near them, on the sand,
> Half sunk, a shattered visage lies, whose frown,
> And wrinkled lip, and sneer of cold command,
> Tell that its sculptor well those passions read
> Which yet survive, stamped on these lifeless things,
> The hand that mocked them, and the heart that fed.

Shadows moved over Roy's face.

"Read the rest," he said.

I read:

> And on the pedestal these words appear:
> "My name is Ozymandias, king of kings:
> Look on my works, ye Mighty, and despair!"
> Nothing beside remains. Round the decay
> Of that colossal wreck, boundless and bare
> The lone and level sands stretch far away.

When I finished, Roy let two or three long dark blocks pass.

"Turn around, let's go home," I said.

"Why?"

"This poem sounds just like the studio *and* the graveyard. You ever have one of those crystal balls you shook and the snow lifted in blizzards inside? That's how my bones feel now."

"Bushwah," was Roy's comment.

I glanced over at his great hawk's profile, which cleaved the night air, full of that optimism that only craftsmen seem to have about being able to build a world just the way they want it, no matter what.

I remembered that when we were both thirteen King Kong fell off the Empire State and landed on us. When we got up, we were never the same. We told each other that one day we would write and move a Beast as great, as magnificent, as beautiful as Kong, or simply die.

"Beast," whispered Roy. "Here we *are*."

And we pulled up near the Brown Derby, a restaurant with no huge Brown Derby on top, like a similar restaurant on Wilshire Boulevard, five miles across town, capped with a derby large enough to fit God at Easter, or any studio bigwig on Friday afternoon. The only way you knew this Brown Derby was important was by the 999 cartoon-caricature portraits on every wall inside. Outside was quasi-Spanish nothing. We braved the nothing to step in and face the 999.

The maître d' of the Brown Derby lifted his left eyebrow as we arrived. A former dog lover, he now only loved cats. We smelled funny.

"Of course you have no reservations?" he observed, languidly.

"About *this* place?" said Roy. "Plenty."

That rippled the fur on the maître d's neck, but he let us in anyway.

The restaurant was almost empty. People sat at a few tables, finishing dessert and cognac. The waiters had already begun to renapkin and reutensil some of the tables.

There was a sound of laughter ahead, and we saw three women standing near a table, bending toward a man who was obviously leafing out cash to pay the night's bills. The young women laughed, saying they would be outside window-shopping while he paid up, then, in a flourish of perfume, they turned and ran past me and Roy, who stood nailed in place, staring at the man in the booth.

Stanislau Groc.

"God," cried Roy. "*You!*"

"*Me?!*"

Groc's eternal flame snapped shut.

"What are you doing here?" he exclaimed.

"We were invited."

"We were looking for someone," I said.

"And found me and were severely put out," observed Groc.

Roy was edging back, suffering from his Siegfried syndrome, dearly remembered. Promised a dragon, he beheld a mosquito. He could not take his eyes off Groc.

"Why do you look at me that way?" snapped the little man.

"Roy," I warned.

For I could see that Roy was thinking my thought. It was all a joke. Someone, knowing that Groc ate here some nights, had sent us on a fool's errand. To embarrass us, and Groc. Still, Roy was eying the little man's ears and nose and chin.

"Naw," said Roy, "you won't *do.*"

"For *what*? Hold on! Yes! Is it the *Search*?" A quiet little machine gun of laughter started in his chest and at last erupted from his thin lips.

"But why the Brown Derby? The people who come here are not your kind of fright. Nightmares, yes. And myself, this patch-work monkey's paw? Who could *I* scare?"

"Not to worry," said Roy. "The scare comes later, when I think about you at three A.M."

That did it. Groc ripped off the greatest laugh of all and waved us down in the booth.

"Since your night is ruined, drink!"

Roy and I glanced nervously around the restaurant.

No Beast.

When the champagne was poured, Groc toasted us.

"May you never have to curl a dead man's eyelashes, clean a dead man's teeth, rewax his beard, or rearrange his syphilitic lips." Groc rose and looked at the door through which his women had run.

"Did you see their faces?" Groc smiled after them. "Mine! Do you know why those girls are wildly in love with me and will never leave? I am the high lama of the Valley of the Blue Moon. Should they depart, a door would slam, mine, and their faces fall. I have warned them also that I have hooked fine wires below their chins and eyes. Should they run too far too fast to the end of the wire—their flesh would unravel. And instead of being thirty, they would be forty-two!"

"Fafner," growled Roy. His fingers clutched the table as if he might leap up.

"What?"

"A friend," I said. "We thought we might see him tonight."

"Tonight is over," said Groc. "But stay. Finish my champagne. Order more, charge me. Would you like a salad before the kitchen shuts?"

"I'm not hungry," said Roy, the wild disappointed Shrine Opera *Siegfried* look in his eyes.

"Yes!" I said.

"Two salads," Groc said to the waiter. "Blue cheese dressing?" Roy shut his eyes. "Yes!" I said.

Groc turned to the waiter and thrust an unnecessarily large tip into his hand.

"Spoil my friends," he said, grinning. Then, glancing at the door where his women had trotted out on their pony hooves, he shook his head. "I must go. It's raining. All that water on my girls' faces. They will melt! So long. Arrivederci!"

And he was gone. The front doors whispered shut.

"Let's get out. I feel like a fool!" said Roy.

He moved and spilled his champagne. He cursed and cleaned it up. I poured him another and watched him take it slowly and calm down.

Five minutes later, in the back of the restaurant, it happened.

The headwaiter was unfolding a screen around the farthermost table. It had slipped and half folded back together, with a sharp crack. The waiter said something to himself. And then there was a movement from the kitchen doorway, where, I realized, a man and woman had been standing for some few seconds. Now, as the waiter realigned the folding screen, they stepped out into the light and hurried, looking only ahead at that screen, toward the table.

"Ohmigod," I whispered hoarsely. "Roy?"

Roy glanced up.

"Fafner!" I whispered.

"No." Roy stopped, stared, sat back down, watching as the couple moved swiftly. "Yes."

But it was not Fafner, not the mythological dragon, the terrible serpent, that quickened himself from kitchen to table, holding his lady's hand and pulling her along behind him.

It was what we had been looking for for many long weeks and arduous days. It was what I might have scribbled on paper or typed on a page, with frost running up my arm to ice my neck.

It was what Roy had been seeking every time he plunged his long fingers into his clay. It was a blood-red bubble that rose steaming in a primeval mud pot and shaped itself into a face.

And this face was all the mutilated, scarred, and funeral faces of the wounded, shot, and buried men in ten thousand wars since wars began.

It was Quasimodo in his old age, lost in a visitation of cancer and a prolongment of leprosy.

And behind that face was a soul who would have to live there forever.

Forever! I thought. He'll *never* get out!

It was our Beast.

It was all over in an instant.

But I took a flash photo of the creature, shut my eyes, and saw the terrible face burned on my retina; burned so fiercely that tears brimmed my eyes and an involuntary sound erupted from my throat.

It was a face in which two terribly liquid eyes drowned. A face in which these eyes, swimming in delirium, could find no shore, no respite, no rescue. And seeing that there was nothing to touch which was not reprehensible, the eyes, bright with despair, swam in place, sustained themselves at the surface of a turmoil of flesh, refused to sink, give in, and vanish. There was a spark of the last hope that, by swiveling this way or that, they might sight some peripheral rescue, some touch of self-beauty, some revelation that all was not as bad as it seemed. So the eyes floated, anchored in a red-hot lava of destroyed flesh, in a meltdown of genetics from which no soul, however brave, might survive. While all the while, the nostrils inhaled themselves and the wound of mouth cried Havoc, silently, and exhaled.

In that instant I saw Roy jerk forward, then back, as if he had been shot, and the swift, involuntary motion of his hand to his pocket.

Then, the strange ruined man was gone, the screen up in place, as Roy's hand came out of his pocket with his small sketch pad and pencil and, still staring at the screen as if he could x-ray through it, never looking at his hand as it drew, Roy outlined the terror, the nightmare, the raw flesh of destruction and despair.

Like Doré, long before him, Roy had the swift exactitude, in his traveling, running, inking, sketching fingers, that required only a glance around at London crowds and then the turned faucet, the upside-down glass and funnel of memory, which spurted out his fingernails and flashed from his pencil as every eye, every nostril, every mouth, every jaw, every face, was printed out fresh and complete as from a stamped press. In ten seconds, Roy's hand, like a spider plunged in boiling water, danced and scurried in epilepsies of remembrance and sketch. One moment, the pad was empty. The next, the Beast, not all of him, no, but most, was there!

"Damn!" murmured Roy, and threw down his pencil.

I looked at the Oriental screen and then down at the swift portrait.

What lay there was close to being a half-positive, half-negative scrawl of a horror briefly glimpsed.

I could not take my eyes away from Roy's sketch, now that the Beast was hidden and the maître d' was taking orders from behind the screen.

"Almost," whispered Roy. "But not quite. Our search is over, junior."

"No."

"Yes."

For some reason I scrambled to my feet. "Goodnight."

"Where you going?" Roy was stunned.

"Home."

"How you going to get there? Spend an hour on the bus? Sit down." Roy's hand ran across the pad.

"Stop that," I said.

I might as well have fired off a gun in his face.

"After weeks of waiting? Like hell. What's got into you?"

"I'm going to throw up."

"Me, too. You think I like this?" He thought about it. "Yeah. I'll be sick, but this first." He added more nightmare and underlined the terror. "Well?"

"Now I'm really scared."

"Think he's going to come out from behind the screen and get you?"

"Yes!"

"Sit down and eat your salad. You know how Hitchcock says, when he finishes having the artist draw the setups for the scenes, the film is finished? Our film is done. *This* finishes it. It's in the can."

"How come I feel ashamed?" I sat back down, heavily, and would not look at Roy's pad.

"Because you're not him and he's not you. Thank God and count his mercies. What if I tear this up and we leave? How many more months do we search to find something as sad, as terrible as this?"

I swallowed hard. "Never."

"Right. This night won't come again. Now just sit still, eat, and wait."

"I'll wait but I won't be still and I'm going to be awfully sad."

Roy looked at me straight. "See these eyes?"

"Yes."

"What do you see?"

"Tears."

"Which proves I care as much as you do, but can't help myself. Simmer down. Drink."

He poured more champagne.

"It tastes awful," I said.

Roy drew and the face was there. It was a face that was in an entire stage of collapse; as if the occupant, the mind behind the apparition, had run and swum a thousand miles and was now sinking to die. If there was bone behind the flesh, it had been shattered and reassembled in insect forms, alien facades masked in ruin. If there was a mind behind the bone, lurking in caverns of retina and tympanum, it signaled madly from out the swiveling eyes.

And yet, once the food was placed and the champagne poured, Roy and I sat riven by the bursts of incredible laughter that ricocheted off the walls behind the screen. At first the woman did not respond but then as the hour passed, her quiet amusement grew almost to match his. But his laughter at last sounded true as a bell, while hers risked hysteria.

I drank heavily to keep myself in place. When the champagne bottle was emptied, the maître d' brought another and waved my hand away as I groped for my empty wallet.

"Groc," he said, but Roy did not hear. He was filling page after page of his pad, and as the time passed and the laughter rose, his sketches became more grotesque, as if the shouts of pure enjoyment drove his remembrance and filled a page. But at last the laughter quieted. There was a soft bustle of preparatory leavetaking behind the screen and the maître d' stood at our table.

"Please," he murmured. "We must close. Would you mind?" He nodded toward the door and stood aside, pulling the table out. Roy stood up. He looked at the Oriental screen.

"No," said the maître d'. "The proper order is you depart first."

I was halfway to the door and had to turn back. "Roy?" I said. And Roy followed, backing off as if departing from a theatre and the play not over.

As Roy and I came out, a taxicab was pulling up to the curb. The street was empty save for a medium-tall man in a long camel's-hair coat standing with his back to us, close to the curb. The portfolio tucked under his left arm gave him away. I had seen that portfolio day after day in the summers of my boyhood and young manhood in front of Columbia studios, Paramount, MGM, and all the rest. It had been filled with beautifully drawn portraits of Garbo, Colman, Gable, Harlow, and at one time or another a thousand others, all signed in purple ink. All kept by a mad autograph collector now grown old. I hesitated, then stopped.

"Clarence?" I called.

The man shrank, as if he didn't wish to be recognized.

"It *is* you, isn't it?" I called, quietly, and touched his elbow. "Clarence, right?"

The man flinched, but at last turned his head. The face was the same, with gray lines and bone paleness to make it older.

"What?" he said.

"Remember me?" I said. "Sure you do. I used to run around Hollywood with those three crazy sisters. One of them made those flowered Hawaiian shirts Bing Crosby wore in his early films. I was in front of Maximus every noon in the summer of 1934. You were there. How could I forget. You had the only sketch of Garbo I ever saw, signed—"

My litany only made things worse. With every word, Clarence shrank inside his big camel's-hair coat.

He nodded nervously. He glanced at the door of the Brown Derby nervously.

"What're you doing here so late?" I said. "Everyone's gone home."

"You never know. I got nothing else to do—" said Clarence.

You never know. Douglas Fairbanks, alive again, might stroll along the boulevard, much better than Brando. Fred Allen and Jack Benny and George Burns might come around the corner from the Legion Stadium, where the boxing matches were just over, and the crowds happy, just like the old times, which were lovelier than tonight or all the nights to come.

I got nothing else to do. Yes.

"Yeah," I said. "You never know. Don't you remember me at all? The nut? The super-nut? The Martian?"

Clarence's eyes jerked around from my brows to my nose to my chin, but not to my eyes.

"N-no," he said.

"Goodnight," I said.

"Goodbye," said Clarence.

Roy led me away to his tin lizzie and we climbed in, Roy impatiently sighing. No sooner in than he grabbed his pad and pencil and waited.

Clarence was still at the curb, to one side of the taxi, when the Brown Derby doors opened and the Beast came out with his Beauty.

It was a fine rare warm night or what happened next might not have happened.

The Beast stood inhaling great draughts of air, obviously full of champagne and forgetfulness. If he knew he had a face out of some old long-lost war, he showed no sign. He held on to his lady's hands and steered her toward the taxi, babbling and laughing. It was then that I noticed, by the way she walked and looked at nothing, that—

"She's blind!" I said.

"What?" said Roy.

"She's blind. She can't see him. No wonder they're friends!

He takes her out for dinners and never tells her what he's really like!"

Roy leaned forward and studied the woman.

"My God," he said, "you're right. Blind."

And the man laughing and the woman picking up and imitating the laughter, like a stunned parrot.

At which moment, Clarence, his back turned, having listened to the laughter and the onrush of words, turned slowly to regard the pair. Eyes half shut, he listened again, intently, and then a look of incredible surprise crossed his face. A word exploded from his mouth.

The Beast stopped his laughter.

Clarence took a step forward and said something to the man. The woman stopped laughing, too. Clarence asked something else. Whereupon the Beast closed his hands into fists, cried out, and lifted his arms into the air as if he might pound Clarence, pile-drive him, into the pavement.

Clarence fell to one knee, bleating.

The Beast towered over him, his fists trembling, his body rocking back and forth, in and out of control.

Clarence cried out and the blind woman, reaching out on the air, wondering, said something, and the Beast shut his eyes and let his arms drop. Instantly, Clarence leaped up and ran off in the dark. I almost jumped to go after him, though for what reason I did not know. The next instant, the Beast helped his blind friend into the taxi, and the taxi roared off.

Roy jumped the starter and we roared after.

The taxi turned right at Hollywood Boulevard, and the red light and some pedestrians stopped us. Roy gunned the engine as if to clear a path, cursed, and finally, when the crosswalk was empty, ran the red light.

"Roy!"

"Stop calling my name. Nobody saw us. We *can't* lose him! God, I *need* him! We got to see *where* he goes! *Who* he is! There!"

Up ahead, we saw the taxi making a right at Gower. Up ahead, also, Clarence was still running but did not see us as we passed.

His hands were empty. He had dropped and left his portfolio behind outside the Derby. How long before he misses it, I wondered.

"Poor Clarence."

"Why 'poor'?" said Roy.

"He's in this, too. Otherwise, why was he outside the Brown Derby? Coincidence? Hell, no. Someone told him to come. God, now he's lost all those great portraits. Roy, we got to go back and save them."

"We," said Roy, "got to go straight on ahead."

"I wonder," I said, "what kind of note Clarence got? What did it say to *him?*"

"What did *what* say?" said Roy.

Roy ran another red light at Sunset in order to catch up with the taxi, which was halfway to Santa Monica Boulevard.

"They're headed for the studio!" said Roy. "No."

For the taxicab, when at Santa Monica, had turned left past the graveyard.

Until we reached St. Sebastian's, just about the least-significant Catholic church in L.A. Suddenly, the taxi swung left down a side street just beyond the church.

The taxicab stopped about a hundred yards down the side street. Roy braked and curbed. We saw the Beast take the woman in toward a small white building obscured by night. He was gone only a moment. A door opened and closed somewhere, and the Beast returned to the taxi, which then glided to the next corner, made a swift U-turn and came back at us. Luckily, our lights were out. The taxi flashed by. Roy cursed, banged the ignition, revved the car, made a calamitous U-turn of his own, with me yelling, and we were back at Santa Monica Boulevard, in time to see the taxi pull up in front of St. Sebastian's and dislodge its passenger, who then fled up the walk into the lit entry of the church, not looking back. The taxi drove away.

Roy glided our car, lights out, into another dark place under a tree. "Roy, what're you—?"

"Silence!" hissed Roy. "Hunch. Hunch is everything. That guy no more belongs in a church at midnight than I belong in the burlesque chorus—"

Minutes passed. The church lights did not go out.

"Go *see*," suggested Roy.

"Go *what?*"

"Okay, *I'll* go!"

Roy was out of the car, shucking his shoes.

"Come *back!*" I yelled.

But Roy was gone, in his stocking feet. I jumped out, got rid of my shoes, and followed. Roy made it to the church door in ten seconds, me after, to flatten ourselves against an outside wall. We listened. We heard a voice, rising, falling, rising.

The Beast's voice! Urgently spelling calamities, terrible commitments, dreadful errors, sins darker than the marble sky above and below.

The priest's voice gave brief and just as urgent answers of forgiveness, predictions of some better life, where Beast, if not reborn as Beauty, might find some small sweet joys through penance.

Whisper, whisper, in the deeps of the night.

I shut my eyes and *ached* to hear.

Whisper, whisper. Then—I stiffened in disbelief.

Weeping. A wailing that went on and on and might never stop.

The lonely man inside the church, the man with the dreadful face and the lost soul behind it, let his terrible sadness free to shake the confessional, the church, and *me*. Weeping, sighing, but to weep again.

My eyelids burst with the sound. Then, silence, and—a *stir*. Footsteps.

We broke and ran.

We reached the car, jumped in.

"For Christ's sake!" hissed Roy.

Shoving my head down, he crouched. The Beast was out, running alone across the empty street.

When he reached the graveyard gate, he turned. A passing

car fixed him as with a theatre's spotlight. He froze, waited, then vanished inside the graveyard.

A long way off, inside the church doors, a shadow moved, the candles went out, the doors shut.

Roy and I looked at each other.

"My God," I said. "What sins could be so *huge* that someone confesses them *this* late at night? And the *weeping!* Did you *hear?* Do you think—he comes to forgive God, for handing him that face."

"That face. Yeah, oh, yeah," said Roy. "I *got* to know what he's up to, I can't *lose* him!"

And Roy was out of the car again.

"Roy!"

"Don't you see, dummy?" cried Roy. "He's our film, our monster! If he gets away?! *God!*"

And Roy ran across the street.

Fool! I thought. What's he *doing?*

But I was afraid to yell so long after midnight. Roy vaulted over the graveyard gate and sank down in shadow like someone drowning. I shot up in my seat so hard I hit my head on the car roof and collapsed, cursing; Roy, dammit. Dammit, Roy.

What if a police car comes now, I thought, and asks me, What you up to? My answer? Waiting for Roy. He's in the graveyard, be out any second. He *will*, will he? Sure, just you *wait!*

I waited. Five minutes. Ten.

And then, incredibly, there came Roy back out, but moving as if he had been electroshocked.

He walked slowly, a sleepwalker, across the street. He didn't even see his own hand on the car door handle, turning it to let him in. He sat in the front seat of the car, staring over at the graveyard.

"Roy?"

He didn't hear.

"What'd you see over there, just now?"

He didn't answer.

"Is he, him, *it*, coming out?"

Silence.

"Roy!" I hit his elbow. "*Speak!* What!"

"He," said Roy.

"Yes?"

"Unbelievable," said Roy.

"*I'd* believe."

"No. Quiet. He's mine now. And, oh God, what a monster we'll have, junior." He turned to look at me at last, his eyes flashlights, the soul burning out of his cheeks and coloring his lips. "Won't we have a film, pal?"

"Will we?"

"Oh," he cried, face blazing with revelation. "Yeah!"

"Is that all you got to say? Not what went *on* in the graveyard, not what you saw? Just, oh yeah?"

"Oh," said Roy, turning to gaze back across at the graveyard. "Yeah."

The church lights in the tiled patio went out. The church was dark. The street was dark. The lights on the face of my friend were gone. The graveyard was filled with night shadowing toward dawn.

"Yeah," whispered Roy.

And drove us toward home.

"I can hardly wait to get to my clay," he said.

"No!"

Shocked, Roy turned to look at me. Rivers of street light ran over his face. He looked like someone underwater, not to be touched, reached, saved.

"You telling me, positively, I *can't* use that face for our film?"

"It's not just the face. I got this feeling . . . if you do it, we're dead. God, Roy, I'm really scared. Someone wrote you to come find him tonight, don't forget. Someone wanted you to see him. Someone told Clarence to come there tonight, too! Things are running too fast. Pretend we were never at the Brown Derby."

"How," asked Roy, "could I possibly do that?"

He drove faster.

The wind ripped in the windows, tore at my hair and my eyelids and my lips.

Shadows ran across Roy's brow and down his great hawk's nose and over his triumphant mouth. It seemed like Groc's mouth, or The Man Who Laughs.

Roy felt me looking at him and said: "Busy hating me?"

"No. Wondering how I could have known you all these years and still not know you."

Roy lifted his left hand full of the Brown Derby sketches. They flapped and fluttered in the wind outside the window.

"Shall I let go?"

"You know and I know, you got a box-brownie in your head. Let those fly and you got a whole new roll, waiting, behind your left eyeball."

Roy waved them. "Yeah. The next set will be ten times better." The pad pages flew off in the night behind us.

"Doesn't make me feel any better," I said.

"Does me. The Beast is ours now. We own him."

"Yeah, who gave him to us? Who sent us to see? Who's watching us watching him?"

Roy reached out to draw half a terrible face on the moisture inside the window.

"Right now, just my Muse."

Nothing more was said. We rode in cold silence, all the rest of the way home.

17

The telephone rang at two in the morning.

It was Peg, calling from Connecticut just before dawn.

"Did you ever have a wife, named Peg," she cried, "left home ten days ago for a teachers' conference in Hartford? Why haven't you *called*?"

"I did. But you weren't in your room. I left my name. Christ, I wish you were home."

"Oh, dear me," she said slowly, syllable by syllable. "I leave town and right off you're in deep granola. You want mama to fly home?"

"Yes. No. It's just the usual studio junk." I hesitated.

"Why are you counting to ten?" she asked.

"God," I said.

"There's no escaping Him or me. You been dieting like a good boy? Go drop a penny in one of those scales that print your weight in purple ink, mail it to me. Hey," she added, "I mean it. You want me to fly home? Tomorrow?"

"I love you, Peg," I said. "Come home just as you planned."

"But what if you're not there when I get there? Is it still Halloween?"

Women and their intuition!

"They've held it over for another week."

"I could tell by your voice. Stay out of graveyards."

"What made you say *that*!?"

My heart gave a rabbit jump.

"Did you put flowers on your parents' graves?"

"I forgot."

"How *could* you?"

"Anyway, the graveyard they're in is a better graveyard."

"Better than what?"

"Any other, because they're there."

"Put a flower for me," she said. "I love you. Goodbye!"

And she ran down the line in a hum and a quiet roar and was gone.

At five in the morning, with no sun in view, and with the cloud cover from the Pacific in permanent position over my roof, I blinked at the ceiling and arose and found my way, without my glasses, to my typewriter.

I sat in the gloom before dawn and wrote: "RETURN OF THE BEAST."

But had he ever been away?

Hadn't he moved ahead of me everywhere in my life, calling me on with whispers?

I typed: "CHAPTER ONE."

"What is there that is so beautiful about a perfect Beast? Why do boys and men answer to it?

"What is there that runs us in fevers for half a lifetime with Creatures, Grotesques, Monsters, Freaks?

"And now, the mad wish to pursue and trap the most terrible face in the world!"

I took a deep breath, and dialed Roy's number. His voice was underwater, far away.

I said: "It's all right. Anything *you* want, Roy. It's okay."

And hung up and fell back in bed.

I stood outside Roy Holdstrom's Stage 13 the next morning and read the sign he had painted.

BEWARE. RADIOACTIVE ROBOTS.
MAD DOGS. INFECTIOUS DISEASES.

I put my ear to the Stage 13 door and imagined him in that vast silent cathedral darkness, fiddling away at his clay like an awkward spider, trapped in his own love and the birthings of his love.

"Go to it, Roy," I whispered. "Go to it, Beast."

And walked, while I was waiting, through the cities of the world.

18

And walking, thought: God, Roy's midwifing a Beast that I fear. How do I stop shaking and accept Roy's delirium? How do

I run it through a screenplay. Where do I *place* it? In what town, what city, somewhere in the world?

Lord, I thought, walking, now I know why so few mysteries have been written in American settings. England with its fogs, rains, moors, ancient houses, London ghosts, Jack the Ripper? Yes!

But America? There's no true history of haunts and great hounds. New Orleans, maybe, with enough fogs, rains, and swampland mansions to run up cold sweats and dig graves, while the Saints march forever out. And San Francisco where the fog-horns rouse and die each night.

Los Angeles, maybe. Chandler and Cain country. But . . .

There was only one true place in all America in which to hide a killer or lose a life.

Maximus Films!

Laughing, I turned at an alley, and walked through a dozen backlot sets, making notes.

England hid here and far Wales and moorish Scotland and raining Eire, and the ruins of the old castles, and the tombs in which dark films were vaulted and ghosts ran in creeks all night down projection room walls, gibbering their chops as night watchmen passed singing funeral hymns, riding old deMille chariots with smoke-plumed steeds.

So it would be tonight as the phantom extras banged the time clocks out, and the tombyard fog sifted in over the wall from the lawn sprinklers tossing cold beads on the still day-hot graves. Any night here you could cross London to meet the Phantom switchman, whose lantern fired the locomotive that shrieked at him like an iron fort and rammed Stage 12 to melt down into the pages of an old October issue of *Silver Screen*.

So I wandered the alleys, waiting for the sun to sink and Roy to step forth, hands bloody with red clay, to shout a birth!

At four o'clock I heard distant rifle fire.

The gunshots were Roy whacking a croquet ball back and forth across a Number 7 backlot meadow. He slammed the ball again and again, and froze, feeling my gaze. He lifted his head to blink at me. His look was not that of the obstetrician but a carnivore that has just killed and eaten well.

"I did it, by God!" he cried. "Trapped him! Our Beast, your Beast, *mine*! Today, the clay, tomorrow the film! People will ask: Who *did* that! Us, son, us!"

Roy clenched his long bony fingers on the air.

I walked forward slowly, dazed.

"Trapped? My God, Roy, you still haven't *told*. What'd you see when you ran after him the other night!?"

"In time, pal. Look, I finished half an hour ago. One look and you'll beat your typewriter to death. I called Manny! He'll see us in twenty minutes. I went nuts, waiting. I had to come bang the balls. There!" He struck another mighty blow, a croquet ball flew. "Someone stop me before I kill!"

"Roy, calm down."

"No, I'll *never* calm down. We'll make the greatest horror film in history. Manny will—"

A voice yelled: "Hey, what're you two doing *here*?"

Manny's Rolls-Royce, a traveling white theatre, glided by, purring under its breath. Our boss's face glared out one small theatre window.

"Do we have a meeting or *no*?!"

"Do we walk or ride?" Roy said.

"Walk!"

The Rolls glided away.

19

We took our time walking to Stage 13.

I kept watching Roy to see if I could get a hint of what he had been up to in the long night. Even when we were boys, he rarely showed his true feelings. He'd fling his garage doors wide to show me his latest dinosaur. Only when my breath exploded did he allow himself a yell. If I loved what he had made, it didn't matter what anyone else said.

"Roy," I said, walking. "You *okay?*"

We found Manny Leiber fuming outside Stage 13. "Where the hell *you* been!?" he cried.

Roy opened the door of Stage 13, glided in, and let the heavy door slam.

Manny glared at me. I jumped forward and pulled the door open for him.

We stepped into night.

There was darkness except for a single light bulb, hung above Roy's armatured clay-modeling stand, sixty feet across a desert floor, a semi-Martian landscape, near the shadowed Meteor Crater.

Roy peeled off his shoes and darted across the landscape like a ballet master, fearful of crushing a fingernail tree here, a car as big as a thimble there.

"Get your shoes off!" he shouted.

"Like *hell!*"

But Manny yanked off his shoes, and tiptoed across the miniature world. Much had been added since dawn; new mountains, new trees, plus whatever lay waiting beneath the wet cloth under the light.

We both arrived, in our stocking feet, at the armatured stand. "Ready?" Roy searched our faces with his lighthouse eyes.

"Dammit to hell, *yes!*" Manny snatched at the moist towel.

Roy knocked his hand away.

"No," he said. "*Me!*"

Manny pulled back, blushing with anger.

Roy lifted the moist towel as if it were a curtain rising on the greatest show on earth.

"Not Beauty and the Beast," he cried, "but The Beast that is Beautiful!"

Manny Leiber and I gasped.

Roy had not lied. It was the finest work he had ever done, a proper thing to glide from a far-traveling light-year ship, a hunter of midnight paths across the stars, a dreamer alone behind his terrible, awful, most dreadfully appalling mask.

The Beast.

That lonely man behind the Oriental Brown Derby screen, laughing, on what seemed a hundred nights ago.

The creature who had run away on the midnight streets to enter a graveyard and stay among the white tombs.

"Oh, my God, Roy." My eyes filled with tears shocked free by the impact, as fresh and new as when the Beast had stepped forth to raise his riven face into the night air. "Oh, God—"

Roy was staring with wild love at his wondrous work. Only slowly did he turn to regard Manny Leiber. What he saw stunned both of us.

Manny's face was white cheese. His eyes swiveled in their sockets. His throat croaked as if a wire choked his neck. His hands clawed his chest as if his heart had stopped.

"What've you *done!*" he shrieked. "Jesus! My God, oh Christ! What is this? Tricks? Jokes? Cover it up! You're fired!"

Manny hurled the damp towel at the clay Beast.

"It's crap!"

With stiff, mechanical movements, Roy covered the clay head. "I didn't—"

"You *did!* You want *that* on the screen? Pervert! Pack your things! Get *out!*" Manny shut his eyes, shuddering. "*Now!*"

"You demanded this!" said Roy.

"Well, now I demand you destroy it!"

"The best, my greatest work! Look at it, dammit! It's beautiful! It's *mine!*"

"No! The studio's! Dump it! The film is scrubbed. You're *both* fired. I want this place empty in an hour. Move!"

"Why," asked Roy, quietly, "are you overreacting?"

"Am I?"

And Manny plowed across the stage, his shoes tucked under his arm, smashing miniature houses and scattering toy trucks as he strode.

At the far stage door he stopped, sucked air, glared at me.

"*You're* not fired. You'll get a new job. But *that* son of a bitch? *Out!*"

The door opened, let in a great Gothic-cathedral spray of light, and slammed shut, leaving me to survey Roy's collapse and defeat.

"My God, what've we *done*! What the hell?" I shouted to Roy, to myself, to the red clay bust of the Monster, the discovered and revealed Beast. "*What!?*"

Roy was trembling. "Jesus. I work for half a lifetime to do something fine. I train myself, I wait, I see, at last I really *see*. And the thing comes out of my fingertips, my God, how it came! What is this thing here in the damn clay? How come it gets born, and *I* get killed?"

Roy shuddered. He raised his fists, but there was no one to strike. He glanced at his prehistoric animals and made an all-sweeping gesture, as if to hug and protect them.

"I'll be *back!*" he cried hoarsely to them and wandered off.

"Roy!"

I followed as he blundered into daylight. Outside, the late-afternoon sun was blazing hot, and we moved in a river of fire. "Where you going?"

"Christ knows! Stay here. No use you getting dumped on! This is your first job. You warned me last night. Now I know it was sick, but why? I'll hide somewhere on the lot so that tonight I can sneak my friends out!" He looked longingly at the shut door behind which his dear beasts lived.

"I'll help," I said.

"No. Don't be seen with me. They'll think you put me up to this."

"Roy! Manny looked as if he could kill you! I'm calling my detective pal, Crumley. Maybe he can help! Here's Crumley's phone number." I wrote hastily on some crumpled paper. "Hide. Call me tonight."

Roy Holdstrom leaped into his Laurel and Hardy flivver and steamed toward the backlot at ten miles an hour.

"Congratulations," someone said. "you silly goddamn son of a bitch!"

I turned. Fritz Wong stood in the middle of the next alley. "I yelled at them and at last you have been assigned to rewrite my lousy film *God and Galilee*. Manny just ran over me in his *Rolls*. He screamed your new job at me. So . . ."

"Is there a monster in the script?" My voice trembled.

"Only Herod Antipas. Leiber wants to see you."

And he hustled me along toward Leiber's office.

"Wait," I said.

For I was looking over Fritz's shoulder at the far end of the studio alley and the street outside the studio where the crowd, the mob, the menagerie gathered every day, forever.

"Idiot!" said Fritz. "Where are you going?"

"I just saw Roy fired," I said, walking. "Now I need to get him rehired!"

"*Dummkopf.*" Fritz strode after me. "Manny wants you *now!*"

"Now, plus five minutes."

Outside the studio gate, I glanced across the street.

Are you there, Clarence? I wondered.

20

And there indeed they stood.

The loonies. The jerks. The idiots.

That mob of lovers worshiping at studio shrines.

Much like the late-night travelers that had once jostled me along to haunt the Hollywood Legion Stadium boxing matches to see Cary Grant sprint by, or Mae West undulate through the crowd like a boneless feather boa, or Groucho lurk along by Johnny Weissmuller, who dragged Lupe Velez after him like a leopard pelt.

The goons, myself among them, with big photo albums, stained hands, and little scribbled cards. The nuts who stood happily rain-drenched at the première of *Dames* or *Flirtation Walk*, while the Depression went on and on even though Roosevelt said it couldn't last forever and Happy Days would come again.

The gorgons, the jackals, the demons, the fiends, the sad ones, the lost ones.

Once, I had been one of them.

Now, there they were. My family.

There were still a few faces left from the days when I had hid in their shade.

Twenty years later, my God, there stood Charlotte and her ma! They had buried Charlotte's dad in 1930 and taken root in front of six studios and ten restaurants. Now a lifetime later, there was Ma, in her eighties, stalwart and practical as a bumbershoot, and Charlotte, fifty, as flower-fragile as she had always seemed to be. Both were frauds. Both hid boilerplates behind their rhino-ivory smiles.

I looked for Clarence in that strange dead funeral bouquet. For Clarence had been the wildest: lugging huge twenty-pound photo portfolios from studio to studio. Red leather for Paramount, black for RKO, green for Warner Brothers.

Clarence, summer and winter, wrapped in his oversize camel's-hair coat, in which he filed pens, pads, and miniature cameras. Only on the hottest days did the wraparound coat come off. Then Clarence resembled a tortoise torn from its shell and panicked by life.

I crossed the street to stop before the mob.

"Hello, Charlotte," I said. "Hiya, Ma."

The two women stared at me in mild shock.

"It's me," I said. "Remember? Twenty years back. I was here. Space. Rockets. Time—?"

Charlotte gasped and flung her hand to her overbite. She leaned forward as if she might fall off the curb.

"Ma," she cried, "why—it's—the *Crazy!*"

"The Crazy." I laughed, quietly.

A light burned in Mom's eyes. "Why land's sake." She touched my elbow. "You *poor* thing. What're you doing *here?* Still *collecting—?*"

"No," I said, reluctantly. "I work there."

"Where?"

I nodded over my shoulder.

"There?" cried Charlotte in disbelief.

"In the mailroom?" asked Ma.

"No." My cheeks burned. "You might say . . . in the script department."

"You *mimeograph* scripts?"

"Oh, for heaven's sake, Ma." Charlotte's face burst with light. "He means *writing*, yes? Screenplays?!"

This last was a true revelation. All the faces around Charlotte and Ma took fire.

"Ohmigod," cried Charlotte's ma. "*Can't* be!"

"Is," I almost whispered. "I'm doing a film with Fritz Wong. *Caesar and Christ.*

There was a long, stunned silence. Feet shifted. Mouths worked.

"Can—" said someone, "we have . . ."

But it was Charlotte who finished it. "Your autograph. *Please?*"

"I—"

But all the hands thrust out now, with pens and white cards.

Shamefacedly, I took Charlotte's and wrote my name. Ma squinted at it, upside down.

"Put the name of the picture you're working on," said Ma. "*Christ and Caesar.*"

"Put 'The Crazy' after your name," Charlotte suggested.

I wrote "The Crazy."

Feeling the perfect damn fool, I stood in the gutter as all the heads bent, and all the sad lost strange ones squinted to guess my identity.

To cover my embarrassment, I said: "Where's Clarence?"

Charlotte and Ma gaped. "You remember *him?*"

"Who could forget Clarence, and his portfolios, and his coat," I said, scribbling.

"He ain't called in yet," snapped Ma.

"Called in?" I glanced up.

"He calls on that phone across the street about this time, to see has so-and-so arrived, come out, stuff like that," said Charlotte. "Saves time. He sleeps late, cause he's usually out front restaurants midnights."

"I know." I finished the last signature, glowing with an inadmissible elation. I still could not look at my new admirers, who smiled at me as if I had just leaped Galilee in one stride.

Across the street the glass-booth phone rang.

"That's Clarence now!" said Ma.

"Excuse me—" Charlotte started off.

"Please," I touched her elbow. "It's been years. Surprise?" I looked from Charlotte to her Ma and back. "*Yes?*"

"Oh, all right," grumped Ma.

"Go ahead," said Charlotte.

The phone rang. I ran to lift the receiver.

"Clarence?" I said.

"Who's *this*!?" he cried, instantly suspicious.

I tried to explain in some detail, but wound up with the old metaphor, "the Crazy."

That buttered no bread for Clarence. "Where's Charlotte or Ma? I'm sick."

Sick, I wondered, or, like Roy, suddenly afraid.

"Clarence," I said, "where do you live?"

"Why?!"

"Give me your phone number, at least—"

"*No one* has that! My place would be *robbed*! My photos. My *treasures!*"

"Clarence," I pleaded, "I was at the Brown Derby last night." Silence.

"Clarence?" I called. "I need your help to identify someone."

I swear I could hear his little rabbity heart race down line. I could hear his tiny albino eyes jerk in their sockets.

"Clarence," I said, "please! Take my name and phone numbers." I gave them. "Call or write the studio. I saw that man almost hit you last night. Why? Who . . . ?"

Click. Hum.

Clarence, wherever he was, was gone.

I moved across the street like a sleepwalker.

"Clarence won't be here."

"What d'ya mean?" accused Charlotte. "He's always here!"

"What'd you *say* to him!?" Charlotte's Ma showed me her left, her evil, eye.

"He's sick."

Sick, like Roy, I thought. Sick, like me.

"Does anyone know where he lives?"

They all shook their heads.

"I suppose you could *follow* him and see!" Charlotte stopped and laughed at herself. "I mean—"

Someone else said, "I seen him go down Beachwood, once. One of those bungalow courts—"

"Does he have a last name?"

No. Like everyone else in all the years. No last name.

"Damn," I whispered.

"Comes to that—" Charlotte's Ma eyed the card I had signed. "What's *your* monicker?"

I spelled it for her.

"Gonna work in films," sniffed Ma, "oughta get you a *new* name."

"Just call me Crazy." I walked away. "Charlotte. Ma."

"Crazy," they said. "Goodbye."

21

Fritz was waiting for me upstairs, outside Manny Leiber's office.

"They are in a feeding frenzy inside," he exclaimed. "What's *wrong* with you!?"

"I was talking to the gargoyles."

"What, are they down off Notre Dame *again?* Get *in* here!"

"Why? An hour ago Roy and I were on Everest. Now he's gone to hell and I'm sunk with you in Galilee. Explain."

"You and your winning ways," said Fritz. "Who knows? Manny's mother died. Or his mistress took a few wrong balls over the plate. Constipation? High colonics? Choose one. Roy's fired. So you and I do Our Gang comedies for six years. *In!*"

We stepped into Manny Leiber's office.

Manny Leiber stood with the back of his neck watching us.

He stood in the middle of a large, all-white room, white walls, white rug, white furniture, and a huge all-white desk with nothing on it but a white telephone. A sheer blizzard of inspiration from the hand of some snow-blind artist over in Set Design.

Behind the desk was a four-by-six mirror so that if you glanced over your shoulder you could see yourself working. There was only one window in the room. It looked down on the back studio wall, not thirty feet off, and a panoramic view of the graveyard. I could not take my eyes away.

But Manny Leiber cleared his throat. With his back still turned he said: "Is *he* gone?"

I nodded quietly at his stiff shoulders.

Manny sensed my nod and exhaled. "His name will not be mentioned here again. He never was."

I waited for Manny to turn and circle me, working off a passion he could not explode. His face was a mass of tics. His eyes did not move with his eyebrows or his eyebrows with his mouth or his head twisting on his neck. He looked dangerously off-balance as he paced; at any moment he might fly apart. Then he noticed Fritz Wong watching us both, and went to stand by Fritz as if to provoke him to a rage.

Fritz wisely did the one thing I noticed often when his world became too real. He removed his monocle and slipped it into his breast pocket. It was like a fine dismantling of attention, a subtle rejection. He shoved Manny in his pocket with the monocle.

Manny Leiber talked and paced. I half whispered, "Yeah, but what do we do with Meteor *Crater*!"

Fritz warned me with a jerk of his head: *Shut up.*

"So!" Manny pretended not to hear, "Our next problem, our *main* problem is . . . we have no *ending* for *Christ and Galilee.*"

"Say that *again*?" asked Fritz, with deadly politeness.

"No ending!" I cried. "Have you tried the Bible?"

"We *got* Bibles! But our screenwriter couldn't read the small print on a Dixie cup. I saw that *Esquire* story of yours. It was like Ecclesiastes."

"Job," I muttered.

"Shut up. What we need is—"

"Matthew, Mark, Luke, and *me*!"

Manny Leiber snorted. "Since when do beginning writers reject the greatest job of the century? We need it yesterday, so Fritz can start shooting again. Write good and someday you'll own all *this*!"

He waved.

I looked out over the graveyard. It was a bright day, but invisible rain washed the tombstones.

"God," I whispered. "I hope not."

That did it. Manny Leiber paled. He was back on Stage 13, in the dark, with me, Roy, and the clay Beast.

Silently, he ran to the restroom. The door slammed.

Fritz and I traded glances. Manny was sick behind the door.

"*Gott*," exhaled Fritz. "I should have listened to Goering!"

Manny Leiber staggered back out a moment later, looked around as if surprised the place was still afloat, made it to the telephone, dialed, said, "Get in here!" and headed out.

I stopped him at the door.

"About Stage 13—"

Manny had his hand over his mouth as if he might be sick again. His eyes widened.

"I know you're going to clean it out," I said, quickly. "But I got a lot of stuff on that stage. And I want to spend the rest of the day talking with Fritz here about Galilee and Herod. Could you leave all the junk so I can come tomorrow morning and claim my stuff? *Then* you can clean out."

Manny's eyes swiveled, thinking. Then, hand over his mouth, he jerked his head once, yes, and turned to find a tall thin pale man coming in. They whispered, then with no goodbyes, Manny left. The tall pale man was I. W. W. Hope, one of the production estimators.

He looked at me, paused, and then with some embarrassment said, "It seems, ah, we have no ending for your film."

"Have you tried the *Bible*?" Fritz and I said.

22

The menagerie was gone, the curb was empty in front of the studio. Charlotte, Ma, and the rest had gone on to other studios, other restaurants. There must have been three dozen of them scattered across Hollywood. One would surely know Clarence's last name.

Fritz drove me home.

Along the way he said, "Reach in the glove compartment. That glass case. Open."

I opened the small black case. There were six bright crystal monocles in six neat red velvet cups nested there.

"My luggage," said Fritz. "All that I saved and took to bring to America when I got the hell out with my ravenous groin and my talent."

"Which was huge."

"Stop." Fritz dutch-rubbed my skull. "Give only insults, bastard child. I show you these—" he nudged the monocles—"to prove all is not lost. All cats, and Roy, land on their feet. What else is in the glove compartment?"

I found a thick mimeographed script.

"Read that without throwing up and you'll be a man, my son.

Kipling. Go. Come back, tomorrow, two-thirty, the commissary. We talk. Then, later, we show you the rough cut of *Jesus on the Dole* or *Father, Why Hast Thou Forsaken Me. Ja?*"

I got out of his car in front of my house.

"*Sieg Heil*," I said.

"That's more *like* it!" Fritz drove away, leaving me to a house so empty and quiet I thought: Crumley.

Soon after sunset, I rode out to Venice on my bike.

I hate bikes at night, but I wanted to be sure no one followed.

Besides, I wanted time to think just what I would say to my detective friend. Something like: Help! Save Roy! Get him re-hired. Solve the riddle of the Beast.

That made me almost turn back.

I could hear Crumley now, heaving great sighs as I spun my impossible tale, throwing up his hands, slugging back the beer to drown his contempt for my lack of real hammered-out Swedish-steel-spiked facts.

I parked my bike out in front of his small thornbush-hidden safari bungalow a mile from the ocean and walked up through a grove of African lilacs, along a path dusted, you felt, by okapi beasts just yesterday.

As I raised my hand to knock, the door blew open.

A fist came out of the darkness with a foaming beer can in it. I could not see the man who held it. I snatched it away. The hand vanished. I heard footsteps fade through the house.

I took three sips to get strength to enter.

The house was empty.

The garden was not.

Elmo Crumley sat under a thornbush tree, wearing his banana

trader's hat, eying the beer that he held in his sunburnt hand, and drinking silently.

There was an extension telephone on a rattan table at his elbow. Looking steadily, wearily at me from under his white hunter's topee, Crumley dialed a number.

Someone answered. Crumley said: "One more migraine. Putting in for sick leave. See you in three days, okay? Okay." And hung up.

"I guess," I said, "that headache is me."

"Any time you show up . . . seventy-two hours' leave."

He nodded. I sat. He went to stand at the rim of his own private jungle, where the elephants trumpeted and unseen flights of giant bumblebees, hummingbirds, and flamingos died long before any future ecologists declared them dead.

"Where," said Crumley, "the hell have you *been?*"

"Married," I said.

Crumley thought it over, snorted, strolled over, put his arm around my shoulder, and kissed me on the top of my head.

"Accepted!"

And laughing, he went to drag out a whole case of beer.

We sat eating hotdogs in the little rattan gazebo at the back of his garden.

"Okay, son," he said, finally. "Your old dad has missed you. But a young man between blankets has no ears. Old Japanese proverb. I knew you'd come back someday."

"Do you forgive me?" I said, welling over.

"Friends don't forgive, they forget. Swab your throat out with this. Is Peg a great wife?"

"Been married a year and yet to have our first fight over money." I blushed. "She makes most of it. But my studio salary is up—one hundred fifty a week."

"Hell! That's ten bucks more than *I* make!"

"*Only* for six weeks. I'll soon be back writing for *Dime Mystery.*"

"And writing beauts. I've kept up in spite of the silence—"

"You get the Father's Day card I sent?" I said quickly.

He ducked his head and beamed. "Yeah. Hell." He straightened up. "But more than familial emotions brought you here, *right?*"

"People are dying, Crumley."

"Not *again!*" he cried.

"Well, almost dying," I said. "Or have come back from the grave not really alive, but papier-mâché dummies—"

"Hold 'er, Newt!" Crumley darted into the house and ran back with a flask of gin, which he poured into his beer as I talked faster. The sprinkler system came on in his Kenya tropical backyard, along with the cries of veldt animals and deep-jungle birds. At last I was finished with all the hours from Halloween to now. I fell silent.

Crumley let out a grievous sigh. "So Roy Holdstrom's fired for making a clay bust. Was the Beast's face *that* awful?"

"Yes!"

"Aesthetics. This old gumshoe can't help with that!"

"You got to. Right now Roy is still *in* the studio, waiting for a chance to sneak all of his prehistoric models out. They're worth thousands. But Roy's there illegally. Can you help me figure out what in hell this all *means?* Help Roy get his job back?"

"Jesus," sighed Crumley.

"Yeah," I said. "If they catch Roy trying to move things out, lord *God!*"

"Damn," said Crumley. He added more gin to his beer. "You know who that guy was in the Brown Derby?"

"No."

"You got any notions about anyone who *might* know?"

"The priest at St. Sebastian's."

I told Crumley about the midnight confession, the voice speaking, the weeping, and the quiet response of the church father.

"No good. No way." Crumley shook his head. "Priests don't know or don't give names. If I went in, asking, I'd be out on my ass in two minutes. Next."

"The maître d' at the Derby might. And he was recognized by someone outside the Derby that night. Someone I knew when

I was a kid hanging out on my roller skates. Clarence. I've been asking around for his last name."

"Keep asking. If he knows who the Beast is, we'd have something to go on. Christ, it's dumb. Roy fired, you tossed into a new job, all from a clay bust. Overreaction. Riots. And how come all that uproar about a dummy on a ladder?"

"Exactly."

"And I thought," sighed Crumley, "when I saw you standing in the door, I was going to be happy that you came back into my life."

"*Aren't* you?"

"No, dammit." He softened his voice. "Yeah, hell. But I sure wish you'd left that pile of horse manure outside."

He squinted at the rising moon over his garden and said: "Boy oh boy . . . You sure got me *curious*." And added: "Smells like blackmail!"

"Blackmail!?"

"Why go to all the trouble of writing notes, provoking innocents like you and Roy, propping fakes up on ladders, getting you to reproduce a Creature, if it didn't *lead* somewhere? What's the use of a panic if you don't cash in on it. There must be more notes, more letters, right?"

"I saw none."

"Yeah, but you were the tool, the means, to get things stirred. You didn't spill the beans. Someone else did. I bet there's a blackmail note out there somewhere tonight, says: 'Two hundred thousand in unmarked fifties will buy you no more reborn corpses on walls.' So . . . tell me about the studio," Crumley said, at last.

"Maximus? Most successful studio in history. Still is. *Variety* headlined their profit last month. Forty million net. No other studio near."

"Those *honest* figures?"

"Deduct five million, you've still got a studio rich as hell."

"Any big problems, recently, ruckuses, upheavals, troubles? You know, any other people fired, films canceled?"

"It's been steady on and quiet for months."

"Then that must be it. The profits! I mean. Everything going along nice and easy and then something happens, doesn't look like much, scares everybody. Someone thinks, my God, *one man on a wall*, there goes the neighborhood! Got to be something under the carpet somewhere, something buried—" Crumley laughed. "Buried is right. Arbuthnot? You think someone dug up some old really dirty scandal that nobody ever even heard of, and is threatening the studio, not very subtly, with releasing the dirt?"

"What kind of scandal, twenty years old, could make a studio think it was going to be destroyed if it was revealed?"

"If we wade in the sewer long enough we'll know. Trouble is, sewer-hopping was never my hobby. Was Arbuthnot, alive, clean?"

"Compared to other studio heads? Sure. He was single and had girlfriends, but you expect that of any bachelor, and they were all nice Santa Barbara horsewomen, *Town and Country* types, handsome and bright, showered twice a day. No dirt."

Crumley sighed again, as if someone had dealt him the wrong cards and he was ready to fold his hand and fade. "What about that car crash Arbuthnot was in? *Was* it an accident?"

"I saw the news photos."

"Photos, hell!" Crumley looked out at his homemade jungle and checked the shadows. "What if the accident *wasn't* an accident? What if it was, well, manslaughter. What if everyone was dead drunk and then dead?"

"They had just come from a big liquor bash at the studio. That much got in the papers."

"Try this," mused Crumley. "Studio bigwig, rich as Croesus, with all-time grosses for Maximus, out of his mind with hooch, playing chicken with the other car, driven by Sloane, ricochets off him and everyone hits the telephone pole. That's not the kind of news you want front-paged. Stock markets dive. Investors vanish. Films die. The silver-haired boy falls off his pedestal, et cetera, et cetera, so there's a coverup. Now, late in time, someone who was there, or uncovered the facts this year, is shaking down the studio, threatening to tell more than photos and skidmarks. Or what if—?"

"What if?"

"It wasn't an accident and it wasn't horse-around drunkenness that slammed them to hell. What if someone did it to them on purpose?"

"Murder!?" I said.

"Why not? Studio heads that tall, that big, that wide, make lots of enemies. All the yes-men around them eventually think rat crap and malice. Who was next in line for power at Maximus that year?"

"Manny Leiber? But he wouldn't kill a fly. He's all hot air!"

"Give him the benefit of one fly and one hot air balloon. He's the studio head now, right? Well! A couple of slashed tires, some loosened bolts, and bang! the whole studio falls in your lap for a lifetime!"

"That all sounds logical."

"But if we could find the guy that did it, he'd prove it *for* us. Okay, buster, what next?"

"I suppose we check the old local newspapers from twenty years ago to see what's missing. And if you could kind of prowl around the studio. Unobtrusively, that is."

"With these flat feet? I think I know the studio gate guard. Worked at Metro years ago. He'd let me in and zip his lip. What else?"

I gave him a list. The carpenters' shop. The graveyard wall. And the Green Town house where Roy and I had *planned* to work, and where Roy might be now.

"Roy's still there, waiting to steal back his beasts. And, Crum, if what you say is true, night chicken rides, manslaughter, murder, we got to blow Roy out of there now. If the studio people go in Stage 13 tonight and find the box in which Roy hid that papier-mâché body after he stole it, what *won't* they do to him?!"

Crumley grunted. "You're asking me to not only get Roy rehired but help him stay alive, right?"

"Don't *say* that!"

"Why not? You're all over the ball field, playing pitcher and running to bat flies and fumble balls. How in hell do I catch Roy? Wander around the sets with a butterfly net and some cat food! Your studio friends know Roy, *I* don't. They can stomp him long before I get out of the bull pen. Give me just *one* fact to start with!"

"The Beast. If we found out who *he* is, we might find why Roy was fired for making that clay bust."

"Yeah, yeah. What else? About the Beast—"

"We saw him go into the graveyard. Roy followed him, but wouldn't tell me what he saw, what the Beast was up to. Maybe, maybe it was the Beast put that papier-mâché duplicate of Arbuthnot up on the graveyard wall—and sent notes to blackmail people!"

"Now you're cooking!" Crumley rubbed his bald head with both hands, rapidly. "Identify the Beast, ask where he borrowed the ladder and how he made the look-alike Arbuthnot papier-mâché corpse! Well! *well!*" Crumley beamed.

He ran to the kitchen for more beer.

We drank and he gazed at me with paternal affection. "I was just thinking . . . how great it is to have you home."

I said, "Hell, I haven't even asked you about your novel—"

"Downwind from Death?"

"That's not the title I gave you!"

"Your title was too good. I'm giving it back. *Downwind from Death* will be published next week."

I leaped to grab Crumley's hands.

"Crumb!! Oh, God! You *did* it! You got some *champagne?!*"

We both peered in his icebox.

"If you churn beer and gin in a Waring blender, is *that* champagne?"

"Why not *try?*"

We tried.

24

And the phone rang.

"It's for you," said Crumley.

"Thank God!" I grabbed the phone. "Roy!"

Roy said, "I don't want to live. Oh, God, this is terrible. Get over here before I go mad. Stage 13!"

And he was gone.

"Crumley!" I said.

Crumley led me out to his car.

We rode across town. I couldn't get my teeth unclenched to speak. I held so hard to my knees that the circulation ran dead.

At the studio gate I told Crumley, "Don't wait. I'll call in an hour and let you know . . ."

I walked away and bumped into the gate. I found a phone booth near Stage 13 and ordered a taxi to wait outside Stage 9, a good one hundred yards away. Then I walked through the doors of Stage 13.

I stepped into darkness and chaos.

25

I saw ten dozen things which were a devastation to my soul.

Nearby, the masks, skulls, jackstraw legbones, floating ribs, skull faces of the Phantom had been uprooted and hurled across the stage in frenzies.

Further over, a war, an annihilation, had just fallen in its own dusts.

Roy's spider towns and beetle cities were trodden into the earth. His beasts had been eviscerated, decapitated, blasted, and buried in their own plastic flesh.

I advanced through ruins, scattered as if a night bombing had rained utter destruction upon the miniature roofs, turrets and Lilliputian figurines. Rome had been smashed by a gargantuan Attila. The great library at Alexandria was not burned; its tiny leaflet books, like the wings of hummingbirds, lay in drifts across the dunes. Paris smoldered. London was disemboweled. A giant Napoleon had stomped Moscow flat forever. In sum, five years' work, fourteen hours a day, seven days a week, had been wasted in, what? Five minutes!

Roy! I thought, you must never see this!

But he had.

As I advanced across the lost battlefields and strewn villages I saw a shadow on the far wall.

It was a shadow from the motion picture *The Phantom of the Opera* when I was five. In that film some ballerinas, backstage, twirling, had frozen, stared, shrieked, and fled. For there, hung like a sandbag from the flies, they saw the body of the night watchman, slowly swaying, high in the stage flies. The memory of that film, that scene, the ballerinas, the dead man hung high in shadows, had never left me. And now, at the far north side of this sound stage, an object drifted on a long spider line. It shed an immense, twenty-foot darkness on the empty wall, like a scene from that old and frightening picture.

Oh, no, I whispered. It *can't* be!

It *was*.

I imagined Roy's arrival, his shock, his outcry, his smothering despair, then his rage, with new despairs to drown and win after his call to me. Then his wild search for rope, twine, wire, and at last: downslung and drifting peace. He could not live without his wondrous midges and mites, his sports, his dears. He was too old to rebuild it all.

"Roy," I whispered, "that *can't* be you! You always wanted to *live*."

But Roy's body turned slowly, shadowed and high. *My Beasts are slain*, it said.

They were never *alive*!

Then, whispered Roy, *I* was never alive.

"Roy," I said, "would you leave me *alone* in the world!?"

Maybe.

"But you wouldn't let someone hang you!?"

Perhaps.

And if so, how come you're still here? How come they haven't cut you *down?*

Which means?

You're freshly dead. You haven't been found. I'm the first to see!

I ached to touch his foot, his leg, to be *sure* it was Roy! Thoughts of the papier-mâché man in the coffin shot through my head.

I inched my hand out to touch . . . but then . . .

Over by his desk was the sculpture platform on which had been hidden his last and greatest work, the Beast, the Monster from the midnight Derby, the Creature who went in churches beyond the wall and across a street.

Someone had taken a ballpeen hammer and struck it a dozen blows. The face, the head, the skull, were banged and smashed until only a shapeless mound remained.

Jesus God, I whispered.

Was this the final crime that made Roy self-destroy?

Or had the destroyer, waiting in the shadows, struck Roy unaware amidst his ruined towns, and hanged him on the air?

I trembled. I stopped.

For I heard the stage door spring wide.

I pulled off my shoes and ran, quietly, to hide.

26

It was the surgeon-medico-physician, the high-noon abortionist, the needle-pushing defrocked high-priest doctor.

Doc Phillips glided into the light on the far side of the stage, glancing about, seeing the ruin, then finding the hanged body above, he nodded, as if this death were an everyday calamity. He stepped forward, kicking the ruined cities as if they were mere garbage and irrelevant trash.

Seeing this, I coughed up a curse. I clapped my hand to my mouth and jerked back in shadow.

I peered through a crack in the set wall.

The doctor had frozen. Like a buck in a forest clearing, he peered around through his steel-rimmed glasses, using his nose as well as his eyes. His ears seemed to twitch on the sides of his shaven skull. He shook his head. He shuffled, shoving Paris, knocking London, arriving to reach and examine the terrible hanged thing in midair. . . .

A scalpel flashed in his hand. He seized a prop trunk, opened it, shoved it under the hanged body, grabbed a chair, stepped up on it, and slashed the rope above Roy's neck.

There was a dreadful crash when Roy hit the trunk bottom.

I coughed up my grief. I froze, sure that this time he had heard and would come, a cold steel smile in his hand. I gripped my breath tight.

Leaping down, the doc bent to examine the body.

The outside door banged wide. Feet and voices echoed.

The cleanup men had arrived, and whether this was their regular time, or if he had called them to work, I did not know.

Doc slammed the lid, hard.

I bit my knuckles and jammed my fingers in my mouth to muffle my terrible bursts of despair.

The trunk lock snapped. The doctor gestured.

I shrank back as the team of workmen crossed the set with brooms and shovels to thrust and toss Athens' stones, Alhambra's walls, Alexandria's libraries and Bombay's Krishna shrines into a dumpster.

It took twenty minutes to clean and cart off the lifework of Roy Holdstrom, taking with it, on a creaking trolley, the trunk in which, crumpled and invisible, lay my friend's body.

When the door slammed a last time, I gave an agonized shout

of grief against the night, death, the damned doctor, the vanishing men. I ran with fists to strike the air and stopped, blind with tears. Only when I had stood shaking and weeping for a long while did I stop and see an incredible thing.

There was a stack of interfaced doorway facades leaned against the north wall of the stage, like the sills and doors through which Roy and I had plunged the day before.

In the center of the first doorway was a small familiar box. It looked as if it had been left by accident. I knew it was there as a gift.

Roy!

I lunged forward to stand, looking down, and *touch* the box. *Whisper—tap.*

Whatever lay inside *rustled.*

Are you *in* there, body from the ladder on the wall in the rain? *Whisper-tap-murmur.*

Damn it! I thought, won't I *ever* be rid of *you*!?

I grabbed the box and ran.

I reached the outer door and threw up.

Eyes shut, I wiped my mouth, then opened the door slowly. Far down the alley the workmen turned a corner toward the carpenters' shop and the big iron incinerator.

Doc Phillips, behind them, gave silent directions.

I shivered. If I had arrived five minutes later, I might have come at the very moment *he* had found Roy's body and the destroyed cities of the world. My body would have gone into the trunk with Roy's!

My taxi was waiting behind Stage 9.

Nearby was a phone booth. I stumbled in, dropped a coin, called the police. A voice came on saying, "Yes? Hello, yes, hello, yes!"

I swayed drunkenly in the booth, looking at the receiver as if it were a dead snake.

What could I say? That a sound stage was cleared and empty? That an incinerator was probably burning right now, long before patrol cars and sirens could help?

And then what? Me, alone here with no armor, no weapons, no proof?

Me fired and maybe dead and over that wall to the tombs on permanent loan?

No!

I gave a shriek. Someone battered me with a hammer until my skull was red clay, torn like the flesh of the Beast. Staggering to get out, I was yanked to strangle on my own fright in a coffin locked, no matter how I banged the glass.

The phone-booth door flew wide.

"You were pushing the wrong *way!*" my taxi driver said.

I gave some sort of crazy laugh and let him lead me out.

"You forgot something."

He brought me the box, which had fallen in the booth.

Whisper-rustle-tap.

"Oh, yeah," I said. "*Him.*"

On the way out of the studio, I lay down on the back seat. When we got to the first outside street corner, the driver said, "Which way do I turn?"

"Left." I bit the back of my wrist. The driver was staring into his rear-view mirror.

"Jesus," he said, "you look awful. You gonna be sick?"

I shook my head.

"Someone die?" he guessed.

"Dead, yes."

"Here we are. Western Avenue. I go north?"

"South." Toward Roy's apartment way out at Fifty-fourth. What then? Once inside, mightn't I smell the good doctor's cologne hanging in the hall like an unseen curtain? And his workmen, down a dark corridor, carrying things, waiting to lug me away like a piece of wrecked furniture?

I shivered and rode, wondering if and when I would ever grow up. I listened to my insides and heard:

The sound of breaking glass.

My parents had died a long time back and their deaths seemed easy.

But Roy? I could never have imagined a downpour of fright like this, so much grief you could drown in it.

Now I feared to go back to the studio. The crazed architecture of all those countries nailed together, now falling to crush me. I imagined every southern plantation, each Illinois attic crammed with maniac relatives and smashed mirrors, every closet hung with tenterhooked friends.

The midnight gift, the toy box with the papier-mâché flesh and death-maddened face, lay on the taxicab floor.

Rustle-tap-whisper.

A thunderclap shook my chest.

"No, driver!" I said. "Turn *here*. To the ocean. To the sea."

When Crumley opened his front door, he examined my face and wandered off to the telephone.

"Make that *five* days' sick leave," he said.

He came back with a full tumbler of vodka and found me sitting in the garden taking deep breaths of good salt air, trying to see the stars, but there was too much fog moving in over the land. He looked at the box on my lap, took my hand, placed the vodka in it and guided it to my mouth.

"Drink that," he said, quietly, "then we'll put you to bed. Talk in the morning. What's that?"

"Hide it," I said. "If someone knew it was here, we might both disappear."

"But what is it?"

"Death, I guess."

Crumley took the cardboard box. It stirred and rustled and whispered.

Crumley lifted the lid off the carton and peered down in. Some strange papier-mâché thing stared back up at him.

Crumley said, "So that's the former head of Maximus Studios, is it?"

"Yes," I said.

Crumley studied the face for another moment and nodded quietly. "That's death, all right."

He shut the lid. The weight inside the box shifted and whispered something like "sleep" in its rustling.

No! I thought, don't *make* me!

27

We talked in the morning.

28

At noon, Crumley dropped me in front of Roy's apartment house out at Western and Fifty-fourth Street. He examined my face carefully.

"What's your name?"

"I refuse to identify myself."

"You want me to wait?"

"You go on. The sooner you walk around the studio and check things out, the better. We shouldn't be seen together, anyway. You got my list of checkpoints and the map?"

"Right here." Crumley tapped his brow.

"Be there in an hour. My grandma's house. Upstairs."

"Good old grandma."

"Crumley?"

"Yeah?"

"I love you."

"It won't get you into heaven."

"No," I said. "But it got me through the night."

"B.S.," said Crumley, and drove away.

I went inside.

My hunch last night had been right.

If Roy's miniature cities had been devastated, and his Beast pounded back to bloody clay . . .

There was a smell of the doctor's cologne in the hall. . . .

The door to Roy's apartment was ajar.

His apartment was eviscerated.

"My God," I whispered, standing in the middle of his rooms looking around. "Soviet Russia. History rewritten."

For Roy had become an unperson. In libraries, tonight, books would be torn and sewn back together, so that the name of Roy Holdstrom would vanish forever, a sad rumor lost, a figment of the imagination. No more.

No books remained, no pictures, no desk, no paper in the trash can. Even the toilet roll in the bathroom had been stripped. The medicine cabinet was Mother Hubbard bare. No shoes under the bed. No bed. No typewriter. Empty closets. No dinosaurs. No dinosaur drawings.

Hours before, the apartment had been vacuumed, scrubbed, then polished with a high-quality wax.

A fury of rage had fired the sound stage to bring down his Babylon, Assyria, Abu Simbel.

A fury of cleanliness here had snorted up the last dust of memory, the merest breath of life.

"My God, it's awful, isn't it?" The voice spoke behind me.

A young man stood in the door. He was wearing a painter's smock, much used, and his fingers were smudged with color, as was the left side of his face. His hair looked uncombed and his eyes had a kind of animal wildness, like a creature who works in the dark and only on occasion comes out at dawn.

"You better not stay here. They might come back."

"Hold on," I said. "I know you, yes? Roy's friend . . . Tom . . ."

"Shipway. Better get out. They were crazy. Come on."

I followed Tom Shipway out of the empty apartment.

He unlocked his own door with two sets of keys. "Ready? Set! Go!"

I jumped in.

He slammed the door and lay against it. "The landlady! I can't let her see!"

"See?!" I looked around.

We were in Captain Nemo's undersea apartments, his submarine cabins and engine rooms.

"Good God!" I cried.

Tom Shipway beamed. "Nice, huh?"

"Nice, hell, it's incredible!"

"I knew you'd like it. Roy gave me your stories. Mars. Atlantis. And that thing you wrote on Jules Verne. Great, huh?"

He waved and I walked and saw and touched. The great red-velvet-covered Victorian chairs, brass-studded and locked to the ship's floor. The brass periscope shining down out of the ceiling. The huge fluted pipe organ, center stage. And just beyond, a window that had been converted into an oval submarine porthole, beyond which swam tropical fish of various sizes and colors.

"Look!" said Tom Shipway. "Go on!"

I bent to peer into the periscope.

"It works!" I said. "We're under water! Or it seems! Did you do all this? You're a genius."

"Yeah."

"Does . . . does your landlady know you've done this to her apartment?"

"If she did, she'd kill me. I've never let her *in.*"

Shipway touched a button on the wall.

Shadows stirred beyond in the green sea.

A projection of a giant spider loomed, gesticulating.

"The Squid! Nemo's antagonist! I'm stunned!"

"Well, *sure!* Sit down. What's going on? Where's Roy? Why did those bums come in like dingos and leave like hyenas?"

"Roy? Oh, yeah." The weight of it knocked me back. I sat down, heavily. "Jesus, yes. Roy. What happened here last night?"

Shipway moved around the room quietly, imitating what he remembered.

"You ever see Rick Orsatti sneaking around L.A. years ago? The racketeer?"

"He ran with a gang . . ."

"Yeah. Once, years ago, at twilight, downtown, coming out of an alley, I saw six guys dressed in black, one guy leading them, and they moved like fancy rats dressed in leather or silk, all funeral-colored, and their hair oiled back, and their faces pasty white. No, otters is more like it, black weasels. Silent, slithering, snakelike, dangerous, hostile, like black clouds smoking out a chimney. Well, that was last night. I smelled a perfume so strong it came under the door."

Doc Phillips!

". . . and I looked out and these big black sewer rats were easing down the hall carrying files, dinosaurs, pictures, busts, statues, photographs. They stared at me from the sides of their little eyes. I shut the door and watched through the peekhole as they ran by on black rubber sneakers. I could hear them prowling for half an hour. Then the whispers stopped. I opened the door to an empty hall and a big tidal wave of that damn cologne. Did those guys kill Roy?"

I twitched. "What made you say *that*?"

"They looked like undertakers, is all. And if they killed off Roy's apartment, well, why not undertake Roy? Hey," Shipway stopped, looking in my face. "I didn't mean—but, well, is Roy—?"

"Dead? Yes. No. Maybe. Someone as alive as Roy just can't die!"

I told him about Stage 13, the ruined cities, the hanged body.

"Roy wouldn't do that."

"Maybe someone did it *to* him."

"Roy wouldn't hold still for *any* sons-of-bitches. Hell." And a tear rolled out of one of Tom Shipway's eyes. "I *know* Roy! He helped me build my first sub. *There!*"

On the wall was a miniature Nautilus, some thirty inches long, a high school art student's dream.

"Roy can't be dead, can he?!"

Then a telephone rang somewhere in Nemo's undersea cabins. Shipway picked up a large mollusc shell. I laughed, then stopped laughing.

"Yes?" he said into the phone, and then, "Who *is* this?"

I all but knocked the phone from his hand. I yelled into it; a shout to life. I listened to someone breathing, far away.

"Roy!"

Click. Silence. Hummmmm.

I jiggled the receiver wildly, gasping.

"Roy?" said Shipway.

"His breathing."

"Damn! You can't tell *breathing*! Where from?"

I banged the phone down and stood over it, eyes shut. Then I grabbed it again and tried to dial the wrong end of the mollusc. "How does this damn thing work?" I yelled.

"Who you calling?"

"A taxi."

"To go where? *I'll* take you!"

"Illinois, dammit, Green Town!"

"That's two thousand miles away!"

"Then," I said, dazed, putting the seashell down, "we'd better get going."

29

Tom Shipway dropped me at the studio.

I ran down through Green Town just after two. The whole town was freshly painted white, waiting for me to come knocking at doors or peering through lace-curtained windows. Flower pollen sifted on the wind as I turned up the sidewalk of my long-gone grandparents' home. Birds flew off the roof as I mounted the stairs.

Tears welled in my eyes as I knocked on the stained-glass front door.

There was a long silence. I realized that I had done the wrong thing. Boys, when they call boys to play, don't knock on doors. I backed off down in the yard, found a small pebble, and threw it hard up against the side of the house.

Silence. The house stood quietly in the November sunlight.

"What?" I asked the high window. "*Really* dead?"

And then the front door opened. A shadow stood there, looking out.

"Is it!" I yelled. I stumbled across the porch as the screen door opened. I yelled again, "Is it?" and fell into Elmo Crumley's arms.

"Yeah," he said, holding on. "If it's me you're looking for."

I made inarticulate sounds as he pulled me in and shut the door.

"Hey, take it easy." He shook my elbows.

I could hardly see him through the steam on my glasses. "What're you doing *here*?"

"You told me. Stroll around, look, then meet you here, right? No, you don't remember. Christ, what in hell you got in this place that's decent?"

Crumley rummaged the fridge and brought me a peanut butter cookie and a glass of milk. I sat there, chewing and swallowing and saying, over and over, "Thanks for coming."

"Shut up," said Crumley. "I can see you're a wreck. What in hell do we do next? Pretend everything's okay. Nobody knows you saw Roy's body, or what you thought was his body, right? What's your schedule?"

"I'm supposed to report in on a new project right now. I've been transferred. No more Beast film. I'm working with Fritz and Jesus."

Crumley laughed. "That's what they ought to title the film. You want me to prowl some more like a damn tourist?"

"Find him, Crumley. If I let myself really believe Roy was gone I'd go nuts! If Roy's *not* dead, he's hiding out, scared. You got to scare him even more, to get him out of hiding before he's really damn well killed for good. Or, or—he's *really* dead right now, so someone killed him, yes? He wouldn't hang himself, ever. So his murderer is here, also. So find the murderer. The guy who destroyed the clay head of the Beast, smashed the red clay skull, then stumbled on Roy and hoisted him up to die. Either way, Crumley, find Roy before he's killed. Or, if Roy's dead, find his damned murderer."

"That's some helluva choice."

"Try some autograph-collector agencies, yes? Maybe one of them would know Clarence, his last name, his address. Clarence. And then try the Brown Derby. That maître d' won't talk to guys like me. He *must* know who the Beast is. Between him and Clarence we can solve the murder, or the murder that *might* happen any minute!"

"At least these are leads." Crumley lowered his voice, hoping to get me to lower mine.

"Look," I said. "This place is lived in since yesterday. There's litter neither of us tossed when Roy and I worked here together." I opened the miniature-fridge door. "Candy bars. Who else would put chocolate in a fridge?"

"You!" Crumley snorted.

I had to laugh. I shut the fridge door.

"Yeah, hell, me. But he said he'd hide out. Maybe, just maybe he did. Well?"

"Okay." Crumley stepped to the screen door. "What do I look for?"

"A big gangling six-foot-three whooping crane with long arms and long skinny fingers and a big hawk nose, getting bald early, and ties that don't go with his shirts and shirts that don't go with his pants and—" I stopped.

"Sorry I asked." Crumley handed me a handkerchief. "Blow."

30

A minute later, I headed out of upper Illinois country away from my grandparents' house.

On the way, I passed Stage 13. It was triple-locked and sealed. Standing there, I imagined what it must have been like for Roy, going in to find some maniac had destroyed his reasons for living.

Roy, I thought, come back, build more beautiful Beasts, live forever.

Just then, a phalanx of Roman troops ran by, double-time, counting cadence, laughing. They flowed swiftly, a bright river of gold-and-crimson—plumed helmets. Caesar's guard never looked better, moved faster. As they ran, my eye caught the last guardsman in flight. His great long legs jerked. His elbows flapped. And what looked to be a hawk's beak plowed the wind. I gave a muted cry.

The troops rushed around a corner.

I ran to the intersection.

Roy?! I thought.

But I could not yell and let people know an idiot hid and ran amongst them.

"Damn fool," I said weakly. "Dumb," I muttered, going in the commissary door.

"Stupid," I said to Fritz, who sat drinking six cups of coffee at the table where he held his conferences.

"Enough flattery!" he cried. "Sit! Our first problem is Judas Iscariot is being cut *out* of our film!"

"Judas!? Has he been fired?"

"Last I heard he was down in La Jolla soused and hang-gliding."

"Ohmigod."

And then I really exploded. Great earthquakes of hilarity burst from my lungs.

I saw Judas hang-glide the salt winds, Roy in the Roman phalanx running, myself drenched by rain as the body fell from the
wall, and again Judas, high above La Jolla, drunk on wind, flying.

My barking laugh alarmed Fritz. Thinking me choked on my
own bewildered upchuck, he pounded my back.

"What's *wrong?*"

"Nothing," I gasped. "Everything!"

The last of my cries faded.

Christ himself had arrived, his robes rustling.

"Oh, Herod Antipas," he said to Fritz, "you summoned me
to trial?"

The actor, as tall as an El Greco painting, and as haunted by
sulfurous lightning and storm clouds, which shifted in his pale
flesh, slowly sank into a chair, without looking to see if it was
there. His sitting was an act of faith. When his invisible body
touched, he smiled with pride at the accuracy of his aim.

A waitress instantly placed before him a small plate of salmon
with no sauce and a tumbler of red wine.

J. C., eyes closed, chewed one bite of fish.

"Old director, *new* writer," he said at last. "You have called
me to confer on the Bible? Ask. I know it *all.*"

"Thank God, *someone* does," said Fritz. "Most of our film was
shot overseas by a hyperflatulent director who couldn't get it up
with an erector set. Maggie Botwin's in Projection Room 4. Be
there in one hour," he signaled me with his monocle, "to see
the whole shipwreck. Christ walked on water, but how about
deep shit? J. C., pour sweet oil in this boy's unholy ear." He
touched my shoulder. "And you, child, solve the problem of the
missing Judas, write an ending for the film that will stop the
mobs from rioting to get their money back."

A door slammed.

And I was alone, scrutinized by J.C.'s blue-skies-over-
Jerusalem stare.

Calmly he chewed his fish.

"I can see," he said, "you're wondering why I'm here. I am
the Christian. *Me?* I'm an old shoe. Comfortable with Moses,

Mahomet, and the Prophets. I don't think about it, I am *it*."

"Have you always been Christ then?"

J. C. saw I was sincere and chewed some more. "*Am* I Christ? Well, it's like putting on a comfortable robe for life, never having to dress up, always at ease. When I look down at my stigmata, I think *yes*. When I don't shave mornings, my beard is an affirmation. I can't imagine any other life. Oh, years ago, of course, I was curious." He chewed another bite. "Tried everything. Went to the Reverend Violet Greener on Crenshaw Boulevard. The Agabeg Temple?"

"*I* been there!"

"Great showmen, eh? Séances, tambourines. Never *took*. Been to Norvell. He still around?"

"Sure! With his big blinky cow eyes and his pretty boyfriends begging cash in tambourines?"

"You sound like *me*! Astrology? Numerology? Holy Rollers? That's fun."

"Been to Holy Rollers, also."

"Like their mud wrestling, talking in tongues?"

"Yeah! But how about the Negro Baptist Church, Central Avenue? Hall Johnson choir jumps and sings Sundays. Earthquakes!"

"Hell, boy, you dog my *steps*! How come *you* been all *those* places?"

"Wanted answers!"

"You read the Talmud? Koran?"

"They came too late in my life."

"Let me tell you what *really* came late—"

I snorted. "The Book of Mormon!?"

"Holy mackerel, right!"

"I was in a Mormon little-theatre group when I was twenty. The Angel Moroni put me to sleep!"

J. C. roared and slapped his stigmata.

"Boring! How about Aimee Semple McPherson!?"

"High school friends dared me to run up on stage to be 'saved.' I ran and knelt. She slapped her hand on my head. Lord, save the sinner, she cried. Glory, Hallelujah! I staggered down and fell into my friends' arms!"

"Hell," said J. C. "Aimee saved me twice! Then they buried her. Summer of '44? In that big bronze coffin? Took sixteen horses and a bulldozer to lug it up that graveyard hill. Boy, Aimee grew fake wings, natural-like. I still visit her temple for old nostalgia's sake. God, I miss her. She touched me like Jesus, in Pentecostal trimmings. What a lark!"

"And now here you are," I said, "full-time Christ at Maximus. Since the golden days with Arbuthnot."

"Arbuthnot?" J. C.'s face darkened with memory. He shoved back his plate. "Come now. Test me. Ask! Old Testament. New."

"The book of Ruth."

He recited two minutes of Ruth.

"Ecclesiastes?"

"I'll do the whole thing!" And he did.

"John?"

"Great stuff! The Last Supper after the Last Supper!"

"What?" I said, incredulous.

"Forgetful Christian! The Last Supper was *not* the Last Supper. It was the *Penultimate* Supper! Days after the Crucifixion and entombment, Simon called Peter, on the Sea of Tiberias with the other disciples, experienced the miracle of the fishes. On shore, they witnessed a pale illumination. Approaching, they saw a man standing by a spread of burning charcoals and fish. They spoke to the man and knew it was Christ, who gestured and said, 'Take of these fish and feed thy brethren. Take of my message and move through the cities of the world and preach therein forgiveness of sin.' "

"I'll be damned," I whispered.

"Delightful, yes?" said J. C. "The Penultimate Supper first, the da Vinci supper, and then the Final Final Last Last Supper of fish baked on the charcoal bed on the sands near the Sea of Tiberias after which Christ departed to stay on forever in their blood, hearts, minds, and souls. Finis."

J. C. bowed his head, then added: "Go rewrite the books, but especially John! Not mine to give, only yours to take! Out, before I rescind my blessing!"

"*Have* you blessed me?"

"All the while we talked, son. All the while. Go."

31

I stuck my head in Projection Room 4 and said, "Where's Judas?"

"That's the password!" cried Fritz Wong. "Here are three martinis! Drink!"

"I hate martinis. And anyway, first, I got to get this out of my system. Miss Botwin," I said.

"Maggie," she said, quietly amused, her camera in her lap.

"I've heard about you for years, admired you a lifetime. I just have to say I'm glad for this chance to work—"

"Yes, yes," she said, kindly. "But you're wrong. I'm no genius. I'm . . . what do you call those things skate across ponds looking for insects?"

"Water striders?"

"Water striders! You'd think the damn bugs would sink, but they move on a thin film on top of the water. Surface tension. They distribute their weight, stretch out their arms and legs so they never break the film. Well, if that isn't me, what is? I just distribute my weight, stretch out all fours, so I don't break the film I skate on. I haven't sunk from sight yet. But I'm not the best and it's no miracle, just plain dumb early-on luck. Now thanks for the compliment, young man, put your chin back up, and do as Fritz commands. The martinis. You'll soon see, I've worked no wonders on what comes next." She turned her slender profile to call quietly toward the projection room. "Jimmy? *Now*."

The lights dimmed, the screen hummed, the curtains parted.

The rough cut flashed on the screen, with a partially finished musical score by Miklos Rozsa. *That* I liked.

As the film advanced, I snuck glances at Fritz and Maggie. They looked as if they were bucking on a wild horse. I did the same, pushed back in my seat by a tidal wave of images.

My hand stole one of the martinis.

"Thatsa boy," whispered Fritz.

When the film finished, we sat silently as the lights came up.

"How come," I said at last, "you shot so much of the new footage at twilight or night?"

"I can't stand reality." Fritz's monocle blinked as he glared at the blank screen. "Half this film's schedule now is sunset. Then, the day's spine is cracked. At sundown, I heave great sighs: survived another day! I work until two each night, without facing real people, real light. I had some contact lenses made two years ago. Threw them out the window! Why? I saw pores in people's faces, my face. Moon craters. Pockmarks. Hell! look at my recent films. No sunlit people. *Midnight Lady. The Long Dark. Three a.m. Murders. Death Before Dawn.* Now, child, what about this goddamn Galilean turkey *Christ in the Garden, Caesar up a Tree!?*"

Maggie Botwin stirred despondently in the shadows and unpacked her hand camera.

I cleared my throat. "Must my narration paper over all the holes in this script?"

"Cover Caesar's ass? Yes!" Fritz Wong laughed and poured more drinks.

Maggie Botwin added, "And we're sending you to discuss Judas with Manny Leiber."

"Why!!?"

"The Jewish Lion," said Fritz, "might enjoy eating an Illinois Baptist. He might listen while he pulls off your legs."

I slugged down my second drink.

"Say," I gasped, "this isn't half bad."

I heard a whirring sound.

Maggie Botwin's camera was focused to catch my moment of incipient inebriation.

"You carry your camera everywhere?"

"Yep," she said. "No day has passed in forty years that I have not trapped the mice among the mighty. They don't dare fire me. I'd cut together nine hours of damn fools on parade and première it at Grauman's Chinese. Curious? Come *see*."

Fritz filled my glass.

"Ready for my closeup." I drank.

The camera whirred.

32

Manny Leiber was sitting on the edge of his desk, guillotining a big cigar with one of those one-hundred-dollar gold Dunhill cigar cutters. He scowled as I walked in and around the office, studying the various low sofas.

"What's wrong?"

"These sofas," I said. "So low you can't get up." I sat. I was about a foot from the floor, staring up at Manny Leiber, who loomed like Caesar, astride the world.

I grunted myself up and went to collect cushions. I placed three of them on top of each other and sat.

"What the hell you *doing*?" Manny scuttled off his desk.

"I want to look you in the eye when I talk. I hate breaking my neck down there in the pits."

Manny Leiber fumed, bit his cigar, and climbed back up on the desk rim. "Well?" he snapped.

I said, "Fritz just showed me a rough cut of his film. Judas Iscariot's missing. Who killed him?"

"What!?"

"You can't have Christ without Judas. Why is Judas suddenly the invisible disciple?"

For the first time I saw Manny Leiber's small bottom squirm

on the glass-top desk. He sucked his unlit cigar, glared at me, and let it blow.

"*I* gave orders to cut Judas! I didn't want to make an anti-Semitic film!"

"What!" I exploded, jumping up. "This film is being released next Easter, right? That week, one million Baptists will see it. Two million Lutherans?"

"Sure."

"Ten million Catholics?"

"Yes!"

"*Two* Unitarians?"

"Two—?"

"And when they all stagger forth on Easter Sunday and ask, 'Who cut Judas Iscariot out of the film?' how come the answer is: *Manny Leiber!*"

There was a long silence. Manny Leiber threw down his unlit cigar. Freezing me in place, he let his hand crawl to the white telephone.

He dialed three studio digits, waited, said, "Bill?"

He took a deep breath. "—*rehire* Judas Iscariot."

With hatred, he watched me replace the three cushions on the three easy chairs. "Is that all you came to talk about?"

"For now." I turned the doorknob.

"Whatta you heard from your friend Roy Holdstrom?" he said, suddenly.

"I thought you knew!" I said, then stopped.

Careful, I thought.

"The fool just ran off," I said, quickly. "Took everything from his apartment, left town. Stupid idiot. No friend of mine, now. Him and that damn clay Beast he made!"

Manny Leiber studied me carefully. "Good riddance. You'll like working with Wong better."

"Sure. Fritz and Jesus."

"What?"

"Jesus and Fritz."

And I went out.

33

I walked slowly back to my grandparents' house somewhere in the past.

"You sure it was Roy running by an hour ago?" asked Crumley.

"Hell, I dunno. Yes, no, maybe. I'm not coherent. Martinis, middle of the day, that's not for me. And—" I hefted the script— "I got to cut two pounds off this and add three ounces. Help!"

I glanced at a pad Crumley was holding.

"What?"

"Called three autograph agencies. They all knew Clarence—"

"Great!"

"Not so. All said the same. Paranoid. No last name, phone number, or address. Told them all he was terrified. Not of being burgled, no, but murdered. *Then* burgled. Five thousand photos, six thousand autographs, his nest eggs. So maybe he didn't recognize the Beast the other night, but was afraid the Beast knew him, knew where he lived, and might come get him."

"No, no, that doesn't fit."

"Clarence, whatever-his-name is, the agency people said, always took cash, gave cash. No checks, no way to trace him that way. Never did things by mail. Showed up, regular, to make deals, then disappeared for months. Dead end. Dead end, too, the Brown Derby. I walked nice and soft, but the maître d' hung up on me. Sorry, kid. Hey—"

Just then, on schedule, the Roman phalanx reappeared, far off, double-timing. With jovial shouts and curses they approached.

I leaned wildly out, holding my breath.

Crumley said: "Is that the bunch you mentioned, and Roy with them?"

"Yeah."

"Is he with them *now*?"

"I can't *see*—"

Crumley exploded.

"Goddamn, what the hell is that stupid jerk doing running around the studio anyway? Why doesn't he get the hell out, escape, dammit?! What's he sticking around for? To get himself killed?! He's had his chance to run, but he's putting you, *and* me, through the wringer. Why!?"

"Revenge," I said. "For all the murders."

"*What* murders!?"

"Of all of his creatures, all his most dear friends."

"Crap."

"Listen, Crum. How long you been in your house in Venice? Twenty, twenty-five years. Planted every hedge, every bush, seeded the lawn, built the rattan hut out back, put in the sound equipment, the rain makers, added the bamboo and the orchids, and the peach trees, the lemon, the apricot. What if I broke in one night soon and tore up everything, cut down the trees, trampled the roses, burned the hut, threw the sound deck out in the street, what would you do?"

Crumley thought about it and his face burned red.

"Exactly," I said, quietly. "I don't know if Roy will ever get married. Right now, his children, his whole life has been stomped down in the dust. Everything he ever loved was murdered. Maybe he's in here now, solving these deaths, trying, just as we are, to find the Beast, and kill him. Maybe Roy's gone forever. But if I were Roy, yeah, I'd stay on, hide, and keep searching until I buried the killer with the killed."

"My lemon trees, huh?" said Crumley, looking off toward the sea. "My orchids, my rain forest? Done in by someone? Well."

The phalanx ran by below in the late sunlight and away into the blue shadows.

There was no great gawky whooping-crane warrior with them.

The footsteps and yells faded.

"Let's go home," said Crumley.

* * *

At midnight, a sudden wind blew through Crumley's African garden. All the trees in the neighborhood turned over in their sleep.

Crumley studied me. "I can feel something coming."

It came.

"The Brown Derby," I said, stunned. "My God, why didn't I think sooner!? The night Clarence ran off in a panic. He dropped his portfolio, left it lying on the walk by the Brown Derby entrance! Someone must've picked it up. It might still be there, waiting for Clarence to calm down and dare to sneak back for it. His address would *have* to be in it."

"Good lead," Crumley nodded. "I'll follow up."

The night wind blew again, a very melancholy sigh through the lemon and orange trees.

"And—"

"And?"

"The Brown Derby again. The maître d' might not talk to *us*, but I know someone who ate there every week for years, when I was a kid—"

"Oh, God," Crumley sighed. "Rattigan. She'll eat you alive."

"My love will protect me!"

"God, put that in a sack and we'll fertilize the San Fernando Valley."

"Friendship protects. You wouldn't hurt me, would you?"

"Don't count on it."

"We got to do something. Roy's hiding. If they, whoever they are, find him, he's dead."

"You, too," said Crumley, "if you play amateur detective. It's late. Midnight."

"Constance's wake-up hour."

"Transylvania time? Hell." Crumley took a deep breath. "Do I drive you?"

A single peach fell from a hidden garden tree. It thumped.

"Yes!" I said.

34

"At dawn," said Crumley, "if you're singing soprano, don't call."

And he drove off.

Constance's house was, as before, a perfection, a white shrine set to glow on the shoreline. All of its doors and windows stood wide. Music played inside the huge stark white living room: some old Benny Goodman.

I walked the shore as I had walked a thousand nights back, checking the ocean. She was there somewhere racing porpoises, echoing seals.

I looked in at the parlor floor, littered with four dozen circus-bright pillows, and the bare white walls where, late nights until dawn, the shadow shows passed, her old films projected from the years before I was born.

I turned because a wave, heavier than the rest, had slammed on the shore. . . .

To deliver forth, as from the rug tossed at Caesar's feet . . .

Constance Rattigan.

She came out of the wave like a loping seal, with hair almost the same color, slick brown and water combed, and her small body powdered with nutmeg and doused in cinnamon oil. Every autumn tint was hers in nimble legs and wild arms, wrists, and hands. Her eyes were a wicked wise merry small creature's brown. Her laughing mouth looked stained by walnut juice. She was a frisking November surf creature rinsed out of a cold sea but hot as burnt chestnuts to touch.

"Son of a bitch," she cried. "You!"

"Daughter of the Nile! You!"

She flung herself against me like a dog, to get all the wetness off on someone else, grabbed my ears, kissed my brow, nose, and mouth, then turned in a circle to show all sides.

"I'm naked, as usual."

"I noticed, Constance."

"You haven't changed: you're looking at my eyebrows instead of my boobs."

"You haven't changed. The boobs look firm."

"Not bad for a night-swimming fifty-six-year-old former movie queen, huh? C'mon!"

She ran up the sand. By the time I reached her outdoor pool she had brought out cheese, crackers, and champagne.

"My God." She uncorked the bottle. "It's been a hundred years. But I knew someday you'd come back. Got marriage out of your blood? Ready for a mistress?"

"Nope. Thanks."

We drank.

"You seen Crumley in the last eight hours?"

"Crumley?"

"Shows in your face. Who died?"

"Someone twenty years ago, at Maximus Films."

"Arbuthnot!" cried Constance in a burst of intuition.

A shadow crossed her face. She reached for a bathrobe and clothed herself, suddenly very small, a girl child who turned to look down along the coast, as if it were not sand and tide, but the years themselves.

"Arbuthnot," she murmured. "Christ, what a beauty! What a creator." She paused. "I'm glad he's dead," she added.

"Not quite," I stopped.

For Constance had whirled, as if shot.

"No!" she cried.

"No, a thing like him. A thing propped up on a wall to scare me, and now, you!"

Tears of relief burst from her eyes. She gasped as if struck in the stomach.

"Damn you! Go inside," she said. "Get the vodka."

I brought the vodka and a glass. I watched her throw back two slugs. I was suddenly sober forever, tired of seeing people drink, tired of being afraid when night came.

I could think of nothing to say so I went to the edge of her pool, took off my shoes and socks, rolled up my pants, and soaked my feet in the water, looking down, waiting.

At last Constance came and sat beside me.

"You're back," I said.

"Sorry," she said. "Old memories die hard."

"They sure as hell do," I said, looking along the coastline now myself. "At the studio this week, panic attacks. Why would everyone fly apart at a wax dummy in the rain that looked like Arbuthnot?"

"Is *that* what happened?"

I told her the rest, as I had told it to Crumley, ending with the Brown Derby and my need for her to go there with me. When I finished, Constance, paler, finished one more vodka.

"I wish I knew what I'm supposed to be scared about!" I said. "Who wrote that note to get me to the graveyard, so I'd introduce a fake Arbuthnot to a waiting world. But I didn't tell the studio I found the dummy, so *they* found and tried to hide it, almost wild with fear. Is the memory of Arbuthnot that terrible so long after his death?"

"Yes." Constance put her trembling hand on my wrist. "Oh, yes."

"Now what? Blackmail? Does someone write Manny Leiber and demand money or more notes will reveal the studio's past, Arbuthnot's life? Reveal what? A lost reel of film maybe from twenty years ago, on the night Arbuthnot died. Film at the scene of the accident, maybe, which, if shown, would burn Constantinople, Tokyo, Berlin, and the whole backlot?"

"Yes!" Constance's voice was far back in some other year. "Get out now. Run. Did you ever dream a big black two-ton bulldog comes in the night and eats you up? A friend of mine had that dream. The big black bulldog ate him. We called it World War II. He's gone forever. I don't want *you* gone."

"Constance, I can't quit. If Roy's alive —"

"You don't *know* that."

"—and I get him out of there and help him get his job back

because it's the only right thing to do. I got to. It's all so unfair."

"Go out in the water, argue with the sharks, you'll get a better deal. You really want to go back to Maximus studios after what you just told me? God. Do you know the *last* day I was ever there? The afternoon of Arbuthnot's funeral."

She let that sink me. Then she threw the anchor after it.

"It was the end of the world. I never saw so many sick and dying people in one place. It was like watching the Statue of Liberty crack and fall. Hell. He was Mount Rushmore after an earthquake. Forty times bigger, stronger, greater than Cohn, Zanuck, Warner, and Thalberg rolled in one knish. When they slammed his casket lid in that tomb across the wall, cracks ran all the way uphill to where the Hollywoodland sign fell. It was Roosevelt, dying long before his death."

Constance stopped for she could hear my uneasy breathing.

Then she said: "Look, is there a brain in my head? Did you know Shakespeare and Cervantes died on the same day? Think! It's all the redwoods in the world cut so the thunder never stops. Antarctica melts down in tears. Christ gapes his wounds. God holds his breath. Caesar's legions, ghosts, ten million, rise, with bleeding Amazons for eyes. I wrote that when I was sixteen and a sap, when I found out that Juliet and Don Quixote fell dead on the same day, and I cried all night. You're the only one ever heard those silly lines. Well, that's how it was when Arbuthnot died. I was sixteen again and couldn't stop crying or writing junk. There went the moon, the planets, Sancho Panza, Rosinante and Ophelia. Half the women at his funeral were old mistresses. A between-the-sheets fan club, plus nieces, girl cousins, and crazy aunts. When we opened our eyes that day it was the second Johnstown flood. Jesus, I do run on. I hear they still got Arbuthnot's chair in his old office? Anyone sat in it since with a big enough butt and a brain to fit?"

I thought of Manny Leiber's behind. Constance said:

"God knows how the studio survived. Maybe by Ouija board, with advice from the dead. Don't laugh. That's Hollywood, reading the Leo-Virgo-Taurus forecasts, not stepping on cracks be-

tween takes. The studio? Give me the grand tour. Let grandma
smell the four winds in the fifty-five cities, take the temperature
of the maniacs in charge, then on to the Brown Derby maître d'. I
slept with him once, ninety years back. Will he remember the old
witch of the Venice shore and let us sit at tea with your Beast?"

"And say what?"

A long wave came in, a short wave rustled on the shore.

"I'll say," she closed her eyes, "stop scaring my future-writing
dinosaur-loving honorary bastard son."

"Yes," I said, "please."

In the beginning was the fog.

Like the Great Wall of China, it moved over the shore and
the land and the mountains at 6 A.M.

My morning voices spoke.

I crept around Constance's parlor, groping to find my glasses
somewhere under an elephant herd of pillows, but gave up and
staggered about to find a portable typewriter. I sat blindly stab-
bing out the words to put an end to *Antipas and the Messiah.*

And it was indeed A Miracle of Fish.

And Simon called Peter pulled in to the shore to find the
Ghost by the charcoal bed and the baked fish to be given as gifts,
with the word as deliverance to a final good, and the disciples
there in a gentle mob and the last hour upon them and the
Ascension near and the farewells that would linger beyond two
thousand years to be remembered on Mars and shipped on to
Alpha Centauri.

And when the Words came from my machine I could not see
them, and held them close to my blind wet eyes as Constance
dolphined out of a wave, another miracle clothed in rare flesh,
to read over my shoulder and give a sad-happy cry and shake
me like a pup, glad of my triumph.

I called Fritz.

"Where the hell are you!" he cried.

"Shut up," I said, gently.

And I read aloud.

And the fish were laid to bake on the charcoals that blew in the wind as fireflies of spark were borne across the sands and Christ spoke and the disciples listened and as dawn rose Christ's footprints, like the bright sparks, were blown away off the sands and he was departed and the disciples walked to all points away and *their* paths were lifted by the winds and *their* footprints were no more and a New Day truly began as the film ended.

Far off, Fritz was very still.

At last he whispered, "You . . . son . . . of . . . a . . . bitch."

And then: "When do you bring that *in?*"

"In three hours."

"Get here in *two*," cried Fritz, "and I will kiss your four cheeks. I go now to un-man Manny and out-Herod Herod!"

I hung up and the phone rang.

It was Crumley.

"Is your Balzac still *Honoré?*" he said. "Or are you the great Hemingway fish dead by the pierside, bones picked meatless?"

"Crum," I sighed.

"I made more calls. But what if we get all the data you're looking for, find Clarence, identify the awful-looking guy in the Brown Derby, how do we let your goony-bird friend Roy, who seems to be running around the studio in hand-me-down togas, how do we let him know and yank him the hell out? Do I use a giant butterfly net?"

"Crum," I said.

"Okay, okay. There's good news and there's bad. I got to thinking about that portfolio you told me your old pal Clarence dropped outside the Brown Derby. I called the Derby, said I had lost a portfolio. Of course, Mr. Sopwith, the lady said, it's here!"

Sopwith! So that was Clarence's name.

"I was afraid, I said, I hadn't put my address in the portfolio."

"It's here, said the lady, 1788 Beachwood? Yeah, I said. I'll be right over to get it."

"Crumley! You're a genius!"

"Not quite. I'm talking from the Brown Derby phone booth *now*."

"And?" I felt my heart jump.

"The portfolio's gone. Someone else got the same bright idea. Someone else got here ahead of me. The lady gave a description. It wasn't Clarence, the way you said. When the lady asked for identification, the guy just walked out with the portfolio. The lady was upset, but no big deal."

"Ohmigod," I said. "That means *they* know Clarence's address."

"You want me to go and tell him all this?"

"No, no. He'd have a heart attack. He's scared of me, but I'll go. Warn him to hide. Christ, anything could happen. 1788 Beachwood?"

"You got it."

"Crum, you're the cat's pajamas."

"Always was," he said, "always was. Strange to report the folks down at the Venice station expect me back to work an hour ago. The coroner phoned to say a customer won't keep. While I'm working, you help. Who else in the studio might know what we need to know? I mean, someone you might trust? Someone who's lived the studios' history?"

"Botwin," I said instantly, and blinked, amazed at my response.

Maggie and her miniature whirring camera, trapping the world day after day, year after year, as it reeled by.

"Botwin?" said Crumley. "Go ask. Meanwhile, Buster—?"

"Yeah?"

"Guard your ass."

"It's guarded."

I hung up and said, "Rattigan?"

"I've started the car," she said. "It's waiting at the curb."

36

We rioted toward the studio late in the afternoon. With three bottles of champagne stashed in her roadster, Constance swore happily at every intersection, leaning over the steering wheel like those dogs that love the wind.

"Gangway!" she cried.

We roared down the middle of Larchmont Boulevard, straddling the dividing line.

"What," I yelled, "are you *doing*?!"

"Once there were trolley tracks on each side of the street. Down the middle was a long line of power poles. Harold Lloyd drove in and out, cat-cradling the poles, like *this*!"

Constance swerved the car left.

"And *this*! and *this*!"

We swerved around half a dozen ghosts of long-gone poles, as if pursued by a phantom trolley car.

"Rattigan," I said.

She saw my solemn face.

"Beachwood Avenue?" she said.

It was four in the afternoon. The last mail of the day was heading north on the avenue. I nodded to Constance. She parked just ahead of the mailman, who trudged along in the still warm sun. He greeted me like a fellow Iowa tourist, plenty cheerful considering the junk mail he unloaded at every door.

All I wanted was to check Clarence's name and address before I knocked at his door. But the postman couldn't stop babbling. He told how Clarence walked and ran, what he looked like around the mouth: quivering. Nervous ears that itched up and down on his skull. Eyes mostly white.

The mailman punched my elbow with the mail, laughing. "A Christmas fruitcake, ten years stale! Comes to his bungalow door in a big wrap-around camel's-hair coat like Adolphe Menjou wore in 1927, when we boys ran up the aisles to pee, away from the 'mush' scenes. *Sure*. Old Clarence. I said 'Boo!' once and he slammed the door. I bet he showers in that coat, afraid to see himself naked. Scaredy Clarence? Don't knock too loud—"

But I was gone. I turned in quickly at the Villa Vista Courts and walked up to number 1788.

I did not knock on the door. I scratched with my fingernail on the small glass panes. There were nine of them. I did not try them all. The shade was pulled down behind so I couldn't see in. When there was no answer I tapped my forefinger, a bit louder.

I imagined I heard Clarence's rabbit heart pounding inside, behind the glass.

"Clarence!" I called. And waited. "I know you're in there!"

Again, I thought I heard his pulse racing.

"Call me, dammit!" I cried, at last, "before it's too late! You know who this is. The studio, dammit! Clarence, if *I* can find you, *they* can, too!"

They? Who did I mean by "they"?

I pounded the door with both fists. One of the glass panes cracked.

"Clarence! Your portfolio! It was at the Brown Derby!"

That did it. I stopped pounding for I heard a sound that might have been a bleat or a muffled cry. The lock rattled. Another lock rattled after that, and a third.

At last the door cracked open, held by an inside brass chain.

Clarence's haunted face looked down a long tunnel of years at me, close by but so far away I almost thought his voice echoed. "Where?" he pleaded. "*Where?*"

"The Brown Derby," I said, ashamed. "And someone stole it."

"Stole?" Tears burst from his eyes. "My portfolio!? Oh God," he mourned. "You've done this to me."

"No, no, listen—"

"If they try to break in, I'll kill myself. They can't have them!"

And he glanced tearfully over his shoulder at all the files I could see crowded beyond, and the bookcases, and the walls full of signed portraits.

My Beasts, Roy had said at his own funeral, my lovelies, my dears.

My beauties, Clarence was saying, my soul, my life!

"I don't want to die," mourned Clarence, and shut the door.

"Clarence!" I tried a last time. "Who's *they*? If I knew, I might save you! Clarence!"

A shade banged up across the court.

A door half opened in another bungalow.

All I could say then, exhausted, was, in a half whisper: "Good-bye . . ."

I went back to the roadster. Constance was sitting there looking at the Hollywood Hills, trying to enjoy the weather.

"What was *that* all about?" she said.

"One nut, Clarence. Another one, Roy." I slumped into the seat beside her. "Okay, take me to the nut factory."

Constance gunned us to the studio gate.

"God," gasped Constance, staring up, "I hate hospitals."

"Hospitals?!"

"Those rooms are full of undiagnosed cases. A thousand babies have been conceived, or born, in that joint. It's a snug home where the bloodless get transfusions of greed. That coat of arms above the gate? A lion rampant with a broken back. Next: a blind goat with no balls. Then: Solomon chopping a live baby in half. Welcome to Green Glades mortuary!"

Which sent a stream of icewater down my neck.

My pass motored us through the front gate. No confetti. No brass bands.

"You should have told that cop who you were!"

"You see his face? *Born* the day I fled the studio for my nunnery. Say 'Rattigan' and the sound track dies. Look!"

She pointed at the film vaults as we swerved by. "My tomb! Twenty cans in one crypt! Films that died in Pasadena, shipped back with tags on their toes. So!"

We braked in the middle of Green Town, Illinois.

I jumped up the front steps and put out my hand. "My grand-parents' place. Welcome!"

Constance let me pull her up the steps to sit in the porch swing, feeling the motion.

"My God," she breathed, "I haven't ridden one of these in years! You son of a bitch," she whispered, "what are you doing to the old lady?"

"Heck. I didn't know crocodiles cried."

She looked at me steadily. "You're a real case. You believe all this crap you write? Mars in 2001. Illinois in '28?"

"Yep."

"Christ. How lucky to be inside your skin, so goddamned naïve. Don't ever change." Constance gripped my hand. "We stupid damn doomsayers, cynics, monsters laugh, but we need you. Otherwise, Merlin dies, or a carpenter fixing the Round Table saws it crooked, or the guy who oils the armor substitutes cat pee. Live forever. Promise?"

Inside, the phone rang.

Constance and I jumped. I ran in to grab the receiver. "Yes?" I waited. "Hello?!"

But there was only a sound of wind blowing from what seemed like a high place. The flesh on the back of my neck, like a caterpillar, crawled up and then down.

"Roy?"

Inside the phone, wind blew and, somewhere, timbers creaked.

My gaze lifted by instinct to the sky.

One hundred yards away. Notre Dame. With its twin towers, its statue saints, its gargoyles.

There was wind up on the cathedral towers. Dust blowing high, and a red workmen's flag.

"Is this a studio line?" I said. "Are you where I think you are?"

Way up at the very top, I thought I saw one of the gargoyles . . . move.

Oh, Roy, I thought, if that is you, forget revenge. Come away.

But the wind stopped and the breathing stopped and the line went dead.

I dropped the phone and stared out and up at the towers.

Constance glanced and searched those same towers, where a new wind sifted flurries of dust devils down and away.

"Okay, no more bull!"

Constance strode back out on the porch and lifted her face toward Notre Dame.

"What the hell goes *on* here!" she yelled.

"Shh!" I said.

37

Fritz was way out in the midst of a turmoil of extras, yelling, pointing, stomping the dust. He actually had a riding crop under his arm, but I never saw him use it. The cameras, there were three of them, were just about ready, and the assistant directors were rearranging the extras along the narrow street leading into a square where Christ might appear sometime between now and dawn. In the middle of the uproar Fritz saw me and Constance, just arrived, and gestured to his secretary. He came running, I handed over the five script pages, and the secretary scuttled back through the crowd.

I watched as Fritz leafed through my scene, his back to me. I saw his head suddenly hunch down on his neck. There was a long moment before Fritz turned and, without catching my eye, picked up a bullhorn. He shouted. There was instant silence.

"You will all settle. Those who can sit, sit. Others, stand at ease. By tomorrow, Christ will have come and gone. And this is the way we will see him when we are finished and go home. Listen."

And he read the pages of my last scene, word for word, page for page, in a quiet yet clear voice and not a head turned nor did one foot stir. I could not believe it was happening. All my words about the dawn sea and the miracle of the fish and the strange pale ghost of Christ on the shore and the bed of fish baking on the charcoals, which blew up in warm sparks on the wind, and the disciples there in silence, listening, eyes shut, and the blood of the Saviour, as he murmured his farewells, falling from the wounds in his wrists and onto the charcoals that baked the Supper after the Last Supper.

And at last Fritz Wong said my final words.

And there was the merest whisper from the mob, the crowd, the phalanx, and in the midst of that silence, Fritz at last walked through the people until he reached my side, by which time I was half-blind with emotion.

Fritz looked with surprise at Constance, jerked a nod at her, and then stood for a moment and at last reached up, pulled the monocle from his eye, took my right hand, and deposited the lens, like an award, a medal, on my palm. He closed my fingers over it.

"After tonight," he said quietly, "you will see for me."

It was an order, a command, a benediction.

Then he stalked away. I stood watching him, his monocle clenched in my trembling fist. When he got to the center of the silent crowd, he snatched the bullhorn and shouted, "All right, *do* something!"

He did not look at me again.

Constance took my arm and led me away.

38

On the way to the Brown Derby, Constance, driving slowly, looked at the twilight streets ahead and said: "My God, you believe in everything, don't you? How? Why?"

"Simple," I said. "By not doing anything I hate or disbelieve in. If you offered me a job writing, say, a film on prostitution or alcoholism, I couldn't do it. I wouldn't pay for a prostitute and don't understand drunks. I do what I love. Right now, thank God, it's Christ at Galilee during his going-away dawn and his footprints along the shore. I'm a ramshackle Christian, but when

I found that scene in John, or J. C. found it for me, I was lost. How could I *not* write it?"

"Yeah." Constance was staring at me so I had to duck my head and remind her, by pointing, that she was still driving.

"Hell, Constance, it's not money I'm after. If you offered me *War and Peace*, I'd refuse. Is Tolstoy bad? No. I just don't understand him. *I* am the poor one. But at least I *know* I can't do the screenplay, for I'm not in love. You'd waste your money hiring me. End of lecture. And here," I said, as we sailed past it and had to turn around, "is the Brown Derby!"

It was an off evening. The Brown Derby was almost empty and there was no Oriental screen set up way in the back.

"Damn," I muttered.

For my eyes had wandered over to an alcove on my left. In the alcove was a smaller telephone cubby where the reservation calls came in. There was a small reading lamp lit over a podium desk, on which just a few hours ago Clarence Sopwith's picture album had probably lain.

Lying there waiting for someone to steal it, find Clarence's address and—

My God, I thought, *no*!

"Child," said Constance, "let's get you a drink!"

The maître d' was presenting a bill to his last customers. The eye in the back of his head read us and he turned. His face exploded with delight when he saw Constance. But almost instantly, when he saw me, the light went out. After all, I was bad news. I had been there outside on the night when the Beast had been accosted by Clarence.

The maître d' smiled again and charged across the room to dislocate me, and kissed each one of Constance's fingers, hungrily. Constance threw her head back and laughed.

"It's no use, Ricardo. I sold my rings, years ago!"

"You remember me?" he asked, astonished.

"Ricardo Lopez, also known as Sam Kahn?"

"But then, *who* was Constance Rattigan?"

"I burned my birth certificate with my underpants." Constance pointed at me. "This is—"

"I know, I know," Lopez ignored me.

Constance laughed again, for he was still holding her hand. "Ricardo here was an MGM swim-pool lifeguard. Ten dozen girls a day drowned so he could pump them back to life. Ricardo, lead on."

We were seated. I could not take my eyes off the rear wall of the restaurant. Lopez caught this and gave the corkscrew on the wine bottle a vicious twist.

"I was only an audience," I said, quietly.

"Yes, yes," he muttered, as he poured for Constance to taste. "It was that stupid other one."

"The wine is beautiful," Constance sipped, "like you." Ricardo Lopez collapsed. A wild laugh almost escaped him.

"And who was that other stupid one?" Constance put in, seeing her advantage.

"It was nothing." Lopez sought to regain his old dyspepsia. "Shouts and almost blows. My best customer and some street beggar."

Ah, God, I thought. Poor Clarence, begging for limelight and fame all his life.

"Your *best* customer, my dear Ricardo?" said Constance, blinking.

Ricardo gazed off at the rear wall where the Oriental screen stood, folded.

"I am destroyed. Tears do not come easily. We were so careful. For years. Always he came late. He waited in the kitchen until I checked to see if there was anyone here he knew. Hard to do, yes? After all, I do not know everyone he knows, eh? But now because of a stupid blunder, the merest passing idiot, my Great One will probably never return. He will find another restaurant, later, emptier."

"This Great One . . ." Constance shoved an extra wine glass at Ricardo and indicated he fill it for himself, "has a name?"

"None." Ricardo poured, still leaving my glass empty. "And I *never* asked. Many years he came, at least one night a month, paying cash for the finest food, the best wines. But, in all those years, we exchanged no more than three dozen words a night.

"He read the menu in silence, pointed to what he wanted, behind the screen. Then he and his lady talked and drank and laughed. That is, if a lady was with him. Strange ladies. Lonely ladies . . ."

"Blind," I said.

Lopez shot me a glance.

"Perhaps. Or worse."

"What could be worse?"

Lopez looked at his wine and at the empty chair nearby.

"Sit," said Constance.

Lopez glanced nervously around at the empty restaurant. At last, he sat, took a slow tasting of the wine, and nodded.

"Afflicted, would be more like it," he said. "His women. Strange. Sad. *Wounded*? Yes, wounded people who could not laugh. He *made* them. It was as if to cure his silent, terrible life he must cheer others into some kind of peculiar joy. He proved that life was a joke! Imagine! To *prove* such a thing. And then the laughter and him going out into the night with his woman with no eyes or no mouth or no mind—still imagined they knew joy—to get in taxis one night, limousines, always a different limousine company, everything paid for in cash, no credits, no identification, and off they would drive to silence. I never heard anything that they said. If he looked out and saw me within fifteen feet of the screen: *disaster!* My tip? A single silver dime! The next time, I would stand thirty feet away. Tip? Two hundred dollars. Ah, well, here's to the sad one."

A sudden gust of wind shook the outer doors of the restaurant. We froze. The doors gaped wide, fluttered back, settled.

Ricardo's spine stiffened. He glanced from the door to me, as if I were responsible for the emptiness and only the night wind.

"Oh, damn, damn, damn it to hell," he said, softly. "He has gone to ground."

"The Beast?"

Ricardo stared at me. "Is *that* what you call him? Well . . ."
Constance nodded at my glass. Ricardo shrugged and poured me
about an inch. "Why is that one so important that you drag in
here to ruin my life? Until this week, I was rich."

Constance instantly probed the purse in her lap. Her hand,
mouselike, crept across the seat on her right side and left something there. Ricardo sensed it and shook his head.

"Ah, no, not from you, dear Constance. Yes, *he* made me rich.
But once, years ago, you made me the happiest man in the
world."

Constance's hand patted his and her eyes glistened. Lopez
got up and walked back to the kitchen for about two minutes.
We drank our wine and waited, watching the front door gape
with wind and whisper shut on the night. When Lopez came
back he looked around at the empty tables and chairs, as if they
might criticize his bad manners as he sat. Carefully, he placed
a small photograph in front of us. While we looked at it, he
finished his wine.

"That was taken with a Land camera last year. One of our
stupid kitchen help wanted to amuse his friends, eh? Two pictures taken in three seconds. They fell on the floor. The Beast,
as you call him, destroyed the camera, tore one picture, thinking
there was only one, and struck our waiter, whom I fired instantly.
We offered no bill and the last bottle of our greatest wine. All
was rebalanced. Later I found the second picture under a table,
where it had been kicked when the man roared and struck. Is
it not a great pity?"

Constance was in tears.

"Is *that* what he looks like?"

"Oh, God," I said. "Yes."

Ricardo nodded: "I often wanted to say: Sir, *why* do you live?
Do you have nightmares of being beautiful? Who is your woman?
What do you do for a living, and is it living? I never said. I stared
only at his hands, gave him bread, poured wine. But some nights
he forced me to look at his face. When he tipped he waited for

me to lift my eyes. Then he would smile that smile like a razor cut. Have you seen fights when one man slashes another and the flesh opens like a red mouth? His mouth, poor monster, thanking me for the wine and lifting my tip high so I had to see his eyes trapped in that abattoir of a face, aching to be free, drowning in despair."

Ricardo blinked rapidly and jammed the photo into his pocket.

Constance stared at the place on the tablecloth where the picture had been. "I came to see if I knew the man. Thank God, I did not. But his voice? Perhaps some other night . . .?"

Ricardo snorted. "No, no. It is ruined. That stupid fan out front the other night. The only time, in years, such an encounter. Usually, that late, the street, empty. Now, I am sure he will not return. And I will go back to living in a smaller apartment. Forgive this selfishness. It's hard to give up two-hundred-dollar tips."

Constance blew her nose, got up, grabbed Lopez's hand, and thrust something into it. "Don't fight!" she said. "That was a great year, '28. Time I paid my lovely gigolo. Stay!" For he was trying to shove the money back. "Heel!"

Ricardo shook his head, and hugged her hand to his cheek.

"Was it La Jolla, the sea, and good weather?"

"Body surfing every day!"

"Ah, yes, the bodies, the warm surf."

Ricardo kissed each and every one of her fingers.

Constance said, "The flavor starts at the elbow!"

Ricardo barked a laugh. Constance punched him lightly in the jaw and ran. I let her go out the door.

Then I turned and looked over at that alcove with the small lamp, the desk, and the filing cabinet.

Lopez saw where I was looking, and did the same.

But Clarence's picture portfolio was gone, out in that night, with the wrong people.

Who will protect Clarence now, I wondered. Who will save him from the dark and keep him, living, until dawn?

Myself? The poor simp whose girl cousin beat him at hand wrestling?

Crumley? Dare I ask him to wait all night in front of Clarence's bungalow court? Go shout at Clarence's door? You're lost. Run!

I did not call Crumley. I did not go yell at Clarence Sopwith's bungalow porch. I nodded to Ricardo Lopez and went out into the night. Constance, outside, was crying. "Let's get the hell out of here," she said.

She swabbed her eyes with an inadequate silk handkerchief. "That damn Ricardo. Made me feel old. And that damn photograph of that poor hopeless man."

"Yes, that face," I said, and added, ". . . Sopwith."

For Constance was standing right where Clarence Sopwith had stood a few nights ago.

"Sopwith?" she said.

39

Driving, Constance cut the wind with her voice:

"Life is like underwear, should be changed twice a day. Tonight is over, I choose to forget it."

She shook tears from her eyes and glanced aside to see them rain away.

"I forget, just like that. There goes my memory. See how easy?"

"No."

"You saw the mamacitas in the top floor of that tenement you lived in a couple years back? How after the big Saturday night blowout they'd toss their new dresses down off the roof to prove how rich they were, and didn't care, and could buy another tomorrow? What a great lie; off and down with the dresses and them standing fat- or skinny-assed on the three-o'clock-in-the-morning roof watching the garden of dresses, like silk petals going downwind to the empty lots and alleys. Yes?"

"Yes!"

"That's me. Tonight, the Brown Derby, that poor son of a bitch, along with my tears, I throw it all away."

"Tonight isn't over. You can't forget that face. Did you or did you not recognize the Beast?"

"Jesus. We're on the verge of our first really big heavyweight fight. Back off."

"*Did* you recognize him?"

"He was unrecognizable."

"He had eyes. Eyes don't change."

"Back off!" she yelled.

"Okay," I groused. "I'm off."

"There." More tears fled away in small comets. "I love you again." She smiled a windblown smile, her hair raveling and unraveling in the flood of air that sluiced us in a cold flow over the windshield.

All the bones in my body collapsed at that smile. God, I thought, has she always won, every day, all her life, with that mouth and those teeth and those great pretend-innocent eyes?

"Yep!" laughed Constance, reading my mind.

"And look," she said.

She stopped dead in front of the studio gates. She stared up for a long moment.

"Ah, God," she said at last. "That's no hospital. It's where great elephant ideas go to die. A graveyard for lunatics."

"That's over the wall, Constance."

"No. You die *here* first, you die over *there* last. In between—" She held to the sides of her skull as if it might fly apart. "Madness. Don't go in there, kid."

"Why?"

Constance rose slowly to stand over the steering wheel and cry havoc at the gate that was not yet open and the night windows that were blind shut and the blank walls that didn't care.

"First, they drive you crazy. Then when they have driven you nuts they persecute you for being the babbler at noon, the hysteric at sunset. The toothless werewolf at the rising of the moon.

"When you've reached the precise moment of lunacy, they fire you and spread the word that you are unreasonable, uncooperative, and unimaginative. Toilet paper, imprinted with your name is dispatched to every studio, so the great ones can chant your initials as they ascend the papal throne.

"When you are dead they shake you awake to kill you again. Then they hang your carcass at Bad Rock, OK Corral, or Versailles on backlot 10, pickle you in a jar like a fake embryo in a bad carny film, buy you a cheap crypt next door, chisel your name, misspelled, on the tomb, cry like crocodiles. Then the final inglory: Nobody remembers your name on all the pictures you made in the good years. Who recalls the screenwriters for *Rebecca?* Who remembers who wrote *Gone With the Wind?* Who helped Welles become Kane? Ask anyone on the street. Hell, they don't even know who was president during Hoover's administration.

"So there you have it. Forgotten the day after the preview. Afraid to leave home between pictures. Who ever heard of a film writer who ever visited Paris, Rome, or London? All piss-fearful if they travel, the big moguls will forget them. Forget them, hell, they never *knew* them. Hire whatchamacalit. Get me whatsisname. The name above the title? The producer? Sure. The director? Maybe. Remember it's deMille's *Ten Commandments*, not Moses'. But F. Scott Fitzgerald's *The Great Gatsby?* Smoke it in the Men's. Snuff it up your ulcerated nose. Want your name in big type? Kill your wife's lover, fall downstairs with his body. Like I say, that's the flickers, silver screen. Remember, you're the blank spaces between each slot-click of the projector. Notice all those pole-vault poles by the back wall of the studio? That's to help the high jumpers up across into the stone quarry. Mad fools hire and fire 'em, dime a dozen. They can be had, because *they* love films, *we* don't. That gives us the power. Drive them to drink, then grab the bottle, hire the hearse, borrow a spade. Maximus Films, like I said. A graveyard. And, oh yeah, for lunatics."

Her speech over, Constance remained standing as if the studio walls were a tidal wave about to fall.

"Don't go in there," she finished.

There was quiet applause.

The night policeman, behind the ornate Spanish ironwork was smiling and clapping his hands.

"I'll only be in there a while, Constance," I said. "Another month or so, and I'll head South to finish my novel."

"Can I come with you? One more trip to Mexicali, Calexico, South of San Diego, almost to Hermosillo, bathing naked by moonlight, ha, no, *you* in raggedy shorts."

"I only wish. But it's me and Peg, Constance, Peg and me."

"Ah, well, what the hell. Kiss me."

I hesitated so she gave me a smack that could flush a whole tenement tank system and make the cold run hot.

The gate was opening.

Two lunatics at midnight, we drove in.

As we pulled up near the wide square full of milling soldiers and merchants, Fritz Wong came leaping over in great strides. "God damn! We're all set for your scene. That drunken Baptist Unitarian has disappeared. You know where the son-of-a-bitch hides?"

"You called Aimee Semple McPherson's?"

"She's dead!"

"Or the Holy Rollers. Or the Manly P. Hall Universalists. Or—"

"My God," roared Fritz. "It's midnight! Those places are shut."

"Have you checked Calvary," I said. "He *goes* there."

"Calvary!" Fritz stormed away. "Check *Calvary*! Gethsemane!" Fritz pleaded with the stars. "God, why this poisoned

Manischewitz? Someone! Go rent two million locusts for tomorrow's plague!"

The various assistants ran in all directions. I started off, too, when Constance grabbed my elbow.

My eyes wandered over the facade of Notre Dame.

Constance saw where I was looking.

"Don't go up there," she whispered.

"Perfect place for J. C."

"Up there it's all face and no backside. Trip on something and you fall like those rocks the hunchback dropped on the mob."

"That was a film, Constance!"

"And you think this is *real?*"

Constance shuddered. I longed for the old Rattigan who laughed all the time. "I saw something just now, up on the belltower."

"Maybe it's J. C." I said. "While the others are ransacking Calvary, why don't I take a look?"

"I thought you were afraid of heights?"

I watched the shadows run up along the facade of Notre Dame.

"Damn fool. Go ahead. Get Jesus down," murmured Constance, "before he stays like a gargoyle. Save Jesus."

"He's saved!"

A hundred feet off, I looked back. Constance was already warming her hands at a hearth of Roman legionnaires.

40

I lingered outside Notre Dame, afraid of two things: going in and going up. Then I turned, shocked, to sniff the air. I took a deeper breath and let it out. "Good Grief. Incense! And candle smoke! Someone's been—J. C.?"

I moved through the entryway and stopped.

Somewhere high in the strutworks, a great bulk moved.

I squinted up through the canvas slats, the plywood fronts, the shadows of gargoyles, trying to see if anything at all stirred up there in the cathedral dark.

I thought, Who lit the incense? How long ago did the wind blow the candles out?

Dust filtered in a fine powder down the upper air.

J. C.? I thought, If you fall, who will save the Saviour?

A silence answered my silence.

So . . .

God's number one coward had to hoist himself, ladder step by ladder step, up through the darkness, fearful that any moment the great bells might thunder and knock me loose to fall. I squeezed my eyes shut and climbed.

At the top of Notre Dame I stood for a long moment, clutching my hands to my heartbeat, damned sorry to be up and wanting to be down there where the great spread of Romans, well-lit and full of beer, stormed through the alleys to smile at Rattigan, the visiting queen.

If I die now, I thought, none of them will hear.

"J. C.," I called quietly into the shadows.

Silence.

I rounded a long sheet of plywood. Someone was there in the starlight, a dim shape seated with his legs dangling over the carved cathedral facade, exactly where the malformed bellringer had sat half a lifetime ago.

The Beast.

He was looking out at the city, at the million lights spread across four hundred square miles.

How did you get here, I wondered. How did you get past the guard at the gate or, no, what? over the wall! Yes. A ladder and the graveyard wall!

I heard a ballpeen hammer strike. I heard a body dragged. A trunk lid slammed. A match lighted. An incinerator roared.

I sucked my breath. The Beast turned to stare at me.

I stumbled and almost fell off the cathedral rim. I grappled one of the gargoyles.

Instantly, the Beast sprang up.

His hand seized my hand.

For a single breath we teetered on the cathedral rim. I read his eyes, fearful of me. He read mine, fearful of him.

Then he snatched his hand back as if burned with surprise. He backed off swiftly and we stood half-crouched.

I looked into that dreadful face, the panicked and forever imprisoned eyes, the wounded mouth, and thought:

Why? Why didn't you let me go? or *push* me? You *are* the one with the hammer, aren't you? The one who came to find and smash Roy's terrible clay head? No one but you could have run so wild! Why did you save me? Why do I *live*?

There could be no response. Something clattered below. Someone was coming up the ladder.

The Beast let out a great heaving whisper: "No!"

And fled across the high porch. His feet thudded the loose planks. Dust exploded down through the cathedral darkness.

More climbing noises. I moved to follow the Beast at the far ladder. He looked back a final time. His eyes! What? What about his eyes?

They were different and the same, terrified and accepting, one moment focused, one moment confused. His hand swung up on the dark air. For a moment I thought he might call, shout, shriek at me. But only a strange choked gasp unraveled from his lips. Then I heard his feet plunging down step by step away from this unreal world above to a more terribly unreal world below.

I stumbled to pursue. My feet shuffled dust and plaster of paris. It flowed like sand seeping through an immense hourglass to pile itself, far below, near the baptistery font. The boards under my feet rattled and swayed. A wind flapped all the cathedral canvas around me in a great migration of wings, and I was on the ladder and jolting down, with each jolt a cry of alarm or a curse trapped in my teeth. My God, I thought, me and him, that thing, on the ladder, running away from *what*?

I glanced up to see the gargoyles lost to view and I was alone, descending in darkness, thinking: What if he waits for me, down there?

I froze. I looked down.

If I fall, I thought, it'll take a year to reach the floor. I only knew one saint. His name popped from my lips: *Crumley!*

Hold tight, said Crumley, a long way off. Take six deep breaths.

I sucked in but the air refused to go back out of my mouth. Smothered, I glanced at the lights of Los Angeles spread in a four-hundred-mile bed of lamps and traffic, all those people multitudinous and beautiful, and no one here to help me down, and the lights! street by street, the lights!

Far out on the rim of the world, I thought I saw a long dark tide move to an untouchable shore.

Body surfing, whispered Constance.

That did it. I jolted down and kept moving, eyes shut, no more glances into the abyss, until I reached and stood, waiting to be seized and destroyed by the Beast, hands outraised to kill, not save.

But there was no Beast. Just the empty baptismal font, cupping a half pint of cathedral dust, and the blown candles and the lost incense.

I looked up a last time through the half facade of Notre Dame. Whoever was climbing had reached the top.

Half a continent away, a mob on Calvary hill let go like a Saturday-afternoon football reunion.

J. C., I thought, if you're not here, where?

41

Whoever had been sent to search Calvary hadn't searched very well. They had come and gone and the hill lay empty under the stars. A wind prowled through, pushing dust ahead of it, around the bases of the three crosses that, for their presence, felt as if they might have grown there long before the studio was built around them.

I ran to the bottom of the cross. I could see nothing at the top, the night was dark. There were only fitful gleams of light from far off where Antipas ruled, Fritz Wong raved, and the Romans marched in a great cloud of beer from the Makeup Buildings to the Tribunal Square.

I touched the cross, swayed, and called up, blindly: "J. C.!" Silence.

I tried again, my voice trembling.

A small tumbleweed blew by, rustling.

"J. C.!" I almost yelled.

And at last a voice came down out of the sky.

"Nobody by that name on this street, up this hill, on *this* cross," the voice murmured, sadly.

"Whoever you are, dammit, come *down!*"

I groped up trying to find rungs, fearful of the dark around me. "How'd you get *up* there?"

"There's a ladder and I'm not nailed in place. Just holding on to pegs and there's a little footrest. It is very peaceful up here. Sometimes I stay nine hours fasting for my sins."

"J. C.!" I called up, "I can't stay. I'm afraid! What're you doing?"

"Remembering all the haylofts and chicken feathers I rolled in," said J. C.'s voice in the sky. "See the feathers falling down like snowflakes? When I leave here I go to confession *every* day! I got ten thousand women to unload. I give exact measurements, so much backside, bosom, groan, and groin, until the priest grabs his seething armpits! If I can't climb a silk stocking, I'll at least get a cleric's pulse so hyperventilated he ruptures his turn-around collar. Anyway, here I am, up, out of harm's way. Watching the night that watches me."

"It's watching me, too, J. C. I'm afraid of the dark in the alleys and Notre Dame, I was just there.

"Stay outa there," said J. C., suddenly fierce.

"Why? You been watching its towers tonight? You see something?"

"Just stay outa there, is all. Not safe."

I know, I thought. I said, looking around suddenly, "What else you see, J. C., night or day up there?"

J. C. glanced swiftly off at the shadows.

"What," his voice was low, "would there be to see in an empty studio, late?"

"Lots!"

"Yes!" J. C. turned his head south to north and back. "*Lots!*"

"On Halloween night—" I plunged on—"you didn't happen to see—" I nodded north some fifty yards—"a ladder on top of that wall? And a man trying to climb?"

J. C. stared at the wall. "It was raining that night." J. C. lifted his face to the sky to feel the storm. "Who'd be nuts enough to climb up there in a storm?"

"You."

"No," said J. C. "I'm not even here *now!*"

He put his arms out, grasped the crossbars, leaned his head forward and shut his eyes.

"J. C.," I called. "They're waiting on set seven!"

"Let them wait."

"Christ was on time, dammit! The world called. And He arrived!"

"You don't believe all that guff, do you?"

"Yes!" I was astonished with what vehemence I exploded it upward along his limbs to his thorn-crowned head.

"Fool."

"No, I'm not!" I tried to think what Fritz would say if he were here, but there was only me, so I said:

"*We* arrived, J. C. We poor stupid human beings. But whether it's us arriving or Christ, it's all the same. The world, or God, needed us, to see the world, and know it. So we arrived! But we got mixed up, forgot how incredible we were, and couldn't forgive ourselves for making such a mess. So Christ arrived, after us, to say what we should have known: *forgive*. Get on with your work. So Christ's arrival is just *us* all over again. And we've kept on arriving for two thousand years, more and more of us, mostly in need of forgiveness of self. I'd be frozen forever if I couldn't forgive myself all the dumb things I've done in my life. Right now, you're up a tree, hating yourself, so you stay nailed on a cross because you're a self-pitying pig-headed dim-witted thespian bum. Now get the hell down before I climb up to bite your dirty ankles!"

There was a sound like a mob of seals barking in the night. J. C., his head thrown back, sucked air to refuel his laughter.

"That's some speech for a coward!"

"Don't fear me, mister! Beware of yourself, Jesus H. Christ!"

I felt a single drop of rain hit my cheek.

No. I touched my cheek, tasted my fingertip. Salt.

J. C., above, leaned out, staring down.

"God." He was truly stunned. "You *care!*"

"Damn right. And if *I* leave, Fritz Wong will come, with his horsewhip!"

"I don't fear his arrival. Only *your* departure."

"*Well*, then! Come down. For *me!*"

"You!?" he exclaimed softly.

"You're up high. Over on set seven, whatta you see?"

"Fire, I think. Yes."

"That's the bed of charcoals, J. C." I reached out to touch the base of the cross and call softly up along its length to that figure with its head raised. "And the night almost over and the boat pulling in to the shore after the miracle of the fish, and Simon called Peter moving along the sand with Thomas, and Mark, and Luke and all the rest to the bed of baking fish. The—"

"—Supper after the Last Supper," murmured J. C., high against the autumn constellations. I could see Orion's shoulder over his shoulder. "You *did* it!?"

He stirred. I pursued quietly: "And *more!* I've got a true ending now, for you, never filmed before. The Ascension."

"Can't be done," murmured J. C.

"Listen."

And I said:

"When it is time for the Going Away, Christ touches each of his disciples and then walks up along the shore, away from the camera. Set your camera low in the sand, and it looks as if he were climbing a long slow hill. And as the sun rises, and Christ moves off toward the horizon, the sand burns with illusion. Like highways or deserts, where the air dissolves in mirages, imaginary cities rise and fall. Well, when Christ has almost reached the top of a dune of sand, the air vibrates with heat. His shape melts into the atoms. And Christ has gone. The footprints he left in the sand blow away in the wind. That's your second Ascension following the Supper after the Last Supper. The disciples weep and move off to all the cities of the world, to preach forgiveness of sin. And as the new day begins, *their* footprints blow away in the dawn wind. THE END."

I waited, listening to my own breath and heart.

J. C. waited, also, and at last said, with wonder, softly, "I'm coming down."

42

There was a vast glare from the waiting outdoor set ahead, where the extras, the bed of fish baking on charcoals, and Mad Fritz were waiting.

A woman stood in the mouth of the alley as J. C. and I approached. She was silhouetted against the light, only a dark shape.

Seeing us, she ran forward, then stopped when she saw J. C.

"Good gravy," said J. C. "It's that Rattigan woman!"

Constance's eyes glanced from J. C. to me and back again, almost wildly.

"What do I do now?" she said.

"What—"

"It's been such a crazy night. Crying an hour ago at a terrible photo, and now—" she stared at J. C. and her eyes flowed freely—"having wanted to meet you all my life. And here you are."

The weight of her words caused her to sink slowly to her knees. "Bless me, Jesus," she whispered.

J. C. reared back as if summoning the dead from their shrouds. "Get up, woman!" he cried.

"Bless me, Jesus," Constance said. And then, almost to herself, "Oh, Lord, I'm seven again and in my white first communion dress and it's Easter Sunday and the world is good just before the world got bad."

"Get up, young woman," said J. C. quieter.

But she did not move and closed her eyes, waiting.

Her lips pantomimed, Bless me.

And at last J. C. reached out slowly, forced to accept and gently accepting, to put his hand on the top of her head. The gentle pressure forced more tears from her eyes, and her mouth quivered. Her hands flew up to hold and keep his touch on her head a moment more.

"Child," said J. C. quietly, "you are blessed."

And looking at Constance Rattigan kneeling there, I thought, Oh, the ironies of this lost world. Catholic guilt plus actor's flamboyance.

Constance rose and, eyes still half shut, turned toward the light and moved toward the waiting bed of glowing charcoals.

We could but follow.

A crowd was gathered. All the extras who had appeared in other scenes earlier that night, plus studio executives and hangers-on. As we approached, Constance moved aside with the grace of someone who had just lost forty pounds. I wondered how long she would remain a little girl.

But now I saw, stepping into the light, across the open-air set, beyond the charcoal pit, Manny Leiber, Doc Phillips, and Groc.

Their eyes were so steadily upon me that I hung back, fearful of taking credit for finding the Messiah, saving the Saviour, and trimming the budget for the night.

Manny's eyes were full of doubt and distrust, the Doc's with active venom, and Groc's with good brandy spirits. Perhaps they had come to see Christ, and myself, roasted on a spit. In any event, as J. C. moved steadily to the rim of the fiery pit, Fritz, recovering from some recent fit, blinked at him myopically and cried, "About time. We were about to call off the barbecue. Monocle!"

No one moved. Everyone looked around.

"Monocle!" Fritz said again.

And I realized he wished the loan of the lens he had so grandly handed me a few hours ago.

I darted forward, planted the lens in his outstretched palm, and jumped back as he jammed it into his eye as ammunition. He fired a gaze at J. C. and heaved out all the air in his lungs.

"Do you call that Christ! It's more like Methuselah. Put on a ton of skin pancake color thirty-three and fish-hook his jawline. Holy jumping Jesus, it's time for the dinner break. More failures, more delays. How dare you show up late! Who in hell do you think you are?"

"Christ," said J. C. with proper modesty. "And don't you forget it."

"Get him out of here! Makeup! Dinner break! Back in an hour!" shouted Fritz, and all but hurled the lens, my medal, back into my hands, to stand bitterly regarding the burning coals as if he might leap to incineration.

And all the while the wolfpack across the pit, Manny counting the lost dollars as each moment fell like blizzards of paper money to be burned, and the good Doc itching his scalpel in his fisted pockets, and Lenin's cosmetologist with his permanent Conrad Veidt smile carved in the pale thin melon flesh about his chin. But now their gaze had shifted from me to fix with a terrible and inescapable judgment and condemnation upon J. C.

It was like a death squad letting go an endless fusillade.

J. C. rocked and swayed as if struck.

Groc's assistant makeup men were about to guide J. C. away when—

The thing happened.

There was a soft hiss as something like a single drop of rain struck the bed of burning coals.

We all looked down and then up—

At J. C., whose hands were thrust out over the charcoals. He was studying his own wrists with great curiosity.

They were bleeding.

"Ohmigod," Constance said. "*Do* something!"

"What?" cried Fritz.

J. C. said, calmly, "Shoot the scene."

"No, damnit!" cried Fritz. "John the Baptist, with his head off, looked better than you!"

"Then," J. C. nodded across the set to where Stanislau Groc and Doc Phillips stood, as merry Punch and dark Apocalypse, "then," said J. C. "let them sew and bandage me until we're ready."

"How do you *do* that?" Constance was staring at his wrists.

"It comes with the text."

"Go make yourself useful," J. C. said to me.

"And take that woman with you," ordered Fritz. "I don't know her!"

"Yes, you do," said Constance. "Laguna Beach, July 4th, 1926."

"That was another country, another time." Fritz slammed an invisible door.

"Yes." Constance paused. The cake fell in the oven. "Yes, it was."

Doc Phillips arrived at J. C.'s left wrist. Groc arrived at his right.

J. C. would not look at them; he fixed his gaze on the high fog in the sky.

Then he turned his wrists over and held them out so they might see his life dripping from the fresh stigmata.

"Careful," he said.

I walked out of the light. A small girl followed, becoming a woman along the way.

43

"Where are we going?" said Constance.

"Me? Back in time. And I know who runs the Moviola to make it happen. You? Right here, coffee and sinkers. Sit. I'll be right back."

"If I'm not here," said Constance, seated at an outdoor extras' picnic table, and wielding a doughnut. "Look for me at the men's gym."

I moved off alone, in the dark. I was running out of places to go, places to search. Now I headed toward one place on the lot I had never been. Other days were there. Arbuthnot's film ghost hid there and perhaps myself, as a boy, wandering the studio territories at noon.

I walked.

And suddenly wished I hadn't left what remained of Constance Rattigan's laughter behind.

Late at night a motion picture studio talks to itself. If you move along the dark alleys past the buildings where the editing rooms on the top floors whisper and bray and roar and snack-chatter until two or three or four in the morning, you hear chariots rushing by in the air, or sand blowing across Beau Geste's ghost-haunted desert, or traffic coursing the Champs-Elysées all French horns and derogatory cries, or Niagara pouring itself down the studio towers into the film vaults, or Barney Oldfield, on his last run, gunning his racer around Indianapolis to the shout of faceless mobs, while further on as you walk in darkness someone lets loose the dogs of war and you hear Caesar's wounds open like rosebuds in his cloak, or Churchill bulldogging the airwaves as the Hound bays over the moors and the night people keep working these shadowed hours because they prefer the company of Moviolas and flicker-moth screens and closeup lovers to the people stranded at noonday, stunned by reality outside the walls. It is a long-after-midnight collision of buried voices and lost musics caught in a time cloud between buildings, released from high open doors or windows while the shadows of the cutter-editors loom on the pale ceilings bent over enchantments. Only at dawn do the voices still and the musics die as the smilers-with-the-knives head home to avoid the first traffic of realists arriving at 6 A.M. Only at sunset will the voices start again and the musics rise in tender strokes or tumults, as the firefly light from the Moviola screens wash over the watchers' faces, igniting their eyes and prompting razors in their lifted fingers.

It was down an alley of such buildings, sounds, and musics that I ran now, pursued by nothing, gazing up, as Hitler raved from the east, and a Russian army sang across the soft high night winds west.

I jolted to a stop and stared up at . . . Maggie Botwin's editing room. The door stood wide.

I yelled. "Maggie!"

Silence.

I moved up the stairs toward the flickering firefly light and the stuttering chatter of the Moviola as the shadows blinked on her high ceiling.

I stood for a long moment in the night, gazing in at the one place in all this world where life was sliced, assembled, then torn apart again. Where you kept doing life over until you got it right. Peering down at the small Moviola screen, you turn on the outboard motor and speed along with a fierce clacking clap as the film slots through, freezes, delineates, and rushes on. After staring into the Moviola for half a day, in a subterranean gloom, you almost believe that when you step outside life itself will reassemble, give up its moron inconsistencies, and promise to behave. Running a Moviola for a few hours encourages optimism, for you can rerun your stupidities and cut off their legs. But the temptation, after a time, is to never step out in daylight again.

And now at Maggie Botwin's door, with the night behind me and her cool cave waiting, I watched this amazing woman bent to her machine like a seamstress sewing patchwork lights and shades while the film sluiced through her thin fingers.

I scratched at her screen door.

Maggie glanced up from her bright wishing well, scowled, trying to see through the mesh, then gave a glad cry.

"I'll be damned! This is the first time in forty years a writer ever showed up here. You'd think the damn fools would be curious about how I cut their hair or shorten their inseams. Wait!"

She unlocked the screen and pulled me in. Like a sleepwalker I stepped to the Moviola and blinked down.

Maggie tested me. "Remember him?"

"Erich Von Stroheim," I gasped. "The film made here in '21. Lost."

"I found it!"

"Does the studio know?"

"Those *s.o.b.s*? No! Never appreciated what they *had*!"

"You got the whole film?"

"Yep! The Museum of Modern Art gets it when I drop dead. Look!"

Maggie Botwin touched a projector fixed to her Moviola so it threw images on the wall. Von Stroheim strutted and weather-cocked along the wainscot.

Maggie cut Von Stroheim and made ready to put on another reel.

As she moved, I suddenly leaned forward. I saw a small bright green film can, different from the rest, lying on the counter amongst two dozen other cans.

There was no printed label, only an ink-stick drawing on the front of a very small dinosaur.

Maggie caught my look. "What?"

"How long have you had that film?"

"You want it? That's the test your pal Roy dropped by three days ago for developing."

"Did you look at it?"

"Haven't you? The studio's nuts to fire him. What was the story on that? Nobody's said. Only thirty seconds in that can. But it's the best half minute I've ever seen. Tops *Dracula* or *Frankenstein*. But, hell, what do *I* know?"

My pulse beat, rattling the film can as I shoved it in my coat pocket.

"Sweet man, that Roy." Maggie threaded new film into her Moviola. "Give me a brush, I'd shine his shoes. Now. Want to see the only existing *intact* copy of *Broken Blossoms*? The missing outtakes on *The Circus*? The censored reel from Harold Lloyd's *Welcome Danger*? Hell, there's lots more. I—"

Maggie Botwin stopped, drunk on her cinema past and my full attention.

"Yeah, I think you can be trusted." And she stopped. "Here I am, rattling on. You didn't come here to listen to an old hen lay forty-year-old eggs. How come you're the only writer ever came up those stairs?"

Arbuthnot, Clarence, Roy, and the Beast, I thought, but could not say.

"Cat got your tongue? I'll wait. Where was I? Oh!"

Maggie Botwin slid back a huge cupboard door. There were at least forty cans of film stashed in five shelves, with titles painted on the rims.

She shoved one tin into my hands. I looked at some huge lettering, which read: *Crazy Youths*.

"No, look at the *small* print typed on the *tiny* label on the *flat* side," said Maggie.

"*Intolerance!*"

"My own, *uncut* version," Maggie Botwin said, laughing. "I helped Griffith. Some great stuff was cut. Alone, I printed back what was missing. This is the only complete version of *Intolerance* extant! And *here!*"

Chortling like a girl at a birthday party, Maggie yanked down and laid out: *Orphans of the Storm* and *London After Midnight*.

"I assisted on these films, or was called for pickup work. Late nights I printed the outtakes just for me! Ready? Here!"

She thrust a tin marked *Greed* into my hands.

"Even Von Stroheim doesn't own this twenty-hour version!"

"Why didn't other editors think to do this?"

"Because they're chickens and I'm cuckoo," crowed Maggie Botwin. "Next year, I'll ship these out to the museum, with a letter deeding them over. The studios will sue, sure. But the films will be safe forty years from now."

I sat in the dark and was stunned as reel after reel shuttled by.

"God," I kept saying, "how *did* you outwit all the sons-of-bitches?"

"Easy!" said Maggie, with the crisp honesty that was like a general leveling with his troops. "They screwed directors, writers, everyone. But they had to have *one* person with a pooper-scooper to clean up after they lifted their legs on prime stuff. So they never laid a glove on me while they junked everyone's dreams. They just thought love was enough. And, God, they *did* love. Mayer, the Warners, Goldfish/Goldwyn ate and slept film. It wasn't enough. I reasoned with them; argued, fought, slammed the door. They ran after, knowing I loved more than they could. I lost as many fights as I won, so I decided I'd win 'em *all*. One by one, I saved the lost scenes. Not everything. Most pictures should get catbox awards. But five or six times a year, a writer would write or a Lubitsch add his 'touch,' and I'd hide that. So, over the years I—"

"Saved masterpieces!"

Maggie laughed. "Cut the hyperbole. Just decent films, some funny, some tear jerkers. And they're all here tonight. You're surrounded by them," Maggie said, quietly.

I let their presence soak in, felt their "ghosts" and swallowed hard.

"Run the Moviola," I said. "I never want to go home."

"Okay." Maggie swept back more sliding doors above her head. "Hungry? Eat!"

I looked and saw:

The March of Time, June 21st, 1933.

The March of Time, June 20th, 1930.

The March of Time, July 4th, 1930.

"No," I said.

Maggie stopped in mid-gesture.

"There was no *March of Time* in 1930," I said.

"Bull's-eye! The boy's an expert!

"Those are not *Time* reels," I added. "It's a cover. For what?"

"My own home movies, shot with my eight-millimeter camera, blown up to thirty-five millimeters, and hid behind *March of Time* titles."

I tried not to lean forward too quickly. "You got a whole film history of this studio then?"

"In 1923, 1927, 1930, name it! F. Scott Fitzgerald, drunk in the commissary. G. B. Shaw the day he commandeered the place. Lon Chaney in the makeup building the night he showed the Westmore brothers how to change faces! Dead a month later. Wonderful warm man. William Faulkner, a drunk but polite sad screenwriter, poor s.o.b. Old films. Old history. Pick!"

My eyes roved and stopped. I heard the air jet from my nostrils.

October 15, 1934. Two weeks before Arbuthnot, the head of the studio, was killed.

"That."

Maggie hesitated, pulled it out, shoved the film into the Moviola, and cranked the machine.

We were looking at the front entrance of Maximus Films on an October afternoon in 1934. The doors were shut, but you could see shadows inside the glass. And then the doors opened and two or three people stepped out. In the middle was a tall, burly man, laughing, eyes shut, head back to the sky, shoulders quivering with his merriment. His eyes were slits, he was so happy. He was taking a deep breath, almost his last, of life.

"You know him?" asked Maggie.

I peered down into this small half-dark, half-lit cave in the earth.

"Arbuthnot."

I touched the glass as one touches a crystal ball, reading no future, only pasts with the color leached out.

"Arbuthnot. Dead, the same month you shot this film."

Maggie cranked backward and started over. The three men came out laughing again and Arbuthnot wound up grimacing into her camera on that long-forgotten and incredibly happy noon.

Maggie saw something in my face. "Well? Spit it out."

"I saw him this week," I said.

"Bosh. You been smoking those funny cigars?"

Maggie moved three more frames through. Arbuthnot raised his head higher into an almost raining sky.

And now Arbuthnot was calling and waving to someone out of sight.

I took a chance. "In the graveyard, on Halloween night, there was a wire-frame papier-mâché scarecrow with his face."

Now Arbuthnot's Duesenberg was at the curb. He shook hands with Manny and Groc, promising them happy years. Maggie did not look at me, but only at the dark-light dark-light pictures jumping rope below.

"Don't believe anything on Halloween night."

"Some other people saw. Some ran scared. Manny and others have been walking on land mines for days."

"Bosh, again," Maggie snorted. "What else is new? You may have noticed I stay in the projection room or up here where the air's so thin they get nosebleeds climbing up. That's why I like loony Fritz. He shoots until midnight, I edit until dawn. Then we hibernate. When the long winter ends each day at five, we rise, timing ourselves to the sunset. One or two days a week, you will also have noticed, we make our pilgrimage to the commissary lunch to prove to Manny Leiber we're alive."

"Does he really run the studio?"

"Who else?"

"I dunno. I just get a funny feeling in Manny's office. The

furniture looks unused. The desk is always clean. There's a big
white telephone in the middle of the desk, and a chair behind
the desk that's twice the size of Manny Leiber's bottom. He'd
look like Charlie McCarthy in it."

"He does act like hired help, doesn't he? It's the telephone,
I suppose. Everyone thinks films are made in Hollywood. No,
no. That telephone is a direct line to New York City and the
spiders. Their web crosses the country to trap flies here. The
spiders never come west. They're afraid we'd see they're all
pygmies, Adolph Zukor size."

"Trouble is," I said. "*I* was at the bottom of a ladder, in the
graveyard, with that mannequin, dummy, whatever, in the rain."

Maggie Botwin's hand jerked on the crank. Arbuthnot waved
much too swiftly across the street. The camera panned to see:
the creatures from another world, the uncombed crowd of autograph collectors. The camera prowled their faces.

"Wait a minute!" I cried. *"There!"*

Maggie cranked two more frames to bring up close the image
of a thirteen-year-old boy on roller skates.

I touched the image, a strange loving touch.

"That can't be you," said Maggie Botwin.

"Just plain old homely, dumpy me."

Maggie Botwin let her eyes shift over to me for a moment and
then back down through twenty years of time to some October
afternoon with a threat of rain.

There was the goof of all goofs, the nut of all nuts, the crazy
of all crazies, forever off balance on his roller skates, doomed to
fall in any traffic, including pedestrian women who passed.

She cranked backward. Again Arbuthnot was waving to me,
unseen, on some autumn afternoon.

"Arbuthnot," she said quietly, "and you . . . almost together?"

"The man on the ladder in the rain? Oh, yes."

Maggie sighed and cranked the Moviola. Arbuthnot got in his
car and drove away to a car crash just a few short weeks ahead.

I watched the car go, even as my younger self across the street,
in that year, must have watched.

"Repeat after me," said Maggie Botwin, quietly. "There was no one up some ladder, no rain, and you were never there."

"—never there," I murmured.

Maggie's eyes narrowed. "Who's that funny-looking geek next to you, with the big camel's-hair overcoat and the wild hair and the huge photo album in his arms?"

"Clarence," I said, and added, "I wonder, right now, tonight, if . . . he's still alive?"

The telephone rang.

It was Fritz in the final stages of hysteria.

"Get over here. J. C.'s stigmata are still open. We got to finish before he bleeds to death!"

We drove to the set.

J. C. was waiting on the edge of the long pit of charcoal. When he saw me he shut his beautiful eyes, smiled, and showed me his wrists.

"That blood looks almost real!" cried Maggie.

"You could almost say that," I said.

Groc had taken over the job of pancaking the Messiah's face. J. C. looked thirty years younger as Groc patted a final powder puff at his shut eyelids and stood back to smile in triumph at his masterwork.

I looked at J. C.'s face, serene there by the embered fire, while a slow, dark syrup moved from his wrists into his palms. Madness! I thought. He'll die during the scene!

But to keep the film in budget? Why not? The mob was gathering again and Doc Phillips loped forward to check the holy spillage and nod yes to Manny. There was life yet in these holy limbs, some sap remained: Roll 'em!

"Ready?" cried Fritz.

Groc stepped back in the charcoal wind, between two vestal virgin extras. Doc stood like a wolf on his hind legs, his tongue in his teeth, his eyes swarming and teeming from side to side.

Doc? I thought. Or Groc? Are they the true heads of the studio? Do they sit in Manny's chair?

Manny stared at the bed of fire, longing to walk on it and prove himself King.

J. C. was alone in our midst, far off within himself, his face so lovely pale it tore a seam in my chest. His thin lips moved, memorizing the fine words John gave to me to give to him to preach that night.

And just before he spoke, J. C. raised his gaze across the cities of the studio world and up along the facade of Notre Dame, to the very peak of the towers. I gazed with him, then glanced swiftly over to see:

Groc transfixed, his eyes on the cathedral. Doc Phillips the same. And Manny between them, shifting his attention from one to the other, then to J. C. and at last, where some few of us looked, up, among the gargoyles—

Where nothing moved.

Or did J. C. see some secret motion, a signal given?

J. C. saw something. The others noticed. I saw only light and shadow on the false marble facade.

Was the Beast still there? Could he see the pit of burning coals? Would he hear the words of Christ and be moved to come and tell the weather of the last week and calm our hearts?

"Silence!" cried Fritz.

Silence.

"Action," whispered Fritz.

And finally, at five-thirty in the morning, in the few minutes just before dawn, we filmed the Last Supper after the Last Supper.

44

The charcoals were fanned, the fish freshly laid, and as the first light rose over Los Angeles from the east, J. C. slowly opened his eyes with a look of such compassion as would still his lovers and betrayers and give them sustenance as he hid his wounds and walked off along a shore that would be filmed, some days later, in some other part of California; and the sun rose, and the scene was finished with no flaw, and there was not a dry eye on the outdoor set, but only silence for a long moment in which J. C. at last turned, and with tears in his eyes, cried:

"Won't someone yell 'cut!'?"

"Cut," said Fritz Wong, quietly.

"You've just made an enemy," said Maggie Botwin beside me.

I glanced across the set. Manny Leiber was there glaring at me. Then he spun about, stalked away.

"Be careful," said Maggie. "You made three mistakes in forty-eight hours. Rehired Judas. Solved the ending of the film. Found J. C., brought him back to the set. Unforgivable."

"My God," I sighed.

J. C. walked off through the crowd of extras, not waiting for praise. I caught up with him.

Where going? I said, silently.

To rest awhile, he said just as silently.

I looked at his wrists. The bleeding had stopped.

When we reached a studio crossroads, J. C. took my hands and gazed off at the backlot somewhere.

"Junior—?"

"Yes?"

"That thing we talked about? The rain? And the man on the ladder?"

"Yes!?"

"I saw him," said J. C.

"My God, J. C.! Then what did he *look* like? What—"

"Shh!" he added, forefinger to his serene lips.

And returned to Calvary.

Constance drove me back to my house just after dawn.

There didn't seem to be any strange cars with spies waiting in them on my street.

Constance made a big thing of wallowing all over me at my front door.

"Constance! The neighbors!"

"Neighbors, my patootie!" She kissed me so hard my watch stopped. "Bet your wife doesn't kiss like that!"

"I'd have been dead six *months* ago!"

"Hold yourself where it matters, as I slam the door!"

I grabbed and held. She slammed and drove off. Almost instantly I was filled with loneliness. It was like Christmas going away forever.

In my bed I thought: J. C., damn you! Why couldn't you have said more?

And then: Clarence! Wait for me!

I'm coming back!

One last try!

45

At noon I went to Beachwood Avenue.

Clarence had not waited.

I knew that when I forced the half-open door of his bungalow court apartment. Snowstorms of torn paper, crushed books, and slashed pictures lay against it, much like the Stage 13 massacre, where Roy's dinosaurs lay kicked and stomped to ruin.

"Clarence?"

I shoved the door wider.

It was a geologist's nightmare.

There was a foot-thick layer of letters, notes signed by Robert Taylor and Bessie Love and Ann Harding way back in 1935 or earlier. That was the top stratum.

Further down, spread in a glossy blanket, lay thousands of photographs that Clarence had snapped of Al Jolson, John Garfield, Lowell Sherman, and Madam Schumann-Heink. Ten thousand faces stared up at me. Most were dead.

Under more layers were autograph books, film histories,

posters from ten dozen flickers, starting with Bronco Billy Anderson and Chaplin and fidgeting up through those years when the clutch of lilies known as the Gish Sisters paled across the screen to lachrymose the immigrant heart. And at last, beneath *Kong, The Lost World, Laugh Clown Laugh*, and under all the spider kings, talcumed toe dancers and lost cities I saw:

A shoe.

The shoe belonged to a foot. The foot, twisted, belonged to an ankle. The ankle led to a leg. And so on up along a body until I saw a face of final hysteria. Clarence, hurled and filed between one hundred thousand calligraphies, drowned in floods of ancient publicity and illustrated passions that might have crushed and drowned him, had he not already been dead.

By his look, he might have died from cardiac arrest, the simplest recognition of death. His eyes were sprung flash-photo wide, his mouth in a frozen gape: *What are you doing to my tie, my throat, my heart?! Who are you?*

I had read somewhere that, dying, the victim's retina photographs its killer. If that retina could be stripped and drowned in emulsion, the murderer's face would rise from darkness.

Clarence's wild eyes begged to be so stripped. His destroyer's face was frozen in each.

I stood in the flood of trash, staring. Too much! Every file had been tumbled, hundreds of pictures chewed. Posters torn from walls, bookcases exploded. Clarence's pockets had been yanked out. No robber had ever brutalized like this.

Clarence, who feared to be killed in traffic, and so waited at street signals until the traffic was absolutely clear so he could run his true pals, his pet albums of faces, safely across.

Clarence.

I turned round-about, wildly hoping to find a single clue to save for Crumley.

The drawers to Clarence's desk had been jerked free and their contents eviscerated.

A few pictures remained on the walls. My eyes roved and fixed on one.

Jesus Christ on the Calvary backlot.

It was signed, "To Clarence, PEACE from the one and only J. C."

I knocked it from its frame, stuffed it in my pocket.

I turned to run, my heart pounding, when I saw a last thing. I grabbed it.

A Brown Derby matchbox.

Anything else?

Me, said Clarence, all cold. Help *me*.

Oh, Clarence, I thought, if only I could!

My heart banged. Afraid someone might hear, I fell out the door.

I ran from the apartment house.

Don't! I stopped.

If they see you run, *you* did it! Walk slow, stand still. Be sick. I tried, but only dry heaves and old memory came up.

An explosion. 1929.

Near my house a man hurled from his wrecked car, shrieking: "I don't want to die!"

And me on the front porch, with my aunt, crushing my head to her bosom so I couldn't hear.

Or when I was fifteen. A car smashing a telephone pole and people exploding against walls, fire hydrants, a jigsaw of torn bodies and strewn flesh . . .

Or . . .

The ruin of a burned car, with a charred figure sitting grotesquely upright behind the wheel, quiet inside his ruined charcoal mask, shriveled-fig hands melted to the steering wheel . . .

Or . . .

Suddenly I was smothered with books and photographs and signed cards.

I walked blindly into a wall and groped along an empty street, thanking God for emptiness, until I found what I thought was a phone booth and took two minutes searching my pockets for a nickel that was there all the time. I shoved it in the slot, dialed.

It was while I was dialing Crumley, that the men with the brooms showed up. There were two studio vans and an old beat-up Lincoln that swept by on their way to Beachwood Avenue. They turned at the corner leading around to Clarence's apartment. Even the sight of them made me squeeze-sink accordion-wise in the booth. The man in the beat-up Lincoln could have been Doc Phillips, but I was so busy hiding, sinking to my knees, I couldn't tell.

"Let me guess," said Crumley's voice on the line. "Someone *really* die?"

"How'd you *know*?"

"Calm down. When I come there will it be too late, all the evidence destroyed? Where are you?" I told him. "There's an Irish pub down the way. Go sit. I don't want you out in the open if things are as bad as you say. You okay?"

"I'm dying."

"Don't! Without you, how would I fill my days?"

Half an hour later Crumley found me half inside the Irish pub front door and regarded me with that look of deep despair and paternal affection that came and went across his face like clouds on a summer landscape.

"Well," he grouched, "where's the body?"

At the bungalow court we found the door to Clarence's bungalow ajar, as if someone had left it unlocked on purpose.

We pushed.

And stood in the middle of Clarence's apartment.

But it was not empty, eviscerated the way Roy's place had been.

All the books were in their cases, the floor clean, no torn letters. Even the framed pictures, most of them, were back on their walls.

"Okay," sighed Crumley. "Where's all the junk you said?"

"Wait."

I opened one drawer of a four-layer file. There were photos, battered and torn, crammed in place.

I opened six files to show Crumley I hadn't been dreaming.

The stomped-on letters had been stuffed in each one.

There was only one thing missing.

Clarence.

Crumley eyed me.

"Don't!" I said. "He lay right where you're standing."

Crumley stepped over the invisible body. He went through the other files, as I had done, to see the torn cards, the hammered and bludgeoned photos, stashed out of sight. He let out a great heavy-anvil sigh and shook his head.

"Someday," he said, "you'll blunder into something that makes sense. There's no body, so what can I do? How do we know he hasn't gone on vacation?"

"He'll never come back."

"Who says? You want to go to the nearest station and file a complaint? They'll come look at the torn stuff in the files, shrug, say one less nut off the old Hollywood tree, tell the landlord and—"

"The landlord?" said a voice behind us.

An old man stood in the door.

"Where's Clarence?" he said.

I talked fast. I raved, maundered, and described all of 1934 and 1935 and me rambling on my roller skates, pursued by a maniac cane-wielding W. C. Fields and kissed on the cheek by Jean Harlow in front of the Vendome restaurant. With the kiss, the ball bearings popped from my skates. I limped home, blind to traffic, deaf to my school chums.

"All right, all right, I get the picture!" The old man glared around the room. "You don't look like sneaks. But Clarence lives as if a mob of photo snatchers might rape him. So—"

Crumley handed over his card. The old man blinked at it and gripped his false teeth with his gums.

"I don't want no trouble here!" he whined.

"Don't worry. Clarence called us, afraid. So we came."

Crumley glanced around.

"Have Sopwith call me. Okay?"

The old man squinted at the card. "*Venice* police? When will they clean 'em up?"

"What?"

"The canals! Garbage. The canals!"

Crumley steered me out.

"I'll look into it."

"Into what?" the old man wondered.

"The canals," said Crumley. "Garbage."

"Oh, yeah," said the old man.

And we were gone.

46

We stood on the sidewalk watching the apartment house as if it might suddenly roll down a runway, like a ship sliding into the sea.

Crumley didn't look at me. "Same old lopsided relationship. You're a wreck because you *saw* a body. I'm one because I *didn't*. Crud. I suppose we could wait around for Clarence to come back?"

"Dead?"

"You want to file a missing-person report? What you got to go on?"

"Two things. Someone stomped Roy's miniature animals and destroyed his clay sculpture. Someone else cleaned the mess. Someone scared or strangled Clarence to death. Someone *else* cleaned up. So two groups, or two individuals: The one who destroys; the one who brings the trunks, brooms, and vacuum cleaners. Right now all I can figure is the Beast came over the wall, kicked Roy's stuff to death on his own, and ran off, leaving things to be found, cleaned away, or hid. Same thing here. The Beast climbed down off Notre Dame—"

"Climbed down?"

"I saw him face to face."

For the first time, Crumley looked a little pale.

"You're going to get yourself killed, god damn it. Stay off high places. For that matter, should we be standing here in broad daylight, gabbing? What if those mop-up guys come back?"

"Right." I began to move.

"You want a lift?"

"It's only a block to the studio."

"I'm heading downtown to the newspaper morgue. There must be something there on Arbuthnot and 1934 we don't know. You want me to search for Clarence, on the way?"

"Oh, Crum," I said, turning. "You know and I know, by now they've burned him to ashes and burned the ashes. And how do we get in to shake down the clinkers in the backlot incinerator? I'm on my way to the Garden of Gethsemane."

"Is that safe?"

"Safer than Calvary."

"Stay there. Call me."

"You'll hear me, across town," I said, "without a phone."

47

But first, I stopped at Calvary.

The three crosses were empty.

"J. C.," I whispered, touching his picture folded in my pocket, and realized suddenly that a rich presence had been following me for some time.

I looked around at Manny's mob of fog, his gray-shadow Chinese-funeral Rolls-Royce, crept up behind me. I heard the back door suck its rubber gums as the soundless door exhaled wide, letting out a cool burst of refrigerated air. Not much larger than an Eskimo Pie, Manny Leiber peered out from his elegant icebox. "Hey, you," he said.

It was a hot day. I leaned into the refrigerated Rolls-Royce cubby and refreshed my face while I improved my mind.

"I got news for you." I could see Manny's breath on the artificial winter air. "We're shutting down the studio for two days. General cleanup. Repainting. Crash job."

"How can you do that? The expense—"

"Everyone will be paid full time. Should've been done years ago. So we shut down—"

For what? I thought. To get everyone off the lot. Because they know or suspect Roy is still alive, and someone has told them to find and kill him?

"That's the dumbest thing I ever heard," I said.

I had found that insult was the best answer. Nobody suspected you of anything if you, in turn, were dumb enough to insult.

"Whose idea was this dumb idea?" I said.

"Whatta you mean?" cried Manny, pulling back into his refrigerator. His breath steamed in jets of frost on the air. "Mine!"

"You're not that dumb," I pursued. "You wouldn't do a thing like that. You care about money too much. Someone had to order you to do that. Someone above you?"

"There's no one above me!" But his eyes slid, while his mouth equivocated.

"You take full credit for all this, that'll cost maybe half a million in one week?"

"Well," Manny flinched.

"It's gotta be New York." I let him off. "Those dwarfs on the telephone from Manhattan. Crazed monkeys. You're only two days away from finishing *Caesar and Christ*. What if J. C. goes on another binge while you're repainting the stages—?"

"That charcoal pit was his last scene. We're writing him out of our Bible. *You* are. And another thing, as soon as the studio reopens, you go back on *The Dead Ride Fast*."

His words breathed out to chill my face. The chill spread down my back.

"Can't be done without Roy Holdstrom." I decided to play it even more blunt and naïve. "And Roy's dead."

"What?" Manny leaned forward, fought for control, then squinted at me. "Why do you say that?"

"He committed suicide," I said.

Manny was even more suspicious. I could imagine him hearing the report from Doc Phillips: Roy hanged on Stage 13, cut down, carted off, burned.

I continued as naïvely as possible: "You still got all his animals locked in Stage 13?"

"Er, yes," Manny lied.

"Roy can't live without his Beasts. And I went to his apartment the other day. It was empty. Someone had stolen all of Roy's other cameras and miniatures. Roy couldn't live without those, either. And he wouldn't just run off. Not without telling me, after twenty years of friendship. So, hell, Roy's dead."

Manny examined my face to see if he could believe it. I worked up my saddest expression.

"Find him," said Manny, at last, not blinking.

"I just said—"

"Find him," said Manny, "or you're out on your ass, and you'll never work at any other studio the rest of your life. The stupid jerk's not dead. He was seen in the studio yesterday, maybe hanging around to break in Stage 13 and get his damned monsters. Tell him all is forgiven. He comes back with a raise in salary. It's time we admit we were wrong and we need him. Find him, and your salary is raised, too. Okay?"

"Does that mean Roy gets to use that face, that head, he made out of clay?"

Manny's color level sank. "Christ, no! There'll be a new search. We'll run ads."

"I don't think Roy will come back if he can't create *his* Beast."

"He'll come, if he knows what's good for him."

And get himself killed an hour after he punches the time clock? I thought.

"No," I said. "He's really dead—forever."

I hammered all the nails into Roy's coffin, hoping Manny would believe, and not close down the studio to finish the search. A dumb idea. But then insane people are always dumb.

"Find him," said Manny and lay back, frosting the air with his silence.

I shut the icebox door. The Rolls floated off on its own whispering exhaust, like a cold smile vanishing.

Shivering, I made the Grand Tour. I crossed Green Town to New York City to Egyptian Sphinx to Roman Forum. Only flies buzzed on my grandparents' front-door screen. Only dust blew between the Sphinx's paws.

I stood by the great rock that was rolled in front of Christ's tomb.

I went to the rock to hide my face.

"Roy," I whispered.

The rock trembled at my touch.

And the rock cried out, No hiding place.

God, Roy, I thought. They *need* you, at last, for ten seconds anyway before they stomp you into paste.

The rock was silent. A dust-devil squirreled through a nearby Nevada false-front town, and laid itself out like a burning cat to sleep by an old horse trough.

A voice shouted across the sky: "Wrong place! Here!"

I glanced a hundred yards over to another hill, which blotted out the city skyline, a gentle rolling sward of fake grass that stood green through every season.

There, the wind blowing his white robes, was a man in a beard.

"J. C.!" I stumbled up the hill, gasping.

"How do you like this?" J. C. pulled me the last few yards, reaching out with a grave, sad smile. "The Mount of the Sermon. Want to hear?"

"There's no time, J. C."

"How come all those other people two thousand years back listened and were quiet?"

"They didn't have watches, J. C."

"No." He studied the sky. "Only the sun moving slow and all the days in the world to say the needful things."

I nodded. Clarence's name was stuck in my throat.

"Sit down, son." There was a big boulder nearby and J. C. sat and I crouched like a shepherd at his feet. Looking down at me, almost gently, he said, "I haven't had a drink today."

"Great!"

"There are days like that. Lord, I been up here most of the day, enjoying the clouds, wanting to live forever, because of last night, the words, and you."

He must have sensed my swallowing hard for he looked down and touched my head.

"Oh, *oh*," he said. "You going to tell me something will make me drink again?"

"I hope not, J. C. It's about your friend Clarence."

He snatched his hand away as if burned.

A cloud covered the sun and there was a surprising small spatter of rain, a total shock in the midst of a sunlit day. I let the rain touch me without moving, as did J. C., who lifted his face to get the coolness.

"Clarence," he murmured. "I've known him forever. He was around when we had real Indians. Clarence was out front, a kid no more than nine, ten, with his big four-eyes and his blond hair and his bright face and his big book of drawings or photos to be signed. He was there at dawn the first day I arrived, at midnight when I left. I was one of the Four Horsemen of the Apocalypse!"

"Death?"

"Smartass." J. C. laughed. "Death. High on my bony ass on my skeleton horse."

J. C. and I both looked at the sky to see if his Death was still galloping there.

The rain stopped. J. C. wiped his face and went on:

"Clarence. Poor stupid, dependent, lonely, lifeless, wifeless son of a bitch. No wife, mistress, boy, man, dog, pig, no girlie pictures, no muscle monthlies. Zero! He doesn't even wear *Jockey* shorts! Long johns, all summer! Clarence. God."

At last I felt my mouth move.

"You heard from Clarence . . . lately?"

"He telephoned yesterday. . . ."

"What time?"

"Four-thirty. Why?"

Right after I knocked on his door, I thought.

"He telephoned, out of control. 'It's over!' he said. 'They're coming to get me. Don't lecture me!' he screamed. It curdled my blood. Sounded like ten thousand extras fired, forty producer suicides, ninety-nine starlets raped, eyes shut, making do. His last words were 'Help me! save me!' And there I was, Jesus on the end of a line, Christ at the end of his tether. How could I help when I was the cause, not the cure? I told Clarence to take two aspirins and call in the morning. I should have rushed over. Would you have rushed, if you were me?"

I remembered Clarence lying in that huge wedding cake, layer upon layer of books, cards, photos, and hysterical sweat, glued in stacks.

J. C. saw my head shake.

"He's gone, isn't he? You," he added, "did rush over?"

I nodded.

"It was not a natural death?"

I shook my head.

"Clarence!"

It was such a shout as would shake the field beasts and the shepherds asleep. It was the start of a sermon on darkness.

J. C. leaped up, head back. Tears spilled from his eyes.

". . . Clarence . . ."

And he began to walk, eyes shut, down the Mount, away from the lost sermons, toward the other hill, Calvary, where his cross waited. I pursued.

Striding, J. C. asked:

"I don't suppose you got anything on you? Liquor, booze. Hell! It was going to be such a *sweet* day! Clarence, you idiot!"

We reached the cross and J. C. searched in back and snorted a bitter laugh of relief, pulling out a sack that made liquid sounds.

"Christ's blood in a brown bag in an unmarked bottle. What *has* the ceremony come to?" He drank, and drank again. "What do I do now? Climb up, nail myself, and wait for them?"

"*Them?!*"

"God, boy, it's a matter of time! Then I'm spiked through the wrists, hung by my ballistics! Clarence is *dead*! How?"

"Smothered under his photographs."

J. C. stiffened. "Who *says*?"

"*I* saw, J. C., but told no one. He knew something and was killed. What do *you* know!?"

"Nothing!" J. C. shook his head terribly. "No!"

"Clarence, outside the Brown Derby two nights ago, recognized a man. The man raised his fists! Clarence *ran*! Why?"

"Don't try to find out!" said J. C. "Lay off. I don't want you dragged down with me. There's nothing I can do now but wait—" J. C.'s voice broke. "With Clarence killed, it won't be long before they think *I* put him up to going to the Brown Derby—"

"*Did* you!?"

And me? I thought. Did you write to ask me to be there, too!?

"Who was it, J. C. *They*, who is *they*?! People are dying all over the place. My friend Roy, too, maybe!"

"Roy?" J. C. paused, furtively. "Dead? He's lucky. Hiding? No use! They'll get him. Like me. I knew too much for years."

"How far back?"

"*Why?*"

"I might be dead, too. I've stumbled on something but I'm damned if I know what. Roy stumbled on something and he's dead or on the run. My God, someone has killed Clarence because *he* stumbled on something. It's a matter of time before they figure, What the hell, maybe I know Clarence *too* well, and kill me, to be *sure*. Damn it, J. C., Manny's shutting the studio for two days. To clean up, repaint. God, no. It's for *Roy*! Think! Tens of thousands of dollars out the window to find one crazy goof whose only crime was living ten million years back, who ran amok with one clay beast and has a price on his head. Why is Roy so important? Why, like Clarence, does he have to die? You. The other night. You said you were high up on Calvary. You saw the wall, the ladder, the body on the ladder. Could you see the face of that body?"

"It was too far away." J. C.'s voice shook.

"Did you see the face of the man who put the body *on* the ladder?"

"It was dark—"

"Was it the Beast?"

"The *what*?"

"The man with the melted pink wax face and the fleshed-over right eye and the awful mouth? Did he shove that fake body up the ladder to scare the studio, scare you, scare me, and blackmail everyone somehow for some reason? If I must die, J. C., why can't I know why? Name the Beast, J. C."

"And *really* get you dead? *No!*"

A truck veered around the studio backlot corner. It ran by Calvary, throwing dust, blowing its horn.

"Watch out, idiot!" I yelled.

The truck dusted off.

And J. C. with it.

A man thirty years older than I, running fast. Grotesque! J. C. a-gallop, robes flapping in the dusty wind, as if to take off, fly, shouting gibberish to the skies.

Don't go to Clarence's! I almost shouted.

Dumb, I thought. Clarence is too far ahead. You'll never catch up!!

48

Fritz was waiting with Maggie in Projection Room 10.

"Where you been?" he cried. "Guess what? Now we got no *middle* for the film!"

It was good to talk something silly, inane, ridiculous, a madness to cure my growing madness. God, I thought, films are like making love to gargoyles. You wake to find yourself clutched to the spine of a marble nightmare and think: What am I *doing* here? Telling lies, pulling faces. To make a film that twenty million people run to or away from.

And all done by freaks in projection rooms raving about characters who never lived.

So, how fine now to hide here with Fritz and Maggie, shouting nonsense, playing fools.

But the nonsense didn't help.

At four-thirty I excused myself to run to the Men's. There in the vomitorium I lost the color in my cheeks. The vomitorium. That's what all writers call restrooms after they've heard their producer's great ideas.

I tried to get the color back in my face by scrubbing with soap and water. I bent over the washbasin for five minutes, letting my sadness and alarm rush down the drain. After one last session of dry heaves, I washed up again, and staggered back to face Maggie and Fritz, thankful for the dim projection room.

"You!" said Fritz. "Change one scene and you screw up the rest. I showed your last last supper to Manny at noon. Now, because of your goddamn high-quality finale, he says, against his better nature, we got to reshoot some up-front stuff, or the film looks like a dead snake with a live tail. He wouldn't tell you this himself; he sounded like he was eating his own entrails for lunch, or your tripes en casserole. He called you words I don't use, but finally said put the bastard to work on scenes nine, fourteen, nineteen, twenty-five, and thirty. Hopscotch rewrites and reshoots. *If* we reshoot every other scene, we might fool people into thinking we got one half-ass fine film."

I felt the old warm color flushing my face.

"That's a big job for a new writer!" I exclaimed. "The time element!"

"All in the next three days! We've held the cast. I'm calling Alcoholics Anonymous to dog J. C. for seventy-two hours now that we know where he hides—"

I stared, quietly, but could not tell them I had scared J. C. off the lot.

"Seems I'm responsible for a lot of bad this week," I finally said.

"Sisyphus, stay!" Fritz leaned to clap his hands on my shoulders. "Till I get you a bigger rock to push up the goddamn hill. You're not Jewish; don't *try* for guilt." He thrust pages at me. "Write, rewrite. *Re*-rewrite!"

"You sure Manny wants me on this?"

"He'd rather tie you between two horses and fire off a gun, but that's life. Hate a little. Then hate a lot."

"What about *The Dead Ride Fast*? He wants me back on that!"

"Since when?" Fritz was on his feet.

"Since half an hour ago."

"But he can't do that without—"

"Right. Roy. And Roy's gone. And I'm supposed to find him. And the studio is being shut for forty-eight hours to rebuild, repaint what doesn't need repainting."

"Jerks. Dumb asses. Nobody tells me anything. Well, we don't need the stupid studio. We can rewrite Jesus from my house."

The phone rang. Fritz all but strangled it in his fist, then shoved it at me.

It was a call from Aimee Semple McPherson's Angelus Temple.

"I beg your pardon, sir," said a barely restrained woman's voice. "But do you happen to know a man who calls himself J. C.?"

"J. C.?"

Fritz grabbed the phone. I grabbed it back. We shared the earpiece:

"Claims to be the Ghost of Christ reborn and newly repentant—"

"Let me have that!" cried another voice, a man's. "Reverend Kempo here! You know this dreadful anti-Christ? We would have called the police but if the papers found that Jesus had been thrown out of our church, well! You have thirty minutes to come save this miscreant from God's wrath! *And mine!*"

I let the phone drop.

"Christ," I moaned to Fritz, "is resurrected."

49

My taxi drove up in front of the Angelus Temple just as the last stragglers from a few late Bible classes were leaving through a multitude of doors.

Reverend Kempo was out front, wringing his rusty hands and walking as if a stick of dynamite was up his backside.

"Thank God!" he cried, rushing forward. He stopped, suddenly fearful. "You *are* the young friend of that creature in there, yes?"

"J. C.?"

"J. C.! What a criminal abomination! *Yes, J. C.!*"

"I'm his friend."

"What a pity. Quickly, now!"

And he elbow-carried me in and down the aisle of the main auditorium. It was deserted. From on high came the soft sound of feathers, a flight of angel wings. Someone was testing the sound system with various heavenly murmurs.

"Where is—?" I stopped.

For there, center stage, on the bright twenty-four-karat throne of God, sat J. C.

He sat rigidly, eyes looking straight out through the walls of the church, his hands placed, palms up, on either armrest.

"J. C." I trotted down the aisle and stopped again.

For there was fresh blood dripping from each of the cicatrices on his exposed wrists.

"Isn't he awful? That terrible man! Out!" cried the Reverend behind me.

"Is this a Christian church?" I said.

"How *dare* you ask!"

"Don't you think, at a moment like this," I wondered, "that Christ himself might show mercy?"

"Mercy!?" cried the Reverend. "He broke into our service, yelling, 'I am the true Christ! I fear for my life. Gangway!' He ran to the stage to display his wounds. He might as well have *exposed* himself. *Forgive?* There was shock and almost a riot. Our congregation may never come back. If they tell, if the newspapers call, you see? He has made us a laughing stock. Your friend!"

"My friend—" but my voice lacked luster as I climbed up to stand by the ham Shakespearean actor.

"J. C.," I called, as across an abyss.

J. C.'s eyes, fixed on eternity, blinked, refocused.

"Oh, hello, junior," he said. "What's going on?"

"Going *on*?!" I cried. "You've just made yourself one helluva mess!"

"Oh, no, no!" J. C. suddenly saw where he was and held up his hands. He stared as if someone had tossed him twin tarantulas. "Did they scourge me again? Did they follow? I'm dead. Protect me! Did you bring a bottle?"

I patted my pockets as if I carried such items all the time and shook my head. I turned to glance at the Reverend, who with a burst of invective scuttled behind the throne and shoved some red wine at me.

J. C. lunged, but I grabbed and held it as lure.

"This way. Then the cork comes out."

"You would *dare* talk to Christ like that!"

"You would dare to be Christ!?" cried the Reverend.

J. C. reared back. "I do not dare, sir. I *am*."

He arose with a jaunty attempt at hauteur, and fell down the steps.

The Reverend groaned, as if murder moved his heart to move his fists.

I got J. C. up and, waving the bottle, led him safely up the aisle and out.

The cab was still there. Before getting in, J. C. turned to see the Reverend in the doorway, his face blazing with hatred.

J. C. held up both crimson paws.

"Sanctuary! Yes? *Sanctuary?*"

"Hell, sir," shouted the Reverend, "would not have you!"

Slam!

Inside the temple I imagined a thousand angel wings, knocked free, sifting down the now unholy air.

J. C. stumbled into the cab, grabbed the wine, then leaned forward to whisper to the cab driver.

"Gethsemane!"

We drove away. The driver glanced at his map book with one eye.

"Gethsemane," he muttered. "Is that street? avenue? or *place?*"

50

"Even the cross isn't safe, even the cross isn't safe, anymore," mumbled J. C. crossing town, his eyes fixed to his wounded wrists as if he couldn't believe they were attached to his arms. "What's the world coming to?" J. C. peered out the cab window at the flowing houses.

"Was Christ manic-depressive? Like me?"

"No," I said lamely, "not nuts. But you're in the bowl with the almonds and the cashews. What made you go there?"

"I was being chased. They're after me. I am the Light of the World." But he said this last with heavy irony. "Christ, I wish I didn't know so much."

"Tell me. Fess up."

"Then they'd chase *you*, too! Clarence," he murmured. "He didn't run fast enough, either, did he?"

"I knew Clarence, too," I said. "Years ago . . ."

That scared J. C. even more. "Don't tell anyone! They won't hear it from me."

J. C. drank half the wine bottle at a chug, then winked and said, "Mum's the word."

"No, sir, J. C.! You got to tell me, just in case—"

"—I don't live beyond tonight? I *won't*! But I don't want both of us dead. You're a sweet jerkoff. Come unto me, little children, and, by God, *you* show up!"

He drank and wiped the smile off his face.

We stopped along the way. J. C. fought to leap out to buy gin. I threatened to hit him and bought it myself.

The taxi sailed into the studio and slowed near my grandparents' house.

"Why," said J. C., "that looks like the Central Avenue Negro Baptist Church! I can't go in there! I'm not black or Baptist. Just Christ, and a Jew! Tell him where to *go*!"

The taxi stopped at Calvary at sunset. J. C. looked up at his old familiar roost. "Is that the *true* cross?" He shrugged. "Just about as much as I'm the true Jesus."

I stared at the cross. "You can't hide there, J. C. Everyone knows that's where you go, now. We got to find a really secret place for you to stay in case there's a call for retakes."

"You don't understand," said J. C. "Heaven is shut and so is Hell. They'd find me in a rathole or up a hippo's behind. Calvary, plus wine, is the only place. Now, get your foot off my toga."

He put the rest of the wine down his cackle, then moved out and up the hill.

"Thank God, I've finished all my major scenes," said J. C. "It's all over, son." J. C. took my hands in his. He was immensely calm now, having veered from the heights to the depths and now steadied somewhere between. "I shouldn't have run away. And you shouldn't be seen here talking to me. They'll bring extra hammers and nails and you'll play the second extra thief on my left. Or Judas. They'll bring a rope and suddenly you're Iscariot."

He turned and put his hands on the cross and one foot on the little climbing peg on one side.

"One last thing?" I said. "*Do* you know the Beast?"

"God, I was there the night he was *born*!"

"Born?"

"Born, dammit, what did it sound like?"

"Explain, J. C., I got to know!"

"And die for knowing, you sap," said J. C. "Why do you want to die? *Jesus* saves, yes? But if I'm Jesus and I'm lost, you're all lost! Look at Clarence, the poor bastard. The guys that got him are running scared. And, scared, they panic and when they panic they hate. You know anything about *real* hatred, junior? This is it, no amateur nights, no time off for good behavior. Someone says kill and it's kill. And you wander around with your stupid naïve notions about people. God, you wouldn't know a real whore if she bit you or a real killer if he knifed you. You'd die, and dying, say: oh, *that's* what it's like, but it's too late. So listen to old Jesus, fool."

"A convenient fool, a useful idiot. That's what Lenin said."

"Lenin!? You see! At a time like this, when I'm screaming: There's Niagara Falls! where's your barrel!? you jump off the cliff with no parachute. Lenin!? gah! Which way to the madhouse?"

J. C. trembled as he finished the wine.

"Useful," he swallowed, "idiot."

"Now, listen," he said, for it was hitting him now. "I won't tell you again. If you stay with me, you're squashed. If you knew what I knew, they'd bury you in ten different graves across the wall. Cut you up in neat sections, one to a plot. If your mom and dad were alive, they'd burn them. And your wife—"

I grabbed my elbows. J. C. pulled back.

"Sorry. But you are vulnerable. God, I'm still sober. I said 'nulverable.' Your wife is back when?"

"Soon."

And it was like a funeral gong sounding at high noon.

Soon.

"Then hear the last book of Job. It's over. They won't stop until they kill everyone. Things got out of hand this week. That body on the wall you saw. It was put there to—"

"Blackmail the studio?" I quoted Crumley. "They afraid of Arbuthnot, this late in time?"

"Scared gutless! Sometimes dead folks in graves have more power than live folks above. Look at Napoleon, dead a hundred and fifty years, still alive in two hundred books! Streets and babies named for him! Lost everything, gained in losing! Hitler? Will be around ten thousand years. Mussolini? Will be hanging upside down in that gas station the rest of our lives! Even Jesus." He studied his stigmata. "I haven't done bad. But now I got to die again. But I'll be screwed six ways from Sunday if I take a sweet sap like you along. Now, shut up. Is there another bottle?"

I displayed the gin.

He grabbed it. "Now help me up on my cross and get the hell out!"

"I can't leave you here, J. C."

"There's nowhere else to *leave* me."

He drank most of the pint.

"That'll kill you!" I protested.

"It's *pain*killer, kid. When they come to get me, I won't even be here."

J. C. began to climb.

I clawed at the worn wood of the cross, then hit it with my fists, my face pointed up.

"Dammit, J. C. Hell! If this *is* your last night on earth—are you *clean!*"

He slowed in his climb. "What?"

It exploded from my mouth: "When did you last confess!? When, *when?*"

His head jerked from south to north so his face was toward the cemetery wall and beyond.

I surprised myself: "Where? *Where* did you confess?"

His face was fixed rigidly, hypnotically, to the north, which made me leap to scramble up, seizing the climb pegs, groping with my feet.

"What are you *doing*?" J. C. shouted. "This is *my* place!"

"Not anymore, there, there, and *here!*"

I swung around behind him so he had to turn to yell: "Get down!"

"*Where* did you confess, J. C.?"

He was staring at me but his eyes slid north. I swiveled my gaze to fix it along the great stretch of crossbar where an arm and a wrist and a hand could be spiked.

"God, yes!" I said.

For, lined up as in a rifle's sight was the wall, and the place on the wall where the wax and papier-mâché dummy had been hoisted in place, and, further on across a stone meadow, the facade and the waiting doors of St. Sebastian's church!

"Yes!" I gasped. "Thanks, J. C."

"Get down!"

"I am." And I took my eyes away from the wall but not before I saw his face turn once again to the country of the dead and the church beyond.

I descended.

"Where you going!?" said J. C.

"Where I should've gone days ago—"

"You stupid jerk. Stay away from that church! It's not safe!"

"A church not safe?" I stopped going down and looked up.

"Not that church, no! It's across from the graveyard and, late nights, open for any damn fool who drops in!"

"*He* drops in there, doesn't he?"

"He?"

"Hell." I shivered. "Before he goes in the graveyard nights, he first goes to confession, yes?"

"Damn you!" shrieked J. C. "Now you *are* lost!" He shut his eyes, groaned, and began the last positioning on the dark pole in the midst of dusk and coming night. "Go ahead! You want terror? You want fright? Go hear a real confession. Hide, and when he comes in late, oh so damn late, and you listen, your soul will just shrivel, burn, and die!"

Which made me clutch the pole so hard slivers stung my palms. "J. C.? You know everything, don't you? Tell, in Jesus Christ's name, J. C. tell before it's too late. You know why the body was shoved up on the wall and maybe the Beast shoved it there to scare, and just who the Beast is? Tell. Tell."

"Poor innocent stupid son-of-a-bitch kid. My God, son." J. C. looked down at me. "You're going to die and not even know all the reasons why."

He stretched his hands out, one to the north, one to the south, to grip the crossbar as if to fly. Instead an empty bottle fell to break at my feet.

"Poor sweet son of a bitch," he whispered to the sky.

I let go and dropped the last two feet. When I hit the ground I called up a last time, dead-bone tired: "J. C.?"

"Go to hell," he said, sadly. "For I sure don't know where heaven is—"

I heard cars and people nearby.

"Run," whispered J. C. from the sky.

I could not run. I simply wandered off away.

51

I met Doc Phillips coming out of Notre Dame. He was carrying a plastic bag and had the look of one of those men who roam through public parks with nail sticks, jabbing trash to thrust in bags to be burned. He looked startled, for I had one foot up on the steps as if I were going to mass.

"Well," he said, much too quickly and heartily. "Here's the boy wonder who teaches Christ to walk on water and puts Judas Iscariot back in the criminal lineup!"

"Not me," I protested. "The four apostles. I just pick up their sandals to follow."

"What're you doing here?" he said bluntly, his eyes flicking up and down my body, and his fingers working on the trash bag. I smelled incense, and his cologne.

I decided to go whole hog.

"Sunset. Best time to prowl. God, I love this place. I plan to own it someday. Don't worry, I'll keep you on. When I do, I'll tear down the offices, make everyone really live history. Let Manny work over on Tenth Avenue, New York, there! Put Fritz in Berlin, there! Me, Green Town. Roy? if he ever returns, the nut. Build a dinosaur farm yonder. I'd run wild! Instead of forty films a year, I'd make twelve, all masterpieces! I'd make Maggie Botwin vice president of the studio, she's that brilliant, and haul Louis B. Mayer out of retirement. And—"

I ran out of gas.

Doc Phillips stood with his mouth dropped as if I had handed him a ticking grenade.

"Anyone mind if I go in Notre Dame? I'd like to climb up and pretend I'm Quasimodo. Is it safe?"

"No!" said the Doc, much too quickly, circling me like a dog circling a fire hydrant. "Not safe. We're doing repairs. We're thinking of tearing the whole thing down."

He turned and walked away. "Nuts. You're *nuts!*" he cried and vanished in the cathedral entrance.

I stood watching the open door for about ten seconds, then froze.

Because from inside I heard a sort of grunt and then a groan and then a sound like cable or rope rattling against walls.

"Doc?!"

I stepped into the entrance, but could see nothing.

"Doc?"

A shadow ran up into the cathedral heights. It was like a big sandbag being hauled up in shadows.

It reminded me of Roy's body hung swinging over on Stage 13.

"Doc!?"

He was gone.

I stared up in darkness at what looked like the bottoms of his shoes sliding higher and higher.

"Doc!"

Then, it happened.

Something struck the cathedral floor.

A single black slip-on shoe.

"Christ!" I yelled.

I pulled back to see a long shadow hauled into the cathedral sky.

"Doc?" I said.

52

"Catch!"

Crumley threw a ten-dollar bill at my taxi driver, who hooted and took off.

"Just like the movies!" Crumley said. "Guys throw money at taxis and never get change. Say thanks."

"Thanks!"

"Christ," Crumley examined my face. "Get inside. Get *that* inside." Crumley handed me a beer.

I drank and told Crumley about the cathedral, Doc Phillips, hearing some sort of cry and a shadow sliding up in shadows. And the single black shoe falling to the dusty cathedral floor.

"I saw. But who could tell?" I finished. "The studio is nailing itself shut. I thought Doc was a villain. One of the other villains must have got him. By now, there's no body. Poor Doc. What am I saying? I didn't even *like* him!"

"Christ almighty," said Crumley, "you bring me the *New York Times* crossword puzzle, when you *know* all I can do is the *Daily News*. You drag dead bodies through my house like a cat proud of its kills, no rhyme, no reason. Any lawyer would heave you out the window. Any judge would brain you with his gavel.

Psychiatrists would refuse you shock privileges. You could motor down Hollywood Boulevard with all these red herrings and not get arrested for pollution."

"Yeah," I said, sinking into depression.

The phone rang.

Crumley handed it over.

A voice said: "They seek him here, they seek him there, they seek that scoundrel everywhere. Is he in heaven, is he in hell—"

"That damned elusive Pimpernel!" I yelled.

I let the phone drop as if a bomb had blown it away. Then I snatched it up again.

"Where *are* you?" I yelled.

Humm. Buzz.

Crumley clapped the phone to his ear, shook his head.

"Roy?" he said.

I nodded, staggering.

I bit one of my knuckles, trying to build a wall in my head for what was coming.

The tears arrived.

"He's alive, he's *really* alive!"

"Quiet." Crumley shoved another drink into my hand. "Bend your head."

I bent way over so he could massage along back of my skull. Tears dripped off my nose. "He's alive. Thank God."

"Why didn't he call sooner?"

"Maybe he was afraid." I talked blindly to the floor: "Like I said: They're closing in, shutting the studio. Maybe he wanted me to think he was dead so they wouldn't touch me. Maybe he knows more about the Beast than we do."

I jerked my head.

"Eyes shut." Crumley worked on my neck. "Mouth shut."

"My God, he's trapped, can't get out. Or doesn't want to. Hiding. We got to *rescue* him!"

"Rescue my ass," said Crumley. "Which city is he in? Boston or the backlot? Uganda on the north forty? Ford's Theatre? Get ourselves shot. There's ninety-nine goddamn places he could hide, so we run around like sore thumbs, yodeling for him to come out, get killed? *You* go on that studio tour!"

"Cowardly Crum."

"You *betcha!*"

"You're breaking my neck!"

"Now you've caught 'on!"

Head down, I let him pummel and thumb all the tendons and muscles into a warm jelly. From the darkness in my skull I said, "Well?"

"Let me think, god damn it!"

Crumley squeezed my neck hard.

"No panics," he muttered. "If Roy's in there, we got to peel the whole damn onion layer by layer and find him in the right time and place. No shouts or the avalanche comes down on us."

Crumley's hands gentled behind my ears now, a proper father.

"The whole thing, it must be, has to do with the studio being terrified of Arbuthnot."

"Arbuthnot," mused Crumley. "I want to see his tomb. Maybe there's something in there, some clue. You sure he's still there?"

I sat up and stared at Crumley.

"You mean: *Who's* in Grant's tomb?"

"That old joke, yes. How do we know General Grant is still there?"

"We *don't*. Robbers stole Lincoln's body twice. Seventy years back they had actually toted it to the graveyard gate when they were caught."

"Is that *so?*"

"Maybe."

"Maybe?!" shouted Crumley. "God I'm going to grow me more hair so I can tear it out! Do we go to check Arbuthnot's tomb?

"Well—"

"Don't say 'well,' dammit!" Crumley scrubbed his bald pate furiously, glaring. "You been yelling that the man on the ladder in the rain was Arbuthnot. *Maybe!* Why not someone got wind of homicide and stole the body to get the proof. Why not? Maybe that car crash came not from being drunk but dying at the wheel. So whoever does the twenty-year-late autopsy has murder evidence, blackmail proof, then they make the fake body to scare the studio and rake in the cash."

"Crum, that's terrific."

"No, guesswork, theory, B.S. Only one way to be sure." Crumley glared at his watch. "Tonight. Knock on Arbuthnot's door. See if he's home, or someone fetched him out to get his guts read for omens and scare Caesar's half-cracked legions to pee blood."

I thought of the graveyard. At last I said: "No use going unless we take a real detective, to check."

"Real detective?" Crumley stepped back.

"A seeing-eye dog."

"Seeing-eye?" Crumley examined my face. "This dog, would he live at Temple and Figueroa? Third floor up?"

"In a midnight graveyard, no matter what you see, you need a nose. He's *got* it."

"Henry? The greatest blind man in the world?"

"Always *was*," I said.

53

I had stood in front of Crumley's door and it had opened.

I had stood on Constance Rattigan's shore and she had stepped from the sea.

Now I edged along the carpetless floor of the old tenement where once I had lived with future dreams on my ceiling, nothing in my pockets, and empty paper waiting in my Smith-Corona portable.

I stopped in front of Henry's door and felt my heart beating rapidly, for just below was the room where my dear Fannie had died and this was the first time I had returned since those long sad days of good friends leaving forever.

I knocked on the door.

I heard the scrape of a cane, and the muted clearing of a throat. The floor creaked.

I heard Henry's dark brow touch the inner door panel.

"I know that knock," he murmured.

I knocked again.

"I'll be damned." The door swung wide.

Henry's blind eyes looked out on nothing.

"Let me take a deep breath."

He inhaled. I exhaled.

"Holy Jesus," Henry's voice trembled like a candle flame in a soft breeze. "Spearmint gum. *You!*"

"Me, Henry," I said gently.

His hands groped out. I seized both.

"Lord, son, you are *welcome!*" He cried.

And he grabbed and gave me a hug, then realized what he had done and pulled back. "Sorry . . ."

"No, Henry. Do it again."

And he gave me a second long hug.

"Where you been, boy, oh, where you been, it's been so long, and Henry's here in this damn big place they going to tear down soon."

He turned and wandered back to a chair and ordered his hands to find and examine two glasses. "This as clean as I think it is?"

I looked and nodded, then remembered and said, "Yep."

"Don't want to give you no germs, son. Let's see. Oh, *yeah.*" He yanked a table drawer open and extracted a large bottle of the finest whiskey. "You drink this?"

"With you, yes."

"That's what friendship is all about!" He poured. He handed the glass to the empty air. Somehow my hand was there.

We waved our drinks at each other and tears spilled down his black cheeks.

"I don't suppose you knew nigger blind men cry, did you?"

"I know now, Henry."

"Let me see." He leaned forward to feel my cheek. He tasted his finger. "Salt water. Damn. You're as easy as I am."

"Always was."

"Don't ever get over it, son. Where you been? Has life hurt you? How come you're here—" He stopped. "Oh, *oh!* Trouble?"

"Yes and no."

"Mostly yes? It's all right. I didn't figure, once you run free, you'd be back soon. I mean, this ain't the front end of the elephant is it?"

"It's not the back, either."

"Near on to it." Henry laughed. "Jesus, it's good to hear your voice, son. I always did think you smelled good. I mean, if innocence was ever put up in a pack, it was you, chewing two sticks of spearmint at a time. You're not sittin'. Sit. Let me tell you my worries, then you tell yours. They tore down the Venice pier, they tore up the Venice short-line train tracks, tear up everything. Next week, they rip up this tenement. Where do all the rats go? How do we abandon ship with no lifeboats?"

"You sure?"

"They got termites working overtime, below. Got dynamite squads on the roof, gophers and beavers gnawing in the walls, and a bunch of trumpeters learning Jericho, Jericho, practicing out in the alley to bring this tumbling down. *Then* where do we go? Not many of us left. With Fannie gone, Sam drunk to death, and Jimmy drowned in the bathtub, it was only a short haul before everyone felt put upon, nudged, you might say, by old man Death. Creeping melancholy is enough to clean out a rooming house in jig time. Let one sick mouse in, you might as well sign up for the plague."

"Is it that bad, Henry?"

"Bad leaning into worse, but that's okay. It's time to move on, anyway. Every five years, just pack your toothbrush, buy new socks and git, that's what I always say. You got a place to put me, boy? I know, I know. It's all white out there. But, hell, I can't see, so what's the difference?"

"I got a spare room in my garage, where I type. It's yours!"

"God, Jesus, and the Holy Ghost coming up fast." Henry sank back in his chair, feeling his mouth. "Is this a smile or is this a *smile*? Only for two days!" he added, quickly. "Got a sister's no-good husband driving from New Orleans to carry me home. So I'll get off your hands—"

He stopped smiling, and leaned forward.

"Armpits somewhere *again*? Out in that world?"

"Not quite armpits, Henry. Something like."

"Not too much like, I hope."

"More," I said, after a beat. "Can you come with me, right now? I hate to rush you, Henry. And I'm sorry to take you out at night."

"Why, son," Henry laughed gently, "night and day are only rumors I heard once, as a child."

He stood, groped around.

"Wait," he said, "till I find my cane. So I can see."

54

Crumley and blind Henry and I arrived near the graveyard at midnight.

I hesitated, staring at the gate.

"He's in there." I nodded toward the tombstones. "The Beast ran there the other night. What do we do if we meet him?"

"I haven't the faintest goddamn idea." Crumley stepped through the gate.

"Hell," said Henry. "Why not?"

And he left me behind in the night, on the empty sidewalk.

I caught up with them.

"Hold on, let me take a deep breath." Henry inhaled and let it out. "Yep. It's a graveyard all right!"

"Does it worry you, Henry?"

"Hell," said Henry, "dead folks ain't nothing. It's live ones ruin my sleep. Want to know how I know this ain't just a plain old garden? Garden's full of flower mixes, lots of smells. Graveyards? Mostly tuberoses. From funerals. Always hated funerals for that smell. How'm I doing, detective?"

"Swell, but . . ." Crumley moved us out of the light. "If we stand here long enough, someone'll think we need burying and do the job. Hup!"

Crumley walked swiftly away among a thousand milk-white tombstones.

Beast, I thought, where are you?

I looked back at Crumley's car and suddenly it was a dear friend I was leaving a thousand miles back.

"You haven't told yet," said Henry. "Why'd you bring a blind man to a graveyard? You need my nose?"

"You and the Baskerville Hound," Crumley said. "This way."

"Don't touch," said Henry. "I got a dog's nose, but my pride is all cat. Watch out, Death."

And he led the way between the gravestones, tapping right and left, as if to dislodge big chunks of night or strike sparks where sparks never struck before.

"How'm I doin'?" he whispered.

I stood with Henry among all the marbles with names and dates and the grass growing quietly between.

Henry sniffed.

"I smell me one big hunk of *rock*. Now. What kind of Braille is *this*?"

He transferred his cane to his left hand while his right hand trembled up to feel the chiseled name above the Grecian tomb door.

His fingers shook over the "A" and froze on the final "T."

"I know this name." Henry spun a Rolodex behind his white billiard-ball eyes. "Would that be the great, long-gone proprietor of the studio across the wall?"

"Yes."

"The loud man who sat in all the boardrooms and no room left? Fixed his own bottles, changed his own diapers, bought the sandbox, two and one half, fired the kindergarten teacher age three, sent ten boys to the nurse, age seven, chased girls at eight, caught 'em at nine, owned a parking lot at ten, and the studio on his twelfth birthday when his pa died and left him London, Rome, and Bombay? *That* the one?"

"Henry," I sighed, "you're marvelous."

"Makes me hard to live with," admitted Henry, quietly. "Well."

He reached up to touch the name again and the date underneath.

"October 31st, 1934. Halloween! Twenty years gone. I wonder how it feels, being dead that long. Hell. Let's ask! Anyone think to bring some tools?"

"A crowbar from the car," said Crumley.

"Good . . ." Henry put out his hand. "But for the helluvit—" His fingers touched the tomb door.

"Holy Moses!" he exclaimed.

The door drifted open on oiled hinges. Not rusted! Not squealing! Oiled!

"Sweet Jesus! Open house!" Henry stood quickly back. "You don't mind, since you got the faculties—you *first*."

I touched the door. It glided further into shadow.

"Here."

Crumley brushed past, switched on his flashlight, and stepped into midnight.

I followed.

"Don't leave me out here," said Henry.

Crumley pointed, "Shut the door. We don't want anyone seeing our flash—"

I hesitated. I had seen too many films where the vault doors slammed and people were trapped, yelling, forever. And if the Beast was out there now—?

"Christ! *Here!*" Crumley shoved the door, leaving the merest quarter-inch crack for air. "Now." He turned.

The room was empty, except for a large stone sarcophagus at

its center. There was no lid. Inside the sarcophagus there should have been a coffin.

"Hell!" said Crumley.

We looked down. There was no coffin.

"Don't tell!" said Henry. "Lemme put on my dark glasses helps me smell better! There!"

And while we stared down, Henry bent, took a deep breath, thought about it behind his dark glasses, let it out, shook his head, and snuffed another draught. Then he beamed.

"Shucks. Ain't nothin' there! Right?"

"Right."

"J. C. Arbuthnot," murmured Crumley, "where *are* you?"

"Not here," I said.

"And never *was*," added Henry.

We glanced at him quickly. He nodded, mightily self-pleased.

"Nobody by that name or any other name, any time, ever here at all. If there had been, I'd get the scent, see? But not so much as one flake of dandruff, one toenail, one hair from one nostril. Not even a sniff of tuberose or incense. This place, friends, was never used by a dead person, not for an hour. If I'm wrong, cut my nose off!"

Ice water poured down my spine and out my shoes.

"Christ," muttered Crumley, "why would they build a tombhouse, put no one in, but pretend they did?"

"Maybe there never was a body," said Henry. "What if Arbuthnot never died?"

"No, no," I said. "The newspapers all over the world, the five thousand mourners. I was there. I saw the funeral car."

"What did they do with the body then?" Crumley said. "And why?"

"I—"

The tombhouse door slammed shut!

Henry, Crumley, and I shouted with the shock. I grabbed Henry, Crumley grabbed us both. The flashlight fell. Cursing, we bent and knocked heads, sucked breaths, waited to hear the door locked on us. We blundered, tussling at the flashlight and then swiveling the beam toward the door, wanting life, light, the night air forever.

We hit the door in a mob.

And, God, it was really locked!

"Jesus, how do we get outa this place?"

"No, no," I kept saying.

"Shut up," said Crumley, "let me think."

"Think fast," said Henry. "Whoever shut us in is gone for help."

"Maybe that was just the caretaker," I said.

No, I thought: the Beast.

"No, gimme that light. Yeah. Hell." Crumley directed the beam up and around. "All outside hinges, no way to get *to* them."

"Well," Henry suggested, "I don't suppose there's more than one door to this place?"

Crumley flashed his light at Henry's face.

"What'd I *say*?" said Henry.

Crumley took the flashlight off Henry's face and moved past him, around the sarcophagus. He flashed the beam up and down the ceiling, the floor, then along the seams and around the small window in back, so small no more than a cat could slide through.

"I don't suppose we can yell out the window?"

"Whoever came to answer I wouldn't want," observed Henry.

Crumley swung his flash, turning in circles.

"Another door," he kept saying. "Must be!"

"Must!" I cried.

I felt the fierce watering in my eyes and the awful dryness in my throat. I imagined heavy footsteps rushing among the tombstones, shadows come to batter, shades running to smother, calling me Clarence, wishing me dead. I imagined the door burst wide and a ton of books, signed photos, signature cards, flooding to drown us.

"Crumley!" I grabbed the flash. "Give me that!"

There was only one last place to look. I peered into the sarcophagus. Then I peered closer and exhaled.

"Look!" I said. "Those," I pointed. "God, I don't know, hollows, indentations, slants, whatever. I never saw things like that in a tomb. And there, look, under the seam, isn't there light coming from under? Well, hell! Wait!"

I leaped up on the rim of the sarcophagus, balanced and looked down at the even, measured forms at the bottom.

"Watch it!" cried Crumley.

"No, *you!*"

I dropped down onto the sarcophagus bottom.

There was a groan of oiled machinery. The room shook when some counterbalance shifted beneath.

I sank down as the sarcophagus floor sank. My feet melted in darkness. My legs followed. I was tilted at an angle when the lid stopped.

"Steps!" I cried. "Stairs!"

"What?" Henry groped down. "Yeah!"

The sarcophagus bottom, laid flat, had looked like a series of half-pyramids. Now that the lid angled, they were perfect steps into a lower tomb.

I took a quick step down. "Come on!"

"Come on?!" said Crumley. "What in hell's *down* there?"

"What in hell's *out* there!" I pointed at the slammed outer door.

"Damn!" Crumley leaped up to fetch Henry. Henry sprang up like a cat.

I stepped down a slow step, trembling, waving the flashlight. Henry and Crumley followed, cursing and blowing air.

Another flight of steps fused with the sarcophagus lid to lead us down another ten feet into a catacomb. When Crumley, last, stepped off, the lid whispered high, banged shut. I squinted at the shut ceiling and saw a counterweight suspended in half light. A huge iron ring hung from the bottom of the vanished staircase. From below, you could grab, use your weight, and yank the stairs down.

All this in a heartbeat.

"I hate this place!" said Henry.

"How would *you* know?" said Crumley.

Henry said: "I still don't like it. Listen!"

Upstairs, the wind, or something, was shivering the outside door.

Crumley grabbed the flashlight and swung it around. "Now *I* hate this place."

There was a door in the wall ten feet off. Crumley gave it a yank and a grunt. It opened. With Henry between we hustled through. The door slammed behind. We ran.

Away from, I thought, or toward the Beast?!

"Don't look!" shouted Crumley.

"Whatta you mean, don't *look*?" Henry thrashed the air with his cane, clubbing the stone floor with his shoes, ricocheting between us. Crumley, in the lead, yelled, "Just *don't* is all!"

But I had seen as we ran, colliding with walls, crashing through a territory of bone heaps and skull pyramids, broken coffins, scattered funeral wreaths; a battlefield of death; cracked incense urns, statue fragments, demolished icons, as if a long parade of doom had, in mid-celebration, dropped its shrapnels to flee, even as we fled with one light caroming off green-mossed ceilings and poking in square holes where flesh had vanished and teeth smiled.

Don't look!? I thought. No, don't stop! I all but knocked Henry aside, drunk with fright. He whipped his cane to crack me in place and pumped his legs like a sighted fiend.

We blundered from one country to another, from a file of bones to a file of tins, from vaults of marble to vaults of concrete and suddenly we were in old-silent-black-and-white territory. Names flashed by with film titles on stacked reel canisters.

"Where in hell are we?" panted Crumley.

"Rattigan!" I heard myself gasp. "Botwin! My God! We're in—Maximus Films! over, under, through the wall!"

And we were indeed in Botwin's film basement and Rattigan's underworld, badly lit photo-landscapes they had traveled in 1920 and '22 and '25. Not burial boneyards but the old film vaults

Constance had named as we rambled. I glanced back in darkness to see real bodies fade even as the film ghosts surged round. Titles sluiced by: *The Squaw Man*, *The Insidious Dr. Fu Manchu*, *The Black Pirate*. Not only Maximus films, but other studios' films, borrowed or stolen.

I was torn. One half fleeing the dark soil behind. One half wanting to reach, touch, see these ancient shadow ghosts that had haunted my childhood to hide me in everlasting matinees.

Christ! I yelled but did not yell. Don't leave! Chaney! Fairbanks! The man in that damned iron mask! Nemo under water! D'Artagnan! Wait for me! I'll be back. If I live, that is! Soon!

All this a babble of fright and frustration, a surge of instant love and instant fear to smother the stupid babble.

Don't look at the beauties, I thought. Remember the dark. Run.

And, dear God, don't stop!

Our echoes caught up with us in a triple rush of panic. We all yelled and streamed in a solid mass the last thirty yards or so, Crumley churning like a crazed ape with his flashlight, Blind Henry and me collapsing with him against a final door.

"God, if it's locked!"

We grabbed.

I froze, remembering old films. Crack the door: a deluge drowns New York, sucks you in salt tides down cisterns. Crack the door and hell fires blast you to mummified bits. Crack the door and all of time's monsters grip you with nuclear claws and hurl you down a pit with no end. You fall forever, screaming.

I sweated the door handle. Guanajuato rustled behind the panel. That long tunnel in Mexico waited where I had once run a gauntlet of horrors, the 110 men, women and children, tobacco-dried mummies yanked from their graves to stand in line and wait for tourists and the day of judgment.

Guanajuato here?! I thought. No!

I pushed. The door drifted away on absolutely silent oiled hinges.

There was a moment of shock.

We stumbled in, gasping, and slammed the door.

We turned.

There was a big chair nearby.

And an empty desk.

With a white telephone in the middle of the desk.

"Where are we?" said Crumley.

"By the way he's breathing, the child knows," said Henry.

Crumley's flashlight played over the room.

"Holy Mother of God, Caesar, and Christ," I sighed.

I was looking at—

Manny Leiber's chair.

Manny Leiber's desk.

Manny Leiber's telephone.

Manny Leiber's office.

I turned to see the mirror that hid the now invisible door.

Half drunk with exhaustion, I stared at myself in that cold glass.

And suddenly it was—

Nineteen twenty-six. The opera singer in her dressing room and a voice behind the mirror urging, teaching, prompting, desiring her to step through the glass, a terrible Alice . . . dissolved in images, melting to descend to the underworld, led by the man in the dark cloak and white mask to a gondola that drifted on dark canal waters to a buried palace and a bed shaped like a coffin.

The phantom's mirror.

The phantom's passage from the land of the dead.

And now—

His chair, his desk, his office.

But not the phantom. The Beast.

I knocked the chair aside.

The Beast . . . coming to see Manny Leiber?

I stumbled and backed off.

Manny, I thought. He who never truly gave, but took, orders. A shadow, not a substance. A sideshow, not a main attraction.

Run a studio!? No. Be a phone line over which voices passed?
Yes. A messenger boy. An errand boy fetching champagne and
cigarettes, sure! But sit in that chair? He had never sat there.
Because . . . ?

Crumley shoved Henry.

"Move!"

"What?" I said, numbly.

"Someone's gonna bust through that mirror, any minute!"

"Mirror!?" I cried.

I reached out.

"No!" said Crumley.

"What's he up to?" asked Henry.

"Looking back," I said.

I swung the mirror door wide.

I stared down the long tunnel, astounded at how far we had
run, from country to country, mystery to mystery, along twenty
years to now, Halloween to Halloween. The tunnel sank through
commissaries of tinned films to reliquaries for the nameless.
Could I have run all that way without Crumley and Henry to
flail away shadows as my breath banged the walls?

I listened.

Far off, did doors open and slam? Was a dark army or a simple
Beast in pursuit? Soon, would a death gun discharge skulls, blow
the tunnel, ram me back from the mirror? Would—

"God damn!" said Crumley. "Idiot! *Out!*"

He knocked my hand down. The mirror shut.

I grabbed the phone and dialed.

"Constance!" I yelled. "Green Town."

Constance yelled back.

"What'd she say?" Crumley peered into my face. "Never
mind," he added, "because—"

The mirror shook. We ran.

55

The studio was as dark and empty as the graveyard over the wall.

The two cities looked at each other across the night air and played similar deaths. We were the only warm things moving in the streets. Somewhere, perhaps, Fritz was running night films of Galilee and charcoal beds and evocative Christs and footprints blowing away on the dawn wind. Somewhere, Maggie Botwin was crouched over her telescope viewing the bowels of China. Somewhere, the Beast was ravening to follow, or lying low.

"Take it easy!" said Crumley.

"We're not being followed," said Henry. "Listen! the blind man says. Where we going?"

"To my grandparents'."

"Well, now that sounds nice," said Henry.

Hustling along, we whispered:

"Good God, does anyone in the studio know about that passage?"

"If so, they never said."

"Lord, think. If nobody knew, and the Beast came every night or every day, and listened behind the wall, after a while he'd know everything. All the deals, the ins and outs, all the stockmarket junk, all the women. Save up the data long enough and you're ready to cash in. Shake the Guy at them, get the money, run."

"The Guy?"

"The Guy Fawkes dummy, the fireworks mannequin, the Guy they toss on the bonfire every Guy Fawkes Day in England, November 5th. Like our Halloween, but religious politics. Fawkes almost blew up Parliament. Caught, he was hanged. We got something like it here. The Beast plans to blow up Maximus. Not literally, but rip it apart with suspicion. Scare everyone. Shake a dummy at them. Maybe he's been shaking them down for years. And nobody the wiser. He's an inside trader using secret information."

"Whoa!" said Crumley. "Too neat. I don't like it. You think no one knows the Beast is behind the wall, the mirror?"

"Yep."

"Then how come the studio, or one part of it, your boss, Manny, has a conniption fit when he sees Roy's clay model of the Beast?"

"Well—"

"Does Manny know the Beast's there and fear him? Did the Beast come into the studio at night, see Roy's work, and destroy it in a rage? And now Manny's afraid Roy will blackmail him because Roy knows the Beast exists and no one else does? What, what, what? Answer, quick!"

"God's sake, Crumley, hush!"

"Hush! What kind of rough talk is *that*?"

"I'm thinking."

"I can hear the cogs turn. Which *is* it? Is everyone ignorant as to who hides behind the mirror listening? and so they fear the unknown? Or do they know and are twice as afraid because the Beast has gathered so much dirt over the years he can go where he damn well pleases, collect his money, run back under the wall? They don't dare cross him. He probably has letters some lawyer will mail the day something happens to him. Witness Manny's panics, hanging out his underwear ten times a day? Well? Which *is* it? Or do you have a third version?"

"Don't make me nervous. I'll go into a funk."

"Hell, kid, that's the last thing I'd want to do," said Crumley, with a twist of lemon in his mouth. "Sorry to shove you into a king-size funk, but I hate keeping time with your quarterhorse half-ass deductions. I've just run through a tunnel chased by a criminal beehive you kicked over. Have we stirred up a nest of Mafia or just a single maniac acrobat? Promises, promises! Where's Roy? where's Clarence, where's the Beast? Give me one, just *one*, body! Well?"

"Wait." I stopped, turned, walked away.

"Where you going?" groused Crumley.

Crumley followed me up the small hill.

"Where in hell are we?"

He peered around through the night.

"Calvary."

"What's that up there?"

"*Three* crosses. You were complaining about bodies?"

"So?"

"I have this terrible feeling."

I put my hand out to touch the base of the cross. It came away sticky and smelling of something as raw as life.

Crumley did the same. He sniffed his fingertips and nodded, sensing what it was.

We looked up along the cross at the sky.

After a while our eyes got used to the darkness.

"There's no body there," said Crumley.

"Yes, but—"

"It figures," said Crumley and stalked off toward Green Town.

"J. C.?" I whispered. "J. C."

Crumley called from down the hill. "Don't just stand there!"

"I'm not just standing here!"

I counted to ten, slowly, wiped my eyes with digging fists, blew my nose, and fell downhill.

I led Henry and Crumley up the path to my grandparents' house.

"I smell geraniums and lilacs." Henry lifted his face.

"Yes."

"And cut grass and furniture polish and plenty of cats."

"The studio needs mousers. Steps, here, Henry, eight up."

We stood on the porch, breathing hard.

"My God." I looked out at Jerusalem's hills beyond Green Town and the Sea of Galilee, beyond Brooklyn. "All along I should have *seen*. The Beast didn't go to the *graveyard*, he was entering the *studio*! What a setup. Using a tunnel no one suspects to spy on his blackmail victims. See how much he had scared them with that body on the wall, grab the money, scare 'em again and pick up more!"

"If," said Crumley, "that's *what* he was doing."

I took a deep trembling breath and at last let it out.

"There's one more body I haven't delivered to you."

"I'd rather not hear," said Crumley.

"Arbuthnot's."

"Crud, that's right!"

"Somebody stole it," I said. "A long time ago."

"No, sirree," said blind Henry. "It was *never* there. That was a clean place, that icehouse tomb."

"So where's Arbuthnot's body been all these years?" asked Crumley.

"You're the detective. Detect."

"Okay," said Crumley, "how's *this*? Halloween booze party. Someone poisons the hooch. Gives it to Arbuthnot at the last second as he leaves. Arbuthnot, driving, dies at the wheel, smashes the other car off the road. There's a coverup. Autopsy shows his body glows with enough poison to pile-drive an elephant. Before the funeral, instead of burying the evidence, they burn it. Arbuthnot, so much smoke, goes up the chimney. So his empty sarcophagus waits in the tomb, where blind Henry here tells all."

"I *did* do that, didn't I?" Henry agreed.

"The Beast, knowing the tomb is vacant and the reason why maybe, uses it as a base, hoists the Arbuthnot look-alike on the ladder, and watches the scalded ants run in a fright picnic over the wall. Okay?"

"That still doesn't find us Roy, J. C., Clarence, or the Beast," I said.

"Lord *deliver* me from this guy!" Crumley pleaded with the sky.

Crumley was delivered.

There was a fearful racket in the studio alleys, some backfires, honks, and a yell.

"That's Constance Rattigan," observed Henry.

Constance parked in front of the old house and cut the motor.

"Even when she turns off the ignition," said Henry, "I can still hear her motor running."

We met her at the front door.

"Constance!" I said. "How did you get past the guard?"

"Easy." She laughed. "He was an old-timer. I reminded him I'd once attacked him in the men's gym. While he was blushing, I roared in! Well, damn, if it isn't the world's greatest blind man!"

"You still working at that lighthouse, directing ships?" asked Henry.

"Give me a hug."

"You sure feel soft."

"And Elmo Crumley, you old s.o.b.!"

"She's never wrong," said Crumley, as she broke all his ribs.

"Let's get the hell out of here," said Constance. "Henry? Lead!"

"I'm *gone!*" said Henry.

On the way out of the studio I murmured, "Calvary."

Constance slowed as we passed the ancient hill.

There was complete darkness. No moon. No stars. One of those nights when the fog comes in early from the sea and covers all of Los Angeles, at a height of about five hundred feet. The airplanes are muffled and the airports closed.

I gazed steadily up the little hill hoping to find Christ in a drunken farewell-tour Ascension.

"J. C.!" I whispered.

But the clouds shifted now. I could see the crosses were empty.

Three gone, I thought. Clarence drowned in paper, Doc Phillips hauled up in Notre Dame's midnight at noon, leaving one shoe. And now . . . ?

"See anything?" asked Crumley.

"Maybe tomorrow."

When I roll the Rock aside. If I have the guts.

There was a waiting silence from everyone in the car.

"Out," suggested Crumley.

I said quietly, "Out."

At the front gate Constance shouted something obscene at the guard, who reeled back.

We went toward the sea and Crumley's.

56

We stopped at my house. As I ran to fetch my 8-millimeter projector, the phone rang.

After the twelfth ring I snatched it up.

"Well?" said Peg. "How come you stood there for twelve rings with your hand on the phone?"

"God, women's intuition."

"What's up? Who *disappeared*? Who's sleeping in Mama Bear's bed? You haven't called. If I were there, I'd throw you out of the house. It's hard to do long distance but, get out!"

"Okay."

That shot her through the chest.

"Hold on," she said, alarmed.

"You said: Get out!"

"Yes, but—"

"Crumley's waiting outside."

"Crumley!" she shrieked, "By the bowels of Christ! Crumley!?"

"He'll protect me, Peg."

"Against your panics? Can he mouth-to-mouth breathe those? Can he make sure you eat breakfast, lunch, or dinner? Lock you out of the refrigerator when you get too chunky? Does he make you change your underwear!?"

"Peg!"

And we both laughed just a little.

"You really going out the door? Mama will be home on Flight sixty-seven, Pan Am, Friday. Be there! with all the murders solved, bodies buried, and rapacious women kicked downstairs! If you can't make it to the airport, just be in bed when mama slams the door. You haven't said I love you."

"Peg. I love you."

"And one last thing—in the last hour: who *died*?"

Outside at the curb, Henry, Crumley, and Constance waited.

"My wife doesn't want me to be seen with you," I said.

"Get *in*." Crumley sighed.

57

On the way west on an empty boulevard with not even a ghost of a car in sight, we let Henry tell what had happened in, under, through the wall and out. It was somehow fine to hear our flight described by a blind man who enunciated with his head as his dark nose snuffed deep and his black fingers sketched the wind, drawing Crumley here, himself there, me below, and the Beast behind. Or something that had lain outside the tomb door like a landslide of yeast to seal our escape. Bull! But as Henry told it we turned cold and rolled up the windows. No use. There was no top to the car.

"And that," declared Henry, taking off his dark glasses for finale, "is why we called you, mad lady from Venice, to come save." Constance glanced nervously in her rear-view mirror. "Hell, we're going too slow!"

She put the car in whiplash. Our heads obeyed.

Crumley unlocked his front door.

"Okay. Spread out!" he growled. "What time *is* it?"

"Late," said Henry. "Night-blooming jasmine gets outa hand round about now."

"Is that true?" yelled Crumley.

"No, but it sure sounds nice." Henry beamed at an unseen audience. "Fetch the beer."

Crumley handed the beers around.

"There'd better be gin in this," said Constance. "Hell. There *is*!"

I plugged in my projector, sprocketed Roy Holdstrom's film, and we turned out the lights.

"Okay?" I clicked the projector switch. "Now."

The film began.

Images flickered on Crumley's wall. There were only thirty seconds' worth of film, and fairly jumpy, as if Roy had animated his clay bust in only a few hours instead of the many days it usually took to position a creature, take its picture, reposition it, and snap another frame, one at a time.

"Holy Jesus," whispered Crumley.

We all sat stunned by what jumped across Crumley's wall.

It was Beauty's friend, the thing from the Brown Derby.

"I can't look," said Constance. But she looked.

I glanced at Crumley and felt as I had felt as a child, with my brother, seated in the dark theatre as the Phantom or the Hunchback or the Bat loomed on the screen. Crumley's face was my brother's face, back thirty years, fascinated and horrified in one, curious and repelled, the sort of look people have when they see but do not want to see a traffic accident.

For up on the wall, real and immediate, was the Man Beast. Every contortion of the face, every move of the eyebrows, every flare of the nostrils, every motion of the lips, was there, as perfect as the sketches that Doré made when he came home from a long night's prowl in the cinder-dark smokestack lanes of London, with all the grotesques stashed behind his eyelids, his empty fingers itching to grab pen, ink, paper, and *begin!* Even as Doré had, with total recall, scribbled faces, so Roy's inner mind had photographed the Beast to remember the slightest hair moving in the nostrils, the merest eyelash in a blink, the flexed ear, and the eternally salivating infernal mouth. And when the Beast stared out of the screen, Crumley and I pulled back. It saw us. It dared us to shriek. It was coming to kill.

The parlor wall went dark.

I heard a sound bubble through my lips.

"The eyes," I whispered.

I fumbled in the dark, rewound the reel, restarted it.

"Look, look, oh, look!" I cried.

The camera image closed in on the face.

The wild eyes were fixed in a convulsive madness.

"That isn't a clay bust!"

"No?" said Crumley.

"It's Roy!"

"Roy!?"

"In makeup, *pretending* to be the Beast!"

"No!"

The face leered, the live eyes rolled.

"Roy—"

And the wall darkened a final time.

Even as the Beast, met in the heights of Notre Dame, with the same eyes, pulled back away and fled. . . .

"Jesus," said Crumley at last, looking at that wall. "So that's what's running loose in graveyards these nights!"

"Or Roy, running loose."

"That's nuts! Why would he do that?!"

"The Beast got him in all this trouble, got him fired, got him almost killed, what better to do than imitate him, be him, in case anyone saw. Roy Holdstrom doesn't *exist* if he puts on the makeup and hides."

"It's still nuts!"

"Nuts all his life, sure," I said. "But now? For real!"

"What's he gain from it?"

"Revenge."

"Revenge?!"

"Let the Beast kill the Beast," I said.

"No, no." Crumley shook his head. "To hell with that. Run the film again!"

I ran it. The images streamed up and down our faces.

"That's not Roy!" said Crumley. "That's a clay bust, animated!"

"No." I shut off the film.

We sat in darkness.

Constance made strange sounds.

"Why," said Henry, "know what that *is*? Crying."

58

"I'm afraid to go home," said Constance.

"Who said you had to?" said Crumley. "Grab a cot, any room, or the jungle compound."

"No," murmured Constance. "That's *his* place."

We all looked at the blank wall where only a lingering retinal image of the Beast faded.

"He didn't follow us," said Crumley.

"He might." Constance blew her nose. "I won't be alone in some damned empty house by a damned ocean full of monsters tonight. I'm getting old. Next thing you know I'll ask some jerk to marry me, God help him."

She looked out at Crumley's jungle and the night wind stirring the palm leaves and the high grass. "He's there."

"Cut it," said Crumley. "We don't know if we were followed through that graveyard tunnel to that office. Or who slammed the tomb door. Could've been the wind."

"It always is. . . ." Constance shivered like someone coming down with a long winter's illness. "Now what?" She sank back in her chair, shuddering, clutching her elbows.

"Here."

Crumley laid out a series of photocopies of newspapers on the kitchen table. Three dozen items, large and small, from the last day in October and the first week in November 1934.

"ARBUTHNOT, STUDIO MAGNATE, KILLED IN CAR CRASH" was the first one. "C. Peck Sloane, associate producer at Maximus studio, and his wife, Emily, killed in same accident."

Crumley tapped the third article. "The Sloanes were buried the same day as Arbuthnot. Services in the same church across from the graveyard. All buried in the same graveyard, over the wall."

"Where'd the accident happen?"

"Three in the morning. Gower and Santa Monica!"

"My God! The corner of the graveyard! And around the block from the studio!"

"Awfully convenient, right?"

"Saved travel. Die outside a mortuary, all they do is cart you in."

Crumley scowled at another column. "Seems there was a wild Halloween party."

"And Sloane and Arbuthnot were there?"

"Doc Phillips, it says here, offered to drive them home, they'd been drinking and refused. The doc drove his own car ahead of the other two cars, to clear the way, and went through a yellow light. Arbuthnot and Sloane followed, against the red. An unknown car almost hit them. The *only* car on the street at 3 A.M.! Arbuthnot's and Sloane's cars swerved, lost control, hit a telephone pole. Doc Phillips was there with his medical kit. No use. All dead. They took the bodies to the mortuary one hundred yards away."

"Dear God," I said. "It's too damn neat!"

"Yeah," mused Crumley. "A helluva responsibility for the pill-pushing dopester Doc. Coincidence, him at the scene. Him in charge of studio medicine *and* studio police! Him delivering the bodies to the mortuary. Him preparing the bodies for burial as funeral director? Sure? He had stock in the graveyard. Helped dig the first graves in the early twenties. Got 'em coming, going, and in between."

Flesh really does crawl, I thought, feeling my upper arms.

"Did Doc Phillips sign the death certificates?"

"I thought you'd never ask." Crumley nodded.

Constance, who had sat frozen to one side, staring at the news clippings, spoke at last, from lips that barely moved: "Where's that bed?"

I led her into the next room and sat her on the bed. She held my hands as if they were an open Bible and took a deep breath.

"Kid, anyone ever tell you your body smells like cornflakes and your breath like honey?"

"That was H. G. Wells. Drove women mad."

"Too late for madness. God, your wife's lucky, going to bed nights with health food."

She laid herself down with a sigh. I sat on the floor, waiting for her to close her eyes.

"How come," she murmured, "you haven't aged in three years, and me? a thousand." She laughed quietly. One large tear moved from her right eye and dissolved into the pillow.

"Aw, shit," she mourned.

"*Tell* me," I prompted. "Say it. What?"

"I was there," Constance murmured. "Twenty years ago. At the studio. Halloween night."

I held my breath. Behind me, a shadow moved into the doorway, Crumley was there, quiet and listening.

Constance stared out past me at another year and another night.

"It was the wildest party I'd ever seen. Everyone in masks, nobody knowing who or what was drinking which or why. There was hooch on every sound stage and barking in the alleys, and if Tara and Atlanta had been built that night they would have burned. There must have been two hundred dress and three hundred undress extras, running booze back and forth through that graveyard tunnel as if Prohibition was in full swing. Even with hooch legal, I guess it's hard to give up the fun, yes? Secret passages between the tombs and the turkeys, like the flop films rotting in the vaults? Little did they know they'd brick the damn tunnel up, a week later, after the accident."

The accident of the year, I thought. Arbuthnot dead, and the studio gun-shot and dropping like a herd of elephants.

"It was no accident," whispered Constance

Constance gathered a private darkness behind her pale face.

"Murder," she said. "Suicide."

The pulse jumped in my hand. She held it, tight.

"Yeah," she nodded, "suicide and murder. We never found out how, why, or what. You saw the papers. Two cars at Gower and Santa Monica, late, and no one to see. All the masked people ran off in their masks. The studio alleys were like those Venetian canals at dawn, all the gondolas empty, and the docks littered with earrings and underwear. I ran, too. The rumors later said Sloane found Arbuthnot with Sloane's wife out back or over the wall. Or maybe Arbuthnot found Sloane with his own wife. My God, if you love another man's wife and she makes love to her own husband at a lunatic party, wouldn't that drive you mad?! So one car tailgates another at top speed. Arbuthnot after the Sloanes at eighty miles an hour. Rear-ended them at Gower, rammed them into a pole. The news hit the party! Doc Phillips, Manny, and Groc rushed out. They carried the victims into the Catholic church nearby. Arbuthnot's church. Where he put money as his fire escape, his escape from hell, he said. But it was too late. They died and were taken across the street to the mortuary. I was long since gone. At the studio the next day Doc and Groc looked like pallbearers at their own funerals. I finished the last scene of the last film I ever made by noon. The studio shut down for a week. They hung crepe on every sound stage and sprayed fake clouds of fog and mist in every street, or is that true? The headlines said the three of them were all happy drunk, going home. No. It was vengeance running to kill love. The poor male bastards and the poor lovesick bitch were buried across the wall where the hooch once ran, two days later. The graveyard tunnel was bricked up and—hell," she sighed, "I thought it was all over. But tonight, with the tunnel open, and Arbuthnot's fake body on that wall, and that terrible man with the sad, mad eyes in your film, it's started again. What's it all mean?"

Her clock ran down, her voice faded, she was going to sleep. Her mouth twitched. Ghosts of words came out, in bits and pieces.

"Poor holy man. Sap . . ."

"What holy man sap?" I asked.

Crumley leaned forward in the doorway.

Constance, deep under, drowning, gave answer:

". . . priest. Poor crock. Dumped on. Studio barging in. Blood in the baptistry. Bodies, my God, bodies everywhere. Poor sap . . ."

"St. Sebastian's? *That* poor sap?"

"Sure, sure. Poor him. Poor everyone," murmured Constance. "Poor Arby, that sad stupid genius. Poor Sloane. Poor wife. Emily Sloane. What was it she said that night? Going to live forever. Boy! What a surprise to wake up nowhere. Poor Emily. Poor Hollyhock House. Poor me."

"Poor what was that again?"

"Hol . . ." Constance's voice slurred . . . "ly . . . ock . . . House. . . ."

And she slept.

"Hollyhock House? No film by that name," I murmured.

"No," said Crumley, moving into the room. "Not a film. Here."

He reached under the night table and pulled the telephone directory out and turned the pages. He ran his finger down and read aloud:

"Hollyhock House Sanitarium. That's half a block over and half a block north of St. Sebastian's Catholic church, yes?"

Crumley leaned close to her ear.

"Constance," he said. "Hollyhock House. Who's there?"

Constance moaned, covered her eyes, and turned away. To the wall she addressed some few final words about a night a long time ago.

". . . going to live forever . . . little did she know . . . poor everyone . . . poor Arby . . . poor priest . . . poor sap . . ."

Crumley arose, muttering. "Hell. Damn. Sure. Hollyhock House. A stone's throw from—"

"St. Sebastian's," I finished. "Why," I added, "do I have this feeling you'll be taking me there?"

59

"You," Crumley said to me at breakfast, "look like death warmed over. You," he pointed his buttered toast at Constance, "look like Justice without Mercy.

"What do *I* look like?" asked Henry.

"Can't see you."

"Figures," said the blind man.

"Clothes off," said Constance, dazed, like someone reading from an idiot board. "Time for a swim. My place!"

We drove to Constance's place.

Fritz telephoned.

"Have you got the middle for my film," he cried, "or was it the beginning? Now we need a redo of the Sermon on the Mount!"

"Does it *need* redoing?" I almost yelled.

"Have you looked at it lately?" Fritz, over the phone, did his imitation of Crumley pulling out his last strands of hair. "Do it! Then write a narration for the whole damn film to cover the ten thousand other pits, pimples, and rump-sprung behinds of our epic. Have you read the *whole* Bible, lately?"

"Not exactly."

Fritz tore some more hair. "Go skim!"

"Skim!?"

"Skip pages. Be at the studio at five o'clock with a sermon to knock my socks off and a narration to make Orson Welles spoil his shoes! Your Unterseeboot Kapitän says: *Dive!*"

He submerged, and was gone.

"Clothes off," said Constance, still half asleep. "Everyone in!"

We swam. I followed Constance as far out in the surf as I could go, then the seals welcomed and swam her away.

"Lord," said Henry, sitting hip deep in water. "First bath I had in years!"

We finished five bottles of champagne before two o'clock and were suddenly almost happy.

Then somehow I sat down, wrote *my* Sermon on the Mount, and read it aloud to the sound of the waves.

When I finished Constance said, quietly, "Where do I sign up for Sunday school?"

"Jesus," said blind Henry, "would have been proud."

"I dub thee," Crumley poured champagne in my ear, "genius."

"Hell," I said modestly.

I went back in and for good measure rode Joseph and Mary into Bethlehem, lined up the wise men, positioned the Babe on a pallet of hay while the animals watched with incredulous eyes, and in the midst of midnight camel trains, strange stars, and miraculous births, I heard Crumley behind me say:

"Poor holy man sap."

He dialed information.

"Hollywood?" he said. "St. Sebastian's church?"

60

At three-thirty Crumley dropped me St. Sebastian's.

He examined my face and saw not only my skull but what rattled inside.

"Stop it!" he ordered. "You got that dumb smug-ass look pasted on your mouth like a circus flier. Which means you trip, but *I* fall downstairs!"

"Crumley!"

"Well, Christ almighty, what about that mill race under the bones and through the wall last night, and Roy in permanent hiding, and Blind Henry cane-whipping the air, fighting off spooks, and Constance who might scare again tonight and show up to yank off my Band-aids. This was *my* idea to bring you here!

but now you stand there like a high I.Q. clown about to jump off a cliff!"

"Poor holy man. Poor sap. Poor priest," I replied.

"Oh, no you don't!"

And Crumley drove off.

61

I wandered through a church that was small in dimension but burning bright with accoutrements. I stood looking at an altar that must have used up five million dollars' worth of gold and silver. The Christ figure up front, if melted down, could have bought half of the U.S. Mint. It was while I was standing there stunned by the light coming off that cross that I heard Father Kelly behind me.

"Is that the screenwriter who telephoned with the problem?" he called quietly from across the pews.

I studied the incredibly bright altar. "You must have had many rich worshipers, father," I said.

Arbuthnot, I thought.

"No, it's an empty church in an empty time." Father Kelly plowed down the aisle and stuck out a big paw. He was tall, six feet five and with the muscularity of an athlete. "We are lucky to have a few parishioners whose consciences make constant problems. They *force* their money on the church."

"You tell the truth, father."

"I'd damn well better or God will get me." He laughed. "It's rough taking money from ulcerating sinners, but it's better than having them throw it at the horses. They've a better chance of winning here, for I *do* scare the Jesus into them. While the psychiatrists are busy talking, I give one hell of a yell, which knocks the pants off half my parish and makes the rest put theirs back on. Come sit. Do you like scotch? I often think, if Christ lived now, would he serve that and would we mind? That's Irish logic. Come along."

In his office, he poured two snifters.

"I can see by your eyes you hate the stuff," observed the priest. "Leave it. Have you come about that fool's film they're just finishing at the studio over there? Is Fritz Wong as mad as some say?"

"And as fine."

"It's good to hear a writer praise his boss. I rarely did."

"You!?" I exclaimed.

Father Kelly laughed. "As a young man I wrote nine screen-plays, none ever shot, or *should* have been shot, at sunrise. Until age thirty-five I did my damnedest to sell, sell-out, get-in, get-on. Then I said to hell with it and joined the priesthood, late. It was hard. The church does not take such as me off the streets frivolously. But I sprinted through seminary in style, for I had worked on a mob of Christian documentary films. Now what of you?"

I sat laughing.

"What's funny?" asked Father Kelly.

"I have this notion that half the writers at the studio, knowing about your years of writing, might just sneak over here not for confession but answers! How do you write *this* scene, how end *that*, how edit, how—"

"You've rammed the boat and sunk the crew!" The priest downed his whiskey and refilled, chortling, and then he and I rambled, like two old screen toughs, over movie-script country. I told him my Messiah, he told me his Christ.

Then he said: "Sounds like you've done well, patching the script. But then the old boys, two thousand years back, did patchwork too, if you remark the difference between Matthew and John."

I stirred in my chair with a furious need to babble, but dared not throw boiling oil on a priest while he dispensed cool holy spring water.

I stood up. "Well, thanks, father."

He looked at my outstretched hand. "You carry a gun," he said, easily, "but you've not fired it. Put your behind back on that chair."

"Do all priests talk like that?"

"In Ireland, yes. You've danced around the tree, but shaken no apples. Shake."

"I think I *will* have a bit of this." I picked up the snifter and sipped. "Well . . . Imagine that I were a Catholic—"

"I'm imagining."

"In need of confession—"

"They always are."

"And came here after midnight—"

"An odd hour." But a candle was lit in each of his eyes.

"And knocked on the door—"

"Would you *do* that?" He leaned slightly toward me. "Go on."

"Would you let me in?" I asked.

I might have shoved him back in his chair.

"Once, weren't churches open all hours?" I pursued.

"Long ago," he said, much too quickly.

"So, father, any night I came in dire need, you would *not* answer?"

"Why wouldn't I?" The candlelight flared in his eyes, as if I had raised the wick to quicken the flare.

"For the worst sinner, maybe, in the history of the world, father?"

"There's no such *creature*." Too late, his tongue froze on this last dread noun. His eyes swiveled and batted. He revised his proclamation to give it a new go-round.

"No such *person* lives."

"But," I pursued, "what if damnation, Judas himself, came begging—" I stopped—"late?"

"Iscariot? I'd wake for him, yes."

"And what if, father, this lost terrible man in need should knock not one night a week but most nights of the year? Would you wake, or ignore the knock?"

That did it. Father Kelly leaped up as if I had pulled the great cork. The color sank from his cheeks and the skin at the roots of his hair.

"You have need to be elsewhere. I will not keep you."

"No, father." I floundered to be brave. "*You* need me to be gone. There was a knock on your door—" I blundered on— "twenty years ago this week, late. Asleep, you heard the door banged—"

"No, no more of this! Get off!"

It was the terrified shout of Starbuck, decrying Ahab's blasphemy and his final lowering for the great white flesh.

"Out!"

"Out? You *did* go out, father." My heart jumped and almost slewed me in my chair. "And let in the crash and the din and the blood. Perhaps you heard the cars strike. Then the footsteps and then the bang and the voices yelling. Maybe the accident got out of hand, if accident it was. Maybe they needed a proper midnight witness, someone to see but not tell. You let in the truth and have kept it since."

I rose to stand and almost fainted. My rise, as if we were on weights and pulleys, sank the priest back, all but boneless, in his chair.

"You were witness, father, were you not? For it's just a few yards off and, on Halloween night, 1934, didn't they bring the victims here?"

"God help me," mourned the priest, "yes."

One moment full of fiery air, Father Kelly now gave up his inflammatory ghost and sank, fold on fold, flesh on flesh, into himself.

"Were they all dead when the crowd carried them in?"

"Not all," said the priest, in shocked recall.

"Thanks, father."

"For what?" He had closed his eyes with the headache of remembrance and now sprang them wide in renewed pain. "Do you know what you've got into?!"

"I'm afraid to ask."

"Then go home, wash your face and, sinful advice, get drunk!"

"It's too late for that. Father Kelly, did you give the last rites to any or all?"

Father Kelly shook his head back and forth, wigwagging as if to sign away the ghosts.

"Suppose I did?!"

"The man named Sloane?"

"Was dead. I blessed him, in spite."

"The other man—?"

"The big one, the famous one, the all powerful—?"

"Arbuthnot," I finished.

"Him, I signed and spoke and touched with water. And then he died."

"Cold and dead, stretched out forever, *really* dead?"

"Christ, the way you put it!" He sucked air and expelled it: "All that—*yes!*"

"And the woman?" I asked.

"Was the worst!" he cried, new paleness firing the old paleness in his cheeks. "Daft. Crazed and worse than crazed. Out of mind and body and not to be put back in. Trapped between the two. My God, it reminded me of plays I'd seen as a young man. Snow falling. Ophelia suddenly dressed in a terrible pale quiet as she steps into the water and does not so much drown as melt into a final madness, a silence so cold you could not cut it with a knife or sound it with a shout. Not even death could shake that woman's newfound winter. You hear *that*? A psychiatrist said that once! The eternal winter. Snow country from which rare travelers return. The Sloane woman, caught between bodies, out there in the rectory, not knowing how to escape. So she just turned to drown herself. The bodies were taken out by the studio people who had brought them in for respite."

He talked to the wall. Now he turned to gaze at me, stricken with alarms and growing hate. "The whole thing lasted, what? an hour? Yet it has haunted me these years."

"Emily Sloane, *mad*—?"

"A woman led her away. An actress. I've forgotten the name.

Emily Sloane did not know she was taken. She died the next week or the week after, I heard."

"No," I said. "There was a triple burial three days later. Arbuthnot alone. The Sloanes together, or so the story goes."

The priest regrouped his tale. "No matter. She died."

"It matters a great deal." I leaned forward. "Where did she die?"

"All I know is she did not go to the morgue across the street."

"To a hospital, then?"

"You've got all I know."

"Not all, father, but *some*—"

I walked to the rectory window to peer out at the cobbled courtyard and the drive leading in.

"If I ever came back, would you tell the same story?"

"I should not have told you anything! I have breached my confessional vows!"

"No, none of what you've said was told in private. It simply happened. You saw it. And now it's done you good to confess at last to me."

"Go." The priest sighed, poured another drink, slugged it back. It did nothing to color his cheeks. He only sagged more awry in his flesh. "I am very tired."

I opened the door of the rectory and looked along the hall toward the altar bright with jewels and silver and gold.

"How is it such a small church has such rich interiors?" I said. "The baptistry alone could finance a cardinal and elect a pope."

"Once," Father Kelly gazed into his empty glass, "I might have gladly consigned you to the fires of hell."

The glass fell from his fingers. He did not move to pick up the pieces. "Goodbye," I said.

I stepped out into sunlight.

Across two empty lots and a third, heading north from the back of the church, there were weeds and long grass and wild clover and late sunflowers nodding in a warm wind. Just beyond was a two-story white frame house with the name in unlit neon above: HOLLYHOCK HOUSE SANITARIUM.

I saw two ghosts on the path through the weeds. One woman leading another, going away.

"An actress," Father Kelly had said. "I forget the name."

The weeds blew down the path with a dry whisper.

One ghost woman came back on the path alone, weeping.

"Constance—?" I called out quietly.

62

I walked around down Gower and over to look in through the studio gate.

Hitler in his underground bunker in the last days of the Third Reich, I thought.

Rome burning and Nero in search of more torches.

Marcus Aurelius in his bath, slitting his wrists, letting his life drain.

Just because someone, somewhere, was yelling orders, hiring painters with too much paint, men with immense vacuum cleaners to snuff the suspicious dust.

Only one gate of the whole studio was open, with three guards standing alert to let the painters and cleaners in and out, checking the faces.

At which point Stanislau Groc roared up inside the gate in his bright red British Morgan, gunned the engine, and cried: "Out!"

"No, sir," said the guard quietly. "Orders from upstairs. Nobody leaves the studio for the next two hours."

"But I'm a citizen of the city of Los Angeles! not this damn duchy!"

"Does that mean," I said through the grille, "if I come in, I can't go out?"

The guard touched his cap visor and said my name. "You can come in, *and* out. Orders."

"Strange," I said. "Why me?"

"Dammit!" Groc started to get out of his car.

I stepped through the small door in the grille and opened the side door of Groc's Morgan.

"Can you drop me at Maggie's editing room? By the time you're back they'll probably let you out."

"No. We're trapped," said Groc. "This ship's been sinking all week, and no lifeboats. Run, before you drown, too!"

"Now, now," said the guard quietly. "No paranoia."

"Listen to him!" Groc's face was chalk-pale. "The great studio-guard psychiatrist! You, get in. It's your last ride!"

I hesitated and looked down into a face that was a crosshatch of emotions. All the parts of Groc's usually brave and arrogant front were melting. It was like a test pattern on a TV screen, blurred, clearing up, then dissolving. I climbed in and slammed the door, which banged the car off on a maniac path.

"Hey, what's the rush!?"

We gunned by the sound stages. Each one was wide open and airing. The exteriors of at least six of them were being repainted. Old sets were being wrecked and carried out into the sunlight.

"On any other day, lovely!" Groc shouted above his engine. "I would have loved this. Chaos is my meat. Stockmarkets crashed? Ferryboats capsized? Superb! I went back to Dresden in 1946 just to see the destroyed buildings and shell-shocked people."

"You didn't?!"

"Wouldn't you like to have seen? Or the fires in London in 1940. Every time mankind behaves abominably, I know happiness!"

"Don't *good* things make you happy? Artistic people, creative men and women?"

"No, no." Groc sped on. "*That* depresses. A lull between stupidities. Just because there are a few naïve fools mucking up the landscape with their cut roses and still-life arts only shows in greater relief the troglodytes, midget worms and sidewinding vipers that oil the underground machineries and run the world to ruin. I decided years ago, since the continents are vast sludge works, I would buy the best-size boots and wallow in it like a babe. But this is ridiculous, us locked inside a stupid factory. I want to laugh at, not be destroyed by, it. Hold on!" We swerved past Calvary.

I almost yelled.

For Calvary was gone.

Beyond, the incinerator lifted great plumes of black smoke.

"That must be the three crosses," I said.

"Good!" Groc snorted. "I wonder—will J. C. sleep at the Midnight Mission tonight?"

I swiveled my head to look at him.

"You know J. C. well?"

"The muscatel Messiah? *I* made him! As I made others' eyebrows and bosoms, why not Christ's hands! So I pared the extra flesh to make his fingers seem delicate: the hands of a Saviour. Why not? Is not religion a joke? People think they are saved. We know they're not. But the crown-of-thorns touch, the stigmata!" Groc shut his eyes as he almost drove into a telephone pole, swerved and stopped.

"I guessed you had done that," I said, at last.

"If you act Christ, *be* Him! I told J. C. I will make you spike marks to show at Renaissance exhibitions! I will sew you the stigmata of Masaccio, da Vinci, Michelangelo! From the Pietà's marble flesh! And, as you've seen, on special nights—"

"—the stigmata bleed."

I knocked the car door wide. "I think I'll walk the rest of the way."

"No, no," Groc apologized, laughing shrilly. "I need you. What an irony! To get me out the front gate, later. Go talk to Botwin, then we run like hell."

I held the door half open, undecided. Groc seemed in such a joyful panic, hilarious to the point of hysteria, I could only shut the door. Groc drove on.

"Ask, ask," said Groc.

"Okay," I tried. "What about all those faces you made beautiful?"

Groc pedaled the gas.

"They'll last forever, I told them, and the fools believed. Anyway, I am retiring, *if* I can get out the front gate. I have bought passage on a round-the-world cruise tomorrow. After thirty years my laughs have turned to snake spit. Manny Leiber? Will die any day. Doc? Did you know? He's gone."

"Where?"

"Who knows?" But Groc's eyes slid north toward the studio graveyard wall. "Excommunicated?"

We drove. Groc nodded ahead. "Now Maggie Botwin I like. She's a perfectionist surgeon, like me."

"She doesn't sound like you."

"If she ever did, she'd die. And you? Well, disillusionment takes time. You'll be seventy before you find you've crossed minefields yelling to an idiot troop, this way! Your films will be forgotten."

"No," I said.

Groc glanced over at my set chin and stubborn upper lip.

"No," he admitted. "You have the look of the true sainted fool. Not *your* films."

We rounded another corner and I nodded to the carpenters, the cleaners, and painters: "Who ordered all this work?"

"Manny, of course."

"Who ordered Manny? Who *really* gives orders here? Someone behind a mirror? Someone inside a wall?"

Groc braked the car swiftly and looked ahead. I could see the stitch marks around his ears, nice and clear.

"It can't be answered."

"No?" I said. "I look around, what do I see? A studio, in the midst of production on eight films. One a huge one, our Jesus epic, with two more days of shooting to go. And suddenly, on a whim, someone says: Slam the doors. And the crazed painting and cleaning happens. It's madness to shut a studio with a budget that runs at least ninety to a hundred thousand dollars a day. What gives?"

"What?" said Groc, quietly.

"Well, I see Doc and he's a jellyfish, poisonous, but no spine.

I look at Manny and his behind is just right for highchairs. You?
There's a mask behind your mask and another under that. None
of you have the dynamite kegs or the electric pump plunger to
knock the whole damn studio down. Yet down it goes. I see a
studio as big as a white whale. Harpoons fly. So there's got to
be a real maniac captain."

"Tell me, then," Groc said, "Who *is* Ahab?"

"A dead man standing on a ladder in the graveyard, looking
over, giving orders. And you all run," I said.

Groc blinked three slow iguana-lizard blinks of his great dark
eyes.

"Not me," he said, smiling.

"No? Why not?"

"Because, you damned fool." Groc beamed, looking at the sky.
"Think! There are only two geniuses smart enough to have man-
ufactured that dead man of yours on that ladder in the rain to
look over the wall and stop people's hearts!" And here Groc was
taken with a paroxysm of laughter that almost killed. "Who could
model a face like that!"

"Roy Holdstrom!"

"Yes! And?!"

"Lenin's—" I stammered—"Lenin's makeup man?"

Stanislau Groc turned the full light of his smile on me.

"Stanislau Groc," I said, numbly. ". . . *You.*"

He bowed his head modestly.

You! I thought. Not the Beast hiding in the tombs, climbing
the ladder to position the scarecrow Arbuthnot and stop the
studio dead, no! But Groc, the man who laughs, the tiny Conrad
Veidt with the eternal grin sewn to his face!

"Why?" I said.

"Why?" Groc smirked. "My God, to stir things *up*! Jesus, it's
been boring here for years! Doc sick with needles. Manny ripping
himself in two. Myself, not getting enough laughs on this ship
of fools. So raise the dead! But you spoiled it, found the body
but told no one. I hoped you'd run yelling through the streets.

Instead, the next day, you clammed up. I had to make a few anonymous calls to get the studio into the graveyard. Then, riots! Pandemonium."

"Did you send the other note to coax me and Roy to the Brown Derby to see the Beast?"

"I did."

"And all," I said, numbly, "for a *joke*?"

"Not quite. The studio, as you have noticed, sits astride that ravenous crack known as the San Andreas fault, ripe for quakes. I felt them months ago. So I propped the ladder and raised the dead. And raised my pay so you might say."

"Blackmail," Crumley whispered in the back of my mind.

Groc squirmed with joy at his own telling: "Scare Manny, Doc, J. C., everyone, including the Beast!"

"The Beast? You wanted to scare *him*?!"

"Why not? The mob! The bunch! Get them all to pay, as long as they didn't find out I was behind it. Run a riot, take the payola, head for the exit!"

"Which means, good God," I said, "you must have known everything about Arbuthnot's past, his death. Was he poisoned? Was *that* it?"

"Ah," said Groc, "theories, speculations."

"How many people know you've bought that round-the-world ticket?"

"Only you, poor sad lovely doomed boy. But I think someone's guessed. Why else is the front gate shut and me trapped?"

"Yes," I said. "They just threw Christ's tomb out with the lumber. They need a body to go with it."

"Me," Groc said, suddenly bleak.

A studio police car had pulled up beside us.

A guard leaned out.

"Manny Leiber wants you."

Groc sank down, his flesh into his blood, his blood into his soul, his soul into nothingness.

"This is it," whispered Groc.

I thought of Manny's office and the mirror behind the desk and the catacombs beyond the mirror.

"Break and run," I said.

"Fool," said Groc. "How far would I get?" Groc patted my hand with trembling fingers. "You're a jerk, but a good jerk. No, from here on, anyone seen with me goes down the maelstrom when they pull the chain. Here."

He shoved his briefcase over on the seat, opened it and shut it again. I saw a flash of bundled one-hundred-dollar bills.

"Grab," said Groc. "It's no use to me now. Hide it fast. High-on-the-hog money for the rest of your life."

"No, thanks."

He gave it another shove against my leg. I pulled away, as if a dagger of ice had stabbed my knee.

"Jerk," he said. "But a good jerk."

I got out.

The police car, creeping ahead, its motor puttering, honked its horn quietly, once. Groc stared at it and then at me, looking at my ears, my eyelids, my chin.

"Your skin won't need work for, oh, thirty years, give or take a year."

His mouth was thick with phlegm. He swiveled his eyes, grasped the wheel with snatching, grappling fingers, and drove away.

The police car turned the corner, his car followed, a small funeral cortège moving toward the back studio wall.

63

I climbed the stairs to Maggie Botwin's palace of reptiles. So called because of all the dropped scenes, the sidewinder film coils in the bin or slithering across the floor.

The small room was empty. The old ghosts had fled. The snakes had gone to ground somewhere else.

I stood in the middle of empty shelves, looking around until I found a note pasted to the top of her silent Moviola.

DEAR GENIUS. TRIED CALLING YOU DURING THE PAST TWO HOURS. WE HAVE QUIT THE BATTLE OF JERICHO AND FLED. WE WILL FIGHT THE FINAL BATTLE AT MY HILLSIDE BUNKER. CALL. COME! SIEG HEIL, FRITZ AND JACQUELINE THE RIPPER.

I folded the note to stash in my diary and read in my old age. I walked down the steps and out of the studio.

There were no storm troopers in sight.

64

Walking along the shore, I told Crumley about the priest, and the path through the weeds and the two women walking there a long time ago.

We found Constance Rattigan on the beach. It was the first time I had ever seen her lying on the sand. Always before she was in her pool or in the sea. Now she lay between, as if she had no strength to go in the water or back to her house. She was so beached, stranded, and pale it hurt me to see.

We crouched down on the sand beside her and waited for her to feel us there, eyes shut.

"You've been lying," Crumley said.

Her eyeballs revolved under her lids. "Which lie do you mean?"

"About your running away in the midst of that midnight party, twenty years ago. You know you stayed until the very end."

"What did I do?" She turned her head away. We could not see if she was looking out at the gray sea, where an early-afternoon fog was rolling in to spoil the hour.

"*They* brought you to the scene of the accident. A friend of yours needed help."

"I never had any friends."

"Come on, Constance," said Crumley, "I've got the facts. I've been collecting facts. Newspapers say there were three funerals on the same day. Father Kelly, over at that church near where the accident really happened, says Emily Sloane died *after* the funerals. What if I got a court order to break into the Sloanes' tomb? Would there be one body there or two? One, I think, and Emily gone where? And who took her? You? On whose orders?"

Constance Rattigan's body trembled. I could not tell if it was some old grief suddenly surfaced in shock, or just the mist now moving around us.

"For a dumb dick, you're pretty smart," she said.

"No, just some days I fall in a nest of eggs and don't break one. Father Kelly told our screenwriter friend here that Emily's mind was gone. So she had to be led. Were you in charge?"

"God help me," whispered Constance Rattigan. A wave fell on the shore. A thicker fog reached the surf-line. "Yes . . ."

Crumley nodded quietly and said: "There must have been a big, a terrible, God knows, a huge coverup, on the spot. Did someone stuff the poorbox? I mean, did the studio promise to, hell, I don't know, redecorate the altar, finance widows and orphans forever? Hand the priest an impossible fortune every week if he forgot that you walked Emily Sloane *out* of there?"

"That—" murmured Constance, eyes wide, sitting up now, searching the horizon—"was part of it."

"And more money in the poorbox, and more and more, if the priest said the accident happened not in front of his church but down the street maybe a hundred yards, so he *didn't* see Arbuthnot ram the other car, kill his enemy, or his enemy's wife gone mad at their deaths. Yes?"

"That—" murmured Constance Rattigan, in another year, "almost does it."

"And did you lead Emily Sloane out of the church an hour later, and, good as dead, did you lead her across an empty lot full of sunflowers and FOR SALE signs—"

"Everything was so close, so convenient, it was a laugh," remembered Constance, not laughing, her face gray. "The graveyard, the undertaking parlor, the church for some quick funerals, the empty lot, the path, and Emily? Hell. She had gone ahead, in her mind, anyway. All I had to do was steer."

"And, Constance," Crumley said, "is Emily Sloane alive today?"

Constance turned her face a frame at a time, like a stop-motion doll, taking about ten seconds to move frame by frame until she was looking right through me, with eyes adjusted to the wrong focus.

"When," I said, "was the last time you took a gift of flowers to a marble sculpture? To a statue that never saw flowers, never saw you, but lived inside the marble, inside all that silence, when was the last time?"

A single tear dropped from Constance Rattigan's right eye.

"I used to go every week. I was always hoping she'd just come up out of the water like an iceberg and melt. But finally I couldn't stand the silence and not being thanked. She made me feel I was dead."

Her head moved frame by frame back in the other direction toward a memory of last year or some year before.

"I think," Crumley said, "it's time for some more flowers. Yes?"

"I don't know."

"Yes, you do. How about. . . . Hollyhock House?"

Quickly, Constance Rattigan jumped up, glanced at the sea, sprinted for the surf, and dived in.

"Don't!" I yelled.

For I was suddenly afraid. Even for fine swimmers the sea could take and not give back.

I ran to the surf-line and started to shuck off my shoes, when Constance, spraying water like a seal and shaking like a dog, exploded from the waves and trudged in. When she hit the hard, wet sand she stopped and threw up. It popped out of her mouth like a cork. She stood, hands on hips, looking down at the stuff on the surf-line as the tide drifted it away.

"I'll be damned," she said, curiously. "That hairball must've been in there all those years!"

She turned to look me up and down, the color coming back into her cheeks. She flicked her fingers at me, tossing sea-rain on my face, as if to freshen me.

"Does swimming," I pointed at the ocean, "*always* make you well?"

"The day it doesn't I'll never come out again," she said quietly. "A quick swim, a quick lay works. I can't help Arbuthnot or Sloane, they're rotten dead. Or Emily Wickes—"

She froze, then changed the name, "Emily *Sloane*."

"Is Wickes her *new* name, for twenty years, at Hollyhock House?" Crumley asked.

"With my hairball out, I need some champagne in. C'mon."

She opened a bottle by her blue-tiled pool and poured our glasses full.

"You going to be fool enough to try to save Emily Wickes Sloane, alive or dead, this late in time?"

"Who'll stop us?" said Crumley.

"The whole studio! No, maybe three people who know she's there. You'll need introductions. No one gets in Hollyhock House without Constance Rattigan. Don't look at me that way. I'll help."

Crumley drank his champagne and said: "One last thing. Who took charge that night, twenty years ago. It must have been bad. Who—"

"Directed it? It had to be directed, sure. People were running over each other, screaming. It was *Crime and Punishment, War and Peace.* Someone had to yell: Not *this* way, *that*! In the middle of the night with all the screams and blood, thank God, he saved the scene, the actors, the studio, all with no film in his camera. The greatest living German director."

"Fritz Wong!?" I exploded.

"Fritz," said Constance Rattigan, "Wong."

65

Fritz's eyrie, halfway up from the Beverly Hills Hotel toward Mulholland, had a view of some ten million lights on the vast floor of Los Angeles. From a long elegant marble porch fronting his villa, you could watch the jets fifteen miles away coming in to land, bright torches, slow meteors in the sky, one every minute.

Fritz Wong yanked his house door wide and blinked out, pretending not to see me.

I handed over his monocle from my pocket. He seized and slotted it.

"Arrogant son of a bitch." The monocle flashed from his right eye like a guillotine blade. "So! It's *you*! The coming-great arrives to bug the soon-vanishing. The ascendant king knocks up the has-been prince. The writer who tells the lions what to say to Daniel visits the tamer who tells them what to *do*. What are you doing here? The film is *kaput*!"

"Here are the pages." I walked in. "Maggie? you *okay*?"

Maggie, in a far corner of the parlor, nodded, pale, but, I could see, recovered.

"Ignore Fritz," she said. "He's full of codswallop and liverwurst."

"Go sit with the Slasher and shut up," said Fritz, letting his monocle burn holes in my pages.

"Yes—" I looked at Hitler's picture on the wall and clicked my heels—"sir!"

Fritz glanced up, angrily. "Stupid! That picture of the maniac housepainter is there to remind me of the big bastards I ran from so as to arrive at little ones. Dear God, the facade of Maximus Films is a clone of the Brandenburg Gate! *Sitzfleisch*, down!"

I downed my *Sitzfleisch* and gaped.

For just beyond Maggie Botwin was the most incredible religious shrine I had ever seen. It was brighter, bigger, more beauteous than the silver and gold altar at St. Sebastian's.

"Fritz," I exclaimed.

For this dazzling shrine was shelved with crème de menthes, brandies, whiskeys, cognacs, ports, Burgundies and Bordeaus, stored in layers of crystal and bright glass tubing. It gleamed like an undersea grotto from which schools of luminous bottles might swarm. Above and around it hung scores and hundreds of fine Swedish cut crystal, Lalique, and Waterford. It was a celebratory throne, the birthing place of Louis the Fourteenth, an Egyptian Sun King's tomb, Napoleon's Empiric Coronation dais. It was a toyshop window at midnight on Christmas Eve. It was—

"As you know," I said, "I rarely drink—"

Fritz's monocle fell. He caught and replanted it.

"What will you have?" he barked.

I avoided his contempt by remembering a wine I had heard him mention.

"Corton," I said, " '38."

"Do you really expect me to open my best wine for someone like you?"

I swallowed hard and nodded.

He hauled off and swung his fist toward the ceiling as if to pound me into the floor. Then the fist came down, delicately, and opened a lid on a cabinet to pull out a bottle.

Corton, 1938.

He worked the corkscrew, gritting his teeth and eying me. "I shall watch every sip," he growled. "If you betray, by the merest expression, that you don't appreciate—ssst!"

He pulled the cork beautifully and set the bottle down to breathe.

"Now," he sighed, "though the film is twice dead, let's see how the boy wonder has done!" He sank into the chair and riffled my new pages. "Let me read your unbearable text. Though why we should pretend we will ever return to the slaughterhouse, God knows!" He shut his left eye and let his right eye, behind the bright glass, shift, and shift again. Finished, he threw the pages to the floor and nodded, angrily, for Maggie to pick them up. He watched her face, meanwhile pouring the wine. "Well!?" he cried, impatiently.

Maggie put the pages in her lap and laid her hands on them, as if they were gospel.

"I could weep. And? I *am*."

"Cut the comedy!" Fritz gulped his wine, then stopped, angry at me for making him drink so quickly. "You couldn't have written that in a few hours!"

"Sorry," I apologized, sheepishly. "Only the fast stuff is good. Slow down, you *think* what you're doing and it gets bad."

"Thinking is fatal, is it?" demanded Fritz. "What, do you *sit* on your brain while you type?"

"I dunno. Hey, this isn't *bad* wine."

"Not bad!" Fritz raged at the ceiling. "A 1938 Corton and he says not bad! Better than all those damn candy bars I see you chewing around the studio. Better than all the women in the world. Almost."

"This wine," I said quickly, "is almost as good as your films."

"Excellent." Fritz, shot through his ego, smiled. "You could almost be Hungarian."

Fritz refilled my glass and gave back my medal of honor, his monocle.

"Young wine expert, why else did you come?"

The time was right. "Fritz," I said, "on October 31st, 1934, you directed, photographed, and cut a film titled *Wild Party*."

Fritz was lying back in his chair, with his legs straight out, the wine glass in his right hand. His left hand crawled up toward the pocket where his monocle should have been.

Fritz's mouth opened lazily, coolly. "Again?"

"Halloween night, 1934—"

"More." Fritz, eyes shut, held out his glass.

I poured.

"If you spill I'll throw you down the stairs." Fritz's face was pointed at the ceiling. As he felt the weight of the wine in the glass, he nodded and I pulled away to refill my own.

"Where," Fritz's mouth worked as if it were separate from the rest of his impassive face, "did you hear of such a dumb film with a stupid title?"

"It was shot with no film in the camera. You directed it for maybe two hours. Shall I tell you the actors that night?"

Fritz opened one eye and tried to focus across the room without his monocle.

"Constance Rattigan," I recited, "J. C., Doc Phillips, Manny Leiber, Stanislau Groc, and Arbuthnot, Sloane, and his wife, Emily Sloane."

"God damn, that's quite a cast," said Fritz.

"Want to tell me why?"

Fritz sat up slowly, cursed, drank his wine, then sat hunched over the glass, looking in it for a long while. Then he blinked and said:

"So at last I get to tell. I've been waiting to vomit all these years. Well . . . *someone* had to direct. There was no script. Total madness. I was brought in at the last moment."

"How much," I said, "did you improvise?"

"Most, no, *all* of it," said Fritz. "There were bodies all over. Well, not bodies. People and lots of blood. I had my camera along for the night, you know, a party like that and you like to catch people offguard, at least I did. The first part of the evening was fine. People screaming and running back and forth through the studio and through the tunnel and dancing in the graveyard with a jazz band. It was wild, all right, and terrific. Until it got out of hand. The accident, that is. By then, you're right, there was no film in my 16-millimeter camera. So I gave orders. Run here. Run there. *Don't* call the police. Get the cars. Stuff the poorbox."

"I guessed at that."

"Shut up! The poor bastard priest, like the lady, was going nuts. The studio always kept lots of cash on hand for emergencies. We loaded the baptismal font like a Thanksgiving feast, right in front of the priest. I never knew, that night, if he even *saw* what we did, he was in such shock. I ordered the Sloane woman out of there. An extra took her."

"No," I said. "A star."

"Yes!? She went. While we picked up the pieces and covered our tracks. It was easier to do, back then. The studios, after all, ran the town. We had one body, Sloane's, to show and another, Arbuthnot's, in the mortuary, we said, and Doc signing the death certificates. Nobody ever asked to see *all* the bodies. We paid off the coroner to take a year's sick leave. That's how it was done."

Fritz drew in his legs, cradled his drink over his groin, and searched the air for the sight of my face.

"Luckily, because of the studio party, J. C., Doc Phillips, Groc, Manny, and all the yes-men were there. I yelled: Bring guards. Bring cars. Cordon off the crash. People come out of houses? Shout them back with bullhorns! Again, on that street, few houses, and the gas station shut. The rest? Law offices, all dark. By the time a real crowd came from blocks away, in their pajamas, I had parted the Red Sea, reburied Lazarus, got new jobs for the Doubting Thomases in far places! Delicious, wondrous, superb! Another drink?"

"What's *that* stuff?"

"Napoleon brandy. One hundred years old. You'll hate it!"

He poured. "If you make a face, I'll kill you."

"What about the bodies?" I asked.

"There was only one dead to start. Sloane. Arbuthnot was smashed, Christ, to a pulp, but still alive. I did what I could, got him across the street to the undertaking rooms; and left. Arbuthnot died later. Both Doc Phillips and Groc worked to save him, in that place where they embalm bodies, but now an emergency hospital. Ironic, yes? Two days later, I directed the funeral. Again, superb!"

"And Emily Sloane? Hollyhock House?"

"The last I saw of her, she was being led off across that empty lot full of wild flowers, to that private sanitarium. Dead next day.

That's all I know. I was merely a director called in to lifeboat the Hindenburg as it burned, or be traffic manager to the San Francisco earthquake. Those are my credits. Now, why, why, why do you ask?"

I took a deep breath, glugged down some Napoleon brandy, felt my eyes faucet with hot water, and said: "Arbuthnot is back."

Fritz sat straight up and shouted, "Are you *mad*!?"

"Or his image," I said, almost squeaking. "Groc did it. For a lark, he said. Or for money. Made a papier-mâché and wax dummy. Set it up to scare Manny and the others, maybe with the same facts you know but have never said."

Fritz Wong arose to stalk in a circle, clubbing the carpet with his boots. Then he stood rocking back and forth, shaking his great head, in front of Maggie.

"Did you know about this!?"

"Junior, here, said something—"

"Why didn't you *tell* me?"

"Because, Fritz," Maggie reasoned, "when you're directing you never want to hear any news, bad or good, from anyone!"

"So that's what's been going on?" said Fritz. "Doc Phillips drunk at lunch three days running. Manny Leiber's voice sounding like a slow L.P. played double speed. Christ, I thought it was me doing things right, which *always* upsets him! No! Holy Jesus, God, oh dammit to hell, that bastard Groc." He stopped to fix on me. "Bringers of bad news to the king are executed!" he cried. "But before you die, tell us more!"

"Arbuthnot's tomb is empty."

"His body—? Stolen?"

"He was never *in* his tomb, ever."

"Who says?" he cried.

"A blind man."

"Blind!" Fritz made fists again. I wondered if all these years he had driven his actors like numbed beasts with those fists. "A blind man!?" The Hindenburg sank in him with a final terrible fire. After that . . . ashes.

"A blind man—" Fritz wandered slowly around the room, ignoring us both, sipping his brandy. "Tell."

I told everything I had so far told Crumley.

When I finished, Fritz picked up the phone and, holding it two inches from his eyes, squinting, dialed a number.

"Hello, Grace? Fritz Wong. Get me flights to New York, Paris, Berlin. *When?* Tonight! I'll wait on the line!"

He turned to look out the window, across the miles toward Hollywood.

"Christ, I felt the earthquake all week and thought it was Jesus dying from a lousy script. Now it's all dead. We'll never go back. They'll recycle our film into celluloid collars for Irish priests. Tell Constance to run. Then buy yourself a ticket."

"To where?" I asked.

"You must have somewhere to go!" bellowed Fritz.

In the middle of this great bomb burst, a valve somewhere in Fritz popped. Not hot but cold air rushed out of his body. His bad eye developed a tic that grew outsize.

"Grace," he cried into the telephone, "don't listen to that idiot who just called. Cancel New York. Get me Laguna! What? Down the coast, dimwit. A house facing the Pacific so I can wade in like Norman Maine at sunset, should Doom itself knock down the door. What? To hide. What good is Paris; the maniacs here would know. But they'd never expect a stupid Unterseeboot Kapitän who hates sunlight to wind up in Sol City, South Laguna, with all those mindless naked bums. Get a limo here now! I expect you to have a house waiting when I reach Victor Hugo's restaurant at nine. Go!" Fritz slammed down the phone to glare at Maggie. "You coming?"

Maggie Botwin was a nice dish of nonmelting vanilla ice cream. "Dear Fritz," she said. "I was born in Glendale in 1900. I could go back there and die of boredom or I could hide in Laguna, but all those 'bums,' as you call them, make my girdle creep. Anyway, Fritz, and you, my dear young man, I was here every night at three A.M. that year, pedaling my Singer sewing machine, sewing up nightmares to make them look like halfway not so disreputable dreams, wiping the smirk off dirty little girls' mouths and dropping it in the trash bins behind the badly dented cots in the men's gym. I have never liked parties, either Sunday-afternoon cocktails or Saturday-night sumo wrestling. Whatever happened that Halloween night, I was waiting for someone, anyone, to deliver me film. It never came. If a car crash happened beyond the wall I never heard. If there was one or a thousand funerals the next week I refused all invitations and cut the stale flowers, here. I didn't go downstairs to see Arbuthnot when he lived, why should I go see him dead? He used to climb up and stand outside the screen door. I'd look out at him, tall in the sunlight, and say, You need a little editing! And he'd laugh and never come in, just tell the dressmaker tailor lady how he wanted so-and-so's face, near or far, in or out, and leave. How did I get away with being alone at the studio? It was a new business and there was only one tailor in town, me. The rest were pants pressers, job seekers, gypsies, fortunetelling screenwriters who couldn't read tea leaves. One Christmas Arby sent up to me a spinning wheel with a sharp spindle and a brass plate on the treadle: "GUARD THIS SO SLEEPING BEAUTY PRICKS NO FINGERS AND GETS NO SLEEP," it said. I wish I had known him, but he was just another shadow outside my screen door and I already had a sufficiency of shadows *in*. I saw only the mobs at his memorial trip out of here and around the block to cold comfort farm. Like everything else in life, including this sermon, it needed cutting." She looked down at her bosom, to hold some invisible beads, hung there for her restless fingers.

After a long silence, Fritz said, "Maggie Botwin will be quiet now for a year!"

"No." Maggie Botwin fixed me with her gaze. "You got any last notes on the rushes we've seen the last few days? You never know, tomorrow we may all be rehired at one-third the salary."

"No," I said lamely.

"To hell with that," said Fritz. "I'm packing!"

My taxi still waited, ticking off astronomical sums. Fritz stared at it with contempt. "Why don't you learn to drive, idiot?"

"And massacre people in the streets, Fritz Wong style? Is this goodbye, Rommel?"

"Only till the Allies take Normandy."

I got into the cab, then probed my coat pocket. "What about this monocle?"

"Flash it at the next Academy Awards. It'll get you a seat in the balcony. What're you waiting for, a hug? There!" He wrestled me, angrily. *"Outen zee ass!"*

As I drove away, Fritz yelled: "I keep forgetting to tell you how much I hate you!"

"Liar," I called.

"Yes," Fritz nodded and lifted his hand in a slow, tired salute, "—I lie."

"I've been thinking about Hollyhock House," said Crumley, "and your friend Emily Sloane."

"Not my friend, but go on."

"Insane people give me hope."

"What!!!!" I almost dropped my beer.

"The insane have decided to stay on," Crumley said. "They love life so much that, rather than destroy it, they go behind a self-made wall to hide. Pretend not to hear, but they *do* hear. Pretend not to see, but see. Insanity says: I hate living but love life. Hate the rules but *do* like *me*. So, rather than drop in graves, I hide out. Not in liquor, nor in bed under sheets, nor in a needle's prick or snuffs of white powder, but in madness. On my own shelf, in my own rafters, under my own silent roof. So, yeah, insane people give me hope. Courage to go on being sane and alive, always with the cure at hand, should I ever tire and need it: madness."

"*Give* me that beer!" I grabbed it. "How many of these you had?"

"Only eight."

"Christ." I shoved it back at him. "Is all this going to be part of your novel when it comes out?"

"Could be." Crumley gave a nice, easy, self-satisfied burp and went on. "If you got to choose between a billion years of darkness, no sun ever again, wouldn't you choose catatonia? You could still enjoy green grass and air that smells like cut watermelons. Still touch your knee, when no one was looking. And all the while you pretend not to care. But you care *so* much you build a crystal coffin and seal it on yourself."

"My God! Go on!"

"I ask, why choose madness? So as not to die, I say. Love is the answer. All of our senses are loves. We love life but fear what it does to us. So? Why not give madness a try?"

After a long silence, I said: "Where the hell is all this talk leading us?"

"To the madhouse," Crumley said.

"To talk to a catatonic?"

"It worked once, didn't it, a couple years ago, when I hypnotized you, so you finally almost recalled a killer?"

"Yeah, but I wasn't nuts!"

"Who says?"

I shut my mouth, Crumley opened his.

"Well," he said, "what if we took Emily Sloane to church?"

"Hell!"

"Don't 'hell' me. We all heard about her charities every year for Our Lady's on Sunset. How she gave away two hundred silver crucifixes two Easters running. Once a Catholic, always a Catholic."

"Even if she's mad?"

"But *she'd* be aware. Inside, behind her wall, she'd sense she was at mass and—talk."

"Rant, rave, maybe . . ."

"Maybe. But she knows everything. That's why she went mad, so she couldn't think or talk about it. She's the only one left, the others are dead, or hidden right in front of us, with their mouths shut for pay."

"And you think she'd feel enough, sense enough, know and remember? What if we drive her even more mad?"

"God, I don't know. It's the last lead we have. No one else will own up. You get half a story from Constance, another fourth from Fritz, and then there's the priest. A jigsaw, and Emily Sloane's the frame. Light the candles and incense. Sound the altar bell. Maybe she'll wake after seven thousand days and talk."

Crumley sat for a full minute, drinking slowly and heavily. Then he leaned forward and said:

"Now, do we get her *out*?"

67

We did not take Emily Sloane to church.

We brought the church to Emily Sloane.

Constance arranged it all.

Crumley and I brought candles, incense, and a brass bell made in India. We placed and lighted the candles in a shadowed room of the Hollyhock House Elysian Fields Sanitarium. I pinned some cotton cloths about my knees.

"What the hell's *that* for?" griped Crumley.

"Sound effects. It rustles. Like the priest's skirt."

"Jesus!" said Crumley.

"Well, yeah."

Then, with the candles lit, and Crumley and me standing well out of the way in an alcove, we fanned the incense and tested the bell. It made a fine, clear sound.

Crumley called quietly. "Constance? *Now.*"

And Emily Sloane arrived.

She did not move of her own volition, she did not walk, nor did her head turn or her eyes flex or motion in the carved marble face. The profile came first out of darkness above a rigid body and hands folded in gravestone serenity upon a lap made virgin by time. She was pushed, from behind, in her wheelchair, by an almost invisible stage manager, Constance Rattigan, dressed in black as for the rehearsal of an old funeral. As Emily Sloane's white face and terribly quiet body emerged from the hall, there was a motion as of birds taking off; we fanned the incense smokes and tapped the bell.

I cleared my throat.

"Shh, she's *listening!*" whispered Crumley.

And it was true.

As Emily Sloane came into the soft light, there was the faintest motion, the tiniest twitch of her eyes under the lids, as the imperceptible beat of the candle flames beckoned silence and leaned shadows.

I fanned the air.

I chimed the bell.

At this, Emily Sloane's body itself—wafted. Like a weightless kite, borne in an unseen wind, she shifted as if her flesh had melted away.

The bell rang again, and the smoke of the incense made her nostrils quiver.

Constance backed away into shadows.

Emily Sloane's head turned into the light.

"Ohmigod," I whispered.

It's her, I thought.

The blind woman who had come into the Brown Derby and left with the Beast on that night, it seemed a thousand nights ago.

And she was not blind.

Only catatonic.

But no ordinary catatonic.

Out of the grave and across the room in the smell and the smoke of incense and the sounding of the bell.

Emily Sloane.

Emily sat for ten minutes saying nothing. We counted our heartbeats. We watched the flames burn down the candles as the incense smoke sifted off.

And then at last the beautiful moment when her head tilted and her eyes dilated.

She must have sat another ten minutes, drinking in things remembered from long before the collision that had left her wrecked along the California coast.

I saw her mouth stir as her tongue moved behind her lips.

She wrote things on the inside of her eyelids, then gave them translation:

"No one . . ." she murmured, "under . . . stands . . ."

And then . . .

"No one . . . ever did."

Silence.

"He was . . ." she said at last, and stopped.

The incense smoked. The bell gave a small sound.

". . . the . . . studio . . . he . . . loved . . ."

I bit the back of my hand, waiting.

". . . place . . . to . . . play. Sets . . ."

Quietness. Her eyes twitched, remembering.

"Sets . . . toys . . . electric . . . trains. Boys, yes. Ten . . ." She took a breath. "Eleven . . . years . . . old."

The candle flames flickered.

". . . he . . . always said . . . Christmas . . . always . . . never away. He'd . . . die . . . if . . . it's not Christmas . . . silly man. But . . . twelve . . . he made . . . parents take back . . . socks . . . ties . . . sweaters. Christmas day. Buy toys. Or he wouldn't talk."

Her voice trailed off.

I glanced at Crumley. His eyes bulged from wanting to hear more, more. The incense blew. I chimed the bell.

"And . . . ?" he whispered for the first time. "*And . . . ?*"

"And . . ." she echoed. She read her lines off the inside of her eyelids. "That's . . . how he . . . ran . . . studio."

The bones had reappeared in her body. She was being structured up in her chair as if her remembrance pulled strings, and the old strengths and the lost life and substance of herself were eased in place. Even the bones in her face seemed to restructure her cheeks and chin. She talked faster now. And, finally, let it all come.

"Played. Yes. No work . . . played. The studio. When his father . . . died."

And as she talked, the words came now in threes and fours and finally in bursts and at long last in runs and thrusts and trills. Color touched her cheeks, and fire her eyes. She began to ascend. Like an elevator coming up a dark shaft into the light, her soul arose, and herself with it, rising to her feet.

It reminded me of those nights in 1925, 1926, when music or voices in far places played or sang in static and you tried to twist and fix seven or eight dials on your super-heterodyne radio to hear way-off Schenectady where some damn fools played music you didn't want to hear but you kept tuning until one by one you locked the dials and the static melted and the voices shot out of the big disc-shaped speaker and you laughed with triumph even though all you wanted was the sound, not the sense. So it was this night, the place, with the incense and the bell and candle fires summoning Emily Sloane up and up into the light. And she was all remembrance and no flesh, so listen, listen, the bell, the bell, and the voice, the voice, and Constance behind the white statue ready to catch it if it fell, and the statue said:

"The studio. Was brand new, Christmas. Every day. He was always. Here at seven. Morning. Eager. Impatient. If he saw people. With shut mouths. He said open! Laugh. Never understood. Anyone depressed, when there was one life. To live. Much not done . . ."

She drifted again, lost, as if this one long burst had tired her to exhaustion. She circulated her blood a dozen heartbeats, filled her lungs, and ran on, like one pursued: "I . . . same year, with him. Twenty-five, just arrived from Illinois. Crazy for films. He saw I was crazy. Kept me . . . near."

Silence. Then:

"Wonderful. All first years . . . The studio grew. He built. Blueprints. Called himself Explorer. Chart maker. By thirty-five. He said. Wanted the world inside . . . walls. No travel. Hated trains. Cars. Cars killed his father. Great love. So, see, lived in a small world. Grew smaller, the more cities, countries he built on lot. Gaul! His. Then . . . Mexico. Islands off Africa. Then . . . Africa! He said. No need travel. Just lock himself inside. Invite people. See Nairobi? *Here!* London? Paris? *There.* Built special rooms each set to stay. Overnight: New York. Weekends: Left Bank . . . wake to Roman Ruins. Put flowers. Cleopatra's tomb. Behind the fronts of each town put carpets, beds, running water. Studio people laughed at him. Didn't care. Young, foolish. He went on building. 1929, 1930! '31, '32!"

Across the room, Crumley raised his eyebrows at me. Lord! I thought I had hit on something new, living and writing in my grandparents' Green Town house!!

"Even a place," murmured Emily Sloane, "Like Notre Dame. Sleeping bag. So high up over Paris. Wake early to sun. Crazy? No. He laughed. Let *you* laugh. Not crazy . . . it was only later . . ."

She sank under.

For a long while we thought she had drowned for good.

But then I chimed the bell again and she gathered her invisible knitting to stitch with her fingers, looking down at the pattern she wove on her breast.

"Later on . . . it . . . truly . . . mad.

"I married Sloane. Stopped being secretary. Never forgave. He kept playing with great toys . . . he said he still loved me. And then that night . . . accident. It. It. It happened.

"And so . . . I died."

Crumley and I waited for a long minute. One of the candles went dark.

"He comes to visit, you know," she said at last to the fading sound of more candles flickering out.

"He?" I dared to whisper.

"Yes. Oh, two . . . three . . . times . . . a year."

Do you know how many years have passed? I wondered.

"Takes me out, takes me out," she sighed.

"Do you talk?" I whispered.

"He does. I only laugh. *He* says . . . He says."

"What?"

"After all this time, he loves me."

"You say?"

"Nothing. Not right. I made . . . trouble."

"You see him clearly?"

"Oh, no. He sits out in no light. Or stands behind my chair, says love. Nice voice. The same. Even though he died and I'm dead."

"And whose voice is it, Emily?"

"Why . . ." she hesitated. Then her face lit. "Arby, of course."

"Arby . . . ?"

"Arby," she said, and swayed, staring at the last lit candle. "Arby. Made it through. Or guess so. So much to live for. The studio. The toys. No matter me gone. He lived to come back to only place he loved. So he made it even after the graveyard. The hammer. The blood. Ah, God! I'm killed. *Me!*" She shrieked and sank down in her chair.

Her eyes and lips sealed tight. She was done and still and back to being a statue forever. No bells, no incense would stir that mask. I called her name, softly.

But now she built a new glass coffin and shut the lid.

"God," said Crumley. "What have we done?"

"Proved two murders, maybe three," I said.

Crumley said, "Let's go home."

But Emily didn't hear. She liked it right where she was.

68

And at long last the two cities were the same.

If there was more light in the city of darkness, then there was more darkness in the city of light.

The fog and mist poured over the high mortuary walls. The tombstones shifted like continental plates. The drywash catacomb tunnels funneled cold winds. Memory itself invaded the territorial film vaults. Worms and termites that had prevailed in the stone orchards now undermined the apple yards of Illinois, the cherry trees of Washington, and the mathematically trimmed shrubs of French châteaus. One by one the great stages, vacuumed, slammed shut. The clapboard houses, log cabins, and Louisiana mansions dropped their shingles, gaped their doors, shivered with plagues and fell.

In the night, two hundred antique cars on the backlot gunned their engines, smoked their exhausts, and gravel-dusted off on some blind path to motherlode Detroit.

Building by building, floor by floor, lights were extinguished, air conditionings stifled, the last togas trucked like Roman ghosts back to Western Costume, one block off this Appian Way, as the captains and the kings departed with the last gate guards.

We were being pushed into the sea.

The parameters, day by day, I imagined, were shutting in.

More things, we heard, melted and vanished. After the miniature cities and prehistoric animals, then the brownstones and skyscrapers, and with Calvary's cross long gone, the dawn tomb of the Messiah followed it into the furnace.

At any moment the graveyard itself might rupture. Its disheveled inhabitants, evicted, homeless at midnight, seeking new real estates across town at Forest Lawn, would board 2 A.M. buses to terrify drivers as the last gates banged shut and the whiskey-film vault-catacomb tunnel brimmed with arctic slush reddened in its flow even as the church across the street nailed its doors and the drunken priest fled to join the maître d' from the Brown Derby up by the Hollywood sign in the dark hills, while the invisible war and the unseen army pushed us farther and farther west, out of my house, out of Crumley's jungle clearing, until at last, here in the Arabian compound with food in short supply but champagne in large, we would make our last stand as the Beast and his skeleton army shrieked down the sands to toss us as lunch to Constance Rattigan's seals, and shock the ghost of Aimee Semple McPherson trudging up the surf the other way, astonished but reborn in the Christian dawn.

That was it.

Give or take a metaphor.

Crumley arrived at noon and saw me sitting by the telephone.

"I'm calling for an appointment at the studio," I said.

"With who?"

"Anyone who happens to be in Manny Leiber's office when that white telephone on the big desk rings."

"And then?"

"Go turn myself in."

Crumley looked at the cold surf outside.

"Go soak your head," he said.

"What're we going to do?" I exclaimed. "Sit and wait for them to crash the door or come out of the sea? I can't stand the waiting. I'd rather be dead."

"*Gimme* that!"

Crumley grabbed the phone and dialed.

When answered, he had to control his yell: "I'm all well. Cancel my sick leave. I'll be in tonight!"

"Just when I need you," I said. "Coward."

"Coward, crap!" He banged down the phone. "Horse handler!"

"Horse *what?*"

"That's all I've been all week. Waiting for you to be shoved up a chimney or dropped downstairs. A horse handler. That's the guy who held the reins when General Grant fell off his horse. Gumshoeing obits and reading old news files is like laying a mermaid. Time to go help my coroner."

"Did you know the word 'coroner' only means 'for the crown'? A guy who did things for the king or queen? Corona. Coronet. Crown. Coroner."

"Hot damn! I gotta call the wire services. Gimme that phone!"

The phone rang. We both jumped.

"Don't answer," said Crumley.

I let it ring eight times and then ten. I couldn't stand it. I picked it up.

At first there was only the sound of an electric surf somewhere off across town, where unseen rains touched implacable tombstones. And then . . .

I heard heavy breathing. It was like a great dark yeast, miles away, sucking air.

"Hello!" I said.

Silence.

At last this thick, fermenting voice, a voice lodged inside nightmare flesh, said: "Why aren't you here?"

"No one told me," I said, my voice trembling.

There was the heavy underwater breathing like someone drowning in his own terrible flesh.

"Tonight," the voice faded. "Seven o'clock. You know where?"

I nodded. Stupid! I *nodded!*

"Well . . ." drawled the lost deep voice, "it's been a long time, a long way . . . around . . . so . . ." The voice mourned. "Before I quit forever, we must, oh we must . . . talk. . . ."

The voice sucked air and was gone.

I sat gripping the phone, eyes tight.

"What the hell was *that?*" said Crumley, behind me.

"I didn't call him," I felt my mouth move. "He called *me!*"

"*Gimme* that!"

Crumley dialed.

"About that sick leave . . ." he said.

70

The studio was shut stone-cold, stripped down dark and dead.

For the first time in thirty-five years, there was only one guard at the gate. There were no lights in any of the buildings. There were only a few lonely lights at the alley intersections leading toward Notre Dame, if it was still there, past Calvary, which was gone forever, and leading toward the graveyard wall.

Dear Jesus, I thought, my two cities. But now, both dark, both cold, no difference between. Side by side, twin cities, one ruled by grass and cold marble, the other, here, run by a man as dark, as ruthless, as scornful as Death himself. Holding dominion over mayors and sheriffs, police and their night dogs, and telephone networks to the banking East.

I would be the only warm and moving thing on my way, afraid, from one city of the dead to the other.

I touched the gate.

"For God's sake," said Crumley, behind me, "don't!"

"I've got to," I said. "Now the Beast knows where everyone is. He could come smash your place, or Constance's, or Henry's. Now, I don't think he will. Someone's made the final trackdown for him. And there's no way to stop him, is there? No proof. No law to arrest. No court to listen. And no jail to accept. But I don't want to be trashed in the street, or hammered in my bed. God, Crumley, I'd hate the waiting and waiting. And anyway, you should have heard his voice. I don't think he's going anywhere except dead. Something awful has caught up with him and he needs to talk."

"Talk!" Crumley shouted. "Like: hold still while I bash you!?"

"Talk," I said.

I stood inside the gate, staring at the long street ahead.

The Stations of the Cross:

The wall I had run from on All Hallows Eve.

Green Town, where Roy and I had truly lived.

Stage 13, where the Beast was modeled and destroyed.

The carpenters' shop, where the coffin was hid to be burned.

Maggie Botwin's, where Arbuthnot's shadows touched the wall.

The commissary, where the cinema apostles broke stale bread and drank J. C.'s wine.

Calvary Hill, vanished, and the stars wheeling over, and Christ long since gone to a second tomb, and no possible miracle of fish.

"To hell with that." Crumley moved behind me. "I'm coming with."

I shook my head. "No. You want to wait around for weeks or months, trying to find the Beast? He'd hide from *you*. He's open to me now, maybe to tell all about the people who have disappeared. You going to get permits to open a hundred graves across the wall? You think the city will hand you a spade to dig for J. C., Clarence, Groc, Doc Phillips?! We'll never see them again unless the Beast shows us. So go wait by the front gate of the graveyard. Circle the block eight or ten times. One exit or another, I'll probably come screaming out, or just walking."

Crumley's voice was bleak. "Okay. *Get* yourself killed!" he sighed. "Naw. Damn. Here."

"A gun?" I cried. "I'm afraid of guns!"

"Take it. Put the pistol in one pocket, bullets in the other."

"No!"

"Take it!" Crumley shoved.

I took.

"Come back in one piece!"

"Yes, *sir*," I said.

I stepped inside. The studio took my weight. I felt it sink in the night. At any moment, all the last buildings, gunshot like elephants, would fall to their knees, carrion for dogs, and bones for night birds.

I went down the street, hoping Crumley would call me back. Silence.

At the third alley, I stopped. I wanted to glance aside toward Green Town, Illinois. I did not. If the steam shovels had demolished and the termites eaten its cupolas, bay windows, toy attics, and wine cellars, I refused to see.

At the administration building a single small outside light glowed.

The door was unlocked.

I took a deep breath and entered.

Fool. Idiot. Stupid. Jerk.

I muttered the litany as I climbed up.

I tried the doorknob. The door was locked.

"Thank God!" I was about to run when—

The tumblers clicked.

The office door drifted open.

The pistol, I thought. And felt for the weapon in one pocket, the bullets in the other.

I half stepped in.

The office was illuminated only by a light over a painting on the far west wall. I moved across the floor, quietly.

There were all the empty sofas, empty chairs, and the big empty desk with only a telephone on it.

And the big chair, which was not empty.

I could hear his breathing, long and slow and heavy, like that of some great animal in the dark.

Dimly I made out the massive shape of the man lodged in that chair.

I stumbled over a chair. The shock almost stopped my heart.

I peered at the shape across the room and saw nothing. The head was down, the face obscured, the big arms and pawlike hands stretched out to lean against the desk. A sigh. In-breath, out-breath.

The head and the face of the Beast rose up into the light.

The eyes glared at me.

He shifted like a great dark yeast settling back.

The massive chair groaned with the shape's turning.

I reached toward the light switch.

The wound-that-was-a-mouth peeled wide.

"No!" The vast shadow moved a long arm.

I heard the phone dial touched once, twice. A hum, click. I worked the switch. No light. The locks in the door sprang in place.

Silence. And then:

There was a great suction of breath, a great exhalation: "You came . . . for the job?"

The *what*?! I thought.

The huge shadow leaned across the dark. I was stared at, but saw no eyes.

"You've come," gasped the voice, "to run the studio?"

Me! I thought. And the voice sounded syllable by syllable:

"—No one now is right for the job. A world to own. All in a few acres. Once there were orange trees, lemon trees, cattle. The cattle are still here. But no matter. It's yours. I give it to you—"

Madness.

"Come see what you'll own!" His long arm gestured. He touched an unseen dial. The mirror behind the desk slid wide on a subterranean wind and a tunnel leading down into the vaults.

"This way!" whispered the voice.

The shape elongated, turning. The chair swiveled and squealed and suddenly there was no shadow in or behind the chair. The desk lay as empty as the decks of a great ship. The uneasy mirror drifted to shut. I jumped forward, afraid that when it slammed the dim lights would extinguish and I would be drowned by the dark air.

The mirror slid. My face, panicked, shone in its glass.

"I can't follow!" I cried. "I'm afraid!"

The mirror froze.

"Last week, yes, you should have been," he whispered. "To-night? Pick a tomb. It's mine."

And his voice now seemed the voice of my father, melting in his sickbed, wishing the gift of death but taking months to die.

"Step through," the voice said quietly.

My God, I thought, I know this from when I was six. The phantom beckoning from behind the glass. The singer, the woman, curious at his soft voice, daring to listen and touch the mirror, and his hand appearing to lead her down to dungeons and a funeral gondola on a black canal with Death at the steering pole. The mirror, the whisper, and the opera house empty and the singing at an end.

"I can't move," I said. It was true. "I'm afraid." My mouth filled with dust. "You died long ago. . . ."

Behind the glass, his silhouette nodded. "Not easy, being dead, but alive under the film vaults, off through the graves. Keeping the number of people who *really* knew small, paying them well, killing them when they failed. Death in the afternoon on Stage 13. Or Death on a sleepless night beyond the wall. Or in this office where I often slept in the big chair. Now . . ."

The mirror trembled; with his breath or with his hand, I could not say. Pulses jumped in my ears. My voice echoed off the glass, a boy's voice: "Can't we talk *here*?"

Again the melancholy half-sighed laugh. "No. The grand tour. You must know everything if you're going to take my place."

"I don't *want* it! Whoever *said*?"

"*I* said. I *say*. Listen, I'm good as dead."

A damp wind blew, smelling of nitrate from the ancient films and raw earth from the tombs.

The mirror slid open again. Footsteps moved off quietly.

I stared through into the tunnel half lit by mere firefly ceiling lights.

The Beast's massive shadow drifted on the incline going down, as he turned.

He gazed at me steadily out of his incredibly wild, incredibly sad eyes.

He nodded down the incline at darkness. "Well, if you can't walk, then run," he murmured.

"From *what*?"

The mouth munched wetly on itself and at last pronounced it: "Me! I've run all my life! You think I can't follow? God! Pretend! Pretend I'm still strong, that I still have power. That I can kill you. *Act* afraid!"

"I am!"

"Then *run*! God damn you!"

He raised one fist to knock shadows off the walls.

I ran.

He followed.

71

It was a dreadful pretend pursuit, through the vaults where all the film reels lay, toward the stone crypts where all the stars from those films hid, and under the wall and through the wall, and suddenly it was behind, and I was ricocheted through catacombs with the Beast flooding his flesh at my heels toward the tomb where J. C. Arbuthnot had never lain.

And I knew, running, it was no tour, sweet Jesus, but a destination. I was not being pursued but herded. To what?

The bottom of the vault where Crumley and blind Henry and I had stood a thousand years ago. I jolted to a halt.

The sarcophagus platform steps waited, empty, in place.

Behind me I felt the dark tunnel churn with footfalls and the fire bellows roar of pursuit.

I jumped on the steps, reaching somehow to climb. Slipping, crying insipid prayers, I groaned to the top, cried out with relief, and shouted myself out of the sarcophagus, onto the floor.

I hit the tomb door. It burst wide. I fell out into the graveyard and stared wildly along through the stones at the boulevard, miles off and empty.

"Crumley!" I yelled.

There was no traffic, no cars parked.

"Oh, God," I mourned. "Crumley! *Where?*"

Behind me there was a riot of feet clubbing the tomb entry. I whirled.

The Beast stepped into the doorway.

He was framed in moonlight. He stood like a mortuary statue reared to celebrate himself, under his carved name. For one moment he seemed like the ghost of some English lord posed on the sill of his ancient country gatehouse, primed to be trapped on film and immersed in darkroom acid waters to rise phantom-like as the film developed in mists, one hand on the door hinge to his right, the other upraised as if to hurl Doom across the cold marble gameyard. Above the cold marble door I once again saw:

ARBUTHNOT.

I must have half cried aloud that name.

At that he fell forward as if someone had fired a starter's gun. His cry spun me to flounder toward the gate. I caromed off a dozen gravestones, scattered floral displays, and ran, yelling, on a double track. Half of me saw this as manhunt, the other as Keystone farce. One image was broken floodgate tides lapping a lone runner. The other was elephants stampeding Charlie Chase. With no choosing between maniac laughters and despairs, I made it down brick paths between graves to find:

No Crumley. An empty boulevard.

Across the street, St. Sebastian's was open, lights on, the doors wide.

J. C., I thought, if only *you* were there!

I leaped. Tasting blood, I ran.

I heard the great clumsy thud of shoes behind, and the gasping breath of a half-blind terrible man.

I reached the door.

Sanctuary!

But the church was empty.

Candles were lit on the golden altar. Candles burned in the

grottos where Christ hid so as to give Mary center stage amidst
the bright drippings of love.

The doors to the confessional stood wide.

There was a thunder of footfalls.

I leaped into the confessional, slammed the door, and sank,
hideously shivering, in the dark well.

The thunder of footsteps—

Paused like a storm. Like a storm, they grew calm and then,
with a weather change, approached.

I felt the Beast paw at the door. It was not locked.

But I was the priest, was I not?

Whoever was locked in here was most holy, to be reckoned
with, spoken to, and stay . . . *safe?*

I heard this ungodly groan of exhaustion and self-doom from
outside. I shuddered. I broke my teeth with prayer for the merest
things. One more hour with Peg. To leave a child. Trifles. Things
larger than midnight, or as great as some possible dawn . . .

The sweet smell of life must have escaped my nostrils. It came
forth with my prayers.

There was a last groan and—

God!

The Beast stumbled into the other half of the booth!

His cramming and forcing his lost rage in shuddered me more,
as if I feared that his terrible breath might burn through the
lattice to blind me. But his huge bulk plunged to settle like a
great furnace bellows sighing down on its creases and valves.

And I knew the strange pursuit was over, and a final time
begun.

I heard the Beast suck breath once, twice, three times, as if
daring himself to speak, or fearful to speak, still wanting to kill,
but tired, oh God, at last tired.

And at last he whispered an immense whisper, like a vast sigh
down a chimney: "Bless me, father, for I have sinned!"

Lord, I thought, dear God, what did priests say in all those
old films half a lifetime ago? From stupid remembrance, what!?

I had this mad desire to fling myself out to sprint down the middle of nothing with the Beast in fresh flight.

But as I seized my breath, he let forth a dreadful whisper: "Bless me, father—"

"I'm not your father," I cried.

"No," whispered the Beast.

And after a lost moment, added: "You're my son."

I gave a jump and listened to my heart knock down a cold tunnel into darkness.

The Beast stirred.

"Who . . ." pause ". . . do you think . . ." pause ". . . *hired* you?"

Dear God!

"I," said the lost face behind the grille, "did."

Not Groc? I thought.

And the Beast began to tell a terrible rosary of dark beads, and I could not but slowly, slowly sink back and back until my head rested on the paneling of the booth, and I turned my head and murmured:

"Why didn't you kill me?"

"That was never my wish. Your friend stumbled on me. He made that bust. Madness. I would have killed him, yes, but he killed himself first. Or made it look as if. He's alive, waiting for you. . . ."

Where!? I wanted to shout. Instead I said: "Why have you saved me?"

"Why . . . One day I want my story told. You were the only one," he paused, ". . . who could tell it, and tell it . . . right. There is nothing in the studio I do not know, or out in the world I do not know. I read all night long and slept in snatches and read more and then whispered through the wall, oh, not so many weeks ago: your name. He'll do, I said. Get him. That is my historian. And my son.

"And it was so."

His whisper, behind a mirror, had given me nomination.

And the whisper was here now, not fourteen inches off, and his breath pulsing the air like a bellows, between.

"Sweet Jerusalem's bone-white hills," said the pale voice. "I hired and fired, all and everyone, for thousands of days. Who else could do it? What else had I to do but be ugly and want to die. It was my work that kept me alive. Hiring you was a strange sustenance."

Should I thank him? I wondered.

Soon, he almost whispered. Then:

"I ran the place at first, secondhand, behind the mirror. I knocked Leiber's eardrums with my voice, predictions on markets, script editings, scanned in the tombs, and delivered to his cheek when he leaned against the wall at two A.M. What meetings! What twins! Ego and super-ego. The horn and the player of the horn. The small dancer. But I the choreographer under glass. My God, we shared his office. He making faces and pretending great decisions, I waiting each night to step forth from behind to sit in the chair by the empty desk with the single phone and dictate to Leiber, my secretary."

"I know," I whispered.

"How could you!?"

"I *guessed*."

"Guessed!? What? The whole crazy, damned thing? Halloween? Twenty, oh God, twenty years ago?!"

He breathed heavily, waiting.

"Yes," I whispered.

"Well, well." The Beast remembered. "Prohibition over but we ran the booze in from Santa Monica, through the tomb, down the tunnel, for the hell of it, laughing. Half of the party on the graves, half in the film vaults, lord! Five sound stages full of yelling men, girls, stars, extras. I only half remember that midnight. You ever think how many people, crazy, make love in graveyards? The silence! Think!"

I waited while he moved remembrance back in years. He said:

"He caught us. Christ, there among the tombstones. Graveyard keeper's hammer, beat my head, my cheek, my eye! Beating! He ran with her. I ran screaming after. They drove. I drove, God. And the smashup and, and—"

He sighed, waiting to slow his heart.

"I remember Doc carrying me to the church, first! and the priest in a frenzy of fear, and then to the mortuary. Get well in tombs! Recover in graves! And the next morgue slab over, damned dead, Sloane! And Groc! trying to fix what couldn't be fixed. Poor bastard Groc. Lenin was luckier! My mouth moving to say cover up, do it! Late. Empty streets. Lie! Say I'm dead! My God, my face! No way to fix! My face! So say I'm dead! Emily? What? Mad? Hide Emily! Cover up. Money, of course. Lots of money. Make it look real. Who'll guess? And a shut-coffin funeral, with me nearby, all but dead in the mortuary, the Doc nursing me for weeks! My God, what madness. Me feeling my face, my head, able to yell 'Fritz' when I saw him. 'You! Take charge!' Fritz did! A maniac-at-work. Sloane, dead, get him out! Emily, poor, lost, mad. Constance! And Constance walked her off to the Elysian Fields. What they called that row of drunk/mad/dope convalescent sanitariums, where they never convalesced and weren't sanitary, but there they went, Emily going nowhere and me raving. Fritz said shut up, and them crying, all looking at my face as if it was something from a meat grinder. I could see my horror in their eyes. Their look said, dying, and I said, like hell! and there was Doc the butcher and Groc the beautician, trying at repairs, and J. C. and Fritz at last said, 'That's it! I've done all I can do. Call a priest!' 'Like hell!' I cried. 'Hold a funeral, but I won't be there!' And all their faces turned white! They knew I meant it. From the mouth, this ruin: a crazed plan. And they thought: If he dies, we die. For you see, Christ Almighty, for us it was the greatest film year in history. Mid-Depression, but we had made two hundred million and then three hundred million, more than all the other film studios combined. They couldn't let me die. I was hitting a thousand over the fence. Where would they find a replacement? Out of all the

fools and jerks, idiots and hangers-on? You *save* him, I'll *fix* him!
Groc told the butcher, Doc Phillips. They midwifed me, re-
birthed me away from the sun, forever!"

Listening, I remembered J. C.'s words: "The Beast? I was
there the night he was born!"

"So Doc saved and Groc sewed. Oh, God! but the faster he
mended, the faster I burst the seams, while they all thought, If
he dies, we sink. And me now *wanting* to die with all my heart!
But lying there under all the tomato paste and torn bone, the
old groin itch for power won. And after some hours of falling
toward death and climbing back, afraid to ever touch my face
again, I said: 'Announce a wake. Pronounce me *gone!* Hide me
here, get me *well!* Keep the tunnel open, bury Sloane! Bury me
with him, *in absentia*, with headlines. Monday morning, God,
Monday I report for work. What? And every Monday from now
on and on. And no one to know! I don't want to be seen. A
murderer with a smashed face? And fix an office and a desk and
a chair and slowly, slowly, over the months, I'll come closer,
while someone sits there, alone, and listens to the mirror and,
Manny, where's Manny? You *listen!* I'll talk through the beams,
whisper through the cracks, shadow the mirror, and you open
your mouth and I talk through your ear, through your head, and
out. You *got* that? *Got* it! Call the papers. Sign the death certificates. Box Sloane. Put me in a mortuary room, rest, sleep,
getting well. Manny. Yes? Fix the office. Go!'

"And in the days before my funeral, I shouted and my small
team listened and got quiet and nodded and said yes.

"So it was Doc to save my life, Groc to fix a face that could
never be fixed, Manny to run the studio, but with my orders,
and J. C. simply because he was there that night and was the
first to find me bleeding, and the one who rearranged the cars,
made the crash look accidental. Only four people knew. Fritz?
Constance? In charge of cleaning up, but we never told them I
survived. The other four got five thousand a week forever. Think!
Five thousand a *week*, in 1934! The average wage then was fifteen

lousy bucks. So Doc and Manny and J. C. and Groc were rich, yes? Money, by God, *does* buy everything! Years of silence! So it was all great, all fine. The films, the studio, from then on, growing profits, and me hidden away, and no one to know. The stock prices up, and the New York people happy, until—"

He paused and gave a great moan of despair.

"Someone discovered something."

Silence.

"Who?" I dared to ask in the dark.

"Doc. Good old surgeon general Doc. My time was up."

Another pause and then:

"Cancer."

I waited and let him speak when he could gather his strength.

"Cancer. Which of the others Doc told, who can say. One of them wanted to run. Grab the cash and vanish. So the scares began. Frighten everyone with the truth. Then—blackmail— then ask for money."

Groc, I thought, but said: "Do you know who it was?"

And then I asked: "Who put the body up on the ladder. Who wrote the letter so I came to the graveyard? Who told Clarence to wait outside the Brown Derby so he could see you? Who inspired Roy Holdstrom to make the bust of the possible monster for an impossible film? Who gave J. C. overdoses of whiskey hoping he would run wild and tell everything? Who?"

With each question, the huge mass beyond the thin panel moved, trembled, took in great soughs of air, sighed it out, as if each breath was a hope for survival, each exhalation an admission of despair.

There was a silence and then he said: "When it all began, with the body on the wall, I suspected everyone. It got worse. I ran mad. Doc, I thought, no. A coward, and too obvious. He had, after all, found and told me my illness. J. C.? Worse than a coward, hiding in a bottle every night. *Not* J. C."

"Where's J. C. tonight?"

"Buried somewhere. I would have buried him myself. I set

out to bury everyone, one by one, get rid of anyone who tried to hurt me. I would have smothered J. C. as I did Clarence. Killed him as I would have killed Roy, who, I thought, killed himself. Roy was alive. *He* killed and buried J. C."

"No!" I cried.

"There are lots of tombs. Roy hid him somewhere. Poor sad Jesus."

"Not Roy!"

"Why not? We'd all kill if we had the chance. Murder is all we dream, but never do. It's late, let me finish. Doc, J. C., Manny, I thought, *which* would try to hit me and run? Manny Leiber? No. A phonograph record I could play any time and hear the same tune. Well then, at last—Groc! He hired Roy, but *I* thought to bring you in for the grand search. How was I to know the final search was for me!? That I would wind up in clay! I went, oh, quite insane. But now—it's over.

"Running, shouting, mad, I suddenly thought: too much. Tired, so damned tired from too many years, too much blood, too much death, and all of it gone and cancer now. And then I met the other Beast in the tunnel near the tombs."

"The other Beast?"

"Yes," he sighed, his head touching the side of the confessional. "Go get him. You didn't think there was just *me*, did you?"

"Another—?"

"Your friend. The one whose bust I destroyed when I saw that he had caught my face, yes. The one whose cities I trampled underfoot. The one whose dinosaurs I degutted . . . *He's* running the studio!"

"That . . . that's not possible!"

"Idiot! Fooled us. Fooled you. When he saw what I had done to his beasts, his cities, the clay bust, *he* went mad. Made himself up as the walking horror. The terrible mask—"

"Mask—" My mouth jerked.

I had guessed but refused the guess. I saw the film face of the

Beast on Crumley's wall. Not a clay bust animated, frame by frame, but—Roy, made up to resemble destruction's father, chaos's child, annihilation's true son.

Roy on film, acting out the Beast.

"Your friend," gasped the man behind the grille, over and over again. "God, what an act. The voice: mine. Spoke through the wall behind Manny's desk and—"

"Got me rehired," I heard myself say. "Got himself rehired!?"

"Yes! How rich! Give him the Oscar!"

My hand raked the grille.

"How did he—"

"Take over? Where was the seam, the crease, the boundary? Met him under the wall, between the vaults face to face! Oh, damn that bright son of a bitch. I hadn't seen a mirror in years. Then, there I was, standing in my own path! Grinning! I struck to smash that mirror! I thought: illusion. A ghost of light in a glass. I yelled and hit, off balance. The *mirror* lifted *its* fist and struck. I woke in the tombs raving, behind bars, put in some crypt and him there, watching. 'Who are you?!' I shouted. But I knew. Sweet vengeance! I had killed his creatures, smashed his cities, tried to smash him. Now, sweet triumph! He ran yelling back at me: 'Listen. I'm off to rehire *myself*! And, yes! give myself a *raise*!' He came twice a day with chocolate to feed a dying man. Until he saw I was truly dying and the fun was lost for him as well as me. Maybe he found that power doesn't stay power, stay great and good and fun. Maybe it scared, maybe it bored him. A few hours ago, he unlocked my bars and led me up for that call to you. He left me to wait for you. He didn't have to tell me what to do. He just pointed down the tunnel toward the church. Confession time, he said. Brilliant. Now he's waiting for you in a final place."

"Where?"

"Damn it to hell! Where's the *one* and only place for such as me, and such as he has become?"

"Ah, yes," I nodded, my eyes watering. "I've been there."

The Beast slumped in the confessional.

"That's it," he sighed. "This last week I hurt many people. I killed some, and your friend the rest. Ask him. He went as mad as I. When this is over, when the police ask, put all the blame on me. No need for two Beasts when one should do. Yes?"

I was silent.

"Speak up!"

"Yes."

"Good. When he saw I was dying, really dying in the tomb and that he was dying from the cancer I had given him, and the game wasn't worth the candle, he had the decency to let me go. The studio *he* had run, *I* had run, had come to a dead jolting halt. We both had to set it in motion again. Now, next week, turn all the wheels. Start back on *The Dead Ride Fast.*"

"No," I murmured.

"Damn it to hell! With my last breath I'll come choke the life out of you. It will be done. *Say* it!"

"It," I said at last, "will be done."

"And now the last thing. What I said before. The offer. It's yours if you want it. The studio."

"Don't—"

"There's no one else! Don't turn it down so quickly. Most men would die to inherit—"

"Die, is right. I'd be dead in a month, a wreck, drinking, and dead."

"You don't understand. You're the only son I have."

"I'm sorry that's true. Why me?"

"Because you're a real honest-to-God idiot savant. A real fool, not a fake one. Someone who talks too much but then you look at the words and they're right. You can't help yourself. The good things come out of your hand into words."

"Yes, but I haven't leaned against the mirror and listened to you for years, like Manny."

"He talks but his words don't mean anything."

"But he's learned. He must know how to run things by now. Let me work for him!"

"Last chance? Last offer?" His voice was fading.

"And give up my wife and my writing and my life?"

"Ah," whispered the voice. And a final "Yes . . ." Adding: "Now, at last. Bless me, father, for I have truly sinned."

"I can't."

"Yes, you can. And forgive. That's a priest's job. Forgive me and bless me. In a moment it'll be too late. Don't send me to everlasting hell!"

I shut my eyes and said, "I bless you." And then I said, "I forgive you, though, God, I don't understand you!"

"Who ever did?" he gasped. "Not me." His head slumped against the panel. "Much thanks." His eyes closed in outer space where there is no sound. I added my own track. The sound of a mighty gate closing on oblivion, tomb doors banging shut.

"I forgive you!" I shouted at the man's terrible mask.

"I forgive you . . ." my voice echoed back from high in the empty church.

The street was empty.

Crumley, I thought, where *are* you?

I ran.

72

There was a last place I had to go.

I climbed the dark interior of Notre Dame.

I saw the shape fixed out near the top rim of the left tower, with a gargoyle not too far away, its bestial chin resting on its horny paws, gazing out across a Paris that never was.

I edged along, took a deep breath, and called: "You . . . ?" and had to stop.

The figure seated there, its face in shadow, did not move.

I took another breath and said, *"Here."*

The figure straightened. The head, the face, came up into the dim glow of the city.

I took a last breath and called quietly, "Roy?"

The Beast looked back at me, a perfect duplicate of the one that had slumped in the confessional a few minutes ago.

The terrible grimace fixed me, the terrible raving eyes froze my blood. The terrible wound of mouth peeled and slithered, insucked and garbled a single word: ". . . Yesssssss."

"It's all over," I said, my voice breaking. "My God, Roy. Come down from here."

The Beast nodded. Its right hand rose up to tear at the face and peel away the wax, the makeup, the mask of horror and stunned amaze. He worked at his nightmare face with a clawing downpull of fingers and thumb. From beneath the shambles, my old high school chum looked back at me.

"Did I look like him?" asked Roy.

"Oh, God, Roy." I could hardly see him for the tears in my eyes. "Yes!"

"Yeah," muttered Roy. "I kind of thought so."

"God, Roy," I gasped, "take it *all* off! I have this terrible feeling if you leave it, it'll stick and I'll never *see* you again!"

Roy's right hand impulsively jerked up to rake his horrid cheek.

"Funny," he whispered, "I think the same."

"How did you come to fix your face that way?"

"Two confessions? You heard one. Want another?"

"Yes."

"Have you become a priest, then?"

"I'm starting to feel like one. You want to be excommunicated?"

"From what?"

"Our friendship?"

His eyes quickened to watch me.

"You *wouldn't*!"

"I might."

"Friends don't blackmail friends about their friendship."

"All the more reason to talk. Start."

Inside his half-torn-away mask, very quietly, Roy said:

"It was my animals that did it. No one had ever touched my

darlings, my dears, ever. I gave my life to imagine them, shape them. They were perfect. I was God. What *else* did I have? Did I ever date the class girl gymnast and cheerleader? Did I have any women in all those years? Like hell. I went to bed with my brontosaurus. I flew nights with my pterodactyls. So imagine how I felt when someone slaughtered my innocents, destroyed my world, killed my ancient bedmates. I wasn't just mad. I was insane."

Roy paused behind his dreadful flesh. Then he said:

"Hell, it was all so simple. It fell together almost from the start, but I didn't say. The night I followed the Beast into the graveyard? I was so in love with the damned monster. I was afraid you'd spoil the fun. Fun!? And people dead because of it! So when I saw him go in his own tomb and not come out, I didn't say. I knew you'd try to put me off, and I had to have that face, my God, that great terrible mask, for our epic masterpiece! So I shut my trap and made the clay bust. Then? Almost got you fired. Me? Off the lot! Then, my dinosaurs stomped on, my sets trampled, my hideous Beast sculpture hammered to bits. I went berserk. But then it hit me: there was only *one* person who *could* have destroyed it. Not Manny, nor anyone we knew. The Beast himself! The guy from the Brown Derby. But how would he *know* about my clay bust? Someone *tell* him? No! I thought back to the night I followed him into the graveyard, near the studio. Lord, it *had* to be! Into the tomb and somehow under the wall, into the studio late nights where, by God, he *saw* my clay replica of his face and exploded.

"*I* did a lot of crazy planning, dear God, right then. I knew that if the Beast found me I was dead. So, I 'killed' myself! Threw 'im off the scent. With me supposedly dead, I knew I could search, find the Beast, get revenge! So I hung myself in effigy. You found it. Then *they* found and burned it, and that night I went over the wall. You know what I found. I tried the tomb in the graveyard, found the door unlocked and went in and down and listened behind the mirror in Manny's office! I was stunned! It was all so beautiful. The Beast was running the studio, unseen. So don't kill the son of a bitch, but wait and grab his power. Not kill the Beast but *be* the Beast, *live* the Beast! And then, my God, run twenty-seven, twenty-eight countries, the world. And at the proper time, of course, come out, be reborn, say I had wandered off in amnesia or some damn-fool story, I don't know, I would've thought of *something*—and the Beast was running down, anyway. I could see that. Dying on his feet. I hid and watched and listened and then poleaxed him in the film vaults under the studio, halfway to the tombs. The makeup! When he saw me standing there in the vaults he was so damned shocked I had my chance to knock him down, lock him in the vaults. Then I went up to test the old power, *my* voice behind the glass. I had heard the Beast talking in and outside the Brown Derby, and then in the tunnel and behind the office wall. I whispered, I muttered, and, hell! *The Dead Ride Fast* was back on schedule. You and me rehired! I got ready to rip off the makeup and come back out as me, when a thing happened."

"What?"

"I found that I *liked* power."

"What?!"

"Power. I *loved* it. Stockbrokers, big corporate men, all that crap. Incredible. I was *drunk!* I loved running the studio, making decisions, and all done without board meetings. All with mirrors, echoes, shadows. Do all the films that should have been done years ago, but never *were!* Rebuild *me*, my universe! Reinvent, recreate my friends, my creatures. Make the studio pay in cash as well as flesh and lives and blood. Figure who was most responsible for trashing my life, then, then, one by one, squash the nitwits, mash the cohorts of the ignorant and the yes-men to the twits. The studio had run me; now *I* ran the studio. God, no wonder Louis B. Mayer was insufferable, the Warner Brothers shooting powdered film clips up their veins all night. Until you've run a studio, buster, you don't know what power is. You not only run a city, a country, but the world beyond that world. Slow motion, you say; people run slow. Fast, you say; people leap the Himalayas, flop in their graves. All because you chopped the scenes, ran the actors, told the starts, guessed the ends. Once I got in, I was high on Notre Dame every night laughing at the peasants, diminishing the giant runts who had hurt my pals and killed the gyroscope that always spun in my chest. But now the gyroscope whirred again, lopsided crazy, off its pivot. Look out there, at what I did, almost everything torn down. The Beast started, but I finished it. I knew if I didn't stop I'd be carted off to a madhouse-dairy to be milked for paranoia. That, and the Beast dying, pleading for one last go with the priest and the bells and candles and confessionals and: forgive. I had to give him back his studio so he could give it back to you."

Roy slowed, licked his dreadful lips, and was silent.

"There's one thing, several things, not clear—" I said.

"Name them."

"How many people did Arbuthnot kill in the past few days. And how many people did—" I had to stop, for I could not say it.

Roy said it for me: "How many did Roy Holdstrom, Beast Number Two, spoil?"

I nodded.

"I didn't kill Clarence, if that's what you're afraid of."

"Thank God."

I swallowed hard and at last said: "At what point—oh, God—when—?"

"When what?"

"At what hour . . . on what day . . . did Arbuthnot stop. . . . and *you* take over?"

Now it was Roy's turn, behind the murdered face, to swallow. "It was Clarence, of course. In the catacombs, I heard voices on the phone systems, at every tomb intersection. Voices *in* the tunnels themselves. One way or another lifting the receivers, or hiding alert, I pulled back or followed the shadows moving to bury. I knew Clarence was due for burial, five minutes after the Beast's rampage at his apartment. I saw and heard, at a distance, Doc hustling through the tunnels, taking Clarence to some damned lost crypt. I knew then they'd soon find I was alive, if they didn't suspect already. I wonder, did they ever check the incinerator to find not my real bones but my mock-up skeleton? And next: *you!* *You* knew Clarence. They might have seen you at his place, or at my apartment. If they added it up they'd have buried you alive. So, you see, I had to take over. I had to become the Beast.

"Not only that, I shut down the studio, to test my power, to see if they jumped at my voice, did what I said. With the studio emptying out it made it easier to kill the villains, take care of my possible assassins."

"Stanislau Groc?" I said.

"Groc . . . ? Yeah. He got us into this in the first place. Hired me for starters, because I could freshen up creatures, just as he tarted up old dead Lenin. Put a bug in Arbuthnot's ear to hire you, maybe. Then made the body that was propped on the wall to scare the studio folks *and* Arbuthnot, then invited us to the Brown Derby for the bestial revelation. Then when I made the clay Beast and frightened everyone, shook them down for cash."

"You killed Groc, then?"

"Not quite. I had him arrested at the gate. When they brought him to Manny's empty office and left him alone and the mirror swung back, he just up and died when he saw me there. Doc Phillips now, ask me about him."

"Doc Phillips?"

"After all, he cleared away my so-called 'body,' right? Him and his eternal pooper-scoopers. I met up with him in Notre Dame. Didn't even try to run. I pulled him up with the bells. I just wanted to scare him. Get him up high and shake until, like Groc, his heart stopped. Manslaughter, not murder. But, being pulled up, he got tangled, got frantic, all but hung himself. Did I do it? Am I guilty?"

Yes, I thought. And then: no.

"J. C.?" I asked, and held my breath.

"No, no. He climbed up on the cross two nights ago and his

wounds just didn't shut. His life ran out of his wrists. He died on the cross, poor man, poor drunken old J. C. God rest him. I found him and gave him a proper resting place."

"Where are they all? Groc and Doc Phillips and J. C."

"Somewhere. Anywhere. Does it matter? It's all bodies out there, a million of 'em. I'm glad one of them isn't—" he hesitated—"you."

"Me?"

"That's what finally made me cease and desist. About twelve hours ago. I found I had you on my list."

"What!?"

"I found myself thinking, If he gets in the way, he dies. That put an end to it."

"Christ, I should hope so!"

"I thought, Wait, he had nothing to do with this whole dumb show. He didn't put the crazy horses on the carousel. He's your pal, your friend, your buddy. He's all that's left of life. That was the turnaround. The road back from madness is knowing you're mad. The road back means no more highway, and you can only turn. I loved you. I love you. So I came back. And opened the tomb and let the true Beast out."

Roy turned his head and looked at me. His gaze said: Am I on report? Will you hurt me for what I have hurt? Are we still friends? What made me do whatever I did? Must the police know? And who will tell them? Must I be punished? Do the insane have to pay? Isn't it all a madness? Mad sets, mad lines, mad actors? Is the play over? Or has it just begun? Do we laugh now or weep? For what?

His face said, Not long from now the sun will be up, the two cities will start, one more alive than the other. The dead will stay dead, yes, but the living will repeat the lines they were still saying just yesterday. Do we let them speak? Or do we rewrite them together? Do I make the Death that rides fast, and when he opens his mouth will your words be there?

What . . . ?

Roy waited.

"Are you really back with me?" I said.

I took a breath, and went on. "Are you Roy Holdstrom again and will you just stay that way and not be anything else but my friend, from now on, yes? Roy?"

Roy's head was down. At last he put out his hand.

I seized it as if I might sway and fall to the streets of the Beast's Paris, below.

We held tight.

With his free hand, Roy worked at the rest of his mask. He balled the substance, the torn-away wax and powder and celadon scar in his fist and hurled it from Notre Dame. We did not hear it land. But a voice, startled, shot up.

"God *damn!* Hey!"

We stared down.

It was Crumley, a simple peasant on the Notre Dame porch below. "I ran out of gas," he called. "I kept going around the block. And then: no gas."

"What," he shielded his eyes, "in hell's going *on* up there?"

73

Arbuthnot was buried two days later.

Or rather reburied. Or rather, placed in the tomb, carried there before dawn by some friends of the church who didn't know who they carried or why or what for.

Father Kelly officiated at the funeral of a stillborn child, nameless and so not recently baptized.

I was there with Crumley and Constance and Henry and Fritz and Maggie. Roy stood far back from us all.

"What're we doing here?" I muttered.

"Just making sure he's buried *forever*," observed Crumley.

"Forgiving the poor son-of-a-bitch," Constance said, quietly.

"Oh, if people out beyond knew what was going on here to-

day," I said, "think of the crowds that might come to see that
it's over at last. Napoleon's farewell."

"He was no Napoleon," said Constance.

"No?"

I looked across the graveyard wall where the cities of the world
lay strewn-flat, and no place for Kong to grab at biplanes, and
no dust-blown white sepulcher for the tomb-lost Christ, and no
cross to hang some faith or future on, and no—

No, I thought, maybe not Napoleon, but Barnum, Gandhi,
and Jesus. Herod, Edison, and Griffith. Mussolini, Genghis
Khan, and Tom Mix. Bertrand Russell, The Man Who Could
Work Miracles, and The Invisible Man. Frankenstein, Tiny Tim,
and Drac—

I must have said some of this aloud.

"Quiet," said Crumley, *sotto voce*.

And Arbuthnot's tomb door, with flowers inside, and the body
of the Beast, slammed shut.

74

I went to see Manny Leiber.

He was still sitting, like a miniature gargoyle, on the rim of
his desk. I looked from him to the big chair behind him.

"Well," he said. "*Caesar and Christ* is done. Maggie's editing
the damn thing."

He looked as if he wanted to shake hands, but didn't know
how. So I went around, collected the sofa cushions, like in the
old days, piled them, and sat on them.

Manny Leiber had to laugh. "Don't you *ever* give up?"

"If I did, you'd eat me alive."

I looked beyond him to the wall. "Is the passage shut?"

Manny slid off the desk, walked over, and lifted the mirror

off its hooks. Behind it, where once the door had been, was fresh plaster and a new coat of paint.

"Hard to believe a monster came through there every day for years," I said.

"He was no monster," said Manny. "And he ran this place. It would have sunk long ago without him. It was only at the end he went mad. The rest of the time he was God behind the glass."

"He never got used to people staring at him?"

"Would *you*? What's so unusual about him hiding out, coming up the tunnel late at night, sitting in that chair? No more stupid or brilliant than the idea of films falling off theatre screens to run the world. Every damn city in Europe is starting to look like us crazy Americans, dress, look, talk, dance like us. Because of films we've won the world, and are too damn dumb to see it. All that being true, what, I say, is so unusual about the given creativity of a man lost in the woodwork?!"

I helped him rehang the mirror over the fresh plaster.

"Soon, when things calm down," said Manny, "we'll call you and Roy back and build Mars."

"But no Beasts."

Manny hesitated. "We'll talk about that later."

"Unh-*unh*," I said.

I glanced at the chair. "You gonna change that?"

Manny pondered. "Just grow my behind to fit. I been putting it off. I guess this is the year."

"A backside big enough to tackle the New York front office?"

"If I put my brains where my butt is, sure. With him gone I got a lot to shoot for. Want to *try* it?"

I eyed the chair for a long moment.

"Naw."

"Afraid once you sit you'll never get up again? Get your can out of here. Come back in four weeks."

"When you'll need a *new* ending for *Jesus and Pilate* or *Christ and Constantine* or—"

Before he could pull back, I shook his hand.

"Good luck."

"I think he *means* it," Manny said to the ceiling. "Hell."

He turned and went to sit in the chair.

"How's it feel?" I asked.

"Not bad." Eyes shut, he felt his whole body sink down into his seat. "A man could get used."

At the door I looked back at his smallness frozen in so much bigness.

"You still hate me?" he asked, eyes shut.

"Yes," I said. "You me?"

"Yeah," he said.

I went out and shut the door.

75

I walked across the street from the tenement, Henry paced me, guided by the sound of my footsteps and the jolting of his valise in my hand.

"We got everything, Henry?" I said.

"My whole life in one suitcase? Sure."

At the curb on the far side we turned.

Someone, somewhere fired an invisible and soundless cannon. Half of the tenement, gunshot, fell.

"Sounds like the Venice pier being torn down," said Henry.

"Yeah."

"Sounds like the roller-coaster coming apart."

"Yeah."

"Or the day they tore up the big red train trolley-car tracks."

"Yeah."

The rest of the tenement fell.

"C'mon, Henry," I said. "Let's go home."

"Home," Blind Henry said and nodded, pleased. "I never had one of those. Sounds nice."

76

I had Crumley and Roy and Fritz and Maggie and Constance over for a last go-round before Henry's relatives arrived to take him back to New Orleans.

The music was loud, the beer was copious, blind Henry was officiating at the discovery of the empty tomb for the fourteenth time, and Constance, half loaded and half-undressed, was biting my ear when the door to my small house burst wide.

A voice cried: "I got an early flight! Traffic was awful. *There* you are! And I know you, you, and *you*."

Peg stood in the door pointing.

"But who," she shouted, "is that half-naked *woman*!?"

A NOTE ABOUT THE AUTHOR

Ray Bradbury has written for motion pictures since 1952 when his *The Beast from 20,000 Fathoms* was filmed by Warner Bros. The following year he screenplayed *It Came from Outer Space* for Universal. In 1953 he lived for a year in Ireland writing the script of *Moby Dick* for John Huston. In 1961 he wrote the narration spoken by Orson Welles and provided an ending for *King of Kings* starring Jeffrey Hunter as Christ. In 1962 his short animated film on the history of flight, *Icarus Montgolfier Wright*, received an Academy of Motion Picture Arts and Sciences nomination, which he shared with all the artists at Format Films. Films have been made of his *Picasso Summer, The Illustrated Man, Fahrenheit 451,* and *Something Wicked This Way Comes.* In 1982 he collaborated with Elaine and Saul Bass on a one-half hour mythological film, *Quest*, for a Japanese museum near Tokyo. The film has since won Gold Medals in Russia and ten other countries. During the eighties he has been creative consultant for the architectural firm The Jon Jerde Partnership which blueprinted the Glendale Galleria, The Westside Pavilion in Los Angeles, and the Horton Plaza in San Diego. Since 1985 he has adapted forty-two of his short stories for his own half-hour show on USA Cable television. He is now writing a musical version of his *The Wonderful Ice Cream Suit* with José Feliciano.